GAVESTON

GAVESTON

CHRIS HUNT

GMP

First published in November 1992 by GMP Publishers Ltd
P O Box 247, London N17 9QR, England

World Copyright © 1992 Chris Hunt

A CIP catalogue record for this book
is available from the British Library

ISBN 0 85449 184 8

Distributed in North America by InBook
P O Box 120470, East Haven, CT 06512, USA

Distributed in Australia by Bulldog Books
P O Box 155, Broadway, NSW 2007, Australia

Printed and bound in the EC on environmentally-friendly paper
by Nørhaven A/S, Viborg, Denmark

TO SYLVIA

Chapter One

DWARD, BY the grace of God etcetera, with Robert the clerk who was Robert the Fool, in this year of Our Lord 1322...our intention being to tell it as it was...

"Or more correctly, as it appeared to us, sire, at the time."
"That is the same thing, Robert. So, proceed."

First of all, let it be set down that Piers Gaveston was the most beautiful creation on God's earth, and if it had not been so, his joys and his pains would have been in proportion the less. Set it down that Gaveston had eyes as green as emeralds and a smile that dazzled like the sun, and then as to his arse —

"No, not the arse, Robert, erase that . . ."

. . . to begin with, at least, we shall exhibit that discretion which has been our discipline these ten years past. And, after all, though it sometimes may have seemed to us that there never was a time when we were not under the spell of that green-eyed Gascon, yet there was such a time.

As a boy, you know, I had conceived a warm affection for my cousin Tom of Lancaster. Thomas, six years older than myself, of noble parentage and vast wide-sweeping lands, heir through Fortune's careless disposal of her favours, to the spoils which the downfall of the mighty leaves for the grabbing. One of these was Kenilworth castle, towards which I rode, nine years old, and my household with me — my servants, squires, my cupbearers, my falconers, my grooms, minstrels, archers, messengers and clerks, and my wise and courtly tutor Sir Guy Ferre.

From Warwick, through the water meadows of the Avon, and past the little scrubby hill where the lands of Lancaster began, our way wound northwards between overhanging trees, edge of the great forest. The leaves of autumn drifted through the sunshafts, and the minstrels drummed and piped a loud and merry noise to fright the wood sprites, and Sir Guy discoursed upon the proper maintenance of roads; and as the trees now, curtain-like, drew back, I found myself wondering once again which of the castles of the realm was most like Camelot. That day I thought it could be Kenilworth.

Roseate and splendid, the castle soared up from a broad encircling lake, save on the north side where it overhung a craggy ditch. Square crenellated turrets topped each corner. The walls of its great battlemented keep were more than twenty feet thick. Sunlight reddened the sandstone and the castle glowed. It was impregnable.

The drawbridge lowered, we rode across and entered.

I ran up the twisting stone stairway and reached Tom's room with a whoop of welcome that made Tom wince. I stood in the doorway, panting, laughing.

Tom lay in bed, an immense dark fur coverlet slung over him, the sunlight circumscribed from a thin sliver of a window. He groaned.

"They said that you were ill," I whispered noisily.

"Come in, come in, and don't be loud."

I tiptoed over to the bed, exaggeratedly silent, making Tom smile.

"Sit down, imp," said Thomas, fondly enough.

"I've come to comfort you."

"And so you do, by being here at all. Your letter was most kind. Are you really so warm-hearted, Ned? However did you become so?"

"What do you mean?"

"If, as they say, we become as our parents, however did you grow so gentle and endearing? Don't tell your father I said that!"

"Oh be assured, I never tell my father anything."

"Give me your hand."

Tom's hand closed over mine, with the clinking of many rings. "You cheer me, Ned. I swear you're prettier than all your sisters. I don't mean to offend. You glitter like a sunbeam."

"Well, that's because of all the gold I'm wearing," I pointed out reasonably.

"No, it's more than that. Your hair is the colour of buttercups and your eyes are speedwells, and you are all smiles and foolery. It pleases me to be with you."

"If I am those things, so could you be, and you never will be so while you stay in bed. What is your illness, cousin? Nobody seemed to know."

"Oh," Tom shrugged and turned away. "It's grief. It's miserable grief."

"For what?"

"For life, what else?"

"I don't understand."

Tom laughed cynically. "No, you don't, and you never will." He sighed, and raised himself to look at me. "Don't you ever feel so? No, I see you don't. You're oddly simple, Ned, clear as a brook. I daresay that for you life is a path marked out for you, and all you need to do is tread. I envy you. But some of us — for me the way is briars and thorns, each day to be freshly hacked, and the process bloody. I don't understand it. I read books to find the answers. For a while I have it, then the clouds come down and I'm lost again. They say the monks are prone to such a secret torment, long days alone, and nights in God's bleak unforgiving presence. Sometimes the pain of it all drives them to self-inflicted death."

I snorted. "You are surrounded by folk who wish you well. Your state is nothing like a monk's."

"The solitude is in the mind," Tom began, then added grumbling: "Why do I try to explain? For you, Ned, a new dog, a minstrel with a song, and all your little sadnesses disperse..."

"I brought my wolfhound to show you," I agreed. "I know you'll like him. But I've other things with me if you don't feel ready for a wolfhound. I brought a book. I'll read it to you."

"Read it to me then; why not?"

I settled into the fur and drew up my knees. Tom shut his eyes and listened to the story of King Mark of Tintagel and Tristan the hero:

"— and Tristan was brought in from the fray sore wounded, and when he was placed upon the bed, King Mark then took him in his arms and wept, and said: So God help me, I would not for the world that Tristan died. And when it seemed that Tristan's wound would not be healed, a wise old woman came into the castle of Tintagel and she said that Tristan must return to the country whence the poisoned spear had come, and there find healing. And so, sad as he was to see the lovely Tristan leave, King Mark ordered a ship to be brought, and filled with food and drink and cloth of gold and gifts, and a harp for him to ease his mind with music. And Tristan set sail for Ireland, beyond the sea. And he was sorry to leave Mark behind, for he had known great happiness with Mark, who loved him."

I caught Tom squinting up at me.

"You aren't reading. You were looking into the air."

I grinned. "I know the story as I know my hands and my face. It's my favourite."

"And mine," said Tom. "What a fool he was to go to Ireland and to find La Belle Isolde and fall in love with her. If he had stayed with Mark..."

"He would never have been healed," I shrugged.

"He loved Mark; Mark loved him. They would have shared pain but love also. Better than what happened. Better love and pain together than betrayal and loss, because of the woman."

"But there was magic in it. Against magic they were powerless. One sip of the enchanted chalice and all was lost."

Tom shuddered. "Come into bed with me, Ned. It's horrid to think of threat and danger."

I slithered beneath the fur and curled against him.

"How good you feel," said Tom, with his arms about me. "Sweet as a rosebud. How odd it is that we are as we are. Do you ever think that you and I are changelings?"

I shifted uncomfortably. "Whatever do you mean?"

"Look at us. My father, affable and easy, and myself so foul and troubled. You so kind and pleasing — and your father spreading terror where he goes!"

"That's a wicked thing to say," I gasped.

"Why? You know that you agree," said Thomas mildly.

"About the terror, yes. But never do I think the other. Never. Changelings? How can we be so? It's impossible. And if you think it, don't ever speak of it to me, or I shall never come and read to you again."

"How angry you've become, Ned. It was just an idle thought. No one supposes either of us other than who we are. Lie still and let me hold you. I'm a brute to vex you. I'll make you glad again. I'll stroke you. Here... and here. You like it, don't you? You like what I do?"

"Yes; I like it very much."

"Then just lie quiet and let me lie against you; and be warm with me. It'll only take a moment."

Tom frowned and grunted. I snuggled to him and I kissed his neck. Tom's lank hair, fair like mine, but not so smooth, fell across my face. Tom sighed and then cried out. I hugged him till he lay at ease. I wasn't sure of course exactly what he did, but his hand had been very busy between his legs, and he was certainly the better for it. He tousled my hair and gave a grudging smile. My nearness, it would seem, had been some help.

"So, have I comforted you?" I enquired a little saucily, guessing well enough the answer. "I said I would."

"You surely have. I think that I could even tolerate your snuffling wolfhound now."

"Lord Edward!" called Sir Guy from the stairway below.

"I'm reading to my cousin," I cried, leaping out of bed. "His sickness has left him. I have performed a miracle."

"An angel, nothing less," Tom muttered with good humour, sitting up in bed. He lightly cuffed my ear. "If I could have you always by me I might even learn to stave off glooms and dreads. I half suspect that you were formed in Heaven."

Whereas in truth I first saw light of day in a half-constructed castle in the mountains of Wales, with the workmen ordered to hammer quietly, and the showers of April trickling through the gaps in the stone. My birth was welcomed, but since there was already an heir to the throne, Prince Alfonso, eleven years old and trained from infancy for his high calling, not seen as an especially momentous event. Alfonso was named for my mother's kin; she was a Spanish princess. Already born, already dead, were John, Henry, Isabella and Berengaria; but there remained a swathe of sisters, Eleanor, Joan, Margaret, Mary and Elizabeth. Within four months of my birth, the precious Prince, the elegant Alfonso, breathed his last, and overnight this baby born in Wales became the hope of the nation and the object of his father's scrutiny.

Whirling me in mighty hands above his head, King Edward swore by all the bones of all the saints the child, now two years old, should be as great a man as he was; and then took off to Gascony, leaving me with a memory of dizziness.

For three years I saw nothing of my parents, and rarely thought of them.

My early world was laced with women: Elizabeth, two years older than myself, with whom I fought; Joan, my favourite, twelve years older, who cuddled me as if I were her own; Eleanor, who, already grown, had her mind on other matters; and Margaret who told me stories. Mary I saw less, as she was given to the church and lived at Amesbury. Here also with us at Windsor were my Welsh nurse Mary Mawnsel and my English nurse Alice.

It was all festivities. I liked Catherning — that ceremony to recall Saint Catherine (though with more merriment than that poor dame enjoyed). Then everything was done in circles — wheel-shaped biscuits to eat, jugglers making wheels of fire with flaming brands, candles hanging on a wheel above our heads, burning in a circle and dropping flecks of scalding beeswax, and the food brought to the tables in a spiralling procession. Christmas came, with a candle big as a maypole glowing on the laden table, the many-coloured waxes trickling down in sculptured waterfalls. Noisy May Days took us to the fields, with men in antlers stamping on the turf to waken the sleeping spirits of the spring. We took boats upon the river and the boatman let me hold the oars; I floundered in the shallows and began to learn to swim; and at the water's edge we fed the swans that later would be roasted at the banquets. In the winter we heard myths and legends in the firelight.

"Let him know the old tales of the bards," the King had ordered. "He must learn to love that scabby land where he was born. You tame a place by understanding its beliefs."

And so I heard about Arianrhod of the Silver Wheel, and Blodenwedd the hag who became an owl, and Gwyn the God of Light, the mighty huntsman, and Llew and the Woman of Flowers, and Rhiannon of the Birds with her swift white horse; and the magic cauldron of Cerridwen; and the enchanted times of the year when the gates to the Otherworld open, and in the moonlit groves or at the standing stones the Otherworldly beings wait and beckon, and wise animals speak and lead the way.

"Heathen tales," nurse Alice said, and crossed herself; but she permitted tales of Arthur and the knights because these were manly and prepared a boy for war; and besides, the King himself was known to reverence them.

"Every castle I had built could well be Camelot," he told me once. "Minstrels may make songs of it and clerks may write it down; but I have left it for all time translated into stone."

All my sisters were beautiful and affectionate, my nurses protective and attentive, but the most binding influence upon me in those early years was my grandmother. The old Queen Eleanor lived then within the convent walls of Amesbury, with her ancient memories of Provence and her passionate love of the sun. Like Guinevere, I thought, revelling in her proximity, snuggling against her fine rich silk, touching the dark softness of her veil, feasting my eyes upon the garnet set in gold upon her gnarled pale forefinger. We sat together in the cloister on a bench of sun-warmed stone and heard the rise and fall of holy singing.

"Pray every day and night for your father and mother, the King and Queen," said Eleanor. "They didn't want to go from you, but they are needed overseas in Gascony."

"What is Gascony?"

"Oh, innocent that I was, Robert!"

12

"Gascony is an English land that France would like to own. And since its people are unruly, a strong hand must keep it in order. That strong hand is your father's."

"Is my father very fierce?" I winced.

"No indeed!" she smiled. "You mustn't think it. But at times he has to be severe. He must prevent rebellion and discord. All kings must do so. Your father is a very great man. One day you will be just like him, and you will learn how difficult it is to be a king."

My painful ignorance persuaded her that I had no concept of my parents. She set about to right the matter.

"Your father is a tall and handsome man, strong, brave and just; all that a king should be. King Henry and I, we nurtured him to love God and his people; he was always a good son to us. When the time came that he should marry we gave great care and consideration to the matter. It's most important, Edward, that a future king should marry well — that is, to give greatest benefit — and it was clear to us that the King of Castile would relinquish his claims to Gascony if our kindred were united. Gascony is a problem to us, Edward, as you will find. Castile wanted it, France intends to have it, and Gascony itself is a turbulent place, full of troublesome barons. But when your father married his Castilian princess we made all calm. Castile now accepts that Gascony is ours...

"Edward was just fifteen. The marriage was blessed by all the stars in heaven, because the Prince and Princess fell in love, and this is rare, my dear, in royal marriages. Young Eleanor has been a joy to us. Perhaps it augured well that she had the same name as myself. She has been the perfect wife to your father; no one could have wished for better. She supports him in all his ventures, goes with him on all his travels, and has borne his children in far off places; in short she is his constant helpmate and support. Why, she travelled with him to the Holy Land when your father took the cross and saved Acre from the Saracen. Your sister Joan was born there. And there your father nearly lost his life — an enemy had sworn to kill him and crept into his tent by night, with a dagger steeped in poison, and this wicked man stabbed King Edward in the shoulder. Your father killed him with one mighty blow, and Eleanor sucked out the poison from the wound made by the dagger. Ah, your father never would allow mere bodily discomfort to annoy him, and within a week was back in the field, the terror of the foe...

"He was always fearless, was my Edward. He was his father's right hand. He put down the de Montfort and he'll take no grumblings from his barons. He knows how to keep our nobles in their place. King

Arthur come again, your father is. The troubadours sing songs about him... Edward, you have grown thoughtful. We have talked enough. Sister Maud's cat has a litter of kittens which are very pretty. We'll go play with them."

This ancient dame with tales to tell of my hero-father was cousin Tom's grandmother too. Sometimes we visited her together. Then Tom grew surly at the talk of fathers, for although Eleanor was surely fond of Edmund of Lancaster it was plain he paled beside his mighty brother. No amount of prompting would elicit more than "Edmund is so loyal. Edmund is all that a brother should be."

And then she might elaborate a little thus: "We worried about him when he was a boy. His shoulder gave him trouble; there was a weakness there. He could never be the warrior that Edward is. He adores Edward, of course. Edward can always rely on him..."

"And he was successful in gaining land," Tom pointed out, quickly sidestepping the reference to the crooked shoulder. "We have all of the de Montfort estates. The Midlands are ours..."

"And very right and fair it is too," said the old lady savagely. "The sons of the crown should appropriate the lands of a traitor. De Montfort was a monster, an ungrateful monster. He betrayed King Henry's trust. He fought against his own anointed King. But right and justice triumphed. It was all due to my Edward, and he only a youth at the time. Edward was stronger than the King himself. Edward was wonderful."

We knew about de Montfort and his horrid end. He had been killed in a dreadful battle and his corpse had been hacked to pieces. They even cut off his cock. This was what happened to wicked men who rose against their king. From infancy Tom and I endured the flaming spectre of de Montfort. He was what happened when a king was weak. King Henry was weak — his widow would never have admitted it, but everybody knew it; and we were warned. De Montfort had been an ulcer on the fair skin of the realm, a putrid pustule that had to be pricked and drained. At heart all kings lived in dread of a de Montfort growing.

A climbing rose framed the window of Queen Eleanor's room at Amesbury.

"Its name is rosa mundi," she explained. "See its whorls, so closely curled, more delicate than silk, finer than old parchment. This came from my home — I mean Provence. Lavender grows wild there on the hillsides. The roses there are fairer than anything we see at Windsor.

I shall give your mother a cutting for the garden at Langley when she returns; you are to make your home there, Ned, and when you see the roses growing you'll remember your old grandame who was always telling you about the olden days... I'm sixty-five — or is it sixty-six? — and though I'm a wrinkled old crone yet I was very beautiful when I was young ... and I could sing; I knew all the troubadour songs. I'll teach you one. My voice still has some sweetness and won't spoil the song by cracking...

> "L'on dit q'amors est dolce chose
> mais je n'en conois la dolcor
> tote joie m'en est enclose,
> n'ainz ne senti nul bien d'amor -
> they say that love is a sweet thing
> but I am not acquainted with its sweetness
> all joy is excluded from me,
> I have never felt any good from love..."

And therefore I knew love songs at a tender age and I could sing the words without the least idea of love's pains and delights.

"You still are beautiful," I told her adoringly.

"Those who truly love us always seem beautiful," said Eleanor, and hugged me. "And now we'll find your sister Mary and I'll take you to see the bee skeps in the meadow and you shall see how bees make honey."

"When your father returns from Gascony," she said one day, "Ask him to tell you everything about King Arthur and his knights. Your father loves those old tales. He is the one to tell you. You see, King Arthur is more than a story sung by minstrels. He was a real person and his knights were as the knights of nowadays must ever strive to be. Your father has a beautiful book about the Grail romances. He took it with him everywhere, even when he went to fight the Saracen ... He loves those old tales."

> "Listen to her, Robert. Is she talking about the man we knew? Is this the man who threw Elizabeth's coronet into the fire? Is this the man who dragged me by the hair?"

"Your father has a passionate reverence for the time of Arthur. He ordered the tomb of Arthur and Queen Guinevere to be opened and reconsecrated, and had them buried in a more fitting setting, there at the enchanted place of Glastonbury, which was once the Isle of Apples... Avalon...

"The Welsh gave him King Arthur's crown, and the red stone from the pommel of his sword. When you were born, your father created his own Round Table in thanks and celebration, and he held a tournament at Nefyn by the sea; knights came from far and wide to joust for prizes and for glory. You are a prince of the land of Arthur. The castle where you were born is like no other castle — beautiful, elegant, pinnacled... Why, it might be Camelot itself...

"Let those knights live for you, Edward. Take them with you in your thoughts. Let them be companions on your path. Lancelot the brave — Tristan the sad knight of Lyonesse — let them speak to you. You'll find they'll help you on your way — faithful Bedevere — Gawain, knight of the Goddess...

"...I was pleased when your father named you Edward," she told me. "This is a special name, rare and unusual, not easy to pronounce. This is because it is a Saxon name. There were many Edwards in those old days; it was as popular as John and Henry are today. But the most celebrated Edward was a saint. My husband, King Henry, venerated him with all the ardour of an acolyte. Each year Saint Edward's day was held with pomp and feast and worship. King Henry built a special shrine for him. Be worthy of the name, child. Be worthy of your father."

My grandame sought to fill my youthful heart with pride. Her intentions were well meaning. But sometimes these encounters left me despondent. My father, it seemed, was a hero, King Arthur come again, invincible in battle, capable and courtly, admired by all. That other Edward, the Saxon king of a bygone age, was more saint than monarch, so holy that even now his name was spoken in hushed tones of reverence. I bore the same name as these two men, each perfect in his own way. But how could I emulate these giants?

When it became apparent that King Edward and Queen Eleanor were expected to return from Gascony, having, naturally, put that place in order, there was tangible unease amongst the happy household where the sisters and the nurses had for so long held sway.

"There will be changes," Joan said, grim, in a voice that implied that such would not be for the better.

"But what is he like?" I cried, unaccountably afraid.

It was much as if the shadow of a giant had dropped upon me, approaching me with slow inevitable steps.

"Don't you remember him at all?" they said in disbelief.

"Well, he's very easy," Joan said laughing. "As long as you don't anger him."

"What angers him?"

"Anything or anyone that goes against him! So, keep silent in his company, agree with all he says, and generally make pretence you don't exist. And you'll do very well."

We waited on the quayside at Dover, my sisters and I, the household and the horses, the nobles of the realm, the bishops, and the townsfolk from their houses. We watched the tall ships drawing nearer.

King Edward, fifty years old, ran up the steps, tall, magnificent in red and gold, his white hair streaming; and he knelt down by me and held both my arms.

"Is he healthy?" he asked over my head. "Is he healthy?"

"Very healthy, sire, exceptionally healthy," they assured him.

"Well, Edward, I am very pleased with you," my father said, and stood, and bent, and heaved me skyward in a whirling embrace that all but cracked my ribs, and pressed me to him till I half suffocated in his beard; but there was no doubt of the warmth of his delight. His face was close to mine. He said with great good humour: "And remember always — when I come home from Gascony I bring gifts!"

And this was so. As I rode up into the town in a crimson cloak with a golden clasp, and seated on a new white palfrey, I truly wondered how I'd ever feared my father.

Some thirteen years previously, Queen Eleanor had acquired the manor of Langley in Hertfordshire, with over a hundred acres of land, and a forest rich in deer, of ancient beech and oak. Within this parkland was a palace, and she set about to make a home there for her son.

Langley Palace stands on Le Corte hill, whose wide and gentle slopes ease down towards the river Gad, which winds by water meadows and a mill through its own valley. The air is clear and pure, and far below in all directions, lies a sea of trees, a shifting shimmering mass of green and gold.

The palace was built of flints, each stone a slab of grey, of ochre, cinnamon and tawny, the chipping of these stones sounding with a metallic musical ring as beyond the wicket gate they worked on the new priory, built of the same stone. The palace gathered round about three courtyards. A flight of covered steps led to the main door, the chambers all on the higher floor. The great hall had tall windows and a timbered roof, and its walls were decorated with fifty four shields and painted with a picture of four knights riding towards a tournament. Little stairways led to the private chambers, which all had hearths and fires; it was a comfortable and lovely place. And there were barns and stables, gardens of vines and roses, with nooks and arbours; and apple orchards on the hillslopes. An outer wall surrounded it, high with battlements. A man came from the village to make traps for wolves; they ran wild in the forest; you could hear them howling as you lay in bed.

Five years old now, I had a room with Turkish carpets on the walls and floors, a blaze of intricate purples, blues and crimsons; and a great chest carved with dragons,snakes and flowers, for my clothes; and I had golden pointed slippers, and silk cushions embroidered with peacocks; no one came back empty-handed from the Holy Land.

A further trophy from the days of the Crusade was a lumbering lugubrious camel who had abode in the stables. His name was Saladin. A groom looked after him, and to make him stand he'd cry: "Yazzah! Yazzah!" and the beast would walk around the courtyard, dignified and swaying, and I rode upon the camel's back and thought myself a potentate.

Joan had been right; changes there were. One by one my sisters were found husbands. Eleanor left England to marry the Count of Bar, and Margaret married the Duke of Brabant, though she didn't leave home till a few years later. At her wedding celebrations they brought in a castle made of pastry, sculpted to look as if it were made of stone; and more knights than I had ever seen attended; and in order to be properly magnificent we changed our clothes three times in one day, not because the clothes were dirty, but to show everybody that we had so many clothes. Joan wed Gilbert the Red, Earl of Gloucester, a giant with flaming hair. All the marriages were a matter of policy. Gilbert the Red was a potential de Montfort, and King Edward knew how to deal with those. Gilbert had to surrender all his lands into the King's hands and then receive them back as a gift of the King. Gilbert was forty-nine. If he died, his lands reverted to the crown.

For myself, the changes were not unpleasant; I grew to know my mother.

An austerely beautiful woman with sleek black hair and a fine intelligence, she read Aristotle's works for pleasure, but she was perfectly content to share with me the tales of Camelot. She loved clothes and jewels and music, perfumes, furs. She showed me how to eat a pomegranate daintily; to this day, you will be impressed to learn, I still possess the skill. She brought gardeners from Aragon — lovely dark-haired men with swarthy skins and bulging muscles — to make Moorish trellises for the vines and roses. She pored over plans for Langley's gardens with the same predatory absorption as my father over the map of Scotland. My father loved her with a deep enduring love beside which his little dalliance with Gilbert the Red's first wife, Alice, counted as nothing.

To see my parents framed by firelight with the wolfhounds dozing on the hearth, I could not help but think the world a peaceful place and my situation in it most acceptable. Whyever had I feared the king's return?

"And now to Edward's marriage... By all the bones of all the saints," King Edward guffawed. "I do believe the boy supposes that I mean him to be wed tomorrow! Come here, son, sit beside me and we'll talk of Scotland. I'm speaking of the future now, so rest your fears. You've years a-plenty with your dogs and camel and your mother's care."

The great hall was dark in the November gloom. The walls with their painted knights, their golds and crimsons, were a dim obscurity of looming shadows where the gusting fire brands glowed. Upon the great oak dining table, scarred and pitted by the cuts of many knives, King Edward slung a parchment and gestured me to join him.

I wriggled up onto the bench beside my father.

"This is Scotland," said my father. "Bring light, God damn you, how are we to read?"

Servants hurried forward, and a candelabra now illumined the unravelled map.

"They've told you that King Alexander died?" he said. "Horse threw him. Fool business. Any man who can't control his nag gets all that he deserves. The matter will turn well for us, boy, for the heir to Scotland is a little wench your own age, and with your marriage we'll have Scotland joined to us, and now that Wales is ours, the country will be one great heap, we ruling it. Yes, all has fallen much to our advantage."

I stole a glance at him. I saw the white bushy hair, the tendrilled beard, the wine-stained bread crumbs tangled in its curls. I was horribly fascinated by the one drooping eyelid, which gave a hooded look to that side of the face, a sleepy falcon's face. The fine-boned cheeks were lean and angular, the nose haughty; and all mannerisms rapid, sudden, inspiring wariness.

"Henceforth your duty is to understand the place you'll rule. It's not like Wales. Wales is a land of the romances. If Llewellyn had shown sense we'd never have needed to fight at all. He was a fool. If he'd been tractable he'd be alive today. But that's all trodden roads now; we must look to what's to come. Scotland — it's a wilderness — a wasteland — but a dangerous wasteland, and a land that might have caused us wars. Not now. By marriage we'll do peaceably what could have cost us lives and gold. I thank Almighty God that things have fallen out so well for us. God's blessing truly is upon us."

Scotland lay spread out before us on the soft uncurled parchment, background to King Edward's jabbing finger, which grew iridescent where the candle flames caught the flash of jewelled rings.

"Here — Carlisle to keep the west, here New Castle to maintain the east. Between, a border land of cattle-grabbing robber lords; beyond, a land of clans and tribes that speak no civil tongue. Here they're little more than Norsemen who have tired of boats and taken to the soil. Here there's a fine church and good farming — these are islands, half over the rim of the world, lost in the northern seas. Here there are forests full of elk and bear and wolves more wild than those in Langley woods. Stirling — we'll go there and flaunt our army — and Perth and Scone where they keep the Stone of Destiny..." Suddenly, disconcertingly he turned and looked me in the eye. "What's in it for us? I can hear you ask it, plain as if you'd spoken. More trouble than it's worth, eh? By God's blood, I'll tell you: Scotland peaceable gives us no cause for anxiety and leaves us free to set our faces towards matters of importance — France and Gascony and a Crusade more glorious than any that has gone before. Scotland hostile or allied with France, and we've a cur that's yapping at our heels, and he'll need whipping!"

My mother sought to soften her husband's harsh account of my new bride's territory by reminding me of the reason for our interest in so unprepossessing an acquisition. That night she sat with me in my room as I lay in my bed, and gave me a portrait of my future bride, an oval framed in silver, small enough to enclose in the palm of my hand.

"Her name is Margaret. She is seven years old. She's King Alexander's granddaughter. Her father is the King of Norway. What a lovely face she has! You can tell her disposition's sweet by those fine eyes, even though the picture is so small. And you will be her husband, and look after her and be a good and true lord, caring for her as a knight must care for his lady."

"I have a picture of an elk also," I confided, showing it. "It is the very largest deer that ever lived."

"Indeed it is," my mother said amused. "But Edward, set about to study the lady, not the elk, for you will find she'll have more relevance."

I pinned the map of Scotland to a chair's back, and became conversant with the country. Here were mountains — here were churches, castles, here the monks' island where the royal dead were buried. The land was wild but I would grow to know it and to love it, and the lady too. We might go riding in the forests and look for elk, and if she found them frightening I would cheer her, and like a true and noble knight I would protect her and make sure she was well content. Throughout that winter, Margaret, Scotland, were my favourite thoughts. In March the treaty that would bring these dreams to life was ratified, and my father sent a ship to Norway to bring home the Maid.

"We'll all go north," he said. "This business is too important to let slip one inch of ceremony. You'll be there to welcome her, Edward."

When my grandmother heard of this, she fretted in her sanctuary. She wrote to my father. "We feel uneasy about his going. When we were there, we could not avoid being ill because of the bad climate. We pray you therefore put him some place south where the climate is temperate, while you go north."

"It made her breathing rasp," my father explained. "She loves the sun, you see. She fears the fogs. But you are strong; the Scottish mists won't trouble you."

"Your father thinks that it would be unwise to permit the Maid to live in Scotland while she is so young. Better that she be under our protection," said my mother pleasantly. "And while she lives in England you shall have ample time to further your acquaintance. She will be your friend."

The notion pleased me. There were so many pleasures there at Langley whose joys could only increase by the sharing — riding in the forest — listening out for the wolves — playing games with bat and ball — watching the thatchers, farrier, gardeners and grooms — sharing a bath in the splendid new bath house which my mother had had installed — hiding in the barns — swimming in the river — taking a small boat out — watching the thatchers, gardeners, farrier and grooms again...

"Now I come to think of it, Robert, all these are pleasures that I still enjoy."

21

My father strode into my chamber, white with fury.

"Cease your fussings. You shall not go north. The wench is dead." He slammed his fist down on the table. "All my plans..." he seethed. "By God's blood, all my plans..." And catching sight of the map pinned to the chair he ripped it clear and slung it to the floor. "You'll not be needing that. That is as worthless now as mouldy hay. And did your mother give you a picture of the girl? Where is it?" I gave it to him.

The King paused with the portrait in his hand. "Poor silly maid. Taken sick on the ship. Died in the Orkney Islands. Back to Bergen with a coffin for a marriage bed. How God sees fit to mock us..."

Detaching the picture from the frame he crumpled it to nothing and tossed it in the fire. He was enormous, like a tree. "By God, it makes you wonder why we ever strive."

Rage soared in him. He kicked the chair out of his path and strode out of the room, leaving me diminished, desolate, in his wake.

I knelt and picked up the discarded silver frame. An empty violated space stared back at me, a reflected emptiness within, a void not to be filled...

"Till Gaveston," said Robert.

Chapter Two

I N HIS grief, as in so many of his outward manifestations, King Edward showed a certain splendour.

Queen Eleanor his wife was dead, dead of a fever, and barely more than a year since they had come back to us from Gascony. Her death was unexpected, up there in the November gloom of murky Nottinghamshire; and her dismal cortege travelled south accompanied by the weeping monarch; while everywhere the coffin rested on the route to Westminster there were crosses to be built in memory of her, lovely graceful monuments in stone.

Six years old, I endured the great state funeral silently. I had never seen my father thus, prostrate with passionate despair, laying claim to misery as if it were his own.

"As if no man had ever lost a wife before," nurse Alice said. And we saw nothing of him for weeks afterwards, as he assuaged his grief at Ashridge, close to God amongst the monks. Poor tormented soul; death in December has a gloom all of its own, and he that's left behind finds nothing of comfort.

King Edward had no need of us. If I had supposed I might be any consolation to the royal widower when we were reunited, I was mistaken.

"What are you snivelling for?" my father said contemptuously and clouted me. "You scarcely knew her."

"Deaths come in threes," said nurse Alice, combing out my hair. "I don't like that one so soon after the young maid of Norway. I wonder who it will be. Deaths come in threes."

I found myself squinting cautiously at the King, eyeing the furrows in his brow, the thick white hair. Were not these signs of age? I looked in vain for trembling limbs, for stumbling tread, for weakness. But King Edward still strode like a soldier, bellowed like a bull, ran, rode, gave orders, made his plans. But if deaths came in threes, as Alice said, who would it be?

Against all odds, I hoped that it would be my father.

In February, in the snow, muffled in many layers of fur, we journeyed across country to visit old Queen Eleanor at Amesbury.

The sky was pale blue, tinged with rose; the sun shone, casting on the distant fields a light sheen of pale amber. The far away white hills looked unreal in their snowy mantle. We rode through woodland where although the snow was rutted with the tracks of carts, beyond the path it lay undisturbed, windblown into sculptured drifts. Some of the tree trunks showed vivid green, as if the Green Knight had passed that way and left his mark. There was one with green antlers, like the head of a deer. There was one I would have sworn to be a figure trapped in the tree-bole, a writhing torso, arms raised, and even, down at hip level, enough whorl of bark to suggest that the figure was male. No sooner had I blinked away this strange fancy than I saw another sight that caused me much astonishment — a squat square little face, puckered into cheeks and wrinkled about the eyes. Nobody else seemed to have noticed these odd shapes. I crossed myself as I had been taught to do when threatened with the unknown. Like a magic thread our path wove its way around curves and over hillocks, and we followed it, in a silence broken only by the jingling of our bridles and the rustle of the undergrowth, and the heavy falls of snow as the wind shook a branch.

Through this mysterious land, I thought, awed, we are travelling to Guinevere.

The ancient dame received us in her chamber where she lay in bed, ice cold, she said, and aching in her bones. King Edward threw a heap of logs upon the brightly burning fire, and kicked them into life. The wet wood crackled and spat, and the sparks cascaded in a wind gust from the hearth.

"'But roses like the roses of Bourgeuil I have not found them here, and I begin to sigh; not that I would go back, but I fain would see flowers fairer than are here'", the old Queen quoted ruefully. "Spring comes so late to England."

King Edward at her bedside held her thin white hand and said: "If I could bring the warm winds from the south at whatever cost and loss of ships I'd do it."

"I know it, dear sire," she answered fondly. "But with all your great indomitable strength, you are not yet God. You've always been a joy to me — no mother ever knew a braver finer son."

King Edward turned away, tears coursing freely down his cheeks.

"Let me see little Edward," said Queen Eleanor, and she hugged me to her in a long embrace. "Remember, child," she said, "Life is not an easy passage. But live it as a knight. Take Gawain with you — Tristan, Lancelot. You will never be lonely in that company..."

In the cold passageway beyond the heavy door we paused, my father and I, and a slow bell chimed far off and echoed hollowly in the silences of pillared stone. King Edward shivered and pulled on his leather gloves.

"Come, Edward."

I hesitated, looking in the direction of the garden. "She lets me see the kittens and the bees."

King Edward frowned dismissively. "Kittens? Bees? What kind of talk is that? Can you not see she's dying?"

Tom of Lancaster understood my grief; she was his grandame also. We lay in my bed at Langley, arms about each other.

"She was very old," said Tom. "It is the way of things."

"But — so many deaths, so close together. Nurse Alice foresaw it — at least, she said another death was due. But Tom, the particular thing that troubles me — "

"What? What is it, Ned?"

"Is it my fault?" I demanded, wriggling from him, hunched and miserable.

"Your fault? However can that be?"

"I loved them all. It seems the ones I love all die. And the ones I don't love," I added gloomily, "stay alive and hearty."

"That is ridiculous and you know it. That would make you a magician. And you are not, are you, Ned? Ned? Have you such power?" Thomas laughed and tickled me and made me giggle, and I knew my fear was foolish. I kissed Tom's cheek. Tom held me close and put his hand between my thighs and stroked me.

"You mustn't ever be afraid," he said.

My fever raged. I lay in sweat-drenched sheets, and tossed and turned. The physician hovered between me and my sister Margaret who also suffered with the tertian ague but whose demise would cause less panic. The King, my father, held me to him, clasping me like a second self. The room was full of candles, prayers and incense, offerings to saints.

"Live, Edward, live!" my father wept, having seen his Queen die of a fever. For the first time, through the mists of delirium, I understood my fearsome father loved me with a frightening intensity.

"Live, Edward!" he commanded, and, appalled at this proximity, too terrified to disobey, I did as I was ordered. Margaret also lived; we were both healthy children.

Travelling players who came to entertain at Langley brought a fortune teller with them, a young woman with a nut brown skin and gaudy bangles at her wrists. She laid three brightly painted blocks of wood on the floor, and Tom and I knelt by her, curious, and she told us we must both beware of bees. Nurse Alice shooed her away and said what was she about — be off or there'd be trouble!

After that, both Tom and I shared an uneasiness near bee skeps, though we laughed about it; neither of us thinking of the alphabet.

The Twelfth Night hobby horse was a marvel to me. He came into the hall prancing and dancing, shaking his golden mane. I knew that he was made of wicker with a cloth around it and that a man was inside to make him work, but he seemed alive. His eyes were made of jewels that flashed in the torchlight. When he drew near to the table his great jaw opened and he bellowed forth real fire. It made me jump. I thought he was magnificent.

"I can think of nothing better," I confided to Tom, "than to be the man inside that horse!"

"You must be more simple than I thought," said Tom.

Within the next five years that northern appendage of the civilized world, that latent power for good or ill — Scotland — kept King Edward much away from home.

A host of claimants to the Scottish throne then asked the King of England to judge which of them had best right to rule, and so my father took his army north and chose John Balliol whom he despised, assessing him as one that he could master. King John did homage for his throne and then, taking advantage of the King of France's invasion of Gascony, set about to ally himself with France. Harassed on all sides, King Edward found himself almost continually at war. Invading Scotland, wrecking Berwick, he took Balliol prisoner and brought him back to England along with the Stone of Destiny and the jewels of the Scottish crown. He left all Scotland garrisoned by Englishmen.

"We shall rule Scotland ourself," my father said in scorn. "These petty kings are no good to man nor beast. Would you credit it — Robert Bruce said Scotland should go to him since he had fought against John Balliol. I told him: Do you think I have nothing to do but win kingdoms for you?"

26

Tom's father, my affable uncle, Edmund of Lancaster, was sent to Paris to negotiate with the devious French King, and my father planned his reconquest of our Gascon province. He helped himself to money from the coffers of the church and gathered up the gold amassed for Holy Crusade to use upon this hugely unpopular undertaking. For what was Gascony but a good source of wine? And what were Gascons but trouble?

My sister Joan bore four children to Gilbert the Red, a son and three daughters. Every one of the three daughters was destined to grow up to marry a man who had been my lover.

When Gilbert the Red died, I being then about eleven years old, King Edward spoke of him to me with some affection.

"He was a soldier, the kind of man I can well tolerate. Some might call him headstrong, rough. And he was so; but that's no bad thing in this thorny world. He was wild when he was young. Thought he knew best. Thought that de Montfort had the answers. Fought at Lewes against us and was the very one who took your grandsire captive. Then he came to his senses and understood de Montfort was a canker, turned against him, and fought by my side at Evesham where we slew de Montfort. But a man like Gilbert has to be contained. I daresay if I'd been a weaker man — more like your grandsire — Gilbert could have been my own de Montfort. No such chance! Once I'd got him safely pacified with Marcher lands he had enough on his plate keeping them in order. Oh, he flared up from time to time, but I could always keep him down. He gave me good support in Wales. We often drunk ourselves to perdition together. A good man was Gilbert, and once married to your sister he was well muzzled. He was a trial to me often, but he was a man, and if you grew to be such a one as he I'd be well pleased ... Joan is still of marriageable age...we'll turn that now to our advantage..."

"Let him do so," Joan shrugged placidly. "I've wed once for his convenience. I am my own woman now. I shall marry whom I please."

I looked at her admiringly. Resist the King's wishes? Go against that leopard? I did not think that I would ever dare do so. But Joan was brave. Then some twenty-five years of age, with Gilbert's death she ruled the mighty Clare inheritance and she had never feared our father's wrath.

"I've lands and wealth," she said, "and I shall go my way."

"She is yet my daughter," stormed the King. "I have had trouble enough from that husband of hers. Now that he's dead she shall not think to act his part as if his spirit yet lived on."

"My spirit is my own," said Joan. "And thanks to it, I lived in harmony enough with Gilbert. Now he's gone and I propose to make my own choices."

"We shall see about that," the King promised, sending envoys to the Count of Savoy upon the subject of her next marriage.

"It is to be hoped, sire, that your envoys love the pleasures of travel for their own sake. I hear that Savoy has many pleasant castles. I hope they will provide the justification for the journey. This may be the moment to let your grace know I am already wed."

I gasped, crouched over my sleeping wolfhound's neck. I buried my lips in his warm hair, my eyes wide as my bold sister made her challenge.

"How may that be?" King Edward asked in a cold steady tone. "I have given no permission on that score, as I recall."

"I requested none," she answered calmly. She was sitting at her tapestry. "Nevertheless I am married." She paused and sorted through her threads. "My husband is a knight of Earl Gilbert's household, Ralph de Monthermer. He is young and kind and has a strong affection for me. I am well content, and there's an end to it."

"No, madam, this is not the end to it, as well you know," King Edward snarled. "By God's blood it is not! A household knight — and you could have had whomsoever I could have plucked for you. What, are you mad? You think I will permit it?"

She shrugged. She was wonderful.

"Stop weaving!" screamed our father, and he heaved the tapestry, frame and all, into the fire. It made a beautiful blaze. I'm surprised more tapestries are not burned. It was most interesting to see it catch fire — horsemen and forest and a writhing unicorn unfolding in merry confusion amongst the leaping flames.

"I never liked it," Joan said.

The wretched Ralph was flung into prison, languishing in Bristol castle. The lands of which Joan boasted were on the instant seized, reverting to the crown.

"King he may be," said Joan to me darkly. "King of all England. But at heart he is a lout, with all the finesse of a foraging hog."

"Let no man think to cross me," said the King to me. "Nor woman either. Learn from this, Edward. There must be obedience to the King. Brook no opposition. By all the bones of all the saints, I will be obeyed; all else is chaos."

The people clamoured in the streets of London against the prospect of war in Gascony. Gascons were lewd and violent — fighters, trouble-makers. Leave them be. Let Philip of France overrun them; it's no more than they deserve. Our business should be to beat the Scots, who threaten from nearby instead of far away across the sea.

At Langley I was taught knightly virtues by the good Sir Guy, along with other boys of good family; and also the politeness of the table — not to spit, nor blow the nose upon the sleeve, nor belch into the face of another, nor scratch the dog, nor spit in to the hand-basin, nor, if having been so reckless as to spit, to tread the spit into the ground.

Meanwhile a knight of the King's household was caught spying for the French and at his trial adjudged guilty. He was slit open and disembowelled and his carcase dangled from a chain amongst the bleeding meat at Smithfield.

I have always had familiarity with the English tongue, the language of the common people, and at Langley ample opportunity to use it, for I wandered freely there amongst the workers on the land. Far from despising them for being peasants and unlettered, I always found them worthy of respect, and lacking the pretension and the arrogance of their so-called betters.

I watched the millwright dress the millstones and recut the furrows in the faces of the stones; the hammering of nails that held the ribs of a boat in place; the shoeing of horses in the glowing hissing farriery; and I learnt the strange and barely pronounceable names of the thatcher's work — the yealm, the spar hook and the shearing hook — and more, I was permitted to tie up the yealms (the tight bunches of thatch) and pass them to the thatcher on his ladder, and to skin the bramble into cord.

It may well have been at the same time that I grew to admire the naked torso of the working man, the pull and stretch of muscle in the shoulder, the furry hairs upon the skin, the gleam of sweat, the careless strength of those to whom the labour of the hands comes easily.

When Tom was at Langley in the summer I took him down to the water mill to show him the young miller at work, with his sleeves rolled up and his tousled hair flopping forward over his face; and the great slats of the paddle wheel by the mossy green-stained wall, and the churning cascades of the white waterfall, and within, the low-beamed creaking innards and the grindstones.

"We had such a flood here in February! Where we are standing, fishes were swimming! On that beam there, kingfishers perched."

"Ned, you are becoming droll," said Tom as we rode off and at a gentle pace traversed the meadow. "Your miller's a fine-looking man, but have you not considered that a king's son talking to a miller is an oddity? As for the mill, where lies the pleasure in discovering, as we supposed, that the mill grinds flour? I knew that before I entered the place; my suspicions are confirmed; and I cannot but feel the subject is irrelevant to such as we."

"At Langley," I explained, "we are a family, all of us, the highest and the low. And since I am allowed to talk to whom I will, I find the so-called humbler folk have much to teach, and I learn all I may."

Tom snorted; but there was affection in his scorn.

Tom was eighteen now, tall and pale, fair-haired, light-browed, with wary eyes and a sensuous mouth that had acquired a slow half-cynical smile. He and his brother Henry were to go to Flanders with the King; he was to be a knight. I envied him.

"Like Lancelot," I thought dreamily. To spend the night in vigil in the Temple Church, to go forth as a hero, seeking glory...

"Have you been in a tournament?" I asked then.

"I have, yes, once."

"What happened?"

"Well," Tom laughed and winced. "I was unseated."

"And hurt?"

"To be sure it hurt! I was very much bruised."

"But you were not wounded."

"Fortunately, no."

"I watched a tournament at Dunstable," I said thoughtfully. "Of course, I longed to be one of the knights. Like the ones on the wall in the great hall, so upright and perfect. Then I saw a combatant who had been unhorsed and pierced by a lance. They carried him on a hurdle and his head hung down. They said it had been a mistake, an accident. I saw it all quite clearly, and the dark stains his passing left in the scattered sand. I thought: for what? To be so hurt — for what?"

"Keep those thoughts to yourself, coz," Thomas laughed, with nonchalance that was a little unconvincing. "It wouldn't do to let your father hear you questioned chivalry."

"I don't," I answered indignantly, adding: "I question pointlessness."

Even at twelve years old I could row strongly up and down the Gad, and Thomas laughed good humouredly as he sat in the stern of my little boat and let the Prince of England act the boatman.

"Don't you wish you were older, Ned?" he asked. "Henry and I will be in Flanders with your father when he goes against the French. You'll miss everything — all the deeds of glory."

"Don't talk to me of Flanders," I panted grimly. "I'm to marry the Count of Flanders' daughter — merely so that we encircle France. I don't want to hear a word about Flanders. And she isn't even pretty."

"Would it matter, Ned?" said Thomas. "All you have to do is get an heir. You aren't required to love the lady."

"I don't even want to think about it."

I moored the boat in a reedy creek where willows overhung the water. We clambered out and made our way up to a hawthorn copse across the rough grass and the sun-dried mud.

"It's rare to be quite so alone," I remarked. "It's one reason why I like to row. I can put yards between me and whoever has the task of keeping an eye upon me."

"Did you want us to be quite alone then?" Thomas asked, and watched me.

"I thought I did...I'm not sure," I said fidgeting.

Tóm put his hands on my shoulders and moved me gently till I stood against a tree. "You grow more beautiful each time I see you," Thomas said. "Just like a flower."

"I'm not," I protested wriggling. "That's silly."

"It isn't. You're smooth as roses." Thomas touched my cheek. "Have you no vanity? Has no one told you that you're very very pretty."

"You have," I giggled, looking up at him, with something of a simper.

Tom bent and kissed me lightly, tentatively.

"So," Tom said severely, tapping my nose. "You permit a man to kiss you in the wood." He grew serious. "Do you kiss others, Edward? Who else have you kissed? There are squires up at the palace with you — barons' sons — aren't there? Who else, Ned?"

"Gilbert de Clare," I answered pouting. "Once."

"Gilbert? That puppy? He can't kiss you; he does not know how."

Tom pounced. Holding me still, he made me part my lips. He slid his tongue between and slowly savoured my mouth.

"Now wind your tongue round mine," he breathed, and I obeyed, a dutiful pupil, and then suddenly flung my arms around my cousin's shoulders, my mouth soft and wide beneath Tom's hard insistent kisses. It occurred to me with some surprise that I must have wanted this to happen.

"Edward, Edward, " Tom said passionately, with his lips on my throat, "there's only I who am good enough for you."

"In what capacity?" I asked him faintly.

"God's truth, as a lover of course!" Tom said and kissed me roughly. "Look what you've done, and now you'd better pay the price."

He forced my head down till I saw the bulging of his crotch. He made me feel it. He said it was all my fault. "You want to see it, don't you, Ned? You want to see it out."

"Yes," I admitted, shamefully excited.

Tom pulled his cock out, long, blue-veined, and glistening at its tip. "I'd like to put it in your arse."

"Oh no, " I whimpered. "I don't think — "

"Why not? Scared? Would I be the first?"

"Yes. Yes, scared, and yes, you would."

"Then on your face then; so kneel down."

"Oh I couldn't..."

Thomas shoved me down upon my knees and held me by my golden hair and worked his cock with rapid skilful thrusts until the juices spewed in flying arcs and, under Tom's careful guidance, pooled upon my upturned face.

"Taste it," Thomas panted.

I savoured it carefully upon my tongue, and blinked it from my eyelashes.

"Only I am good enough for you, Ned," Tom repeated. "Don't forget it." He stepped back, tidied himself up.

I wiped my face, and rubbed my head, noticing only now, that Tom's grip had been painful.

"You liked my prick," said Tom and laughed; I blushed.

"When I go to Flanders," Tom said, "I shall think of you, as a knight would of the love he left at home, who waits for his return. We love each other, Edward. We must be together. We are superior to them all. When I come home I want you to be mine."

I looked at him. "How is that possible?"

"You know what I mean," Tom answered. "Lovers. I long for it," he added fiercely. "I think of you constantly, Ned. You're the only one that's ever cared for me with some conviction. I know you love me. The knowledge keeps me in my right mind when the fit of gloom's upon me. And when I come back, you'll give me what I wanted today. You'll let me have you as I want. Edward?"

"Yes."

"Promise me, promise me!" Tom's eyes were narrowed, glittering.

"I promise," I replied.

It was certainly with mischievous intent that I persuaded Tom to ride the camel Saladin. There was a pompousness about my cousin, born of his clearly held belief that he was just about the most important person in the world.

So meek and docile seemed the beast as it knelt at the groom's command, and anyone skilled on horseback as my cousin was, thought nothing of mounting such a foolish-faced unwieldy animal. As Tom careered upwards, rode, then slipped, and struggled to regain his balance, how I laughed and danced about!

"Nobody rides him well," I sniggered.

Tom jumped down at once, white-faced with rage, and seized me by the collar and shook me savagely.

"Don't ever laugh at me!" he seethed.

"How dare you! Let me go!" I gasped. I stammered out with dignity: "I think you have forgotten who I am." Tom flung me from him, panting in his anger. "I never do!" he cried. "And that's the very devil of it."

Tom venerated Camelot almost as much as I did, but we could never play at knights as children without arguing. Both of us wanted to be King Arthur; and neither would give way.

My father prowled about my chamber, dark of brow.

"I hope you are not growing bookish, Edward," he began, his fingers lifting objects, his eyes peering to the shadows as if looking for confirmation of his dire suspicions; and finding none.

"No sire, I assure you," I protested.

"Then what's this I hear about your lack of interest in jousting?" barked the King.

"Sire there's nothing I like better; I love tournaments."

"So I should hope. I thought as much." The King sat down and looked at me thoughtfully. "You never knew your grandsire. He was a good man, Edward, a good good man. A faithful husband and the best of fathers. Loved beautiful things — churches, coloured windows, velvets, brocades. Always giving presents — to the wrong people. Devoted to the memory of Saint Edward. The thirteenth of October, Edward's day, meant more to him than Yule or any other anniversary. Pious, pure. Always having churches built. Masses three times a day. But Lord, what a pit he got us into with his policy. Couldn't keep the barons down, and where did it land him? They came to court in armour, making their demands at the point of a sword; they made him swear on oath to do as he was told. They ruled the country under the de Montfort. King Henry lived in dread of him.

Thunder and lightning he feared, but Simon worst of all; and he a king. I had to take control for his own good. You know about Evesham — how we finally brought de Montfort down... A foul summer it was, that year; the sky was black as doom — they said it was the blackness of the Crucifixion. Truly it was very dark. We slaughtered them. Take heed of this, my boy; they have to know who's master. Every baron, given half a chance, thinks he knows how to rule, and each one must be subjugated in the way best suited — some you bribe with lands and marriage, some you remove the fangs, and some you crush. King Henry never had the way of it. He thought the world as good and pure as he. I loved that man with all my heart. I wept when he was from me. *He* was a bookish man, a lover of fine things. *He* hated tournaments. *I'd kill you with my bare hands if I thought that you would grow to be as he.*"

"I think Tom told my father that I said that jousting did not please me," I confided to my sister Elizabeth.

"Thomas of Lancaster!" said Elizabeth. "You know, I wouldn't trust him an inch. He's very wealthy now his father's died. There's a rumour spread that Tom's father — Uncle Edmund — was King Henry's eldest son, but that when they saw he had a crooked shoulder they passed him over in favour of our own sire. A story so ridiculous is not to be believed, of course, and few will do so. But a second rumour says that it was Tom himself who first began that wicked story."

King Edward's plan was to attack France on three sides, himself leading an army from the Flanders side, a second army coming up from Gascony.

And now he found himself at odds with his clergy, who baulked at funding such a venture. Their leader was Robert Winchelsea, Archbishop of Canterbury. I thought anyone who dared oppose my father was to be admired, and fool that I was, I admired Winchelsea enormously. To look at him, you'd think he was a fat and jolly man, all rosy-cheeked and cheerful like the merry priest of the tales who drinks all day and sings and fishes and knows other songs than holy ones. It's true that Winchelsea was fat. Otherwise he was a walking conscience, prickly as a hair shirt, jovial enough but horribly austere, and rumoured secretly to whip himself for his soul's sake. He gave to the needy with a rapturous abandon and kept back only two robes for himself, a personal parsimony that still makes me shudder.

My father, thwarted, lost his temper and outlawed all clergy; the Archbishop threatened all the church's enemies with excommunication, and the Pope supported him. My father swore he'd never make pilgrimage to the shrine of Saint Thomas again and asked Winchelsea if he were eager for a martyr's crown. Certain barons also grumbling, King Edward turned to pageantry.

"The time has come," he told me, "for you to win the hearts of the masses."

The sun beat strongly down on London — on crenellated city wall, on spire and tower, on gable, thatch and timber, on a maze of narrow twisting streets, on Pissing Lane beside Saint Paul's, on Ebbgate Street so choked with excrement that none might pass, on Blowbladder Street that led to Cock's Lane stews, on the splendid Guildhall, the shop fronts of West Chepe; and on the gleaming glinting river.

Outside King Rufus' hall at Westminster it shone upon a ceremony.

Spears and helmets, swords and bucklers caught the dazzling rays, with cloth of gold and jewelled brooches, pommels, gauntlets; pennants and canopies and the royal baldaquin showed that here the mighty were at work in all magnificence. Upon a dais spread with purple stood King Edward in a robe of gold and crimson, gesturing like Herod in a Twelfth Night play; and myself beside him, in pale blue satin, with my golden hair combed till it shone, and golden jewels about my person; youthful, beautiful, angelic, thirteen years of age.

"My people!" cried the King.

The sweating masses, pressed about the dais, jostled for a better sight; the soldiers held them back; the nobles and the bishops preened and bloomed, the drummers and the trumpeters fidgeted, waiting for the signal for their fanfare.

"My people..." said the King — no player's voice more resonant, more melodious, no orator more finely tuned to his own purpose. "I have presumed upon your kindliness. I have been rash and thoughtless. The heat of my blood was strong for glory; I was reckless, I confess it. My people will be generous, I said. They understand it is for England's pride that I go forth and take an army against the aggressor — France — that wolf which prowls about the gentle borderlands of Gascony. So I took reckoning from you in taxation. Ah — cruel fortune — for the dismal truth is this: that those who go in holy wars against a savage foe in God's good name must fight with weapons wholly of this earth — with soldiers, archers, yeomen of the field, men like yourselves. And drear though harsher truths must be, these Heavenly representatives must be paid in earthly coin. What would you have me do? Remain at home, and hunt and sport while France goes pillaging against our Gascon brothers? No! I know you would not this of me. For I swore upon my coronation day that I would be a good lord to you and do what was right. And though it break my heart to quit these shores, I must: God wills it. And my love for you is of such mettle that, old as I be, white haired and haggard in the service of my countrymen, yet will I venture, though it be to death itself."

He paused, and turned away, as if emotion choked him. Swiftly then, he reached his hand out to me and leaned upon my shoulder. I supported him, aware from the very muscles of his strong right arm, how little did that monarch need support, and least of all from me.

"My people," said the King. "I leave you Edward!"

Now the tears coursed freely down his face. A moan of generous compassion arose from the assembled throng.

"My son!" the King wept, gently but insistently urging me forward. "But new-grown to manhood, raised to give his life for you, as I shall do, if I am called by God to do so. Your Prince — my son. O! Take him to your hearts!"

"Prince Edward!" cried the multitude, and cheered, and seemed well pleased; and though no dove was seen to rise above the crimson hangings, the King had made his point.

The nobles now came forward — that is, those who were not presently in sullen opposition to the King nor in Gascony already — and one by one knelt down in fealty before me. I received their homage. I stood with, I believe, a natural dignity and possibly some Heavenly radiance emanating from me — it was that kind of occasion. I daresay if a sword within a stone had been produced, I might well have been able to heave out the sword.

So help me, I was moved almost to tears by what we did that day. I watched my father weeping for the populace and never doubted that the tears were true. A successful player must believe the part he plays, and the king was going for high stakes. And therefore while my head said: "What hypocrisy!" my heart admired and added: "What magnificence!"

Reconciliation was the theme now. Young Ralph of Monthermer had been released from Bristol castle and forgiven — if he would come and fight in Flanders and bring fifty knights; and Joan's lands were restored to her. Archbishop Winchelsea and Bishop Langton who hated one another, stood side by side and promised to advise their prince for the general good of all while his father was away. Tears flowed like rain at the beauty of it all; concord manifest in flesh.

"Where shall we go?" bellowed King Edward, drawing his sword and slicing it through the air in a silver arc. "Where shall I lead you?"

"To Gascony!" cried a voice, well planted in the crowd for best effect.

"To Gascony!" screamed the mob with one accord.

I gasped. The spectacle, the fervour, the solemnity sent shivers down my back beneath my ice-blue satin. Truly the people seemed to love me. I felt holy, wonderful. We were invincible, my father and myself. Chosen, worshipped, touched by the finger of God. Our cause was just — the liberation of our Gascon brothers. My father was the hero who would bring them that freedom.

Suddenly, inconsequentially, then, from a distant childhood memory, came a laughing echo of my father's voice:

"Remember, Edward; when I come home from Gascony, I bring gifts..."

Chapter Three

"It was a measure of our naivety, Robert, that we should suppose ourself in any sense of the word a ruler when our father went away. We were left as Regent of England. We thought to give command, make statements, let our views be known, dictate in some small instance policy.

"In truth we were as powerful as the man who leads the carol dance at Yule; nay, not so powerful as that."

LONDON SURGED and throbbed about the fortress of the Tower, into which I had been hustled for my safety's sake. "We are on the brink of civil war," said Walter Langton. Were we? Certainly the Bishop, with his propensity to make pronouncements, made me believe so, and in consequence I shivered in my sheets at night to think of all that might be happening beyond the ramparts of my place of refuge.

The Council, over whom I nominally presided, now set about to save the land from civil war. The recalcitrant earls who would not go to Gascony were in the city, armed, with soldiers, and guards left at each city gate should their retreat be hindered.

The Council parleyed with them. The Council consisted of old Beauchamp of Warwick, Edmund of Cornwall, Warenne of Surrey — all elderly men with aches and pains — and three barons, and three bishops. But in effect the Council was Walter Langton.

Clerk of the King's Chancery, Langton had risen through ambition and King Edward's favour, to the bishopric of Coventry and Lichfield; and now that my father's right hand man, Chancellor Burnell, was dead, Langton reigned supreme as treasurer and my father's most cherished minister. Monstrously rich, holding lands and forests and half of Sussex and Surrey, he primed himself to rise to the occasion. Archbishop Winchelsea detested him, and I, admiring Winchelsea, soon followed suit.

"Let us be fair, Robert, if we may; describing in dispassionate manner one whom we found nauseous."

He was extremely elegant and tall; handsome in a pale-skinned, well-groomed style; his hands slender, his eyes limpid and grey. A rumour had attached itself to him that he admired beautiful women. He certainly possessed more than two robes for himself and dressed as though he enjoyed his clothes. He had a well-modulated voice and made pronouncements of the most definitive nature in a gentle soothing tone and with a self-effacing fatuous smile.

And while this Bishop saved the country from its fate, I watched the city's spires and roof-tops from my stone-walled sanctuary and heard the many bells chime for festivals and funerals, marriages and Masses, a distant cacophony of wind-blown noise.

London! A place of brawls and riot, street fights, clamour and sedition, a place in which no monarch felt at ease. Wharves and taverns, dunghills, dirt, foul rivers, pestilence — could such a city house but rats and villains? Billingsgate, stinking of fish; Dowgate with its choked-up alleys; the Vintry where the wine made every man a drunkard; Walbrook where skinners plied their trade and the blood of slaughtered beasts oozed down the cobbles to the slimy little stream; Cheapside, every man a trader.

I recalled the tales of London's perfidy. Loyal only to itself, a shifting heap of guildsmen, shopkeepers, apprentices, led by a tribe of self-important mayors, owning no appropriate respect to crown nor monarch, ever a source of disaffection. Londoners had once pursued my beautiful grandmother, Queen Eleanor, as she set off for Windsor in her royal barge, and pelted her with stones and filth till she had been obliged to turn back for her own safety; and my father in righteous wrath had led his troops against the men of London who fought at Lewes — for de Montfort's infantry were Londoners — and slaughtered them all in just revenge. "Never trust 'em," said King Edward, "they were sent by God to be our penance, a disease within the body of the monarchy." In any baronial eruption Londoners could not be counted upon to take the King's part — why, they let de Montfort's army in and welcomed it with open arms and garlands...

I waited in my eyrie. The Tower was like a rock, the sea in storm surrounding it.

"The Lord be praised," said Walter Langton. "All is calm again."

I marvelled; and I thanked him; and we set about to govern England.

Immediately I understood why King Edward's war in France had grown so urgent and so necessary. Had he stayed at home, a grim and bitter harvest would have been his to gather. A list of grievances awaited the attention of the monarch, an attack upon his ancient rights, and furthermore, the confirmation of the Great Charter, and nothing to be done without consent of church, earl, baron, knight and burgess.

"My father will never agree to that," I said scornfully.

Walter Langton took me privily aside. "Confirm the Charter in your father's name. Summon the bishops and clerks, the knights from all the counties to bear witness. While it is true King Edward will agree to all that is set down, the fact remains your father is not here. Therefore he will ratify the business from across the sea, and distance lends its deviation, and it will be discovered that the ways and means are always open for manoeuvre. Such is diplomacy."

Mystified, confused, I understood that Walter Langton was in my father's confidence in a way that I myself was not. I formed a strong resentment towards this disagreeable Bishop, born partly of jealousy and partly of a certainty that such should not be so in a regency council of which I, the Prince, was head.

"And so," said Walter Langton, "let us turn our thoughts to Scotland."

There was no question but that the activities of William Wallace must be drastically curtailed.

A robber villain, he had murdered the Sheriff of Lanark, an Englishman; he had attacked the castle of Stirling; and was now leading raids across the border, pillaging and burning in the manner of his kind. An English army must be dispatched at once to deal with him and restore equilibrium in the north.

I thrilled at the prospect. "I shall lead the force myself, of course."

"I hope, Lord Edward, that it will not come to that," said Langton with a light laugh. "We have soldiers there under Surrey's command. Wallace is nothing — a burr, a pinprick. It should be no great matter for my lord of Surrey and Hugh Cressingham to deal with him. All we need to do is to await the happy news."

The news was not so happy. Wallace and his foot soldiers and spearmen defeated a force of knights on horseback at a bridge near Stirling. Surrey, ailing and rheumatic and a most reluctant combatant, fled, and Cressingham was caught and skinned like some poor beast, and tanned, and cut up into shreds — a big man, Hugh, so there was plenty to go round. Then Wallace named himself ruler and continued raiding with more aplomb and insolence than before.

"The time has come," said Langton, "to consider mustering a royal army."

Writs were sent out to all the shires for levies of troops to muster at Newcastle under my leadership. Welsh foot soldiers were summoned, preparations made.

"At last!" I thought, in a fervour of delight. "My chance has come to show my father I am worthy of his trust in me."

I seethed with impatience. I could hardly wait to prove myself with this God-given opportunity. No news had come of any victory in France. It might well be that mine was to be the victory, not his; that age and difficulty were at last to smudge the radiance of my father's military prowess, that he would return to hear the praise resounding for his son's achievements in the north. I could so clearly picture it, the King's return. He would find me seeming older, hardened by campaign, but modest in success.

"Sire!" [*This would be Walter Langton speaking.*] "The Prince has proved himself to be a leader beyond my wildest expectations. In battle a lion. Yourself when young, with all the promise of fulfilment yet to come. A young King Arthur. And here is William Wallace, fettered, chained, begging for clemency. The battle raged long and hard and bloody. The Prince was in the thick of the fighting. An inspiration to his men."

Scotland will be my success, I thought gleefully, quivering with anticipation. My testing ground, my field of prowess, and my glory. And when all's done I shall present the victory to him, and we shall meet as equals...

King Edward sent his message early in the January.

"It is plain to us that Scotland needs firm handling. We shall return, and see to it."

With the greatest contempt for his Flemish allies who had proved themselves ineffective, critical and hostile, King Edward turned his back on all his previous intentions and arrived at Sandwich in the spring. He brought with him a truce with France and the likelihood of not one but two French marriages tucked under his belt. He sped from shrine to shrine amassing Heavenly help for his campaign in Scotland; he received the Great Seal back into his keeping; he assembled an army; and he rode north.

I lay in my bed at Langley with my arms around Gilbert de Clare, Lord of Thomond, three years older than myself, and a companion of my household. It was mid morning; we were lazy stayabeds with no shame at all.

"He was pleased with me, of course," I told Gilbert. "After all, it was not that I had done anything stupid — dropped the Great Seal in the Thames or declared war on Ireland for the whim of it. I had succeeded in remaining on civilized terms with the Bishop of Coventry — no easy matter, since he certainly considered himself the country's ruler and myself a hindrance to be tolerated. I had done all that was required of me. So, yes, he was pleased enough. But it was the careless satisfaction of the master with the dog, a pat on the head, and a stick to catch, and my reward to go away and play. I am dismissed. I am a child again, to learn my manners and my courtly skills, to sport in the fields when I need exercise. So, he would have us play; then we will play."

A group of young companions lived now at Langley with me, boys of rich families, learning with me, under the guidance of Sir Guy and of the men-at-arms who taught us weaponry.

Gilbert was my favourite. Fair-haired like me, he was affable, amenable and good looking. In my bed he shared the boyish pleasures I was growing to enjoy — the touch of hands about the body, and the mischievous playfulness of mock fights, intertwining of arms and legs, and sudden kisses, and the half-wicked thrill of holding cocks beneath the blankets, and the savouring of slow fondling, till the juices came and left us gasping.

Laughing from the great contentment of our romping I lay back breathless.

"If my father could see us!" I giggled. A horrid thought came to my mind. I winced. "I wish that I could stave it off for ever, marriage. First he finds me one and then another, and then he finds me reasons why the matter is no longer relevant. No Flemish count's daughter now that we've dispensed with Flanders; instead a French princess of eight years old. Perhaps," I said morosely, "she'll be struck down before she grows."

"Include it in your prayers; we are too well content to brook an interruption," Gilbert answered comfortably.

"And yet we have one foist upon us," I spluttered indignantly, sitting up. "Another squire to join us here, one of my father's choosing, some sponger that he found in Flanders, some younger son without a penny, and we must find a home for him. A Gascon no less, and I have heard no good of Gascons."

"Quarrelsome and shifty," agreed Gilbert sagely. "Liars, thieves and wastrels every one."

"How many Gascons do you know?" I grinned and thumped him.

"A thousand," Gilbert sniggered, adding: "Not a one."

"'We are well pleased with him', my father writes.'Receive him kindly. He has done us good service.' I know well enough he'll be some snivelling fawning pup, and I can promise you that if my father finds him pleasing, I shall not. Are we an almshouse here, to take all comers, any landless wastrel? He would do better to enter the church, would you not say?"

"Why do you believe him landless?"

"If he has land in Gascony, what does he here? No, Gilbert, he plans to rise in England, and has wormed his way into the King's affections. Gilbert!" I said suddenly."That is no mean achievement!"

"What did I tell you?" Gilbert shrugged and laughed. "Devious and shifty, just as we supposed. And what's his name, this protege of King Edward's?"

"Piers Gaveston." It was probably the first time that I said the name out loud.

"And when does he arrive?"

"My father came back to England a month ago, and this Gascon with him. He should be here already. He must be dawdling on the way."

On my fourteenth birthday I distributed pennies to the poor and then went riding in the woods beyond the palace. A gang of my young companions rode with me. The forest floor was yellow with primroses, and amongst them white sorrel and anemones, with beyond, smudges of purple violets. The sun struck sharp and bright as the trees thinned at the wood's edge. We rode down the hill across the cowslip meadows towards the river which gleamed between its reeds and alders.

Langley village was in sight now, and looking across to it we saw a small procession setting out, with men-at-arms and baggage, figures on horseback, and a little covered coach. We saw it start to wind its slow way up the hill towards the palace.

"Visitors," I grumbled. I foresaw more ceremonies of good intent and well-wishing to which I would be obliged to make more speeches.

"But could it be our Gascon?" Gilbert wondered.

"If so it shows a monstrous lack of courtesy," I said huffily. "On my birthday I do as I please, and I would prefer not to be encumbered with occasions. "

I turned and half looked back. Against the green of Le Corte hill the riders showed as distant silhouettes, a dark unravel thread, the palace its inevitable destination. A sudden shower fell, blurring the sharp impact of the sight. I was not inclined to mysticism; I had no prescience of the way the course of my existence was to change, no shudder of foreboding nor shiver of anticipation. But I did stave off the meeting.

"Return home, those who wish," I cried, and rode as far as Berkhamstead in simple pique, accompanied by Gilbert and two squires; we came home wet and sodden.

We rode up the hill and through the palace gateway; we dismounted. I could not help but see the fresh horses, the little coach, and to notice a certain bustling about within the courtyard. And now Sir Guy approached us, frowning.

"Piers Gaveston is here, Lord Edward..."

"Let him wait," I said, a certain truculence possessing me, a sense of having acted childishly, with no accompanying sense of regret. "I need a bath," I added. "Gilbert, bathe with me."

Sir Guy pursed his lips and without a word conveyed a gentle disapproval.

"I know, I know," I said pettishly. "Courtesy to guests and good behaviour. But would you have me receive a stranger mud-bespattered?"

Servants heated up the fire within the bathhouse. I sat in the steaming water, knee to knee with Gilbert, giggling as I soaped.

"We could stay here all day," I said, the foolish notion reducing me to fits of merriment. "What is the point of being a prince if one cannot remain in one's bath as long as there's warm water? More coriander, John, and rosemary for our hair!"

My young valet leaned over the great bath and poured the scented water through my yellow hair. I squealed with pleasure and flicked the droplets from my eyelashes, splashing fistfuls towards Gilbert who yelled and squirmed and struck out with his heels, until cascades of water drenched the floor and both of us sank down in the foam, weak with laughter.

The last time in my life that I was fancy free, the last uncluttered moments of my boyhood, of my liberty — I wonder that I ever emerged from the tub. However, at length the delights of bath time palled and I arose nude and pink from the herbal brew, a towel about me like a cloak.

"Gilbert, how do I look? Will I make a good entrance?"

"It is more customary to be clad," Gilbert sniggered.

"You think my nakedness would offend?" I said haughtily in mock outrage.

"Indeed my lord," said Gilbert with complete sincerity, "it would cause only admiration."

I grinned in reply; I had a fair idea that I was easy on the eye.

"Then let us dress and go to meet our fate."

We say these things so carelessly, never thinking that we speak the truth.

Dressed in shades of blue, with yellow embroidered shoes, my minions about me, I walked in most regal fashion the length of the great hall, looking neither to right nor left. I mounted the dais; I sat. Peacock shimmered against azure. The gold of my hair glinted in the play of light. I smelt of coriander.

I leaned down a little towards the one who knelt at my feet, head bent. I extended my royal hand for the kiss, with a flash of sapphire and gold.

"Piers Gaveston, Lord Edward," said Sir Guy.

"Gaveston," I said primly. "We greet you well."

The young man raised his head. I gaped, dry-mouthed, heat rising to the throat. A welter of weird things then happened. The room changed colour; it became suffused with radiance. The shields painted around the wall glowed crimson, orange, purple, and the four knights seeking a tournament leapt into motion, with their banners streaming silver-gilt; I swear their horses neighed. Previously unnoticed music danced upon the quivering air with a myriad buoyant notes from flute and shawm and heavenly harp; and a choir began to sing. The rushes on the floor hurled scents of lemon, lavender and rose, so violently it might have been a summer's noontide. Midsummer! Our special time... All that from one glance only.

"My lord —" said Gaveston; and now there were trumpets also, and a forestful of nightingales, and rose petals falling from the rafters, and the taste of Turkish sweets, and another choir a little more ethereal yet; and the first strawberries of June, and silk against the skin; and cherries.

"Please rise," I said faintly, and stood up myself, aware of a burning sensation between the sapphires on my fingers which, I noticed, looking down, glowed with a leaping flame where Gaveston's lips had been. "And sit beside me, on this bench."

"Beside you, my lord?"

"Yes. Why not?" I laughed affectedly. "We are not very formal here."

"My lord," said Gaveston with a dazzling smile. "It is your birthday. I was given leave to arrive when it best suited me. And so I waited, so that I might come with a particular gift, one altogether proper for this most special occasion."

"You have brought me a gift?" I blinked, trying to disperse the golds, silks, cherries, rose petals, and let reality re-form.

"I have, my lord." There was a pause. "Myself."

Chapter Four

ALTHOUGH UPON that day I saw something akin to the Archangel Michael in human form, in fact Piers Gaveston was a young man, fifteen years old.

What was unusual about him — oh Robert! — was that he was startlingly beautiful. The appreciation of beauty being personal to each observer, it might be supposed that some there might have been who did not find him beautiful; yet even those who grew to hate him knew they hated something beautiful; some maybe even hated him simply because of it. There is that in man which takes a pleasure in the smashing of an icon.

While Gaveston sat and talked about his journey from London and the condition of the roads and the weather, I had opportunity to observe more closely what had caused my sensibilities such turmoil.

Piers Gaveston was slight of build but muscular and graceful, perfectly proportioned as far as could be observed with the perfection partially obscured by a lengthy supertunic of dark green sarcenet over a tunic of a paler shade of green, and elegant doeskin boots. He was slim and upright and of medium height. His hands were strong and expressive; he gestured constantly, flamboyantly. His hair was black, strikingly so amongst such a flock of fair-haired fellows. When I dared look more closely, I saw that his eyes were green and dancing, beneath long dark lashes and fine black eyebrows; his nose well shaped. His face was pointed, his chin deeply dimpled. His teeth were white, exquisite; his smile dazzling and rapid; the susceptible melted at it.

"You have come from London..." I began, attempting to root this vision in some actuality.

"I have been in London for a month, since we all came from Flanders."

"But, London!" I winced. "To stay so long in such a vile place!"

"London isn't vile; it's wonderful!" laughed Piers. "Forgive me that I disagree with you, my lord, so early in our friendship, but why ever do you think it less than marvellous?"

"Street brawls and violence and horrid dirty streets."

"My lord, you have a strong right arm, and nobody that wields a sword need ever fear a brawl. The secret is to know yourself capable of dealing with your adversary. Most men are cowards at heart and will retreat if you seem stronger. And moreover," added he all twinkling, "a street brawl can be most exciting! Then afterwards, you count up the survivors, and with arms about each other, off you go to the nearest tavern and you fortify yourselves, and so! Do you know how many taverns London has?"

"No, I can't say that I do."

"Three hundred and fifty-four!"

"And you know them all?" I asked him dubiously.

"Every single one," said Gaveston, straight-faced as a priest at Mass; and we both laughed, for what good was a Gascon who was not a braggart, and Piers knew well enough what was expected.

"I love the way you speak," I could not help confiding. "I hope you don't object to my observing it. But my mother and my beloved grandmother had that southern lilt; I love to hear it from your lips."

"I am honoured to be the cause of further happiness to my Prince."

"You have always lived in Gascony?"

"We have extensive lands there; many castles. Louvigny — Montgaillard — St Loubouer — Hagetmau — Gabaston — Roquefort de Marsan from my mother's family. Our family being very wealthy, we move from castle to castle. My father owns vast forests, mountains, many villages. The castles are more beautiful than any I have seen in England and we cherish all of them dearly. Louvigny is my favourite. They have all been in our family for generations..."

I looked at Piers dubiously. Was this truly so? I wanted to believe him, of course — but what then was he doing here in England, plainly hoping to rise through service to my father? Was I being subjected to that careless bragging which we understood to be a feature of the Gascon character? No, surely not. I shook the unworthy thought away.

"My mother died when I was four years old," said Piers. "Her name was Claramonde de Marsan. She was the most beautiful woman in all Gascony. I remember her very well. She had black hair, so sleek and smooth that it was full of light, and eyes like emeralds. Also," he added carelessly, "also she was a witch."

I gasped. I was the perfect audience.

"My father was heartbroken at her death," continued Piers. "And afterwards, things never went so well for us. I wonder whether we had been protected by her spells till then, for we have been very much in need of magic since. Agnes, who travelled in the covered coach and came with me today, she has been with me since the day that I was born; she was my mother's confidante; she knows the things my mother knew; later I'll tell some of them to you."

Bemused, transfixed, I listened, unable to believe my father knew of this, and wondering what further revelations were to follow.

"It was I that helped my father to escape," said Piers. "They let me visit him. I made pretence that I was halfwit. I took food into the prison every day. The guard grew well habituated to my presence. I could see he was a fool. One day I took two daggers hidden in a pie. We fought our way clear, and by nightfall we were well away. We stole two horses and rode day and night till we came to the coast; there we took ship to England. We lurked about in London and lived by any means we could. One day I'll tell you some of my adventures. I know things about the London backstreets which I think you'd find exciting. Some dark night when we have nothing much to do, I'll tell you... London was full of the preparations for the Gascon war, and naturally we took our places in the army of the King, to save our homeland. My brothers also. We are all excellent swordsmen... I was amongst the crowd when you, my Prince, were presented to the people, and the King wept and vowed that he would die for Gascony. You were like an angel."

"I was?"

"The sun shone on your golden hair."

"They went to some trouble to be sure I made a good impression. My hair was washed until it squeaked; no mouse more vociferous."

"It is important to look beautiful if you would be a knight; almost as important as prowess in arms. The King knows that; he has an eye for pageantry."

"And you went across the sea with him — a squire of the household, I believe? How did that come about?"

"He noticed me," said Piers, as if that were all explanation needed.

"He noticed you?"

"Well — riding by and such. There were so many wild and stupid, the ones calm and well-mannered could not help but be noticed."

"I heard our soldiers were unruly."

"There was unnecessary fighting. It was as if once having left the shores of England they must grow savage. At Sluys they fought amongst themselves and set fire to more than thirty ships. Hundreds died. When we arrived at Bruges we looked a rabble. Some of the Welsh and Irish came in skins and fur that looked as if it had been freshly ripped from the beasts' backs and they were barefoot and inarticulate. The Count of Flanders nearly passed away from shock.

Well, having no mountains in his plate-flat land he never had seen mountain men. He was entirely ineffectual. King Edward rapidly came to despise him — you could tell it."

"I can imagine."

"And when we were so long without a battle, and when the news came that there was to be a truce, our men grew discontented."

"Discontented?" I raised my eyebrows. "I heard it was much more."

"There was a little pillaging," Piers grinned.

"Whole towns were burned!"

"Yes, one or two; that is the way of soldiers," Piers said airily. "But who would have thought the Flemish so unreasonable as to retaliate? They burst upon our troops like fiends from Hell and slaughtered all they saw. And so we had to burn some houses in return. The King was very angry with the Count of Flanders' lack of control. He told him that the men of Ghent must be severely punished for so harassing their guests. The Count of Flanders said he dare not punish them. By all the bones of all the saints, the King said, if you will not do so, then will I, and in such manner they will not forget for a hundred years! He is superb when he is angry, is he not, your father?"

"You seem to find him admirable then?" I said cautiously.

"I do, I do!" Piers cried. "He's a colossus, powerful and strong, brave as a lion. Naturally I admire him; and besides," he added with a smile, "he pays my wages."

I stood up. "Come; it's time you met the others".

The rumours flew before him like a swarm of gnats, this new addition to the ten companions of the Prince.

"He's seen fighting in the streets — he burned cities — he led troops — he's been in brothels — he escaped from a dungeon — he slew the guards. King Edward picked him out for his bravery and cunning, chosen from above all others. He has twenty castles — and his mother was a witch!"

Piers might well have been some hero of romance. Never denying the wildest of surmises he relished all attention, rewarding our blatant curiosity with further stories and a radiant luminousness in which all were invited to bask. He rode into Langley like a questing knight, a traveller from a distant shore, a man blessed by the King, possessing more than his fair share of personal beauty and more clothes than some of us had ever seen. With the striped Italian cloth and the French satins he introduced a sartorial element to what had previously been merely dressing; but if attempt were made to imitate, it soon became apparent that it was in the manner of the wearing wherein lay the particular charm.

"I know what would suit you, my Lord Edward. Let me show you. I always do this with my own clothes, d'you see, design them myself; that way you wear exactly what you want and always look good. Have you thought of tying your hair back with threads of gold?"

As well as clothes, Piers brought with him an elegant tutor and the redoubtable Agnes, his nurse from birth and the friend of his mother the Circean Claramonde. Some thirty-five years old now, Agnes, just as much as Piers, was well content to play the part.

I think she may well have been ugly; but it must have been a feature of the magic which hung about her that in thinking of her I am fully persuaded she was beautiful. And yet she had a shock of black unruly hair that billowed widely from her face, which was gaunt, angular and curiously pale. Her mouth was wide; some of her teeth were black; and yet her smile was enchanting. Her eyes were dark and lively, her expression vivacious, all-knowing. She was thin and tall. She had two cats, both black, that rarely left her side, but perched on her shoulders and about her neck. She was known to brew potions and had a skill in massaging with oils which no doubt contributed to the odour of sandalwood and lavender about Piers. She could play music on a little harp that sat upon her lap. She preserved a certain mystery, keeping herself apart from the castle servants. She patently adored Piers.

Piers was not mysterious. Everything he did was visible, immaculate. He could ride faster and better than anyone, with lance or without; he could beat everyone at swordplay and wrestle anyone to win except myself and here I suspected diplomacy.

Wrestling... This was the first occasion on which we touched each other in close proximity. Our chests and arms were bare. We faced each other, feet in the summer grass, the other boys about us, encouraging us, jeering us good humouredly, Sir Guy a little further off to watch and see fair play. We were both lithe, springy, strong, Piers and myself. With laughing glittering eyes he teased me to attack. We lunged at one another. All in a moment we were clamped together. We were breathing into one another's mouths. Twisting, slippery with sweat, we struggled, heaving, panting, our thighs wrapped around each other's. Excitement made me weak. Piers had the advantage. He tripped me, flung me to the ground. When he sat astride me I felt a strange delightful languor. I wanted to remain there, under him, sun-dazzled in the dusty grass. But there was reputation at stake, and honour. My foolish comrades jumped up and down and bawled advice, believing me discomfited. I was obliged to free myself and so restore my dignity. I broke clear, to cheers that barely compensated for my disappointment, for my loss.

Tilting at the quintain, running, bat and ball, quarterstaff, Piers excelled at all of them. He was forever at the centre of a yelling cheering group that cried him on and jumped up and down and screeched the time-honoured recommendation: "Smite him to gobbets!"

Nimble, lithe, successful, innovative, handsome even streaked with dust, there was no one like him. He ought to have been heartily detested; quite the converse. I suppose it was that the lads who shared my education, except for Gilbert, were all much younger in age, and Gilbert being blessed with a gentle disposition and a pleasant nature, knew no rancour. Far from seeing Piers as rival or supplanter, all now turned to him as a natural leader, eager to follow him in escapade and benefit from his suggestion.

He would of a sudden organise a ball game up and down the meadow or a chase amongst the woods and prizes for the winners and he saw to it that no one was left out; he could sense what each was best at and devise such sports that everyone blossomed at one thing or another.

And in the evening he needed but the lightest persuasion to give colourful accounts of dungeons, battles, disguises, pursuits from bloodthirsty foes, burning cities, betrayals, ambush — all, it seemed, from personal experience.

"...and he was slain with one blow of the swingeing axe which crashed down upon him with a sickening thud; he fell forward, straight across me; I was mown to the ground by his weight and drenched with his blood. Cautiously I wriggled from beneath him — then paused, immobile, feigning death, for my foes were all about me. It was only because I was so smeared with his blood that I was spared, being believed dead as he...

"...so I took the woman's gown and cloak, and in a grove of crab apple trees I put on her clothes and made my way down to the village, walking very daintily. I almost thought I would be captured, for a blacksmith saw me — a great bear of a man — and he must have desired me — well, I was very pretty in my woman's gown; it was the colour of fine Bordeaux — and he stopped me in the square and demanded a kiss. What could I do? I must permit it. And he thanked me and said it was a very good kiss — which, to be honest, I believe it was. I don't know which of us was best pleased; I know his hot embrace had me near fainting for the pleasure of it! And when he let me go I tripped away and through the village, and so escaped..."

Just a few days after his arrival Piers arranged a May Day celebration up in the woods, better than any we had had before. He bribed some yeomen of the chamber to wear horns and masks and run among the trees with flaming brands till elf lights glowed in copse and thicket, and then to give chase. A pleasurable panic ensued and all were rounded up to foregather at a bonfire. Here was Agnes dressed in green, with a magic brew for us which was passed around in a circle, and afterwards Piers led us in a dance, and those who had not fallen down overcome, staggered home with him, half dancing, half asleep, and very well content.

I watched the transformation of our lives in something of a daze. One day I took Piers down to the stables and arranged for him to ride the camel. Out came Saladin led by the groom, and was made to kneel for Piers to mount and was led about the yard with Piers upon him. I stood there, hands on hips, the ribald jeering ready on my lips, and then my mouth wide open in a silent gasp I thought despairingly: "He rides the camel proudly, like a king. He rides as if it is entirely natural to him. *Even on the camel he is beautiful!*"

"Bathe with me, Piers," I invited.

I spent the ensuing hour in the sweetest of confusions. It was all so strange to me. God's soul, but I had never been in love before and I scarcely understood this malady to be the cause of my delicious bewilderment.

Bathing with Gilbert was not like this. Bathing with Gilbert was laughing, splashing, kicking; it left me exhilarated, comfortable and clean. But sitting in the tub with Gaveston...

I was never much of a thinker; it did not come naturally to me to analyse sensation. My cousin Tom was right — a minstrel with a song, a new puppy, a boat on the river, these had been till now the liveliest sources of my enjoyment. Now at fourteen, with all my knightly training — my courtesy, my chivalry, my prowess with horsemanship and sword — and my brief experience of policy, I found myself adrift, unsure, entirely baffled.

There I sat, up to my armpits in the herb-strewn bath, my knees two islands in the scented brew, and there sat Piers, his black hair wet and welded to his skin in ornamental tendrils, his neck slender and his shoulders strong, his arms all muscle, and upon his chest a moist tangle of dark hairs exquisite as a monk's artwork on parchment.

When Piers stood up and climbed out of the bath, a pleasurable quiver ran across my belly, a sensation which seemed to be related to my staring at the perfect rounds of Gaveston's behind, and the well-proportioned prick beneath its generous smudge of curly black hair and those firm and lissome thighs whose dark hairs gleamed with waterdrops. In a moment John the valet slung a towel about him and eclipsed the bright perfection. I was like one left in darkness.

I stood up to follow. I tried to shake myself clear of thoughts and water.

Water was easy.

"Oh yes, all men will go with boys in an army camp," said Gaveston decisively. "Some are too lazy to go looking for camp followers of the female kind; some would fuck anything that moved, no matter who or what; some prefer boys, and believe me, the boys about an army camp are very sweet, especially for pennies."

We were lying in the hay meadow, where the cut grass spread dry and yellow and the bees buzzed in the clover heads. No passer by would have been able to surmise amongst the circle of boys which lad was Prince, which knight's son, which was squire, which valet. I loved the comfortable camaraderie we possessed. At least, it used to be comfortable. I sighed.

"How do they go about finding..? I mean, how do they know which boy is what they're looking for?" It was Robert de Scales that asked.

"Some boys from the town who offer that kind of service come out to the camp and stroll about and catch the eye — they paint their faces heavily, redden their lips, and walk a certain way."

"Which way?"

Ever delighting to display himself, Piers jumped up and minced about until he made everybody laugh. I must have laughed the loudest. It was to hide the growing discomfort that I endured. If I had been a knight at war... if he had been that kind of boy... A wash of shame at this unbidden and unworthy thought possessed me; so I laughed.

Piers paused. "And then they lift their tunics up at the back, like this, and show they have a hole cut in their breeches! And the bum is hanging out!"

Some small embarrassed boys destined to grow up and marry and revere their wives and believe each word of Holy Writ tittered in high voices. Gilbert gave a languid smile. I grew unaccountably warm and knew I would remain so as long as Piers stood there provokingly, all merry, with his tunic up.

"And then," said Piers, curling up cat-like in the meadow grass, "those knights who are interested crook a finger or sidle up alongside, and into the tent they go. This transaction is what is known as *entering foreign parts!*"

We laughed, to show that we were worldly in our understanding.

"Does no one see, nor mind?" we enquired.

"Believe me, anything's permissible in war time," Piers replied. "If any accusation follows, knights may simply shrug and say 'There was no woman by', and there's an end to it. You'd be surprised how many knights with wives at home and many children, take to this kind of pleasure once they join an army."

"Oh, who?"

"I name no names. But it is common practice. And some who are not married and have therefore no burden of fidelity to juggle with, they flit from boy to boy and bring their own servants especially for the purpose. It is no secret that Tom of Lancaster your cousin..." He flung me a careless glance.

"My cousin Tom? What of him?"

"As well as women, he likes boys. Grooms and kitchen lads. Boys with yellow hair."

"You should not speak so," I murmured. Lord, but the sun was hot!

"Then my lips are sealed," said Gaveston, and bowed.

"And what about women?" asked William de Munchensi; and Gaveston obliged with tales of red-headed wenches in torn gowns. My interest palled, and I drifted off into an uneasy reverie and wondered whether cousin Tom had so satiated himself in foreign parts that he had long since forgotten our little encounter against the hawthorn tree, and my promise to him.

"And what of you, Piers?" Gilbert asked, as he and Piers sat on my bed that night drinking wine by candlelight. "I don't recall you spoke about your own experiences in the Flemish fields?"

"Oh, I had offers," Piers said airily.

"Please don't suddenly become enigmatic," I said irritably.

"What would you like to know, my lord?" said Piers obligingly, as if, no matter what, he would provide it. I scowled at him. "Did you go with men or women?" I demanded.

Piers hesitated, surprised by my tone. Did he understand my desperation — was my vulnerability so obvious, so raw?

"With men or women?" I insisted.

Piers laid a hand upon my wrist. "With men, Lord Edward," he said in a low voice. "But not often."

"Was that because you had no woman by?" I cried. There was a pause, and Gilbert laughed brittlely.

"I did not seek out women, no," said Piers. "But since you ask, I have known what it is to lie with a woman. Curiosity prompted me. The experience was agreeable."

"Tell!" said Gilbert warmly.

"I don't want to hear about it," I snapped.

The incorrigible Piers was undaunted. "My lord, I have a tale about a hairy guard who prowled the prison where my father lodged, and who pursued me with his breeches open..."

"And achieved you?" Gilbert asked.

Piers paused, looking at me. "I continue?" he enquired.

"Yes," I muttered sulkily.

"If my lord will smile; otherwise not."

"Oh, tell, then," I grimaced.

"We are talking of a guard of monstrous proportion," Piers declared. "Legs like young oaks. Arms like cut logs. His trunk," he sniggered, "like a trunk."

"Your story is rooted in exaggeration, I think," said I.

"I will branch out then into fine detail," Piers grinned. "This guard of monstrous proportion could not take his eyes from me as I brought food along the passageways that led to my father's cell. He followed me at a small distance. One day he pinioned me against the wall. Remember I was younger then, and not so skilled in dealing with adversity. He held me there and panted in my face. He said I had a very pretty face. He said he had been watching me. He said I walked as whores walked. He said I had the most beautiful arse in the whole world! And being innocent and knowing no better, I believed him."

"Well, it could be verified, I suppose," said Gilbert languidly.

"Not without all the other arses in the world here beside it!" Piers countered quickly.

"I have seen his arse," I said with studied carelessness. "It's not so bad."

"My lord, I thank you for your magnanimity," cried Piers and blew a kiss.

"This guard — this walking tree, who so admired this selfsame arse?" Gilbert prompted.

"He asked if he might be allowed to kiss it. He said all that he required of me was that when I brought food I would pause for a moment in his company and let him kneel behind me for a moment. He said an object of such beauty should be worshipped. And at that point he had not even seen it uncovered. I was astonished!"

"And so are we, at such a fabrication!"

"But it's all true," protested Piers. "I said if I permitted that, what could he give me in return? He said that there were ways to make my father's circumstances easier. I said if that were so, it were a small price to pay and he should have what he desired. So he stood back and I turned round to face the wall and I pulled up my tunic to my waist and he knelt down behind me and unpeeled my hose and planted his thick wet lips upon me."

"On the cheeks or between?" I demanded.

"At first he was curiously respectful, as one at a shrine," Piers answered modestly. "A chaste kiss was enough. But as the days went by he grew more demanding. He would prise my cheeks apart and lick and slobber. But yet he never asked for more nor took advantage of me. It was enough for him to worship me. Between us there occurred a certain closeness, almost an affection."

"Yet you and your father killed him when you escaped," said Gilbert dubiously.

"Oh no," said Piers and shrugged. "That was a completely different guard."

"Your story, whether true or no, has left me aroused," I murmured, sliding back my robe to show the verification. "I think that you should pay the price for having so affected me."

Piers hesitated.

"Why not" I said astonished. "It is permitted. Gilbert and I often... and the others also..."

"My lord," said Piers, "while it is true I told the story for the pleasure I hoped that it would bring, it was a silly story, slight, not worthy of being the occasion of my laying hand upon you; and if I am to touch you, this is not the time."

I was angry and embarrassed. "Oh, very well," I said huffily. "Be pompous and self righteous. Gilbert shall do it. Gilbert..."

But my reluctant member wanted Gaveston's touch or nothing; and would make no response to Gilbert's ministrations.

"Have I leave to retire?" said Piers.

"We shall be glad if you would quit our presence," I declared with feeling.

"I think, my lord, he will not quit your thoughts so easily," said Gilbert in the silence following the closing of the door.

"I don't understand it," I said helplessly. "I don't even like him very much."

"He has bewitched you," Gilbert smiled.

"You think so?" I frowned.

"Ned — I was jesting!" Gilbert protested with a laugh.

"News, my lord! News from the north!"

King Edward had won a victory up by Falkirk. The way of it was this: His spies had told him that the Scots intended to pursue him at a distance from behind the trees.

"They need not do so," he replied. "I shall come out to meet them!"

That night he slept on the bare moors amongst his troops, as he was wont to do, wrapped in his cloak. As he slept, his horse, taking sudden fright from a noise, trod on him where he lay, and broke two of his ribs. Rising above mere pain the King was first in the saddle come the morning, to lead his army into battle.

Some mischievous angel protected my father. He was always surviving incidents which would have killed a weaker or less fortunate man. In Paris once, a bolt of lightning killed two servants just beside him, missing him. Arrows that should by rights have served him as King Richard's death-bolt at Chalus, passed underneath his arm or grazed his elbow. Stumbling horses that did for King Alexander left my father smiling and unhurt. Crumbling masonry missed him by inches. He led a charmed life.

At the head of a fearsome cavalry charge my father put the Scots to flight with sword and slaughter. William Wallace fled to France. King Edward now began to devastate the lands of Robert Bruce in anticipation of that Scotsman proving foolish enough to take up Wallace's cause, and he sent word he would remain in Scotland for the duration of the year.

On the hillside near the palace we boys sat in a circle around Sir Guy's homespun map of battle. Sticks in the white dust represented the English cavalry, twigs the Scottish archers, and three square flintstones in a place of importance at the front of Wallace's army the schiltroms upon which Wallace had relied so heavily and to such small purpose.

"A schiltrom: that is, a tightly-packed square of foot soldiers, spears raised and extended — a hedgehog, in effect. In perfect formation impenetrable. But against the might of the English cavalry they fell apart. Wallace is here, a stream here providing a natural defence for his position, between his army and ours, and he's fortified it with a little makeshift fence. Behind the stream, marshy ground, his army on a little hill, with his archers and cavalry at the back, his schiltroms to the fore to take the brunt of our attack. We sent three prongs, left, right, centre..."

Sir Guy prowled about us, a long hazel switch scraping the lines of the English approach.

"As our cavalry wheeled, our archers shot holes in the schiltroms; they collapsed and were destroyed. The battle was conclusive. It proved once and for all that there is no substitute for the knight at full charge. Cavalry is invincible."

"Cavalry is invincible," we sang as we rode at the quintain, jousted with tipped lances, cantered in the meadows. "Invincible, invincible..."

We bathed every day from the island in the river in the heat of August amongst the yellow water lilies.

We splashed and fought and swam and rode each other in mock combat, and ran about squealing, shaking ourselves to dry; and sprawled in the sun amongst the grasses.

And all the while I was never without awareness of where Gaveston was, and always from the corner of my eye I looked to see whom he was with, what he did, how he seemed, and whether he ever watched me in return. I can't say that he did. His bounty was distributed with sickening liberality to all. Laughing loudest, swimming furthest, remaining naked for the longest time, I never could be truly sure that he had noticed me. I resorted to more obvious expedients, flinging myself in his path, flaunting my blond beauty like a young (and gauche) Triton, posing on tree trunks, catching his eye and inviting him thus to run his gaze the length of me, which, extended, lay before him like a banquet, dappled with shadow under the quivering leaves.

"Love me!" my eyes beseeched. "Look! I am beautiful. Love me!"

But Robert de Scales ran between, and William de Munchensi chased him, and Robert de Clavering jumped upon me, and Gilbert de Clare pulled Piers away to join a romp; and all my hopes went spiralling away amongst the dancing sunshafts.

I have always known exactly what I want, and gone about to get it. They say this is a trait of those born under the sign of Taurus the Bull. Anyone who may have supposed me indecisive has simply misunderstood that single-mindedness must sometimes take a devious route to achieve its end. But in this instance I took the direct path, and rushed the gate head-on.

Formally and with all dignity I sent a message that Piers Gaveston should attend me in the rose garden.

Impeccable choice for such a tryst, the garden was for the most part the creation of the two Queen Eleanors. In the ornamental tapestry of paving stone and flowery grass and trellis, grew in their season vines and strawberries, lavender, violets, peonies and wallflowers. But it was in the tunnel arbour that I waited, a covered walk composed entirely of roses, red and white, with leaves so twined to make a green and petalled darkness.

Dressed in black and gold, and glittering with rings and jewelled braiding, I stood there gleaming in the scented shadows. Gaveston coming in from the sun, a wine-dark silhouette against the foliage, found his eyes meshed in pools of dazzling green, and paused, his hand upon a rose.

"Ah, Gaveston," said I, my voice strained with the nervousness of my anticipation.

"My lord? Is all well?" Piers asked uncertainly.

"You must know why I have sent for you," I said.

"No, my lord. I hope I've not displeased you."

"God give me strength," I groaned, and took one step towards him. "Piers Gaveston, you must have guessed... It cannot have escaped your notice... You must know that I love you?"

Chapter Five

GAVESTON WAS silent, and, half turned away, his face showed nothing. His fingers tightened on the rose.

"Speak!" I cried. "Answer me!"

"My lord, what can I say?"

"What have we here? A speechless Gascon? This must be the first time I have ever known you to be without words!"

"It is also the first time that you have spoken of love, my Prince. Perhaps you are jesting?"

I had the strong impression that he hoped it. Stung, enraged, I responded: "I loved you from the first moment that I saw you. I want you to remain with me always. I think of nothing but you. Day and night. It's like being ill. It's horrible. You must help me. I don't know what to do."

"My lord, I am honoured... and appalled to be the cause of suffering. I don't know what to do. I had not planned this, no, not at all."

"What do you mean? Nobody plans their emotions. It isn't possible. These things occur."

"Yes my lord, they do. But for my own life I did make plans, as one must do when one has merely one's own abilities to bring to the game."

"Perhaps you would be good enough to explain to me what these so important plans were," I said sarcastically. "And how the onset of my love has checked them."

Piers fidgeted. He snapped the rose stem, closing his hand about the rose. "My lord, I told you I had many castles. Circumstances forbid my possessing them in any actuality. In all honesty there is nothing for me in Gascony." In a startling burst of frankness he blurted out: "We lost our lands through fortunes of war. All our castles are possessed by others. My father petitions constantly for the restoration of what is ours. There are so many of us to be provided for — Arnaud Guillaume my elder brother, Guillaume Arnaud born out of wedlock, my two younger brothers Gerard and Raimond and my sister Amy... For those in my position, a younger son, a father dispossessed, the future does not augur well. One prays for war, which brings a kind of merry chaos as a result of which the mighty fall, and those beneath scramble for pickings. Your father's expedition was a God-send, and I was fortunate: I caught his eye. You understand it, Edward, it is no small matter for a landless foreign youth to gain the favour of the King of England. It was a dream come true, more than I ever dared imagine... Pardon me, I called you by your name."

"I think that since I made a declaration of my love to you, some small aberrations from formality may be permitted," I remarked caustically.

"And it's not an easy name to say," Piers grinned. "A Saxon king-saint has much to answer for."

"If we were to become friends you should call me Ned."

"How can we?" Piers declared in some exasperation. "Once I attach myself to you, what am I but an adventurer, a parasite? It was my intention, do you see, to rise by my ability. Your father says that there will be a place for me in his army, a lieutenant of the north perhaps; he said to wait, to pass the intervening time with you, perfect my skills, my accent, and my understanding of the English way of things; then he will make me captain of a troop, and a knight, and after that who knows? At his side my prospects to win glory seemed almost a certainty. Wherever your father is," he laughed, "there will be wars; he is that kind of man. He would not like it, and you know it — he would not like this talk of love!"

Anger surged in me. "How dare you?" I seethed. "How dare you bring my father into this matter? He has dictated often enough whom I am to love, who not; and must he even here intrude his hateful presence and so step between us? Are you so weak and pitiable that you will act to please him and do only as he says? You are bold enough in other matters. I had thought better of you."

"Oh Edward, oh my lord, but I had no idea," said Piers staring hard. "I did not know you hated him."

"I hate him and I am afraid of him."

It was the first time I had ever formulated these half-understood truths aloud. A desperation at my predicament overcame me in the instant. A son who thinks thus of his father...whatever would become of me? Something of my misery must have shown in my face, and Piers responded. He pulled me to him in a rush of friendly sympathy. We stood together with our arms about each other and our faces close. With the lightest of movements our mouths met in a kiss, gentle and thoughtful, and from which we both drew back, still looking at each other.

"And so?" I said, flushed and fever-bright. "Was that so threatening?"

"One single kiss, no," Piers said ruefully. "But I believe that you had more in mind when you made your declaration. Those who say 'I love you' rarely mean 'and there's an end to it; now go your way'. Some consequence is generally expected."

"How ungratefully you receive that declaration!" I muttered. "As if it were an inconvenience." I flared at him. "You think that you will rise under my father's auspices? Well, have you considered that the King is not immortal, and, God willing, he must one day seek salvation elsewhere, and then whom do you suppose will have the power to give you all you seek?"

Gaveston made a dismissive gesture and flung the rose away. "My lord, you must not so demean yourself. You do not need to buy me with promises. If I were to love you in return I would need no bribery. And when I speak of rising, I must make it clear that I am not ambitious, nor greedy for lands. Fame I would like, and glory, but apart from that a living, moderate wealth, no more."

"In my experience, Robert, all men want riches. But I think Piers spoke the truth then; he was not ambitious in the way that some men are. I think at that stage all he wanted was to be Sir Lancelot; but then, at that stage he was very young."

"But as to love," he said and laughed. "It is unfortunate, that's all, that you are not some squire, some baron's son, some — anything that put us on an equal footing."

"We can be so!" I answered passionately. "For I can make you prince in all but name."

"I wish you would not speak so," Piers replied, and now he was a trifle agitated. "No man should be offered such a choice, so freely and so generously, and with so little effort on his part. Oh Edward!" then he groaned. "No one will ever know for sure whether I grow to love you because of what you offer or because you are yourself. Neither I nor you will know it, and I weep for that."

"If I thought for one moment that you would ever love me," I said in a low voice, "I never would enquire the cause."

"Oh my lord," said Gaveston much moved, and took me in his arms, this time with strong emotion, and he held me to him and we kissed as lovers.

In my ignorance of love's ways, I thought to bind him to me by a ceremony. I thought that if he could be persuaded to swear his love aloud, in the presence of some holy object and before a witness, he would never dare deny it in the days to come, and that way I would keep him.

I had not learnt then that we keep most truly those we never chain. I was accustomed to acquiring that which I desired, and therefore without more ado I sought out Piers the following day and put forward my proposition.

"We must make a covenant," I said, as excited as I would have been for a midnight feast. I was like someone who on entering a cave had found a golden ball and, with no idea of its value in the world of men, could only treat it with a boy's enthusiasm, and toss it to and fro. Piers maybe had more wisdom.

"My lord, I'd sooner not," he said uneasily.

"But I want to!" I swear I even stamped my foot. "I want to say I love you with a ceremony. It will only be," I added disarmingly, "you and I and Gilbert. Why do you hesitate?"

"I don't know, my lord. It's not something to which I am accustomed, making vows," Piers admitted.

"You are so brave in every other way," I marvelled. "You ride better than any of us; you win every joust, you fight with sword and mace, you shoot a fine arrow — but the taking of a vow appears to make you frightened."

"The things you speak of I have trained myself to do. I know that I can do them. A promise is another matter. Besides," he added with a barefaced grin, "you know, my lord, that I am something of a liar."

"I don't believe that in this instance you would lie to me," I said wide-eyed and trusting.

"Well, who can say?" shrugged Piers. "But it has always been my true intent to please my Prince; and if he wants a ceremony I shall undertake to make it memorable."

"Yes, yes, in the beginning it was all me. I made him love me. I almost ordered it. Why he went along with it, who can ever truly know? I doubt that he himself knew. He lived for the moment, did Piers, and would have given small heed — as nor did I — to the implications and ramifications of our bonding. Any excuse for a ceremony, he'd have thought, especially one by moonlight and in secret. He certainly didn't love me then, though he said he did. That came later. No, the impetus at first came all from me."

When the new moon was a few days old — the time, said Agnes, best aspected for the making of vows — Piers came to my room at night. I had sent my servants away, and only Gilbert waited there with me. Across a low table we had spread a length of cloth-of-gold. It lay like the mantle of an altar and on it a small carved Persian box and two candles in silver candlesticks.

"I thought you might not come," I murmured greeting him.

"I said I would."

"What have you there?"

"A magic brew!" Piers set it down upon the table-altar. It was a silver chalice, wide-lipped and low, its base broad as its cup, its stem slender.

"Such as priests use!" I breathed, approving. Within was wine, and the leaves of herbs that floated on its surface.

"What is that?" I asked.

"Only the good wine of Gascony. But," Piers added, "Agnes added things to make it special."

"Magic things?" I said awed.

"But naturally."

Gilbert came forward and put his nose toward the chalice and sniffed ostentatiously as if to show that such did not scare him. "It looks like caraway to me," he said. I elbowed him aside.

"Well, Gaveston, come kneel by me," I said.

We knelt together at our altar.

"I wondered whether Gilbert should be priest," I said. "But Gilbert is not holy, and I want to do this properly. So Gilbert shall be our witness, but the holiness comes from our vows, and this."

I opened the carved box and showed what it contained. It was a gold ring set with a sapphire. It was the holiest thing I possessed. "Saint Dunstan forged this with his own hands. Most famous of abbots, most renowned of archbishops, he shall add sanctity to what we do now. The holiness of Dunstan is with us."

"And the enchanted light of the moon," said Piers.

"Is that necessary also then?" I asked uncertainly.

"Oh yes indeed," Piers answered warmly. "The moon calls to mind the Lady. To be truly blessed we must pay respects to both Lord and Lady. My mother would have counted nothing holy unless the Lady's blessing was upon it."

"But is that not witchcraft?" I said uncomfortably.

"Yes. But you need not fear it. My mother's witchcraft was very beautiful and good."

"Very well then , the Lord and the Lady. In the names of Our

Heavenly Father and — whom shall I say?"

"Our Mother the Earth."

" — and Our Mother the Earth, I, Edward, take thee, Piers Gaveston, as my eternal love, in faithfulness and truth from this day forth. In token of which, I give you a ring."

It was a great ruby set in gold.

Piers hesitated. "My lord, it is too rich. I dare not. And besides, it will be seen."

"I want it to be seen. I want all the world to know I love you."

"I have not brought one for you."

"It doesn't matter. Will you wear it?"

"I will."

With a shiver of delight I put the ring on Piers' finger. Now he was mine!

"And with it all my love," I said. "Now you. Now you to say the vows."

There was a pause. Gilbert fidgeted in the shadows.

"I, Piers Gaveston..."

" — take as your eternal love Edward — say it!" I prompted in some agitation.

" — take thee, Prince Edward, as my eternal love. In token of which I receive your ring. In the names of the Lady and the Lord. May She bless our union. For," Piers added gloomily, "He will not."

"Don't say so," I remonstrated. "The Lord blesses all who walk in His ways. Now you, Gilbert, say you witness it."

"I, Gilbert de Clare, am witness to the oaths of Prince Edward and Piers Gaveston," Gilbert said obediently. "Edward the Prince and Piers Gaveston have promised to love each other for all time; I verify it."

"Thank you, Gilbert. Now we are bound. Now we have taken our oath. Next we must drink the wine."

We sipped in turn, then drank more fully.

"Like Tristan and Isolde," said Gilbert with a laugh.

"No!" I cried hotly, turning on him. "Nothing like that! How dare you say we represent those ill-fated souls?"

"I did not mean to offend you, Ned," said Gilbert. "But you are very like the paintings of the hapless pair of lovers, kneeling there, your lips upon the chalice. Their story was sad, my lord, but yours need not be so."

"No," I agreed in some relief. "I know it, Gilbert. I was wrong so to berate you. But it is true that we have drunk from the magic chalice, and there is no turning back."

"My knees are aching," Piers said, sounding more uncomfortable than might be accounted for by mere aching knees. "May I rise?"

"If it is in my power," I answered with a smile. "But first embrace me and so seal our knot."

We kissed, then stood. "Will you stay with me tonight?" I said.

"Yes my lord."

"My services, I take it, are no longer required," said Gilbert quizzically.

I hugged him. "Dear Gilbert. You understand."

With Gilbert gone I paced about then, barefoot on the Turkish carpet. I turned to Piers.

"I want to know your thoughts about — "

"My lord?"

"About *fyn amour* and *fol amour* and friendship. I need to know what you think."

Piers chortled. "This is not, my lord, what I expected at this juncture"

"No — but it has begun to trouble me, and you must say what you think."

"Of course. What do you want to know?"

"You've heard the song of Amis and Amiloun."

"But naturally."

"A love song, isn't it? About two boys. Beautiful boys who loved each other. Loyalty to each other exceeding all other emotion. More than the love of women."

"Yes indeed. Amiloun chooses leprosy and poverty rather than desert Amis. Amis kills his own children in order to heal Amiloun. Their love is very strong. No one could deny it."

"It is an acceptable love," I said heavily. "It can be sung about at table. And it's an ideal. It shows us how we should be. Loyalty makes us as the angels. Like Roland and Oliver — 'for love of thee here will I take my stand — together we endure things good or bad — I leave thee not for all incarnate man'."

"Beautifully rendered, my lord."

"Don't laugh," I begged. "A perfect friendship. 'Friendship, that divine thing...' I was always told to emulate those noble youths — were not you? — as ideals of courtly behaviour. Amis and Amiloun, they were loving, they were beautiful — but they — they were without desire. And this is *fyn amour*. Piers Gaveston — *is that the way it is to be for us?*"

"I don't know, my lord. I don't know how it is to be for us."

"You know so much about the world. Is that all you have to say upon this matter? You are not being very helpful."

"I am treading very cautiously, because you are the prince of England, and you must indicate what is permissible." His voice, in the flickering shadows, sounded vibrant, almost excited. It was as if it had suddenly occurred to him that we were venturing into deep waters and that in such waters, treasures could be discovered.

"I wish I were a carter's son tonight!" I said fervently. "One who has never been taught the distinction between one love or another."

"You fear, my lord, that if I were to take you in my arms we should become inferior — we should sink from *fyn amour* to *fol amour*, which is a rutting transient passion fit only for beasts. You fear that."

"It is because I want the best for us, that neither of us should be less than what we are for loving each other. I want it to be pure as in the stories, and yet I want — I want — *you know what I want!*"

"Poor Edward," Gaveston laughed fondly. "Come here." He put his arms around me. "You have honoured me with a declaration of your love and I know how to treat a gift. Make ready for bed, and we will simply lie as comrades."

I gave a howl of disappointment and wriggled clear of him. "But is that what you want?" A horrid thought struck me. Perhaps he found me repulsive! I gulped. "I never asked you — but — don't I please you? My cousin Tom said I was very pretty."

"Your cousin Tom may say as much; he is almost your equal," said Piers a little sourly. "And he comes of royal blood."

"I hate it when you won't be honest with me because of who I am," I snapped.

"Forgive me," Piers said contritely; but I thought he smiled. "I will force myself — I will attempt to be honest."

"Then first and most important: Do you desire me?"

"Yes of course."

"And second: What do you think of *fyn amour*?"

Piers took me in his arms again and kissed me lightly.

"I think *fyn amour* is for the stories."

The morning sunlight woke me, warm on my face and naked shoulder. I moved in my silken sheets. I wriggled with an unbelievable contentment, and stretched, my arms behind my head. My first night with him; our very first night together... I said his name over and over, savouring it upon my lips, like that sweet balm they make from strawberries.

Piers had slipped away to his own bed long before dawn, leaving me to sleep, to wake and marvel. Soon my chamber valets would be hurrying to my side, and a day of jousting practice, sport, and riding would unfold once more, and all would seem as it had been the day before. But everything was different now. Gaveston had been with me. He had slept...here; his head had lain on this very pillow...here. I recalled his lips on mine...how he had kissed my body...all over! He had used his tongue upon my skin...he had done things to me — stroking, kissing, love-biting — and oh! he had put his mouth about my cock...

I rolled up on to my elbows, thrusting the hair back from my face. Yet what had happened? Was it so much, except in my own quivering fancy? Piers' lips had merely done what Gilbert's hand had done on many a night of cheery intimacy. All the boys did it, didn't they, as soon as they were able? For Piers it probably meant nothing at all. I must try to seem all unconcerned and careless, treat it as I would had it been Gilbert.

But maybe because Gaveston was more experienced, a youth who'd been to war and seen the soldiery at play, the plain truth was that what had been with Gilbert frivolous and slight, with Gaveston was like the embarkation to a world beyond all worlds, myself a hesitant and eager voyager; and I could not pretend it otherwise.

Whatever secrecy we had supposed appropriate for our ceremony proved impossible to maintain in Langley Palace. Rumour spread rapidly. Prince Edward had taken Piers Gaveston in some form of wedlock! Great good humour greeted the discovery and several of the boys thought it a droll idea and one to emulate. Various mock marriages occurred and much exchanging of rings and orisons with, I believe, an equivalent amusement. It was all the fashion for that autumn, as certain styles of hair and shoe; and it provoked a spate of love songs, jealousies and reconciliations; and then, a troop of acrobats and tumblers visiting, the new game was to learn to walk on stilts.

With pride and adoration I stood and watched Piers ride at tilt, his lance held light and steady, and his mailed hands firm upon the reins, the horse obedient to his lightest touch. Whomever Piers rode against he unhorsed, unless through kindliness he refrained, and all those boys admired his skill and generosity.

After combat he removed the cumbersome helmet and shook his black hair free, which from the heat within the metal lay pressed against his brow in moist dark curls; and he jingled across to me, his legs and arms encased in bonded mail; his body also, beneath a white surcoat. He sat down on the bench; I handed him a cup of wine.

"I ask myself which of King Arthur's knights you are," said I, "for truly you are in every way a knight. Jousting, riding, dancing, boldness of spirit, beauty — you excel at all!"

Gaveston laughed comfortably, sweating in his chain mail, wiping his forehead, flashing a smile.

"Me? I am Gawain, knight of the Goddess, and I bear the holy pentagram upon my shield."

"Knight of the Goddess!" Just as my grandmother had once said to me! *Take Gawain with you on your journey — you will never be lonely in such company...*

"Oh yes. Gawain was a servant of the Lady."

"I take it that you do not refer to Our Lady, Mother of Our Lord," I said sitting down beside him.

"My Lady is a queen in Her own right. My mother's goddess. And my mother was a —"

"A witch, yes I know. " I frowned. "I wish you would not boast of it, Piers. What if the story spread, and clouded your fame? What if my father came to hear of it?"

Gaveston slapped my knee. "Don't fear so much! Your father knows of it."

"He knows of it?" I stuttered. "He knows that your mother was a witch and that you make no secret of it?"

"When a woman is beautiful, as my mother was, all men get to hear of her, kings also. He told me that he greeted me well, for my mother's sake. Your father has respect for the Old Religion. Everyone knows it."

"They do not!" I gasped. "He has never said as much to me."

"In France they know. Your father and his forebears all respect the Old Religion. Some of the old Plantagenet kings were witches."

"I don't believe it!" I said staunchly. "They worship at the shrines of saints. They pray to God Our Father. My father loves to go to Walsingham — to all the shrines — to anywhere that's holy."

"It doesn't matter; one may worship both God the Father and the Lady Mother. Myself I pray to both." He nudged me knowingly. "Double the good fortune, eh?"

I shook my head and marvelled. How rash and fearless was Gaveston, I thought, so free in his beliefs, so careless of opinion!

As Piers walked away to unpeel his chain mail and wash himself, I watched him. I thought: Gawain, knight of the Goddess; Gawain, as the song had it, "a man of beauty and of graciousness and gaiety of heart."

The leaves were falling in the autumn winds. In the woods at Langley we hunted, hawked and rode and sometimes Piers and I slipped away from the others and paused amongst the trees to kiss.

"Love me — quickly — love me, Piers," I said, and in the rustling golden glades he'd kiss and fondle me; with hand and lips he did what I asked. A little rumpled we'd return, and say that we'd been climbing trees or checking wolf traps.

In the evening minstrels sang of love and chivalry. And now all love songs had some relevance. The singers — some had come from Aquitaine and knew all the troubadour richness, and others from nearby who sang mere simple songs of wanting — entertained us as we dined, and I would steal a glance at Piers and hope the song touched him as it did me. And if it were possible to do so with some secrecy he'd come to me at night; but not often, because I feared Sir Guy might say something to my father. But perhaps, I told myself, he has noticed nothing; you could never tell.

On All Souls' Night, which in the language of the Old Religion is named Samhain, we joined with people from the village, up in the woods, and we danced around a fire, and a villager wore the horns of a stag and a cloak of deer hide; and Agnes wore a green robe and a garland of berries, and the people knelt to her, and it was understood that for that night she was the Goddess come to earth, and Piers and I knelt also, and it did not seem wrong.

At the palace we had a procession of Jack o' Lanterns, each carrying a turnip candle, and we made a circle of them and played games within. Apple bobbing in a trough of water! Catch the apple in one bite and love will thrive; two bites and love will be brief; three bites and love will turn to hate; four bites and you'll have no love at all — how urgent does this game become when the love object is close by, how meaningful each apple bite! "Who believes these foolish tricks?" I laughed; and yet when Piers and I both gained our apple with one bite I was excessively content. My heart so beat I could scarcely tell whether it was from nervous anticipation or from the sight of him on his knees with his head in the water and his bending bum raised; both, no doubt. I know that apple bobbing never had excited me to fever pitch before.

As Yule approached we made the Three Shepherds play for our enjoyment. I have often thought I should have been a travelling player. I can play brutes, nuns, lions, ladies, all with absolute conviction, as good as any I have seen come off the road; and Piers as much as I had always relished dressing up. We found we had an aptitude for foolery together when we put on our disguises, and nothing would better please us than that we two should play the midwives at the stable. There sat Robert de Scales in blue and silver, with a wig of flaxen hair, cuddling a swathed wooden doll and seated in straw beside a manger. Gilbert as the First Shepherd hustled in a mob of shuffling boys upon their hands and knees, with fleeces on their backs, and Piers and I, the midwives, met them at the stable door with the time-honoured question: "*Quem quaeritis in prosepe, pastores. Dicite.*" Ah, we were midwives would have put the fear of God into a woman near her time — blowzy red-faced strumpets we, with mangy hair and pockmarks, sagging bolsters strapped against our chests, and a wineskin passed one to the other which we swigged with gusto. It was all Gilbert could do to kneel and worship with a proper reverence. You have not seen a Three Shepherds play like that one, ever.

"Gascony," said Sir Guy Ferre.

My tutor and I sat before a map of the same at a table in my chamber.

"Gascony," said Sir Guy, "often synonymous with Aquitaine. To reach it you begin here, London, and then move to here, Dover, and so to Wissant, Paris, Poitiers and Angouleme. Travelling at a rate of forty miles each day a man may reach Gascony in three weeks. Alternately by sea, from Plymouth to Bordeaux, two weeks. This is Bordeaux, here, where the wine fleets assemble; and this is Bayonne, where the ships are built. This is the Garonne, the most important of the rivers, and here the Pyrenees, the southern reaches. Your father has always taken a personal interest in Gascony. Our thriving commercial links have always bound us. In any given year, some hundred thousand tuns of wine come to us from Bordeaux and in return we send them leather, cloth and grain. Because of the internal politics of the place and because of its proximity to France and Spain it's a potential source of trouble to us, and your father has always felt it important to maintain a firm control, unlike some of the barons who would be content enough to let it go its own way. Bearn, particularly, has always been a hotbed of rebellion and unrest. Your grandfather sent Simon de Montfort to govern Gascony some fifty years ago. He ruled with a firmness bordering on tyranny, and a propensity to put the Gascon lords in chains. This is not the way to further good relations. The Gascons brought their grievances to King Henry; and Simon was recalled and tried. He ravaged Gascony and wrecked the vineyards. Gascony therefore became the cause of conflict between de Montfort and King Henry — King Henry was for gentleness; de

72

Montfort for oppression.

"Gascony has a tendency to become the cause of trouble. Their merchants come over, they gibber in their own tongue, they settle near the warehouses, and they have privileges which upset our merchants. Edward..." Sir Guy paused and looked into my eyes. "It might be wise if you were to pay less heed to young Piers Gaveston. I notice that you single him out as your particular companion. Distribute your favours more widely. As I mention, Gascony has always been a source of trouble..."

"You will have heard the news; the King, my father, is on his way south," said I to Piers as we rode along the rutted track in the bleak bare woodlands. "My sisters and I were always wary of his returns. He always made changes."

"I think you need not fear him quite so much," said Piers. "He is a king and must be strong. But he is the most admired monarch of the known world. You should be proud of him. I would be, were he my father."

I remained unconvinced. "He always brings changes; and we have been peaceful for so long. Besides, my cousin Tom is with him, nor am I eager to see him again."

"No, him I do not like," Piers agreed.

"You knew him in Flanders, I believe?"

"I could have known him even better, had I so chose. He would have liked me in his tent."

"He asked you — ?"

"He acquired boys from the town. You saw them entering and leaving, pretty whores who went with anybody. And when he asked me, naturally I refused. It would have made me seem as they. He has no understanding of a person's pride. I was poor, yes, but I was not poor in spirit."

I reflected on the matter at some length. "So Tom of Lancaster asked you to his bed!"

"His bed perhaps, or more likely over his table," said Piers coarsely.

"Some would say it would have been an honour," I said smiling a little. "He is after all the nephew of the King of England."

"You know him well, my Prince, and therefore I have no wish to offend," Piers answered carefully. "But to commence, he isn't pretty — his big pale face, his lecherous lips... And for myself I find him strange. I think he has a certain madness."

"He does admit to melancholy," I agreed.

"It's more than that," said Piers. "Melancholy has a quietude, a passivity. Your cousin has a strength within. And he is very arrogant."

"I sometimes think he's envious of me," I ventured cautiously.

Piers guffawed. "Oh, innocent! But naturally he is envious of you. He strides round like a prince. He shouts his orders. He cuffs with his fists. He dresses well; his horses are superb. And he was always close to the King, at his right hand, as one who would say 'Lean on me, sire, I am always here!' As if he were the royal heir. But he is not the heir."

"And you refused him!" I said impressed. "Bold indeed. What did he say to that?"

"He became tight-lipped," Piers answered drily. "I had offended him, that much was plain to see. I might have been afraid, if I had not been sure of the King's protection. But men as Thomas, I despise them. They think their rank entitles them to take what they please. He is a lord but he has the manners of a churl."

I grew silent. Then I said: "And I suppose you think the same of me?"

"The same as what? In which respect?"

"My rank entitles me. I suppose you think I am like Thomas."

"No indeed I don't," said Piers. "It is terrible to me that you should think that. You are quite different."

"I demanded favours."

"But my lord, you spoke of love and friendship. And besides, we only play; we do the things that all boys do. Thomas wanted more. He said as much."

I let it pass that Piers considered trifling what I believed most beautiful. Instead I smiled. "You mean he asked for — for —"

"For sodomy," said Piers more bold. "And why do you smile?" he added quizzically. "That is no laughing matter!"

"I smile because he asked the same of me," I sniggered. "And I said no. But then he made me give a sort of promise."

"How?"

"He forced me. He pulled my hair. And I said I would, when he came back from Flanders. But I won't, of course."

Gaveston began to laugh. "Yes, that's very droll. Poor Thomas! Asking and asking and obtaining only refusals. I wonder how many more, besides ourselves!"

I giggled. "Maybe dozens!"

"Hundreds..."

"Thousands..."

"There are not thousands at court!"

"But if we include Flanders and France..."

And we continued to laugh, setting each other off to fresh bursts of hilarity, and rode with the good humour of it, careless, laughing at Thomas of Lancaster.

King Edward returned in January and gave thanks and gifts at the shrines of East Anglia for his good fortune in the north. Then he swept everybody off to Westminster Palace, for important works were afoot — two marriages to arrange and no time to waste. Alliance with France was now the way of it: King Edward was to wed the seventeen-year-old sister of the King of France, and Prince Edward of Caernarvon was to be betrothed to the French King's daughter Isabelle, eight years old. I was not asked for my opinion, but I did reflect in gloomy resignation that it looked as if this proposed bride amongst so many other previous possibilities was now most likely to be mine.

Sixty years old, King Edward put his country's welfare first, and for his people's sake, prepared to act once more the role of bridegroom and wed and bed a fresh young girl, and Margaret, as princesses must, no doubt accepted policy's dictates and set about to make the best of it. A wedding was announced for the month of September.

King Edward patted Gaveston's back and said how pleased he was to see him settled well, and Piers preened like a stroked cat.

"Look to him, Edward," said my father all bonhomie. "He's debonair and courtly. Emulate him; he can teach you much."

If your grace but knew, I thought; and bowed.

King Edward chafed in the confines of the palace and the spring airs made him restless. Moreover, he was pursued by tactless barons pressing for his confirmation of the oaths he'd taken through the Regency Council and ratified in Ghent, matters to do with Magna Cartas and Laws of the Forest which would curtail the sovereignty of the monarch should they be followed through.

"Oaths taken under duress, Edward," said he darkly, "are no oaths at all. No man is bound by oaths forced upon him. Remember that. Such oaths should be considered null and void."

"But sire," cried those about him. "You do not purpose to quit this place? The business here attends your grace — the Charters — "

"I find the air at Westminster does not suit me," said the King, and rode away.

"Cousin Edward!"

Thomas of Lancaster caught up with me in the long stone passageway. "Edward! Have you been avoiding me?"

"Of course not, Tom," said I walking.

"Stand still; we need to talk." He caught my sleeve.

"We do?" I paused. We faced each other at the foot of the stairway. A shaft of the bright spring sunshine penetrated from a high window, bringing sweet airs even to Westminster.

"Young Edward, you have grown more beautiful since I have been away," said Thomas with what was plainly admiration.

You have not, I thought. I found Tom's features coarser, and I recalled what Piers had said: his big pale face, the manners of a churl...

"I'm happy so to please you, coz," I said with a certain archness which, I now recalled, came naturally to me in close proximity to my cousin.

"You might yet please me more," said Tom in loaded tones. He was wearing buff-coloured satin; it suited him, but I felt nothing for him.

"How so?" I answered coyly.

"You do remember? What we spoke about at Langley. It seems not so long ago to me. I often thought about it while I was away. Sometimes the memory of it helped me sleep at night."

I thought I knew what he meant by that. I fidgeted.

"We were good friends, were we not?" he murmured, moving closer to me. "You rowed your little boat, you teased me with your eyes — and then we grew more intimate. You do remember... I see you do."

"I do remember, yes," I said and smirked.

"Then you remember that you made me a promise." Tom's face grew of a sudden flushed. He panted somewhat. "I have often thought about that promise, Edward. When I lay in bed I imagined it. I thought about you — your golden hair and your blue eyes... I remembered the softness of your skin... your teasing ways, as if you knew you wanted me, but made pretence of shyness — this combination is irresistible. And then I thought about you kneeling down before me, and your upturned face and your pink tongue as you licked the juices on your lips...and how I wanted more, and you did too, at heart, I know it. And how you made a promise to me, that we should both have satisfaction... I have often thought about that promise, Edward, pictured what it would be like, imagined you beneath me, and we becoming lovers... I think the time has come — the time has come when I might claim fulfilment of that promise..."

Roughly he seized my hand; I pulled away.

I darted from him, elated with a sense of power, a mischievous imp who should have known better and did not.

"Alas," I sniggered. "A promise made under duress is no promise at all. I have it on the very best authority."

And I laughed and ran up the stairs.

"Edward!" Tom called after me, hoarse and strained.

Way above his head, in the crook of the stairs, I turned to look at him. His face looked ghastly, staring after me. I might, with wisdom, have been more uneasy; but instead I laughed and paid no heed.

Chapter Six

IT WAS all very well for Piers Gaveston, who thought King Edward superb, splendid, and the wonder of the age, to say that I became a different person in my father's presence. I couldn't help the effect my father had on me.

My life became now the acting out of a series of directives from the King. Royal progresses to show myself to the people of England; political banquets, speeches to burgesses, visits to folk and places of small interest to me but whose goodwill was deemed necessary. In order to carry out such with appropriate finesse I grew stiff and self-controlled, excessively polite. The obligation to please continually a man whose expectations were, as I believed, higher than I could reach, resulted in my seeking relief in endless games of dicing and chance, where money, horses, garments were the prizes, and myself not always winner. In gaming I forgot myself, which at that time I was ever more glad to do. I played in secret and at fever pitch. Piers saw it all and marvelled.

But he saw it infrequently, for, as a squire of the royal household, he was often whisked away wherever the King went, and this, I suspect, was half the cause of my seeking refuge in the thrill of gambling. You see, I believed that Piers' absences accorded well enough with his own tastes. Piers liked my father and made no secret of it. He was with him when he hunted in Woolmer forest, or at Dover to survey the royal ships. The King dined well, and radiated strength and energy and all the while seemed very pleased with Piers; and Piers, the churl, was happy to confirm the monarch's good impression of his person. Sometimes I swear I hated both of them.

My particular companion in gambling pursuits was Walter Reynolds. A clerk in the King's household he was determined to pursue a career in the church. His aspirations were religious, his attitude wholly secular. As I understood it, he was valued by my father as a man without particular scruple, who could be relied upon to carry out such little tasks as were disagreeable to a more fastidious fellow. Bad company? I did not think so. Worldly and all knowing, witty and diverting, he was a pleasure to be with. His name I thought suited his persona: his face was foxy, with its pointed nose, receding chin and narrow clever eyes, but as with the fox, he was a handsome fellow and looked good in tawny fur. I liked him very much.

The year was dominated by the coming marriage and betrothal. The court was full of French officials and papal envoys. Canterbury, the place of the ceremony, became a thriving hubbub of activity. In the fields around the city the pavilions of the nobles bloomed in bright colours, and the streets around the cathedral filled with traders, stalls and entertainers. A huge jousting area was set up. Cartloads of wine rumbled in; herds of sheep, pigs, cows, oxen, flocks of geese for roasting ambled towards their doom; and slaughtered larks and partridges, rabbits and cygnets dangling from poles borne shoulder-high jostled with overladen baskets of plums, pears, quinces, and sacks of sweet-smelling spices. Travelling musicians plied their trade at every corner; and solemn-eyed monks from Saint Thomas' shrine prayed for time to pass quickly and restore some sense of sanctity.

Early in September the lady whose arrival was the cause of the festivities, Margaret of France, a lovely fair-haired girl, with her entourage and the Dukes of Burgundy and Brittany, came to Canterbury, and King Edward met his bride and led her to the palace of the Archbishop.

On the night before the wedding it was the King's pleasure to drink with his son. Wine-rosy, he gripped my wrist.

"She's a fine looking girl, Edward and they tell me she's like to be a good breeder. It's true I am a little older than she, but I have never found encroaching years a disability — you know it — I can set a pace... And what's the fault, eh, what's wrong with wanting a pretty wench in my bed and not some ancient dame? That's what a man was made for, why God put us on this earth. Any priest will tell you that. There's nothing like it, Edward, as you'll come to know; there's nothing like the feel of a woman in your arms, a big well-made woman you can grip hold of with your hands. Ah," he said, and wiped a sudden tear. "I said I'd never take another wife; I said I'd never marry. There never was a woman like your mother. She'll always be here, in my heart." His tears coursed freely. "She'll understand. She knows I have to make alliances. She'll understand, your mother..." He looked at me, almost beseechingly. "You so resemble her — those high cheek bones, so beautiful..." He traced them with his finger tip. "Tell me she will understand..."

I set my face into a sympathetic smile; while feeling of a sudden sickened.

At the cathedral door Archbishop Winchelsea joined the royal pair in wedlock, and feasting and festivity followed. At the tournament it was observed young Gaveston did well, and ladies enquired who was the handsome Gascon. It was not a happy time for me. I felt I had no claim upon him; I felt he was the world's.

"We are never alone," I whispered to Piers at the banquet. "I always have to share you with a gaping throng."

"There's nothing to be done about it," Piers replied. "It has to be so. What else may we do?"

"I could suggest all kinds of things," I answered sulkily. "But it seems to me this pleases you, this business and noise, the adoration of women, and of course my father's obvious approval of you. Well, you are sure to rise now, are you not, and all your ambitions will be fulfilled!"

Piers smiled disarmingly. My heart ached, for I understood that whether Piers offended me or pleased me it would make no difference; a careless smile would always bind.

By November King Edward had marched north again. And he took Gaveston with him.

"Why don't you refuse?" I screeched at Piers, appalled at his indifference to my feelings. His servants bustled to and fro with armour, banners, clothes, and chests that rattled with pots and chalices. I stumbled round them, raging and ridiculous. "You will be parted from me for — who knows how long? You will be away for Christmas. No one fights in winter. Say you'll join him later. Say you're ill."

"But I am in extreme good health," he laughed. "Who would believe me?"

"You are flirting very dangerously with the possibility of a broken jaw," I promised with clenched fists.

"Ah Edward," Piers said, sickeningly amused. "Be peaceful. I shall soon return." He put a reassuring brotherly arm about me. I shook it off.

"You *want* to go with him!" I seethed. "You want to go to Scotland with my father! Even in November! Even leaving me behind!"

"But naturally," Piers answered simply, adding, as if he thought the explanation superfluous, "we go for glory."

The King took his farewells of wife and son at the gates of Langley in the rain, with Gaveston a little to one side upon a restive roan; I wished that it would throw him.

"The two whom I love most upon this earth," the King wept,

embracing first Margaret, then myself, then she again.

The love that he professed, however, did not prevent the King from leaving, and from taking the choicest household squires with him. Ah, I could not let Piers go in anger. I rushed to him. He leaned down from his saddle and hugged me, warmly, with excited eyes. I didn't blame him. I would have been excited also, going for glory.

The riders gone, the Queen and I now turned back to the palace.

"You must remember," I said to the sorrowing lady, "that Scotland is for him a fever that rages through the limbs."

"But — so soon after our marriage," she marvelled. "And it may well be I am with child, and he knows it. This Scotland must indeed be important with him."

"I believe," said I laconically, "it absolves him from having once again to ratify the Charters, which he would have to do were he at Westminster."

We entered the great hall. "This place is cold," said Margaret. "Sit with me, Edward, in my chamber."

She was not especially beautiful, the Queen. Her face was long, her ears too prominent, but her expression was sympathetic and her eyes a gentle grey.

The fire in her hearth burned bright in the dark of the afternoon. We sat opposite each other, thinking of those that had gone.

"We are of an age, Edward," Margaret said. "We must be friends."

"It would please me very much, madam."

"We have something in common today. We have been left behind by those we love."

I smiled politely. "My father will be sorely missed."

"I shall miss your father," she agreed. "I know that in your eyes it must seem odd to see a stranger in your mother's place and I would not attempt to fill that place. Your mother was a famous lady, beautiful and brave. But I shall love your father to the best of my ability and it will be no hardship to me. Yes I shall be sad that he is gone. But when I said that we have been left here by those we love, for you I did not mean your father. I do not doubt the strength of your respect for him, but your love, I think, is for the Gascon."

I blushed guiltily. "We are like Amis and Amiloun," I said swiftly.

"Yes," she said and laid a hand upon my arm. "He is your friend. The friendship of young men is a fine thing and much to be admired."

It was clearly apparent that she believed that Piers and I exemplified the trait of *fyn amour*. I was certainly happy for her to continue to think so. I experienced some relief at her interpretation of the situation.

"Piers is in every way a knight," I said, "And he comes of good family."

"Trust me, Edward," Margaret said. "I am for you. I hope that you will let me be one sister more."

Hesitantly I understood that Margaret, well meaning and lonely, wished to be an ally. Indeed, her presence there at Langley did remind me of the time when all my sisters were at home. Margaret enjoyed many of my own pleasures; we read stories, we listened to the songs of minstrels, and, sharing a fondness for music and the antics of the jugglers, mummers and clowns that enlivened winter days there, we began to make our preparations for the Yuletide festivities, which we spent at Windsor Park with as much delight as was possible away from those we loved.

"And Isabelle?" I enquired. "She whom I am to marry? Is she as sweet as you?"

But Margaret only laughed, and said that Isabelle was a child and would be sure to change as she grew older.

Robert the Fool came over from France in Margaret's entourage. The first time that I saw him he was upside down and back to front.

Imagine a slim pole held at shoulder level by two men. From this pole dangles an acrobat. His smiling face meets yours, his grin a cheery grimace. He seems to have no feet. His legs are bent behind him, knees over the pole, feet tucked behind his neck. Where his arms were, who knows? He seemed to have none. Contorted thus into an unrecognisable shape, yet still he smiles, as if all's entirely reasonable.

"That was you, Robert. Do I tell it right?"
"In all modesty, sire, one learns these things as an infant...I could no more do it now than fly."

Robert has grown stiff and creaky over the years, and has turned his back on foolery; now I employ him as my clerk. But in those days I almost believed a series of threads ran through his limbs and body, and not bones at all. I had no idea, then, that he was well-lettered and could read and write, and that as a boy, he had been given to the church, and that the church had given him back, for that he somer-saulted when he should have been upon his knees.

Upright, Robert was short of stature, stocky of build. His hair was fair and sparse, combed back from his brow which was broad. Clever brown eyes he has and a bold stare; a squat snub nose and a small mouth with a propensity to smirk. His chin is very long below the lips, his neck thick. In one nostril he wears a small silver ring, and in one ear lobe three silver studs. It is a pleasing face, the features too irregular for beauty, nonetheless a good face. Like all whose talents are used to provoke mirth in others, he sees the human condition with a certain sad perplexity, and I suspect him of a gloominess of nature, which he strongly denies.

With his silly bauble, a fool's head on a stick, the many- jointed Robert teased and cajoled more laughs from me than I would have believed possible without Gaveston.

"You like the Fool," said Margaret warmly. "He's yours; I give him to you."

Robert has been close to me since that particular Christmas; he has been with me through everything that followed; he has seen it all.

Our absent ones fared not so well. The expedition to Scotland proved a brief and inconclusive venture and their Christmas spent at Berwick dismal. Of glory they saw nothing. King Edward raged; but for lack of troops and money he was obliged to make for home, where he arrived in early January.

"But only to make preparations for such an expedition as will bring the cursed Scots to heel once and for all," he promised. "And this time I shall not be parted from my dear ones. Queen Margaret shall accompany me, and Edward, you shall know a man's campaigning. Until that time, be free to play, for come the Spring you'll see a different kind of life."

Free to play...

I had my own royal barge, with velvet curtains for privacy, and seats covered with cushions of silk and cloth-of-gold; and a barge master Absalon of Greenwich to bear us where we would; and I had Gaveston returned, and Gilbert and the companions of Langley, and we set about to please ourselves, with all the fervency of those whose days are numbered.

Spring came green and sharp in the fields about the river. While King Edward, pursued by the stubborn conscientious Archbishop Winchelsea, swore all the oaths he knew and scowlingly confirmed the Charters in exchange for Parliamentary goodwill and money for his army, I lounged on silk with Piers, and the princely barge took us to and fro between Windsor castle and the Tower of London.

"The King, your father, thinks it's time that you became proficient in the arts of love," said Piers with twinkling eyes, "and he has hinted that I be the one to guide you."

"Whatever do you mean?" I gasped. "Is this another jest, I hope? He surely does not suspect or guess — that — ?"

"A guilty conscience is a dreadful thing, my lord," teased Piers. "You credit his grace with supernatural powers if you suppose he sees through distances. I merely mean to say your father has had love much on his mind of late, and his so visible prowess in the bedchamber has recalled to him his younger days. He was fifteen when he first saw your mother, and it has occurred to him that you are fifteen now — why, nearly sixteen — and for all he knows, you have not yet tasted womanflesh. In certain parts of London there are places...and we have leave to visit them."

"And you were such a rat as to agree!" I cried indignantly.

"Your father thinks I am a suitable companion for such an excursion," Piers grinned. "Worldly, courtly, debonair, discreet..."

"A rat," I spat.

"A worldly courtly debonair discreet rat, with fine dark fur."

"A rat no less."

"And I am to introduce you to the very sweetest gutters!"

I had never dreamed it possible to see London so! A city throbbing with sedition, plot and strife, detested by my father and grandfather, a place to fear and shun — this self-same London was a place of pleasure and excitement when, a heavy cloak about my royal person, and guards that followed within call, I walked about the streets with Gaveston as my companion and Walter Reynolds as our guide.

With the barge moored at the wharfside, we moved up into the city, to the mesh of narrow streets that crowded round about St Paul's. I found that every winding alley, nook and twist possessed a name that gave some hint as to what might be found within — Love Lane, Lad Lane, Gropecuntlane — and more or less important depending upon the requirements of the moment, Bread Street, Milk Street, Ironmonger Lane. Every street corner had its tavern — there were Bushes, Lions, Bells and Mitres, Harts and Jugs and Lambs and Bears, and sweet warm ale to be had at each; and brawls for the unwary and enough of a smattering of sedition to suggest King Edward's poor opinion of the place a true one.

We were once drinking in a low den when a fellow in a lively gathering was heard to say: "King Edward — pah! I'd like to see his head stuck on a pole on London Bridge!"

"The devil take you for so foul a wish!" a patriot cried. "On him, lads!" and a fight so fierce ensued that Piers and Walter hustled me away at speed. In good time, as it proved, for we later heard the man who had made so ill considered a remark had been beaten to death by the mob.

Reflecting soberly upon my father's hopes for me I permitted Piers and Walter to lead me to a house of ill repute, for it was true that I had not known what it was to lie with a woman, and it seemed only common sense that when my betrothal blossomed into wedlock I should know what was expected of me.

"They are all good clean girls here," Walter Reynolds said as we traversed the street, "and free from *morbus indecens aie cunnientis*."

"What is that?"

"That is what you might catch if we went to the stews on Bankside or down Blowbladder Street. But here you may be easy."

Scarcely reassured I plodded on between my cheerful companions. Our destination was a stone archway like an old gatehouse standing athwart the street, each foot of the arch containing a spiral stairway leading to the room above, and in this room a merry profusion of young women were gathered about a couple of bath tubs. Some were bathing, some pouring water on the bathing ones, and some laughing, waiting with towels to rub them dry. I had never seen an undressed female in my life, and to do so now in such a situation was something of a shock to my innocence. I stared. I knew that many a youth's fond heart had lifted — and his prick also — at the kind of scene I witnessed; mine did not, and beyond the curiosity which I would have felt at any new experience I felt no emotion other than a certain apprehension.

Piers for his beauty was at once seized and surrounded by the undressed nymphs but though it plainly pleased him he laughingly parried all invitations. Walter meanwhile was in discussion with the mother of the maids, a female of great girth and raucous guffaw, who fawningly proffered me a drink and encouraged me to make my choice. Helplessly I looked about. I had no preference. I was obliged to leave the decision to Piers and Walter who gave the matter great consideration, while each girl entering into the spirit of the contest flaunted her own particular charms. The chosen one then took my hand and led me behind a curtain to a small room where I saw a low bed waiting, and the girl, dropping the bath towel from her, closed the curtain and, naked, eased me to the couch.

My friends were waiting, lounging about the baths, conversing with the women, when I emerged flushed and dignified, and intimated my readiness to leave. Of what occurred behind the curtain, suffice to say that I had performed the deed and now knew what it was one did with women.

"If you wish it, you may request the wench's presence on the barge," said Walter.

"I think not," I replied.

The night air in the street struck cold.

Walter coughed. "There is a place my lord might find more pleasing," he suggested.

"Oh! No more of those!" I said fervently.

"This one is different."

Against the city wall at Aldersgate stood an irregular row of overhanging gabled houses. Walter knocked at the door of one of these and we waited beside its teetering lanthorn. A man let us in, looking shiftily about in all directions before he closed the door behind us. We climbed several rickety steps and entered a low room where some half a dozen boys diced in the straw. Comfortable among dicers I squatted down with them and drinks were passed around, and Gaveston and Reynolds flirted with the master of the boys, one Alfred, a young man barely older than themselves, good-looking, street wise, wary. Piers tapped me on the shoulder.

"Any one of these is yours, my lord."

I grinned and hesitated. I wanted them all.

The boys guessed as much.

"Choose me, my lord!"

"Choose me!"

The boys came clamouring, kneeling round about me.

"Look, my lord, what I can give you!"

"Have you seen a cock this big!"

"Mine's bigger — see!"

"My arse is biggest. Look at that! Every one I go with says they've never had a better one!"

I gaped at the wealth before me. Jutting hairy bums, pricks teased to erection held in front of me, firm thighs, legs apart, and the cheery grins of those who know they have what you want.

"I — thank you all very much. I choose him; but tomorrow I will return, and again, until I know you all."

They cheered good humouredly and passed more ale around, and Alfred led me and my catch by the light of a wavering candle up a dark stairway to a room beneath the thatch, Gaveston and Reynolds waiting below. Mice scuttled on the dusty boards, and with more straw upon the floor I had more the impression of a barn than a brothel. My lad — it was the one with the biggest cock — pulled off his clothes and stood before me naked, flaunting that great prick at me; and then undressed me, dropping to his knees and taking my cock in his mouth. We caressed each other's pricks and sucked in turn, with many a kiss and whispered compliment. We rolled in the straw, laughing, ruffling each other's hair, and very comfortable together. We came back downstairs smiling, and then tempted by the dice, I stayed for a couple of rounds, and when I left that place I was in great good spirits.

"They are like companions," I said to Piers. "I don't know why it should be so, but I am easy there. I liked it better than the women, clean as they most surely were!"

"Then next time," Piers grinned, "we'll come back for the one with the big arse."

This we did. And there to my excitement I learnt that pleasure, like a diamond, can be many faceted. I learnt that what is enjoyable with one can become even more so with two and three, that one may lie and kiss the prick of he who kneels athwart one's face, and yet a third may be about one's loins and yet another crouched behind him, and the grunting, panting, gasping all contribute to the sweetness of coming.

This initiation was not without its effect upon me in the sphere of my more rarefied existence. One evening, when the royal barge was moored in some backwater and a minstrel strumming in the stern, Walter, Piers and I were dozing on the cushions, well hidden in our velvet-curtained safety. A strenuous afternoon of pitching pennies up and down the boards for profit had left us languid. I reached for Piers. Before we knew it I had half undressed him and my lips had found his cock and all my new-found skills were put in practice.

"Why, Ned!" laughed Piers, plainly relishing all that I did for him, "what a competent little whore you are!"

Saucily delighted at the compliment I continued what I was about, and Walter Reynolds watched, and stroked my hair the while. It occurred to me that carnality had been awakened in my nature; and not of the kind my father had intended.

King Edward was in as good a humour as I'd ever seen him. With his young Queen well into her pregnancy and in the best of health withal, and preparations for the great advancement of the army northwards and, if I may say so, the best of expectations of his handsome son, the King had everything that he required for happiness. Benevolence shone from him as he rode.

"God's blessing upon our venture is of the utmost importance," he told me. "I love Walsingham; it has an odour of great sanctity. And here at Saint Edmund's Bury we shall partake of spiritual fare that shall sustain us in the bleak lands of the north this summer."

Passing beneath Abbot Baldwin's great tower my father and I entered the abbey, shrine of the holy Saxon martyr-king. My father's stay would be but brief, a few days only. Sacred as this East Anglian settlement undoubtedly was, it disquieted him, being well known as the place where, a hundred years ago, the barons of the realm had sworn upon Saint Edmund's altar to obtain from King John a certain charter of liberties later ratified at Runnymede. But I requested longer amongst the hallowed stones. My father agreed, delighted at my piety, and rode away, leaving me to revel in divine inspiration. "But for a week, no more; then you must follow."

Gaveston! I thought savagely as I paced between the great pillars... Gaveston! thought I, as I walked in the abbot's vineyard beside the river Lark... Gaveston! I thought, instead of contemplating the hideous death of the saint that lay buried there. He does all that my father orders. Go north, says my father, and so he goes, and cheerfully, as if my wishes counted for nothing! One moment he is my companion in whoring, the next my father's puppy to run where he is bid. He does not love me; that much is plain; well, two may play at faithlessness, and he shall see how much he likes my coolness.

Possible indeed to forget the cause of heart's unease here in this place of prayer. The river flowed beneath the three-arched bridge; the birds of May time sang; the monks made their devotions.

> *Laus tua, deus, resonet coram te, rex*
> *Laudamus te*
> *Qui venisti propter nos, rex angelorum, deus*
> *Benedicimus te*
> *In sede magestatis tue*
> *Adoramus te.*
> — May your praise O God resound in your presence O king
> We praise you
> Who came to earth for our sake, King of the Angels, O God
> We bless you
> On your throne of majesty
> We worship you.

I took my place in the procession which carried the royal standard to and fro amongst the holy caskets. Every relic in the abbey gave its sanctity to the golden leopards on the crimson. Thus blessed by God it would be borne in battle. "Three leopards of fine gold set in red; courant, fierce, haughty and cruel: to signify that like them the King is dreadful to his enemies, for his bite is slight to none who brave his anger..."

How much holiness was required to sanctify that object of war, how much prayer and how much daily, nightly supplication? I lent my voice to the brothers' pleas, acting as some young novice, never as a prince, and finding solace in the ceremonies.

I could be happy here, I thought, as many others had so thought before and would do hence, forgetful of the discipline, the accidie — that inexplicable depression of the spirit that drove some to despair — and the relentless regularity of a life devoted to the service of the Maker. Yes, I thought, I could well take to the life of a monk. Ha! That would serve Piers Gaveston aright! He would come begging, pleading with me to renounce my higher calling. He would miss me soon enough if I devoted myself to God. Moreover, the monk's robe would well suit me, I believed, as it did those who were lean and tall.

Fortified by such brave thoughts I sang and chanted, knelt and prayed for grace, and ate but what the monks ate, sleeping on a hard pallet, rising before dawn, and blessing my freedom from the presence of one whose love was questionable, finding solace in the presence of One whose love was unconditional.

But when the week was over, I rode north.

Queen Margaret gave birth to a son in Yorkshire on the journey and King Edward "hastened like a falcon before the wind" to see the infant Thomas.

In my own comportment also there was something of the falcon's swiftness. Every mile northward brought me nearer to Carlisle, where the army was assembling and where Gaveston would be waiting. Waiting? He came riding out from Carlisle town when my approach had been announced, and I knew him instantly, the rider with the long black hair and the sun upon him, Gawain knight of the Goddess, coming up from Camelot, the flaming pentagram upon his shield as clear as if it truly blazed there, carrying the potential of all promise and all pleasure.

"Gaveston — " I gasped, with the dust and my emotion, little more than a hoarse croak. I leaned to him from the saddle. Piers clasped my hand.

"My lord! The days were long without you. And it is Midsummer — the time to be with those we love."

The voices of the monks grew fainter and more faint in my ears, and spiralled into nothingness.

Midsummer! That magic time! Amongst the hustle and bustle of the gathering of men and weapons, of horses, tents and baggage, of provisions by the cartload, it was always possible to slip away unnoticed. For the celebration of the day, we found a little reed-fringed mere on the moorland near the ancient wall, and here Piers and I said prayers to the Lady and knelt and blessed ourselves with water, and said the old rhyme from our childhood that one spoke at Midsummer:

"green is gold
fire is wet
future's told
dragon's met..."

And then, alone in that great stillness, save for a crew of grazing sheep and the calling of the curlews, we kissed, a long slow savouring kiss; and I began half to believe he truly loved me.

If the year was spent in a flamboyant and useless campaign, I paid no heed. Every moment was exciting to me. I was a soldier at last and I was with Gaveston, and if there were to be glory I would be part of it. All that occurred was a splendid and unfolding background to the growing certainty that Piers had missed my company, that Piers was glad as I was to be reunited. Perot I called him now, in my affection...

With its knights and messengers, foot soldiers, bannerets, troopers and grooms, with carts and packhorses, with tents and stores, our cumbersome procession trailed its way through marsh and moor, crossed stream and ford and sidestepped bog and swamp. It attacked the castle of Caerlaverock with siege engines — great battering rams on wheels, and wooden stages that held catapults which hurled boulders at the castle walls; it sweated in heat and shivered in rain. But this was campaigning! Once, in August, we fought a skirmish up and down a river, and I was in command of the rearguard and we chased the Scots into the woods. I still remember the elation and the praise. I had done well, they said; they said I fought like a lion, that I had well distinguished myself. My father hugged me to him. I was proving myself to be the kind of son he always wanted. I was very well content. We took the Scottish stores and goods and baggage which they left behind them in their flight; this was, in fact, the summit of our achievement.

When camp was to be made for any length of time, shacks made out of timber were constructed for the nobles, and the floors were strewn with flowers. In such a wooden hut, the whispering woods about us, and the bleak dark hills beyond, the waters of some lake a-gleam in moonlight, slept Gaveston and I. And where else should a man sleep but with his companion-in-arms, so literally true with us? And who supposed we sent our servants from us and slept alone?

I reached for him; the night was warm and I was restless, and the moonlight from the window-slit lay on his naked shoulder; and I wanted him. In all our embracings yet, we had stopped short of the ultimate possession; I could do so no longer, and he understood. I hesitated, inexperienced.

"Use oil of sandalwood," he murmured sleepily.

"Piers," I whispered awkwardly. "Are you sure? I am thinking of something which the church considers damnable. In the year of my birth they made a statute which says that anyone discovered in the act of sodomy should be burned alive."

"Then we had better be sure not to be discovered, Ned," said Piers.

Silently and with a gathering excitement I padded amongst the flowers. I eased myself down beside him and he spread his legs beneath me. The perfect rounds of his firm arse pressed against my belly. I parted his cheeks, spilling the rich odour of sandalwood in my clumsy haste; I heard him laughing. Gently and ecstatically I entered him; it was so easy...so reasonable, this damnable offence. Cautiously I moved in him.

"Harder," he said. "More..."

With soft groans of delight I took my pleasure, coming rapidly in my exhilaration. I hugged him to me, covering his neck in passionate kisses.

"Edward!" he whispered, half laughing, half alarmed. "Don't leave me a bite on the back of the neck; I will find it difficult to explain away. Although I suppose in this wild country werewolves may exist, who would believe me?"

"I forgot!" I gasped. He twisted round to meet my kisses. "My turn, I think," he said.

Excitement flared in me again.

"Lie on your back," he said. I lay to his direction; he lifted my legs. "You fuck beautifully," he said; and moved his hands about me, bending his dark head to kiss me underneath my balls. I felt his tongue about me. Then with a swift movement he was over me, confident and sure, with moonlight on the muscles of his leaning arms. His face came close to mine. I put my hands each side of his head and drew him down to me; we kissed; and with sure steady thrusts he moved between my thighs, his warm balls nuzzling the soft hairs of my arse. Then he sighed, and came in pools of pleasure on my belly. He lay on me; we held each other close. What we had just done was punishable in the laws of our land by death.

But who would ever know! Elation seized me, and I knew such happiness as I had never known.

In the early light of dawn we left the shack and stumbled over tent ropes to the edge of the lake to bathe, as was the custom every morning. We were soon joined by many others, knights, pages, squires — mere naked men waist deep in water, splashing, yelling at the cold of it. I could not help but wonder...somehow I could not believe that amongst that great gathering Piers and I were the only ones who had risked our lives that night and known the secret pleasures of the flesh. But as I had told myself, who would ever know? Men keep these secrets close.

King Edward had strategies to plot, maps over which to pore, veterans to give lengthy counsel to him; he had better things to do than cast suspicious eyes upon a son who at the present moment was a wonder and a joy to him, a son as tall and comely as a prince should be, moreover one who wielded well the sword and had proved himself in battle, albeit a small and insignificant one. Thomas of Lancaster, however, had leisure enough to ponder on events.

He strode into my hut, shoving aside the servant at the door. I was seated, Gaveston at my feet amongst the strewn flowers. We both started guiltily, though our conversation had been slight.

"Leave us, Gaveston," said Thomas curtly.

Gaveston jumped up.

"No!" I cried. "Cousin, you forget yourself to give your orders here!"

"Well, I would speak with you, and must he listen?" Thomas answered.

"My lord, I take my leave," said Piers and bowed and hastened out.

"He is too much with you, that one," Thomas observed disapprovingly.

I shrugged. "I believe I may choose my own companions?"

"Don't trust him, Edward," Thomas said. "I knew him in Flanders. He's a nobody, an upstart. He has contrived to please the King, your father, with his pretty ways. He's after all he can get; his family are nothing back in Gascony. Don't be fooled by his agreeable manner; he's the kind of boy who turns his charms on as one turns the stopper on a wine keg. He has his eye on future chance. He never leaves your side. He means to make himself indispensable."

"How well you understand him," I said ironically.

"He is beneath my notice," Thomas answered. "I merely give advice. Edward!" he said pained. "What has happened? Why are we no longer close?"

"You are as dear to me as ever, cousin," I said graciously.

"I think not," Tom replied. "When you were a boy you held me in esteem — affection — you were open in your manner — we were friends —"

"Ah, there you have it," answered I. "When I was a boy! I think you loved me as a sort of puppy or a jester, someone to amuse you. I was glad to please you. But since then, my duties, my responsibilities — I am not as I was; how can I be? But I am still your cousin and your friend."

"It was not the action of a friend to spurn my advances, Ned. We shared an intimacy in our youth. You have not forgotten; I know you have not. What has changed? I have not. Have I grown loathsome? I seem much as I ever was. My love for you as strong," he added pointedly.

"We are both older; that's all," I said. "Boys together do things; it doesn't signify."

"But with us —" said Thomas fiercely. "We are far more than common. Think who we are. We shared a passion born of our high birth, the understanding that only we two are good enough for each other, all else inferior. We are bound by blood."

I moved uneasily. "Whatever can you hope for, cousin? I am betrothed, and must think of what is right. I can offer you nothing, and certainly not a continuation of our boyish indiscretions."

"There are always ways and means," said Thomas in low tones, "for secret passions to burn, none knowing, and appearances maintained."

"That's too dangerous!" I laughed glibly. "I would not care to take the risk."

I could see he was about to persuade me further. I took a breath. "Don't take offence, dear Tom. I understand your meaning — but — I do not wish it. And we shall both be happier if neither of us speaks of this again."

Tom's eyes grew dark. "Am I, so near to you in rank, still not yet good enough?" he breathed.

"It isn't that at all," I answered losing patience. "I have tried to be dispassionate. You don't know me at all if you think that rank plays any part in this. I love the common man. I'll walk alongside any carter on the road. Why do you oblige me to cause you distress? You could come to my bed the humblest thatcher in Langley *did I but desire you!*"

"So that's the way of it," said Thomas almost to himself. "No, I don't believe it...you used to love me; I swear you did. There must be some reason..." He stared at me stupidly. I thought he had a crazed look. "It can't be that there's someone else — there's no one good enough for you but me."

"Please, Tom, go from me," I urged. "We'll talk of it another time."

"That's right," said Tom almost like an idiot. "We'll talk of it another time."

He caught his cloak about him and went from the hut.

I winced and shivered. When Piers returned, a little hesitantly, I said: "Oh why are some folk such a trial!"

"I don't suppose you mean Lord Thomas of Lancaster?" Piers twinkled.

"I received a proposition; I refused; I made him angry. His eyes were like hard black beads."

"Ah, spare him not a thought," Piers laughed. "He's a churl, and when we speak of him we'll call him thus — the Churl."

I grinned. "We shall not speak of him at all."

At New Abbey, near Dumfries, Archbishop Winchelsea's party caught up with our weary and frustrated army, bearing letters from the Pope, condemning our venture into Scotland.

With appropriate respect the King and barons listened as the Latin homily was read aloud. Myself I did not understand it all, though I didn't admit as much. My father thanked the Archbishop for his trouble and assured him that he would give the matter further consideration; thus the public face. Away from the Archbishop the King pounded tables, kicked a bench or two, and shouted: "By the blood of God I will not sue for peace! And for Jerusalem's sake I will not rest but will defend my rights so long as breath of life sustains my body! What does this Archbishop think to gain by plaguing me so? Has he not heard of Thomas Beckett?"

But as the autumn came on and still no battle fought nor any purpose achieved, a truce was called to last till Pentecost, and in a savage frame of mind King Edward gave the order to march south.

He turned to me then, gripping my arm in vice-like concentration. "Son," he said. "My pride, my joy, though all things work against me, in you I have found pride and solace. You have so bravely borne yourself. Those doubts I sometime felt are gone. My dear dear son, my hope for the future, balm to my eyes — continue so to please me, and all other disappointments count as nothing. I feel it in my bones that you will never give me cause to grieve — your nature is to please. Nothing and no one shall break this amity between us now." He smiled, and nodded at Piers Gaveston who stood a little way beyond; and in his great content and satisfaction with his son he set about to reward me and create me Prince of Wales.

Sixteen years of age, I received a ring, a silver rod, a circlet round about my yellow hair, a sword girt about my body, and a ceremony of extreme solemnity. This completed, I began a journey into Wales, with Gaveston and Gilbert and a troop of men-at-arms, and Robert the Fool, and all my household, to meet my people, to accept their homage.

Chapter Seven

WITH THE sea always a little to our right, we made our way along the northern coast of Wales, crossing the boggy marshland of the Clwyd and the roaring gorges of the Conwy; and where we paused, in castle and in church, the men of Wales came, barons, foresters, knights, clerks, bishops, to do homage for their land. Each man must kneel and place his hands between mine and swear allegiance, and they came in hundreds, which meant aching palms for me. Sometimes at one gathering, as many as two hundred made their vows. But I loved it. I was touched by such a demonstration of their loyalty, formal though it of necessity must be. These people are for me, I thought, not for my father. They want me for their prince. This land where I was born is special to me; this is an affair of the heart.

If I needed to escape the endless ceremony I would ride with Piers and Gilbert hard along the low strand that was never far from where we travelled, and the sea rolled in with white-foamed waves, and the wind brought clear cold spray and cries of seabirds.

On the evening of my seventeenth birthday we feasted at Rhuddlan castle and, my pleasure in music and entertainment being known, a crwther was brought to court, a man skilled at the three-stringed fiddle of the countryside. Then Gwynionydd, a bard, sang tales of Y Tylwyth Teg, the Little People, who live in the enchanted circles and the underground lakes and within the mountains and the sacred groves. I was spellbound, touched by the music, which, as the wise know, has the power to translate the listener to other realms, and in those realms he may dance all night, forgetful of his cares and duties, and banquet upon golden fruit and make love on banks of roses; then, the fiddling ceasing, he must return in pain and misery, to find himself an old old man, the hillside a grey tangle of sharp thorns, the food a bitter taste upon his lips and no one to believe his tales.

"If my lord so wishes, I know of a man who has a harp, but he is frail and cannot travel; but he is a good man of the old faith."

"I long to see him; we will go to him."

A hut beneath a rowan tree, halfway up a mountainslope, the grass upon the track knee-deep and wet with rain; the man an ancient, hunched, in darkness save for the glow of a small fire of spluttering wood, the harp a gnarled and ragged thing bent as a bough, the music wild and eerie. I sat, my cloak about me, having given instruction that no man should give away the knowledge of my rank, yet feeling like a prince of old times, one who travelled in disguise upon a quest. I half expected that the cauldron on the hearth was Cerridwen's, with all the answers to the mysteries of life and death within; I half believed that veils of mist would suddenly descend and translate us all into another form. And so we sat and listened, and the harper glad enough to play for us and speaking words that none of us from England understood.

"It's unforgivable that I can't speak their tongue whom I should govern," murmured I. "Piers, this music reaches me as nothing I have heard before. This is a magic place."

"For me also, my lord."

As we came away we rode a little further off between the trees and came upon a birch grove full of lichen-covered rocks, and there dismounted. Out of sight of the waiting attendants we moved close to each other and embraced. We kissed slowly, our lips tasting of the rain. The red-gold sun set in a dazzling blaze between the black shapes of the distant trees, glinting upon half-hidden streams, so that the dark wood danced with gold.

"When I was a child they told me of the white birds of Rhiannon and the stag of Rhydynvre and the old owl of Cwm Cawlwyd and all the lands that come alive by moonlight and disappear at dawn and all the floating islands light as thistledown, but now for the first time I feel them. These are my people; I know it in my heart."

Sir Gruffydd Llwyd, coming to us at Flint, vowed: "We would die for you, my Prince. Call upon us in your time of need and we are yours." And though he may not have spoken for the dark and sullen-eyed that looked out from their wayside hovels as we passed, he spoke at least for many that had thrown their lot in with the power of their overlords; and of an evening, in my gratitude, I sat with Gwynionyd and learnt with all due concentration all the words in the Welsh language that I could get my tongue about. I'm pleased to say that if I ever found myself cast loose in any part of my dear principality I'd have no trouble asking for a tune upon the fiddle.

Too short a time it seemed to me did we pursue the shadowed boundary between mystery and the commonplace. In May we set our faces towards England and arrived at Kenilworth, where Tom of

Lancaster was to be married.

Alice Lacy, daughter of the Earl of Lincoln — a big fat man, a man who was no longer young, a man whose vast estates would one day fall to Tom of Lancaster...

"The King should have prevented it," said Gilbert thoughtfully. "See what Thomas has become in land, in wealth, in revenues! He may live off his own, dependent upon none. Look at what he will own — all the de Montfort lands of Leicestershire with Kenilworth and Lancaster and Pontefract; then all his lands in Yorkshire and the north, in Wales, in Lincolnshire. Why, he may ride from one end of north England to the other, and never set foot, or rather hoof, out of his own terrain. It's fortunate that he is no de Montfort, Ned, but being your cousin, a man loyal and true. What do you think upon this matter?"

But I was much too occupied in sniggering behind my hand at the contemplation of the kind of marriage Alice Lacy was embarked upon. "Sweet coz," I said, and kissed them both, "and sweetest Alice — all my love and kindest wishes for your future happiness. Many many children — days and nights of passion..." and I laughed in great good humour, hoping that my laughter would be supposed mere well-wishing and not what it was.

I had further cause for laughter when Walter Langton was caught up in a scandal. That wretched Bishop who had ruled the country in King Edward's absence and so gently steered me from the helm was accused of murder and adultery, with pluralism, simony, and best of all, I tittered gleefully, with converse with the Devil, who came up at his beck and call and supped and drank with him. Langton was obliged to go to Rome to explain himself to the Pope, the which he did, aided by the dispensing of sums of money to those whom he must persuade of his innocence, the which achieved his purpose and returned him vindicated and absolved, much to Archbishop Winchelsea's disappointment.

The King's cousin the Earl of Cornwall died, making the title vacant, and was buried with ceremony at Ashridge priory, and the manor of Langley which had been in his possession was granted to me as my own by my now doting father.

Elizabeth my sister became a widow and was remarried to Humphrey de Bohun, Earl of Hereford, twenty-six years old and of a taciturn nature. A new son was born to the King and Queen at Woodstock Manor. He was christened Edmund. He was to be my favourite brother.

And I, I gambled and diced and played backgammon, ninepins, chess, and entertained my father and stepmother and my sisters Elizabeth and Joan and Joan's children — Gilbert, Eleanor, Meg and Elizabeth. And at Westminster, ten monks conspired to rob the royal treasury. Their leader was a travelling merchant who planned it to the finest detail, but was caught, the jewels about his person, and paid for his failure with his life, his hide nailed on the Treasury door.

But all the rest was Scotland...

We were always marching in the direction of Scotland or marching back from Scotland or marching across Scotland or up and down the damned place. That was all you had to do to please my father; anyone could have done it. Any fool who spat and cried out Rot the Scot! might hope for knighthood; that was how it was.

> *"And now you are too modest, sire. Let it be set down that you led half the army, golden in the sunshine of your father's approbation; and how your father, fully cognizant of your military prowess, said in utmost confidence: Let the boy win his spurs!"*
>
> *"Ah, yes, it was undoubtedly a happy time."*

Surrounded by my friends — Gaveston on a dapple grey, Reynolds on a piebald, Gilbert on a roan — supported by the experience of old Lacy of Lincoln and the fervour of my contemporaries, Arundel, and Hereford my brother-in-law, and accompanied by the perpetual enigma of my cousin Lancaster and his younger brother Harry, I led a mighty force through Galloway and Annandale, by loch and inlet, castle, moor and forest.

We saw the silver sands of Turnberry, Loch Ryan's scar with its clamorous seabirds, and paused to make pilgrimage to the shoreline cliffs of Whithorn where the cave of Saint Ninian the missionary showed dark and dank beyond the glistening pebbles of the beach. We led our troops to pillage and plunder about the Moray Firth in the time-honoured manner of invading armies; we burned barns and we besieged castles. At the walls of Stirling before it fell to us, my father narrowly escaped death once again — a crossbow bolt lodged in his armour, and he pulled it out and spat and waved it at the foe and swore he'd kill the man that shot it. He was immortal.

I had my court about me as I rode — my clerks and messengers, my servants, minstrels, confessors, my Robert; also a lion on a chain that travelled in a cage with Ralf his handler. It was in our tradition that great beasts accompanied us to war; but one must discriminate: Saladin stayed at home. We pitched tents and pavilions up and down the glens, packing and unpacking, and then setting off again to make our unwieldy way through rough terrain, the leopards of my banner leading, myself in crested helmet and chain mail, with a wonderful sword and gleaming gauntlets, mounted upon a superb white horse.

Thus the pageantry of our display, our show of might. And then there were the moments of rashness.

The camp was set up beside a stream; the sun was warm; the tents pitched in a field of harebells, mayweed, eyebright, yarrow; a field of love, not war.

"You sent for me, my lord," said Piers at the entrance to my bright pavilion.

"I did. Come in."

I closed the tent flap and tied the cords in place. A cooler gloom eclipsed the sunlight, and underfoot the scents of the meadow rose as they were crumpled. My sleeping couch stood in the centre, so strewn with purple satin cloths and cushions as to render it a sultan's low divan. I wore a light robe, nothing more.

"As you see," said I, "we are quite alone." I sat down on the bed. "And I have given orders that no one is to enter."

Piers' eyes glinted. Then he looked about. "But — here?" he blanched. "And now? In the light of day?"

"The better to see each other, my sweet Perot."

"Ah, Edward, how can you ask it? Are you mad? The cloth of the tent alone hides what we do — and outside — "

"Yes, the army in its entirety. Are you afraid?"

A few yards distant and there was the resting army. The yells and guffaws of the soldiers romping in the stream, the splashing of water, the sound of running feet; the rattle and clang of metal as men cleaned chain mail and iron-capped helmets, and the thud of hammer as fresh tents went up — the stable tent, the chapel, council chamber, offices — the chink of bridle as the horses were led by, the shouts and banter of the men, the rhythmic sound of whistle, tabor, lute. All but a breath away.

"Afraid? Yes! You may be sure I am."

"Take off your clothes."

Piers hesitated.

I lay back on the couch and slipped aside my robe. "I've heard about you pretty boys," I said in a low provocative tone. "I've heard about the way you wait about the camp and tease the soldiers with your glances. I know your kind. They told me about you. There's one, they said, Piers Gaveston, the handsomest of all, with wicked eyes and the lewdest arse, and all you have to do is ask him, he has such an itch for it..."

Piers grinned and slowly unbuckled his belt. He removed his tunic. I watched dry-mouthed, almost as if I'd never seen him naked. The sounds outside were totally eclipsed by the pounding of my heart.

"Hurry now," I laughed. "I'm panting like a dog."

Piers stood in his breeches, a sight to be savoured. There was the firmness of his dark-skinned torso, and his muscular arms; the lean slender belly, the little black curls that showed about the navel. But the breeches! The breeches were tight-fitting, hugging arse and thighs to somewhat above the knee, and trimmed with orphrey, as it is called, Phrygian gold, that same rich embroidery that priests use on holy vestments. Luxurious, sybaritic, sensuous...

I licked my lips. "Unpeel, O blessed one."

He stripped for me and pausing just long enough for best effect, strolled over to me through the living flowers. He knelt, his arms around my waist. He caressed my prick with his tongue. I raised him to the bed. "Lie on your belly; let me have my will."

Awed at such perfection I knelt between his thighs, taking in through adoring eyes each portion of his beauty. I ran my hands along the dark hairs of his thighs, I handled each firm cheek and parted them to kiss the cleft between, to put my face against his balls. I reached down for the oil of sandalwood and poured it over Perot's flawless buttocks, stroking it over his skin, kneading it in between, till all was soft and smooth and acquiescent. I eased myself down on him and fucked.

"I wish the tent would blow away," I murmured into his ear. "I wish they all could see us, beautiful, loving, performing on this dais, for their enlightenment."

"By all the saints," gasped Piers. "I pray that no god hears your wish."

"Why, Perot," I teased. "I believe that you are still afraid?"

"If you are not, Ned, we might well ask ourselves which one is crazed!"

"I long to wear you at my side, the fairest of my jewels!"

"Ned, simply be content that we were not discovered!"

My army moved to Perth, a small walled hamlet by the swiftly-flowing Tay, to take up our winter quarters at the castle.

"If we had the skins of bears and the fires of Hell we would be very happy here," said Robert the Fool. "As it is, we must move sharply to keep warm."

"You should dance more," Gaveston laughed.

"Make fools of yourselves if you must," said Robert. "There's always someone to find women to come dance with soldiers. Leap and skip and make a show and entertain; the less work for me! Already a Fool I don't have to work at it as you do, and you'll maybe teach me something. The best dancer gets as his reward a clout from my bauble."

Piers and I joined the revellers in the dance of the carol, winding a merry way up and down the hall; and the minstrels blew and strummed and beat, and the cold wind howled through the hollows of the arches and stirred the holly boughs and bay leaves, and tossed the fire-smoke high.

A series of acrobatic somersaults the length of the table, touching neither meat nor drink, brought Robert in a topsy turvy arc past those who sat and watched the dancers on that Christmas Day.

"All who have light hearts are dancing," Robert thought. "And these remain."

Guy Beauchamp, Earl of Warwick since the death of his father, thirty-one years old, broodingly handsome and reputed to be ruthless. Dark haired, dark browed, with well-formed features, he wore an expression of habitual cynicism, and his preference for black velvet in his impeccable dressing made him panther-sleek. On his long slim fingers gleamed garnet and gold. He rarely smiled; Robert thought him sinister.

Aymer de Valence, Lord of Montignac, heir to the earldom of Pembroke. Thirty-four years old, a tall pale black-haired man, large-nosed and sombre; of a pious inclination. It was said he had intended to become a churchman and his leanings still strayed Heavenward. Gaveston called him Joseph the Jew.

Hugh Despenser, aged forty-four, a quiet stolid man with a thoughtful wrinkled face. Kindly, it was believed, but keeping his own counsel. They said he was ambitious for his son.

Young Hugh Despenser, twenty years old; in shadow, with his face turned away.

Thomas of Lancaster, a frown between his brows, gnawing on a chicken bone, watching those that danced.

"Who's the beauty?" Warwick asked lightly.

Thomas spat the gristle from his mouth. "Piers Gaveston," he answered. "A nobody from Gascony."

It had not occurred to him to ask "which beauty?"

Watchers and dancers, Robert thought, men are of the two kinds and it was ever thus. And he somersaulted once again between the trenchers and the tankards and the steaming pies, and upside down he pulled a face at each of those that sat and gazed, his grimace a mirror of each withdrawn preoccupied expression.

"Be off with you, Fool," Tom of Lancaster said angrily, understanding what was done.

But Guy Beauchamp tossed a silver coin, and said that tricks should be rewarded.

In the morning those that were going riding gathered in the hall, awaiting Warwick whose page said he was still sleeping.

From the doorway to the stairs that led to Warwick's chamber a wretched peasant girl came stumbling forth, barefoot and half clad, her torn gown clutched about herself, her face much bruised, her hair dishevelled. She ran past the assembly in some distress. Guffaws and whistles followed her as she fled. Within a moment Warwick appeared, stepping from the low archway careless and complacent, sleek as a well-groomed dog. Cheers and congratulations greeted him. Warwick bowed.

"My lord has slept well?" Thomas enquired ironically.

Warwick curled his lip. "You would do well to sleep as I do."

"Another time, my lord," I murmured, embarrassed by the little scene, "let your sleeping be less visible."

"Ha!" Warwick snorted. "My Prince envies me? The wench has sisters; I'll get one for you."

"Prince Edward only likes the girls from Gascony!"

I spun round. I could not tell who said it — the gaggle of squires and pages standing there of a sudden looked as innocent as butterflies. I could not quickly enough control my discomfiture. I stuttered stupidly.

"So that's the way of it," said Warwick in amusement.

"Our horses will grow restive," said the senior Hugh Despenser loudly and firmly. "If my lord is ready — ?"

The moment passed in the communal eagerness to be off. Two things were plain to me. The first was that it had been naive of me to suppose that everyone shared Queen Margaret's innocence and believed my close friendship with Perot mirrored that of Amiloun and Amis. The second was that Hugh Despenser had my welfare at heart, and in this I was to find I was not mistaken: of all the men who professed to serve me, Despenser was consistently dependable and loyal, and remained so throughout all that was to pass.

I have no excuse for my stupidity in the company of Thomas on the ride across the moors.

I rode hard and fast; a bitter wind howled, flecked with icy rain. Thomas rode alongside, straining to keep pace.

"Is it true?" he yelled against the wind.

I feigned not to hear him.

"God damn you, is it true?" screeched Thomas.

"Ah — truth!" I laughed. "You would discuss philosophy?"

The wild wind excited me. I relished the thudding hooves, the raw bleak moorland and the billowing sky. My hair flowed out behind me like a golden pennant.

"Do you fuck Gaveston?" screamed Thomas.

"Oh, Thomas, leave me; go away."

He would not, but would ride alongside. "Tell me, Edward! Is it true?"

Seized with a sudden wildness I laughed aloud and looked at Thomas as I rode and cried out: "Yes! I fuck Piers Gaveston! And remember, Thomas — envy is a sin!"

Thomas gaped like a fish. His open mouth seemed to fill half his face. He dropped behind. I rode on, elated, with a kind of madness, laughing like an idiot, shouting to the wind: "I love Gaveston — let the whole world know it!"

Piers shook me roughly awake. I protested mildly, half asleep. He had come in from outside. He was dressed, wearing crimson velvet. He looked dishevelled and unkempt; that is, much unlike himself. God's soul, but he was angry.

"Don't ever speak to me again, nor look at me, nor touch me!" he seethed, hanging over me like Sword and Famine.

"Never, as I live," I answered affably. "What have I done?"

"The Earl of Warwick thinks I am your whore," Piers spat, and strode about, and threw my servant from the room and slammed the door.

I raised myself up to my elbow and moved the fringe of hair out of my eyes. "Do we care what the Earl of Warwick thinks, Perot?" I asked. "He is a lewd and callous brute."

"He is a mad dog!"

"Calm yourself, my love."

"Don't call me that. Look at my face — my swollen lip."

"What happened?" I sat up in bed and hugged my knees.

Piers stood still, turned, and stared at me. "He kissed me! But in hatred!"

"Hatred? You know what they say about love and hate!"

"Believe me, I can tell the difference."

His news sunk in at last. "He kissed you?" I gasped. "Sit down, Perot. Tell me..."

Piers threw himself down on the bed, lying alongside me, propped up on his elbows. Yes, his mouth was much bruised. Beast that I was, I could not help observing that in no way did it lessen his beauty. I longed to caress the split lip; I dared not. He was furious.

"I came down into the hall...the stairway was dark and I came through the door into the brightness; I found myself surrounded by a gang of Warwick's men, that buzzed about me and would not let me pass. Seven or so. There seemed more. They slung me against the wall and held me there, my back against the wall, spread-eagled, and they stood back to make a path for the Earl of Warwick. What he said was horrible."

"You must tell me."

"He said: 'So! Piers Gaveston, the loveliest wench at the Prince's court. It's time we were acquainted.' Well — nothing in a great hall ever goes unobserved and a smirking audience began to gather about. That was what made it so insupportable. So many people saw... I told him I had nothing to say to him and I ordered him to call off his dogs. I was very dignified."

"What did he say?"

"He leered at me, close to my face. He said he had a reputation to maintain. He said: 'All whores love me, and you will be no different.'"

I gasped, properly appalled.

"Yes!" Piers cried. "And he ran his hands about my body, handling me, all over, Ned, but in a kind of horrible contempt that left me speechless. Then with his two hands he cupped my face and kissed me on the mouth, to hurt, you understand. 'That's what you like, isn't it?' he said, and when I pulled away he turned and said to his men: 'I swear I heard that that was what he liked. But some whores pretend a coyness to entice the more. Who yet shall taste him before we let him go?' And then they each took turns to kiss me, Warwick's men, with jests and each encouraging the other; and then they left me, and with hardly a backward glance, as if it had all been of insignificance!"

And that, I think, had rankled with him most of all.

"And that was all?" I saw at once that I had phrased my question foolishly.

"All?" he shrieked into my face. "I was humiliated before the entire household!"

"Yes, yes, forgive me," murmured I. "We must be more discreet in future; we must scotch the rumours."

"They consider me a nothing," Piers growled. "They will see...they don't know me at all if they think that."

"No," I soothed him. "They are quite wrong. But Warwick is a brute; the whole world knows it; it will be forgotten soon."

Piers stared at me disbelievingly. He uncurled; he stood up; then he seized me, shook me, and threw me back in the sheets. "Listen to me!" said my darling, livid in his rage. "I was humiliated. All the world saw it. And laughed. I can't go downstairs now with my mouth like this — everybody will remember and laugh afresh. I shall have to stay in my room. A recluse! A hermit! Disfigured! It was all because of you! And what I want to know, Edward, is this: how will I be avenged?"

I laughed awkwardly. "But what can I do?"

"Edward! The Earl of Warwick has insulted me beyond endurance. And, by implication, you. I ask you: what are you going to do about it?"

I sat and thought. At last I sighed. "While my father has my purse strings and command of me, the truth is there is nothing I can do."

"And where does that leave me?" screeched Piers.

"Be patient, Perot, just be patient. One day he will die."

With Warwick and Lancaster gone from the castle, patience was an easier matter. Piers' natural exuberance soon surfaced to replace his wounded dignity, his lip healed rapidly, and his expectation of a hermit's life proved groundless. He even once said mischievously to me: "And he's not bad looking, is he, the Earl of Warwick?"

The King's goodwill intact yet, I was entrusted with diplomacy and was permitted to treat with the Scottish leader John Comyn, and though William Wallace still remained at large, the conquest of Scotland was considered an accomplished fact when the bulk of Scottish lords surrendered. Pausing only to burn Dunfermline Abbey, King Edward turned his back on Scotland, and together we went south.

I was twenty years old. I was the light of my father's eye. Tall and long-limbed, golden-haired and handsome, soldier and campaigner,

I had about me nothing to prevent an observer from supposing that if Longshanks were to die, the world would see any change at all.

So how came cracks in the noble edifice of familial concord? Whence the surcease of solidarity?

It may have begun with the festivities at Langley when I and Walter Reynolds, who was then treasurer of my wardrobe, put on a pageant for the King and Queen. We chose the morality play where Death and Life contend for Mankind's soul, and the soul is saved by the intervention of the Virgin. I played the Virgin.

"Beautiful..." cooed Walter, combing my hair. "No false hair needed; your own is soft and thick and lovely to the touch. And now to paint your face..."

I surveyed myself thoughtfully in my woman's guise. Of course, I was too tall to pass for a woman. I was almost as tall as my father. But I was very graceful, very slender. I wore a shimmering white gown and a filmy overtunic with the hem embroidered in a band of silver thread. My hair was tied in further threads of silver, bound up in a crispinette, a silver circlet on my brow. I had a silken shift; I rustled when I walked. My eyelids were painted silver, my cheeks whitened, but with a piquant touch of rouge, my lips red as the proverbial cherry. I was very lovely.

The household worked to create Heaven and Hell, the damned souls wearing black, the saved souls white. There was fire for the Mouth of Hell, and a Heavenly Cloud with the sun's beams radiating, and cords from which to dangle angels. There was in Paradise a Fountain, and there were seven deadly sins and seven virtues, played by those who also played the saved and damned souls. Richard Rhymer my especial minstrel, who could charm the soul away with his crwth after the Welsh style, played Heaven's trumpet. Robert the Fool played Death, with the bones and skulls of dead beasts hung about him; Gaveston played Life, in flaming scarlet.

Amongst it all, poor Robert nearly played his part too well and himself to perdition. To find some relaxation from the rehearsing, I proposed we all should swim. The cries of horror that reverberated from the violets I dwelt amongst could be heard at Berkhamstead. Swim in December! Gaveston would not; Reynolds would not. But Robert would, and other brave folk also, and we took ourselves into the icy Gad and swam; at least, I swam, and Robert drowned and must be heaved up from the shingled depths and saved. I saved him. As we panted together naked and shivering on the bank, and towels were fetched and warming drinks, I said to Robert: "You truly are a

Fool, to come into the river not knowing how to swim."

"You saved my life, my lord," said Robert.

"I own it," I replied.

"Then you must take responsibility for your deed. It may have been the Lord's will I should drown."

"I accept that same responsibility," I said. "You shall not leave me." It was, I thought, a moving and meaningful moment.

"Ah, Robert, if I'd known with what continual disrespect you were to treat me, what shameless lack of reverence, and I God's Anointed!"

"You'd have thrown me back in the Gad, I know... Gaveston played Life, we said, in flaming scarlet..."

"Yes, yes. Alright..."

Piers glowed like a burning coal. And Walter Reynolds played God, which he considered to be no more than his due, since he directed all; and Gilbert played Mankind and prayed for salvation, and very pretty was he in his loin cloth.

Graciously I floated in, and interceded with the Most High, and Walter granted mercy.

"God's teeth," King Edward growled, half in affection, it would seem, half in disgust. "That I should ever sit at table with my son in woman's garb, his face more painted than a whore's!"

"It was but for the play," I laughed, tossing back my spangled locks.

"You played the lady to perfection," said Queen Margaret soothingly. "And the King was much entertained. Now laugh, sire, and let not poor Edward think you scorn him for his fine performance. I doubt that I have seen a true woman yet more beautiful than Edward."

King Edward snorted. Maybe he was too much in agreement. "I would wish him less able to play that part. Graces such as he displays sit poorly on the soldier he played at Caerlaverock."

I understood his meaning well enough, and some devil being on my shoulder then, I simpered sweetly and continued gracious and a touch seductive, for the pleasure that possessed me of a sudden to annoy my father. I knew well enough he was disturbed at heart by my all too apparent beauty and its sudden incarnation into female form.

It may have been this which prompted him to take me to one side before he left Langley and to offer me advice. He entered my chamber and sat down and toyed with a table napkin fashioned in the shape of a *fleur de lys*.

"Your bravery I know is not in question," said the King. "I have been witness of your courage in the field; no man more proud than I of the son who shall succeed him. No, what I query is your judgement of the souls of men. It seems to me that time which could be spent in working to understand which men are to be trusted and which doubted is passed by you with men of small integrity. Reynolds, for instance... Use his talents, Edward, but let him not be close with you. I should not have to say as much — a discerning man would know these things. I should not have to tell you whom to take as your adviser."

"But you will, no doubt," I smiled.

"God's breath I will," he said good humouredly enough. "And the best man of all is Walter Langton. Depend upon him, as I do; you shall not regret it."

I sniggered, thinking of that Bishop chatting familiarly with the Devil.

"Hugh Despenser," the King continued, "will be loyal to the core."

I smirked. "He is a youth of my own age."

"The elder Hugh Despenser," frowned the King. "Next the Lord of Montignac, Aymer de Valence, whom I have left in charge of Scotland — that should show you the measure of my trust in him. Then Lacy, Earl of Lincoln."

"He is so fat!" I grinned. "Gaveston — " I shut my mouth. I had been about to say: "Gaveston calls him Burst Belly" — but I refrained; however, thinking upon that I giggled, and, reasonably enough, I suppose, my father clouted me.

"When will you learn respect?" he cried. "I see I waste my time here; it is clear enough that you would rather spend your days with fools and players. But if you can hold my words in your remembrance, do so; it is good advice."

The King stood up and turned away.

"Forgive me," I said sulkily. "It is right that your grace should so inform me. And Tom of Lancaster?"

"Eh?"

"My cousin Thomas. Am I to trust him?"

"Thomas is your kin," shrugged my father. "Blood of our blood; and certainly for us."

"And Warwick?"

"Naturally I put my trust in Beauchamp."

"And — Gaveston?" I ventured.

"Gaveston?" King Edward said scornfully. "I was speaking of those that matter."

If he but knew, thought I, hugging the knowledge to myself like fur, and savouring the voluptuousness of a guilty secret... if he but knew how Gaveston mattered...

Well; he was soon to know...

Chapter Eight

LINCOLN, WHERE the court spent Christmas in the castle on the crag...

The kissing bush of mistletoe hung from the rafters, branches of brightly coloured ribbons twined amongst its silvery berries. The great Yule candle, big as a young birch, burned in its bed of holly. The Yule log smouldered.

The fanfare of horns and shawm, drums and trumpets announced the commencement of the banquet, and the servants glided in with partridge, pheasant, peacock — roasted and then decked out in their feathers as if they lived, their beaks and claws painted gold; with pies of plum and pear, with almond pastes yellow with saffron; with chicken glazed with honey, mustard, rosemary; with salmon soaked in wine, with pastry sugar castles; and spiced cakes. The Boar's Head made its entrance, triumphant as a lord, its mouth gaping with apples.

Jugglers with balls and daggers, jugglers with fire; a magician with white doves; dancers, minstrels, tumblers — ceaselessly the entertainers followed one another, till the fanfare brought the feasting to a close. And everybody danced, the slow and stately measures, the carols and the leaping jigs. And to a cheer of great approval King Edward joined the dancers, and the murmur went about: "How tall and upright yet the king! — how well he bears himself! — he has the secret of eternal youth, no doubt of it!"

I watched morosely. Ah, would he never die, the King? How regularly now that question posed itself to me! How daily a feature of my thoughts it proved! Others half the King's age had had the grace to quit this mortal stage and permitted their offspring the benefits accruing from their demise. I itched for those that were my due.

Not so much the powers of kingship, no, those were not uppermost with me, but more the relinquishment of restraint; for I felt bridled at every turn. I must make it clear that it was no morbid fixation upon my father's strenuous hold on the vital processes, but an entirely reasonable desire for independence, common to any man in health and strength.

My revenues were dealt out to me in fits and starts via Walter

Langton. A sudden order from my father could send me where I might or might not wish to go. The members of my household were changed about without my agreement, without consultation with me. The room I had ordered built at Langley was counter-ordered by my father to be taken down again — and yet Langley was supposed to be my own. And every year the dreary yolk of Scotland's weight to drag us northward. Granted it brought a freedom of a kind, and yes, at first I had enjoyed the pleasures of campaigning — but every year? for ever? and for what? There must be better ways of passing time.

Superimposed upon all these preoccupations was the worst of all, the perpetual unease of always hiding my true feelings about Piers before folk.

"But they knew! Everybody knew."

"Robert, they did not! And who are they? Gilbert knew, and John and William my valets, and..."

"Elizabeth your sister knew it."

"She never said as much."

"Your sister Joan knew. I heard tell she said good luck to you."

"My dearest Joan... Yes, she was ever bold. She said the matter of whom his children loved should be of no concern to a father. She told me to love whom I pleased. She said that Piers was the handsomest man at court. She said she liked him."

"And therefore many, it would seem, knew what you vainly thought a secret. And those who did not know it, supposed it."

"But I was always so discreet..."

"As a donkey shitting."

I crossed myself. What manner of son was I, to sit and wish my father dead! And yet I did wish it. Guilt and remorse made me uneasy. I quit the hall, the warmth and merriment, and climbed the little stair that led to the chapel; here I knelt to pray.

The little room of richly painted wood was full of the scent of incense. The light of a single candle burning on the altar caught the golden cross in its steady light, and the images of saints peered from the shadows — Saint Hugh that holy man of Lincoln — Saint Christopher who guided travellers — Saint John — Saint Joseph — Saint Luke the Wonderworker.

"Santo Christophero, ora pro nobis," murmured I upon my knees. *"Santo Josepho, ora pro nobis."* Then I grinned, for flippancy was never far from me. Saint Joseph, I assumed, would not take kindly to prayers about hostility to fathers, it being his only claim to fame. At

that moment I felt a hand upon my shoulder and jumped.

"You did not hear me enter," observed King Edward, kneeling down beside me ponderously, leaning on the altar rail. Billows of dark velvet settled with him, spreading on the stone.

"I was at prayer," I simpered.

"It is sometimes good to be alone," the King said heavily, pausing, as if considering his words.

"I will leave you then," I said, purposely misunderstanding, and in a great hurry to be off. My father gripped my arm and pulled me back into place. The strength of that grip was enough to make me shudder — a sword-arm tried in battles, all its life.

"I sought you out especially," the King said, "hoping that in this place of sanctity the wish to wring your neck would be a little softened. My temper is not a placid one, and I pray for the serenity to speak pleasantly. I hoped that I would never have occasion to speak to you at all upon this matter."

"Which matter, sire?" I said with a pounding heart.

We gazed ahead of us towards the golden cross.

"An innocent boy whom I entrusted to your keeping and whom it seems that you have much incommoded."

I sniggered.

"Oh? Did I make jest?" my father said with great restraint.

"Forgive me, sire. I have no recollection of being entrusted with an innocent."

"I brought young Gaveston to your household in all good faith. Have you been pestering him with your attention?"

"Such attention as I may have shown to Gaveston has not been ill received," I answered haughtily.

"I have heard other."

"From whom?" I demanded.

"From Gaveston."

"What? You have spoken to Piers — ?" I gasped.

"— who says on oath that he has never welcomed your advances."

"My — advances?" I screeched.

"Let me hear no more of it," King Edward said. "Give no man cause to talk, remember who you are and whence you came. Another time and I shall not speak fair." The King got to his feet.

White faced with rage I also stood, bowing as my father left the room; and then I strode away in search of Gaveston.

At the bottom of the stairs stood Walter Langton with a smirk of such satisfaction upon his face that I believed he knew what had transpired and, more, that he had been the one to broach the subject to the King.

"Do you know aught of this?" I seethed, unable to pass by without expressing something of my feelings.

"A kind son never grieves his father," answered Langton like a Heavenly Virtue in a play, with only one line to say, who therefore overacts it.

"Have you such wide experience of sons, Bishop?" I said with all the relish of youth insulting age for the enjoyment of it. "So the rumours of adultery were true?"

He was, to my gratification, speechless at my rudeness, and his pale cheeks paled the more; it struck me with amusement that I may have hit upon a truth by accident. It did not trouble me.

"In toadying to my father," I continued, "and in your spreading of false rumours I suggest that you remember to whom it is you give offence, and the precariousness of your position thereby. You are a hireling of the monarch, Langton, and as such may be dismissed."

Again I left him speechless, and again I did not care.

Gaveston was amongst the dancers in the hall, smiling and impeccable, paying especial court to ladies. For all my glowerings and hintings you would swear he had a mote in his eye as far as I was concerned. And not until King Edward's entourage had left the castle did he place himself in any situation that was not well frequented by the masses; I might scowl and scowl and turn into a gargoyle for all that he would notice me.

I caught up with him at last in the room where he slept while he was at Lincoln, with squires and servants all about, and for ignoring me and for what he had said to my father, I seized him by the hair and shook him. The Plantagenet rage is a fearful thing — I speak as one who has both dealt and received it — and I made him howl.

"You told my father lies! You said that I importuned you and you found it distasteful!"

"Send away the servants!" screeched Piers writhing in my grip. "What are you thinking of to say that before folk?"

"Be off with you!" I yelled to those about us. "Or stay, it matters not, since all the world knows, sees and has opinions upon what I do."

Some stayed, some fled. Those who stayed hovered in the shadows, silent, like young owls on a beam.

I threw Piers to the floor; he lay there groaning, clutching his head. I stood over him. I bellowed: "You denied our love!"

Piers crawled to his knees and reached for the bed's support.

"Be calm, Ned — hold your anger — let me be."

"So it's true then! So you told him I had molested you and that you were much offended by my beastliness?"

"Not quite that, no," Piers said, a reluctant amusement creeping back into his tone. "Please, Ned, you frighten me. Sit down! You are so tall when you stand up!"

"But how could you say that to him?"

"I didn't say it. He put the words into my mouth — I answered yes and no. Whatever he wanted to hear. Well, what else could I do?" Piers glowered. "He has the power to send me back to Gascony!"

"He would never do that," I said in scorn. "That's idle speculation — timorous talk. He values you, the whole world knows it. You should not have been so lily-livered. You should have answered him plainly, boldly. For my sake, Piers, you should have spoken out with pride!"

"And told the truth?" he answered with a cynical smile.

"Why not?" I answered recklessly. "Are you ashamed of what is true?"

"No," he said cautiously. "But I prefer to temper honesty with expediency."

"Honesty?" I seethed. "You have never understood the word. You were not honest, hinting that I, a brute, forced my unwelcome attention upon you, and you a sweet and sanctimonious virgin!"

Piers grinned. "I know, I know, it's derisible; but it was what he seemed to want to hear and so I let him understand whatever suited him. I was a beast, it's true, and I have wronged you by default, Ned; but Lord, Lord, he is so fierce, your father, and I dared do no other."

I softened slightly. I sat down on the bed. "I begin to think you fear him more than I do."

"He holds my future in his hands," Piers answered soberly. He rubbed his head, which must surely have been throbbing from my treatment of him. "If I were banished from these shores I would be a nothing, a nobody. You, for all that he may rage at you, will always be his son."

"It's intolerable," I muttered. "Why should we have to lie and pretend and hide our true sentiments? Why must we live in fear of what he may or may not do?"

Piers looked up at me expressively; he had no need to answer. The anger went from me.

I took Piers' head into my lap and nursed him, stroking him. "Oh God," I murmured passionately. "If only he would die..."

Very well, I grant that it was stupid of us to break into Walter Langton's forest and hunt and slay his deer; but who could have foreseen the awful consequences? And it was so merry!

Our sport was to be outlaws. We had often talked about the pleasures of the lawless, and imagined what it must be like to live wild in the greenwood. No servants to pry or gossip.

"Or to hand one's clothes and prepare one's food..."

"Yes, Robert; but the pleasure of preparing food for oneself, food one has captured by one's own skill: the sizzling venison over the humble fire, the richness of a rabbit stew with herbs culled from the wilderness, and bread brought by friendly villagers..."

"And the pursuing by the Sheriff's men, the threat of the gallows?"

"...the eluding of the same!"

"The snows in winter, the bare bleeding feet..."

"...the flowers in summer...lovemaking in a blossomed bower... Robert, I will not be dissuaded."

We left our horses, servants; and together, armed with longbows and sheaves of arrows, off we slunk into the forest. We were wearing peasant gear — brown hose bound about with leather thongs, simple jerkins over fustian shirts, and our own doeskin boots. Each of us wore a green hat with the perkiest little feather. I have seen Piers Gaveston in all kinds of clothes, but that hat, that feather, those tight hose, that short brown leather jerkin so became him I am almost tempted to declare I liked him better thus than in any of his satins.

"By all God's angels!" I declared in longing. "If only we were truly peasants and could live together here for ever!"

"Close to the earth and none to work against us," Piers agreed with feeling.

"A little hut of thatch...a dog or two...perhaps a flock of sheep to tend."

"And a clear stream beside and," Piers added laughing, "several more hats and three or four changes of hose."

It was early spring and the forest was in bloom. Everywhere was bursting with the fresh new green, and all the trees in leaf and rustling with the gentle breezes. We ran amongst the verdant paths, we kissed amongst the thickets, chased each other for the pleasure of pursuit and capture, and lay down on a bed of primroses for the especial delight of handling our pricks in the open air, which, like food munched out of doors, has a savour of its own. To suck Piers' cock amongst the primroses in Walter Langton's wood was a most piquant joy to me, to spew my own seed there the same. We dozed awhile, and then, refreshed, we hunted deer.

Hunted! Well, since the beasts were browsing in the clearings, this was not so difficult. Two bucks and a hind we got and would have stopped there anyway; but then to our dismay some half a dozen louts that passed as foresters in Langton's employ, each one with a knife drawn and an ugly mastiff at his heels, came bursting up on us as we stood over our catch, and ordered us to go with them.

"But — don't you know who I am?" I laughed in disbelief.

"This is the Prince of Wales!" explained Piers in tones of proper awe. And some alarm, for it was plain that they did not believe us. Horrid brutes of fellows they were too, and they plainly had no intention of releasing us.

Piers nudged me. "Speak to them in French — show them —"

My harangue in the language of the court had no effect. Indeed, it served only to make them more suspicious. I hesitated. I did believe they would use violence if we resisted.

"Best go with them," said Piers, clearly agreeing. "We can put right their mistake when we see Langton."

"Oh God! Must we be taken before him?" I wailed. "Ah, this is insupportable. Listen to me, men. We are not the peasants we seem. We are in disguise. *God's blood, do we look like peasants?*"

Piers burst out laughing, and I too saw the humour of it. Not so Langton's foresters, who surrounded us now and laid hands upon us, and we went quietly with them, with a gathering sense of foolishness.

I prayed that Langton was from home; he was not. He received us in his great hall, and forewarned by the first of the fellows having gone on ahead, had dressed himself for the occasion in fine robes.

Ringed about by his menials, Piers and I stood, captured peasants before the overlord. I had the grace then to guess the peasant's lot a little less than excellent. Had we been in truth now what we seemed, we could each have lost one eye and one testicle, this being our first offence, and such extreme mercy therefore permissible.

"So it is indeed the Prince of Wales," said Langton; and he could not keep the purr of satisfaction from his tone. "I did not believe my servant. I supposed he must have taken a madman in my woods, to speak so wild a boast."

"Well, it was a romp, no more," I laughed. "And we are nicely caught. I must congratulate you, Bishop, on the vigilance of your foresters."

"They were not vigilant," said Langton smoothly. "They heard your tramplings and the sounds of your trespass from far off. The whole wood rang with it."

"They saw us?" I blanched horrified. God in Heaven — what had they seen?

If Walter Langton took enjoyment from the sight of Piers and I now thoroughly discomfited and looking guilty as thieves caught with their hands in the silver, he must have done so now.

"We merely walked," I answered haughtily.

"And slew three deer, as I understand. Are times so hard at Langley that the King's son must come robbing of his subjects?"

I flushed now. "You but hold your forests for the King and by his kindness. If I choose to sport with my father's deer, that is my business. And it is not your place, Bishop Langton, to question the actions of the King's son."

"However, I do question them," Langton replied. "And your father also I think will be inclined to question them."

"Ah — don't tell my father," I pleaded. "It was nothing, was it? You shall have three deer more. It's a paltry matter, just between ourselves, and hardly worth my father hearing."

"I think otherwise," said Langton. "In matters of waywardness and ill-discipline, that which is allowed to grow unchecked grows only more vile and rampant."

"God's soul, so that's the way of it then?" I seethed. "Perhaps then you should call the Devil to your aid. We know he comes up to your bidding. Where is he? Perhaps you have him lurking nearby?"

It seemed plain that we were to be accused of poaching and no more. Our spirits so revived, we turned to jibing. We looked around, as if for Langton's once-reputed familiar. We whistled as if for a dog.

"My lord the Devil?" called Piers in invitation. "Don't be afraid; you are among friends. Sweet Lucifer — your master Bishop Langton is close by and calls for you."

"How dare you?" Langton seethed. "Impudent pup — vile Gascon — it is you who are the cause of the Prince's wild ways. You have enticed him with your comeliness and your sorcery. Witch's brat! You lead the Prince to evil acts; and the Prince is weak and pliant — "

"I am no such thing," protested I indignantly. "I'm pleased you think my friend is comely — everybody does. Would you like to embrace him? We heard you liked the sins of the flesh!"

"Get out!" said Walter Langton, pointing to the door.

We bowed our way out of the room, flourishing our pretty hats. The brooding foresters stood back, and let us pass.

"God's truth but there is not a day goes by without I ask myself how did I come to spawn you!" screamed the King across the table, glaring till his eyes grew red and all the veins stood out upon his brow.

"Oh God and all the saints grant him apoplexy!" I prayed, and stood my ground and gave him stare for stare.

We were at Midhurst Abbey. Throughout our confrontation holy plainsong echoed down the passageways, and monks, silent as moths, flitted by, hugging the walls, apologetic, self-effacing, taking it all in.

"In Scotland," shouted my father, "barely more than a year ago — I thought I had a son worthy of me. Then I believed against all odds, that you were of such stuff as fashioned kings — how bitterly I was deceived!"

"Any figurehead may lead a troop," I answered scathingly. "But come real policy and I am constantly thwarted. You place more trust in wretched Langton than in me."

"And with good cause, for time and time again I've leaned on him and found him strong."

"If I had been given something of a chance I might have proved the same."

"I never dared to try you. I had heard your skills were dicing, play acting and finding fresh ways to fritter away your money."

"All fathers say that," I shrugged dismissively. "I am no worse than any other son whose income is a pittance and fed to him at the whim of others."

"By Heaven you are worse!" my father cried. "If your faults stopped there...if you were but a simple spendthrift...I would be on my knees in gratitude if all you did to cause me grief was overspend your money. Ah! My life has been a good one, and the time has come to pay for it, I see it all now. You are sent by the Almighty to make clear to me that in man's voyage through this temporal space come equal joys and woes..." King Edward beat his brow.

"I thought it was myself the play actor," I snorted.

"I never was a patient man — but how you try me. I can barely keep my hands from off your throat."

"All this is brought about by Walter Langton, I suppose," said I. "So he went snivelling to you."

"You broke into his forest — let your arrows at his deer — two bucks and a hind — you made no secret of your trespass — you paraded your ill-gotten gains — and when the Bishop reprimanded you, what did you say — ?"

I sniggered. "I told him to call up the Devil to give him help. God's teeth, that man is pomposity itself. How he struts and swaggers, basking in your persevering favour. But we all know of what he has been accused!"

"Slanders and lies, and damn your mouth, boy. Your insults to the good man are the peak of all your other follies too numerous to count. Your action was that of an ill considered simpleton, a birdwit, an idiot. Ha! And in your folly you had an accomplice."

I felt my grin fade.

"Gaveston was with you."

"So he was," I hedged, "and others too."

"Oh yes, I know your little coterie. Gilbert de Clare and your yeomen of the chamber. Well, there has been enough of this. That Gascon has gone wayward in your company and Gilbert is soft in the head. You do no good to either. Henceforth they go elsewhere. As for you, get you to Windsor and let me hear some good of you at last — or if no good, then at least no further proof of your imbecility."

"What do you mean?" I said, suddenly alarmed. "Are you taking Gaveston away? But that's impossible."

"Your company unmans him. It will be for his own good."

"But you are wrong!" I squealed. "You don't understand. He is my friend!"

"By all the bones of all the saints," the King said heavily, "I understand too well. Do you suppose me uninformed? Even if I had not beheld your overfond displays towards the boy, do you not guess that others have spoken to me about what now appears common knowledge?"

"Common knowledge?" I faltered. "Who has spoken to you? Whom do you believe more than myself when I tell you it's all lies, every word, all lies..."

King Edward shrugged. "It was your cousin Tom, who had it from yourself."

"Oh, Tom," I sneered. "And do you suppose him so holy?"

"I have said my words to you. I tell you, stay at Windsor; let me see no sight of you till I can tolerate your presence once again. For by Saint Peter's staff, I cannot bear to look on you."

He turned on his heel and made to go. I lunged across the table as if to pull him back. I gripped the tablecloth bunched in my clenched fist.

"Not Gaveston!" I pleaded weeping. "Don't take Gaveston, I beg you..."

Patently convinced now of my degeneracy, King Edward left me snivelling into the wreck of the tablecloth. Monks, moth-like, flitted by.

Was ever prince so treated! I seethed with fury and humiliation. Windsor Park had never seemed so hateful to me. My household denuded, most of my companions removed, my allowance so reduced I was obliged to sue to friends and sisters for money. I ached for Gaveston who, true to pattern, meekly set off at the King's direction, with a pious look upon his face and many loud expressions of loyalty to the King. Gilbert also knew which way the land lay, and went docilely away.

Refusing to believe my father could be serious in forbidding me the royal presence I trailed about the south of England in my father's wake, expecting forgiveness. It did not come, and so I settled into Windsor as instructed, and wrote begging letters.

Firstly to my sister Elizabeth, a letter which I fully intended that she should show my father, and I hoped that she would understand this, otherwise I never would have composed so fraudulent and honeyed an epistle.

"Very dear sister, do not be dismayed at these news which you tell us they chatter in the parts where you are, about our lord the King our father and us; for it is quite right that he should say and do and ordain concerning us whatever pleases him, and we shall be always ready to obey all his wishes; for whatever he does at his own pleasure, so is it for our profit and for love of us, and be pleased not to listen to anything to the contrary, whatever they may tell you. May the Lord preserve you..."

To the Earl of Lincoln, to my sister Joan, to Walter Reynolds and to Hugh Despenser I fear the requests were more explicit and concerned with little sums of money. But to Elizabeth, who was with the King, upon a matter closer to my heart than monetary allowance:

"We entreat and request you especially to be pleased to beg the King to be pleased to grant our two valets to dwell with us, that is to say Perot de Gaveston — (no, begin again, let it seem that Gaveston was not foremost in our thoughts) — that is to say, Gilbert de Clare and Perot de Gaveston, for if we had these two, with the others whom we have, we should be much relieved from the anguish which we have endured and yet daily suffer, from the restrictions at the pleasure of our lord the King..."

The hot dry summer burned. Flies buzzed on rotted fruits. In response to my letter Hugh Despenser came visiting, and he was all solicitude, all promises, all consolation.

"Only the vilest would suspect that such a kindly meritorious grey-haired gentleman had any other purpose."

"Why do you dislike the Despensers so, Robert? Listen to you, carping on. Despenser lent me money to buy horses and greyhounds, and sent gifts of raisins and wine. He came especially to cheer me and enliven my time at Windsor."

"It was lively before he came. Livelier!"

"I won't hear a word against him; against either of them!"

"How glad we are to see you, in our time of trial!" I cried extending both my hands. "A man knows who his friends are at such times. I greet you well, Hugh Despenser, my father's friend and mine."

Robert now chose to tumble for pennies distractingly up and down between our feet. He and I both being after money from Despenser I could not fault him; our similarity as suppliants, however, irritated me; I may have kicked him.

"You did, sire."

"You deserved it."

"My prince," said the kindly and dependable fellow. "To serve you is our pleasure. May I present my son, whose devotion is equal to my own, who seeks but a chance to prove it."

I beheld the young Hugh Despenser as for the first time, raising the youth from his knees to embrace him in welcome. Hugh was my own age, twenty one, slim and slight, with sleek chestnut hair and heavy eyebrows. His eyes were brown and limpid, his lips perhaps too thick, though the general tenor of his face was handsome. He seemed nervous, diffident, his movements swift and coltish. I patted him — "be at your ease" I said — but all my thoughts were on the subject of who was missing, and not who was there.

The Despensers brought the news of William Wallace's capture, of his trial at Westminster and of his judgement and his execution at Tyburn. His head now grimaced upon London Bridge, "his quarters," said Despenser enumerating them one by one upon his fingers, "dispatched to Stirling, Berwick, Newcastle and Perth."

"It is to be hoped the servants at the gates were warned," said Robert cheerily. "Had they been expecting provisions from the market, the wrapped and gory packet might yet end up in a pie."

I frowned at him for his unseemly fantasy.

"The death of a traitor and outlaw is good news," I said. "May it serve to keep the peace in Scotland."

All those about the table said amen.

The other news of prominence was that Archbishop Winchelsea was in disgrace and banished, and the Bishop of Lichfield and Coventry very satisfied. It was reckoned that my father never would recall the man who had so angered him, and Winchelsea was like to die beyond the seas.

"And have you other news?" I asked then tremulously.

"My lord — ?"

"Of Gaveston," I breathed softly, as one at prayer.

"He was seen dicing," said the younger Hugh.

"Well," I said snappishly. "We all must find amusement these dull days."

"The King, your father, was briefly taken ill," Despenser then added.

"How so?" I said, alert and bright of eye.

"A pain about the chest."

"That laid him low?" I gasped.

Despenser laid his hand upon my wrist. "There is no cause for alarm, my lord. They said it was the lampreys."

"How this heat enervates us older folk," Despenser said, and fanned his face with a scroll of parchment. "But you are young, Lord Edward, as is my son. Down by the river there must be a breeze and I hear you have a boat..."

The royal barge moved slowly down the Thames. They were haymaking in the fields. It was stiflingly hot.

"Even Robert is too flattened by the heat to make us laugh," I said. "How different it would be if Gaveston were here. He likes the heat. It never wearies him. Do you remember, Robert, when we rolled in the buttercup meadow at Langley and Piers undressed and how we covered him with buttercups?"

Poor Hugh said very little. What could he say? Thrust into my company by the clumsy machinations of his father, he was ill at ease, polite and shy, though charming, as only a gawky good looking boy can be; but how could he compete with a phantom of perfection? No one could compete with Perot; he was born to win in any situation that you care to name; yes, any situation, Robert, for even when it might appear that he had lost, he remained victor in beauty; and in simply being who he was, he won.

As a result, that summer day, so hot, so tremulous, quivering in the noon of its perfection, became merely a vessel wherein other summer days were poured, days of less actual brilliance, but of more in essence, because Perot had been there.

Yes, I recall that Hugh lay on the sun-baked boards, leaning on his elbow, near my knee, and the shape of his reclining hip showed through the pale coloured sindon that he wore, and he had eased his collar open so that his throat showed, young and vulnerable. I always felt that he was younger than myself; he seemed gauche, inexperienced in the world's ways, gentle — and I admit that long after the Despensers had quit the castle I retained the image of the open tunic and the boyish throat. But most of all it was the memory of what was not there that I recall — the laughing face, the green eyes full of life and fire, the saucy jibes, the image of his nakedness when I strew buttercups about him and his skin was petalled with the golden dust.

"Dear sire, I feel that in your grace's assessment of the character of Hugh — what did you say? unworldly, quiet and shy — I hesitate to say this, but there is perhaps some inconsistency?"

"We none of us remain exactly as we were, thank God, and I believe that Hugh was all those things on that first day."

"And your judgement never is at fault, of course."

"And yours is not required. Now write. Write how I suffered as the days went by, watching at the windows like the besieged who await relief, waiting for some rider who brought tidings from my father."

"And how we swam in our own sweat, and the strawberries melted between our fingertips, and the butter dribbled like syrup and our guts ached from the flux that started in the kitchens..."

And still no message came. Inactivity brought strange fancies. Would he dare disinherit me? Was there a precedent among our eccentric wayward ancestors for so damnable an act? Dare he pass me over in favour of the infant Tom that was born at Brotherton and showed his loyalty early by refusing the milk of a French wet nurse? How could I better such an act of heroism? As far as I had heard, at that age I drank indiscriminately, the palate showing no such fine discernment. Ah, let my little brother wait — my lord the King loves anybody till they answer back.

"How can you grumble, my Prince?" enquired Robert the Fool. "You have the swans on the river — you have a boat to row — and you have me to cheer you. How can you say you suffer?"

"But I do!" I wailed. "I am without my Perot. I am in disgrace. Disgrace is a cold bleak country, for all that it is summer time. I am forbid my father's presence."

"But you detest your father's presence!" Robert tittered.

"Nevertheless it is the source of all that nourishes."

"Oh Edward, what a Fool you are," sighed Robert. "I could learn from you!"

"Why so?"

"What must a king possess to ensure the survival of his dynasty? What must there be for peace and stability? Who must be waiting in the background to step forward when the moment comes? You may need your father — but the need is equal, just as the detestation is so!"

"Yes, I see the way your thoughts tend."

"He may desire to tread you into the ground, my dear, and make wine of your pulp; but you are his first born and he has no choice but to call you back and welcome you with open arms!"

Before the great gathering that filled the hall at Westminster, my father embraced me in a warm political embrace.

"My first born son, I welcome you with open arms!"

I got a mouthful of his beard, rough as a brush.

Chapter Nine

IT WAS October when he took me back.

"You understand why I have brought you back," he muttered in the antechamber, the one with the painting on the wall of Adam digging.

"I do. Believe me, I have no illusions."

"Expediency, that's why," he said gruffly, thinking I was an idiot and might need explanation.

Expediency — for my lord the King a passion stronger than love, stronger than hate, a burning oily fluid thick enough to drown the festering irritation I inspired in him. And as for myself, well, who would rather sit in the shadows when the world was out there dancing in the sun?

"And what is more," said he, "I desire that it be seen your household is restored to you. All your household." His bushy eyebrows quivered like a curtain hiding the pointed calculation of the expression that would lie there in his sunken eyes. Yes! I saw a gauntness in his face... No! It was not my fancy. The skin was loose over the bones, the flesh was failing. Naked, I guessed, his spare and rangy frame would be all skeleton, and beneath, the blood as thin as water.

"You mean Gaveston," I goaded him.

"I mean Gaveston," he bellowed back. Then, quietening, he added, breathing quickly: "I have always known how to play a part, whichever part the times required of me. It is your folly that you have not learnt to do the same. Give 'em a ceremony, that has always been my watchword and it never fails. Now you and I must be seen to be entirely reconciled. With all the pomp that I can muster. I mean no half measures. You must have Gaveston back, for it to be seen how strong my trust in you and your fine judgement. Ha! And you must take him back, be seen with him, yet give no cause for gossip. You understand me, Edward. You have been a fool, a wastrel and a simpleton, but for the sake of our stability you must work to be otherwise."

"I am none of those things," I replied in even tones.

Men ever see the superficial. Because I match the shades of yellow in my shoes, my hose, my tunic and my tunic braid, there is a general assumption of a certain mental frivolity, at odds with wisdom and perception; I have never seen the logic of this false conclusion.

"You must be what I want," my father said, with narrowed eyes, and patently not hearing what I said. "You must be what I need you to be. Anything else is out of the question. Do you hear me? Must it be said of me that though I create castles out of stone I cannot make a son in my own image? Must they say that of me? No! I will not have it so. You shall be as I demand!"

"And what of me?" I answered passionately. "Why are your thoughts always drawn towards yourself, your fame? Why does the world's voice carry so much weight with you? You appear so strong, but your strength is composed only of what men believe to be true. It's bluster. I am not your second self and never will be, but I do possess strengths of my own. Your Majesty seems blind to them. You are wrong to seek in me an image of yourself. No man creates another in his own image. Except God. And father, for all that you may strive to be so, you are not He."

My father, reddening with rage as I was speaking, now let out a great guffaw.

"So! I am not God, you think?" he said, but not displeased now; the comparison had teased his fancy. "But," he growled, "I am His regent here on earth. Forget it at your peril!"

I bit my lip. All I had implied concerning myself, the natural difference in our nature, had quite passed him by. As always, he had latched upon what most concerned him, his own reputation. He slung a heavy arm about my shoulders.

"Let us go eat," he said. "My stomach's growling."

"What? Are we to meet here in an antechamber, as strangers, as passers-by?" I gasped, confronting Piers. Damn him, he had grown more beautiful. Every absence had the same effect. What did he do, bathe in some secret spring known only to himself the more to taunt me with his startling perfection?

"Ned, are you mad?" he said between his teeth. "Folk are looking at us. Our lightest glances will be noted. Now of all times we must be discreet."

I glowered at him, love and fury warring in me. "How can you be so calm?" I breathed. "Have you not suffered, as I have, to be separated for so long? Have you no more to say than this? Discretion! A cold word to a lover who has lived only for the moment when he sees your face once more."

"I have learned to hide my feelings," Piers said quietly. "And I advise you, Ned, to do the same. They watch us, Ned; they wait for us to play into their hands."

"You love me still?" I demanded urgently. "Nothing has changed?"

"Nothing!" he was quick to reassure me.

"Hug me, even here, even with folk about. Brothers may do as much, and friends."

Piers put his arms around me. Any one may clasp a friend in manly affection; but Piers touched my ear lobe with his lips, and goose flesh ran down my arm to my fingertips.

"I love you." We whispered the words quickly, and, excitement flaring, drew quickly apart.

"We must be severe," said Piers, but now his eyes were dancing. "Treat it as a game we play for the attention of the multitude. Just a game, Ned."

For the months that followed, more than at any other time, we were like players on a little stage, acting out a fiction to make acceptable the unbelievable, our audience composed of every baron with an interest in the swings of policy; and France, which waited with a bride they wished to see wed to a prince of unimpeachable virility; and Scotland, which prayed constantly for chaos anywhere south of Northumbria. The father and son that basked in mutual affection, the Prince that did not love Piers Gaveston, the Gascon youth quite indifferent to his boon companion, the Prince who sought advice from Walter Langton, the Bishop who respected the heir to the throne — these were the parts we played. No one was fooled, of course.

I swear Piers took that same mischievous delight as I did, in encountering me and bowing dutifully and passing me by every whit as unconcerned as those that went from Jericho to Jerusalem. We always loved pretence, illusion; play acting came easily to us. We waited on events.

Scotland showed its hand first. Robert Bruce, Earl of Carrick, a man who had been ally to us, stabbed to death John Comyn, Scotland's leader, at the altar of a church in Dumfries, then had himself crowned King. Scotland rose up in support of him; and so we must to Scotland once again.

But first there came the ceremony of knighthood.

   "In spite of all, I tell you, there was holiness in it. You may laugh, Robert. You remember just as I do how the word was sent about that all young men desirous of knighthood should present themselves at Westminster at Pentecost to take their vows along with the Prince of

Wales, and how they came in hundreds and took London by surprise. The town reeled with the shock of it and, you remember how it was, you may well snigger when I refer to holiness. Of course, you have a point. The stench was foul. For every horse, equivalent steaming dung piles; for every man, no less. So many tents to house them that they had to cut down trees and kick down walls to make a place for them. The swell of folk oozed into every cranny and London like a swollen pig's bladder stretched to take it in."

Noise, it was all noise, and never more so than when it should have been most silent — the night before the ceremony, the vigil in the abbey church.

After all, there were three hundred of us, and I fear that some were a little the worse for drink. We were pressed against each other, kneeling. We grew warm and sweated, and there was constant buzz of conversation, some shouting, a brawl or two. We strained to hear the chanting monks that stood in ranks towards the altar and the ringing of their little bells was lost to us. Being with Piers and Gilbert I found laughing easy, and the night was long, too long to think unceasingly of holy things.

I do recall I thought of cousin Tom. "When we were children we were always playing knights but it ended in disaster, for we came to blows over who should play King Arthur. I had the better claim, I thought, but he said as he was older and stronger he should play the king. We never came to an agreement."

"It was always clear to me," said Piers, "that Arthur's true love was Lancelot, and Guinevere a burden; but no minstrel would ever dare to sing the truth, and so the myth went unchallenged."

"As with Mark and Tristan," I agreed. "I swear they were lovers. It seems to me as clear as day. Ah, how I longed for the moment when I became as they, questing, righteous, pure!"

Gaveston convulsed himself in laughter and I clouted him. He overbalanced and brought down three or four others.

"Tristan's vigil was never thus!" he spluttered, righting himself and warding off the insults from those he had knocked against.

"Make way! Make way for the monks!" yelled men-at-arms. We were too tightly jammed for any monk to enter. At the far doorway tall processional candles glimmered, and a golden cross, the monks coming in to sing the night offices. The next we knew, some half a dozen men on great horses came riding in, bellowing: "Back! Back! Make way!" and, climbing over each other and squealing in protest, would-be vigil keepers pushed and shoved, fleeing the horses. All solemn and self righteous came the monks in slow procession, trying to pretend that all was much as usual as they progressed pointedly towards the altar; and the great chargers snorted and whinnied and milled about, and Piers and I and Gilbert pressed our fists into our mouths, howling and choking with the merriment of it.

But on the morrow, when my father in the palace chapel gird the sword about me and made me Duke of Aquitaine and knight, and at my feet the Earl of Lincoln and my sister's husband Hereford fastened on my spurs, it was another matter. Here was silence, here sanctity. I knelt before my father, the King, awed by his undoubted magnificence. A shiver passed down my spine. I was a knight. I was dedicated to God's holy work, to fight for right, to be as perfect as it was in my power to be. Lancelot, Bedevere, Tristan, I was as they. I stood, aware of all that I now undertook.

Then in my father's gaze I saw such love, such pride. He caught me to him in a sudden hard embrace and, emotion overcoming us, we wept in one another's arms.

It fell to me then to give knighthood to the others, which included my dear Gaveston, and Gilbert, and Hugh Despenser, all of whom I kissed in warm affection, and I whispered to my dear: "Arise, Sir Gawain, servant of the Goddess." I held him to me closely. "My dear companion," I said. "Loyal and faithful we are bound by what is done today."

However, it was then my duty to knight three hundred others. And by the day's end, knighthood had a little lost some awe, for the spirit seems unable to maintain its reverence three hundred times over...

Then came the banquet. You recall tales of how King Arthur used to sit down to the feast of Pentecost with all his knights about him, and the servants brought in a procession of the finest dishes in the land, each plate piled high with all the best that ingenuity and the season might devise; and how the king would forbid the first mouthful till a miracle had been seen, a wonder worthy of an assembly that included Lancelot, Gawain, Bors, Bedevere; and how into the chamber came or weeping damsel, ragged knight, Green Man — we were like that. The air was heady with the new crusade to Scotland, our just war, its purpose to rescue that Holy of Holies, our right to trample Scotland down. After the capons, pheasants, herons, pikes, venison haunches, tench in jelly, eels, carp, lampreys; after the quinces in comfit, pears in syrup, tansy cake, plums, wafers with red hippocras, came in two great roast swans, all netted round about with strands of gold. Upon these birds the company took oaths, each more elaborate than the last.

"By God in Heaven and by these swans I shall avenge the death of John Comyn," King Edward said, "and I call upon you, Edward, my son, my cherished dearest son," — his voice broke and I hurried to support him — "and you, all friends about me at this time of glory and of woe, to swear that if I die in undertaking this great mission you will never let my body rest till we have vanquished Scotland, but will bear my corpse at the head of the army till victory is ours!"

We swore it. God, what a set of oathbreakers were there present! Cousin Tom swore to eat no red meat, Warwick to wear a belt of horsehair next the skin, I to sleep no two nights in one place till we had conquered Scotland, and Lord knows I broke that vow within the week. I daresay of King Arthur's knights who vowed to pause from dining before a wonder had been worked, there was a finger or two that strayed towards a chicken bone or cherry.

Scotland was easy. It always was, in those days. Within a month the Earl of Pembroke, Aymer de Valence, had sent Bruce running for his life with a vicious little affray at Methven that made the would-be King of Scotland fugitive. It proved again what we had learnt at Langley — mounted knights were invincible, invincible!

Lochmaben castle surrendered to me, and we laid the country waste. We dug in around Kildrummie where the Bruce's womenfolk were hid, and took it by September. And all that time my father's health was failing. Was it this that makes the recollection of those days so heady?

Clear of Westminster, Piers and I were like prisoners escaped, the chains of good behaviour left behind in hall and chapel. I procured a horse for him, a superb black charger with white forelegs; he called him Roland. We had Welsh foot soldiers with us, my own dear followers. I would rather have the Welsh alongside me than other soldier. They love to fight, they keep their weapons in good order, they can go for miles without food or drink. Light on their feet they are fierce as wolves; they would rather fight than plough. From my time in Wales I know them as a people generous with their hospitality, shrewd of nature, and magicians on the harp and crwth. I never yet encountered one that could not sing.

We were knights upon adventure. The further north we went, the sweeter seemed the air, the stronger our excitement. As we rode, full of health and expectation, laughing, and in reckless moments, hugging, we knew well enough my father's army travelled slowly, he in a litter, cursing no doubt at his inadequacy. Pains in the legs it was; he had them back at Pentecost when at Hugh's wedding to Eleanor de

Clare, Joan's eldest daughter, after the banquet of the swans, he could not stand. He swore it was a change of shoes that caused it, and the Queen confided to me that she was obliged to rub his calves at night; the muscles were as stiff as wood. But none has ever died of muscle stiffness, I supposed, and thought our only benefit would be that he could not prowl up on us unobserved.

We knew he could not spy on us. He was at Hexham — Perth — Dunfermline — places where we were not! And we thought: well, what can he do? — he is not here! And if anything is said, we shall deny it. What did we do? We simply acted in a natural way and made clear our affection; I do not think that any who observed us had cause to be offended; and as for cousin Tom's sour face, well, I was not afraid of Thomas. Thomas was no fool — at least, I thought so then — and he knew every whit as well as I that our liege lord was carried in a litter, and to whom his sovereignty would go when Heavenly trumpets brayed that kings are mortals. So let him glower if I embraced my dear in sight of him there in the wilderness about Kildrummie castle's walls, while we awaited its inevitable surrender.

The evening being warm, I was at my tent's doorway, sprawled on a wide rug, drinking, much at ease but for the midges, which I wished to Hell, and watching the wrestlers — that is, watching Piers, who wrestled with some boys and valets, winning every throw.

I speak of a naked torso glistening with sweat, and moist curls of black hair about the chest and arms and at the belly, where the hose would never stay in place but teased us there, and with the glimpse of arse cleft, never quite as much as we would like. His hair flopped forward in an unkempt curtain and he shook it like a mane on some perfect wild young stallion, and as he sat astride his victim every muscle of his upper arm and shoulder rippled with exertion, and his firm thighs spread; his hose, torn at the knee, excited the discerning with the blur of flesh. And the buttocks, welded to the hose, so that their perfect shape was clearly sculpted, round and glossy and inviting touch. And the face, all smeared with mud and dust, and his eyes that laughed with the pleasure of the combat, and the panting breathing that called to mind the heat of lust — and the way he raised his head and caught my eye to grin, and the opponent took advantage and seized a fistful of his hair to bring him down and how he toppled and tumbled, all arms and legs, and righted himself within the instant and laughed.

My cousin Tom eased himself down beside me on the trodden earth, and, pulling up a cushion, gestured, and a servant brought him wine.

"It's better when he keeps with his own company," remarked he, with a jerk of the head towards the wrestling.

"What do you mean, Tom? I suppose something derogatory?"

"I mean the Gascon whom you have taken under your wing. If he would remain at that distance and amuse himself with grooms and valets, no one would take exception to his presence."

"You mean yourself? You take exception to his presence?"

"Any man of rank would do so. In this world, where a man's importance is measured by the lands he holds, a poverty-stricken Gascon counts as nothing, and you demean yourself, my cousin, by the worth you seem to place on him."

"Myself I do not judge a man by the extent of his possessions," I said huffily. It was a sore point with me that I could not grant land in quantity without my father's approbation. Otherwise, Piers would be wealthy indeed. "Do you mean, Tom, that you would tolerate Piers Gaveston if he had land?"

"I do."

"I see." I pondered this.

"Ned, I bear no personal resentment toward the boy," said Tom and reached for the dish of wild raspberries. He took one between finger and thumb and studied it. "Every prince should take his pleasure how and where he will. One questions your discretion, for you're very careless of opinion; but if the boy knows his place, there need not be a problem. I have thought about it at some length, believe me."

"You have? And may I ask why it should touch you in any way whatsoever?"

"In any realignment of power," said Tom of Lancaster, and ate the raspberry with a snap of his teeth, "it is vital that you and I be friends."

"You speak in riddles, Tom. I thought you came to grumble about Gaveston."

"Nothing so insignificant as that," said Tom, and picked his teeth. "So here we sit. What do you think of it all? Of that?"

He jerked a thumb towards the castle. All around it, the land was burnt and flattened, and our weapons of war sat idly by, the trenches and the hollows for our mines, the heaps of stones, and further off, our army, bored and sweltering, our horses cropping hay, our tents strewn out, fragments of coloured cloth, our banners limp and mudstained.

"Of that?" I shrugged. "I think we'll take the castle; we have but to wait."

"Exactly. Wait. And is that how you wish to pass your time, your summer? Is there nothing you would rather do? In short, sweet cousin, do you care a fig for Scotland?"

I scratched my chin. "I hadn't thought..."

"You never do, Ned," Thomas laughed and shook his head. "But God forbid, and if the King should die, you will have some decisions to make concerning what we do each summer in the north."

"You mean not fight the Scots?" I chortled. "My father would return from the dead and beat us all into submission at so bold a proposition."

"Your father dead would be of no concern to the living," Tom replied. "I ask you — do you care a toss for Scotland? If they sit behind the wall and get about their own affairs, is not that all that we require of them? Think on it, Ned. What's here for us but heat and rain and bogs, hard earth and small diversion — and midges, damn 'em?" added he and slapped his neck.

"We go because he tells us go," I mused, "and none dare do other."

"We must be friends, coz, you and I," said Tom. "And therefore keep the Gascon in his place. Keep him in the background, like a coney on a tapestry, and there'll be no need for our friendship to grow sour. I want your friendship, Ned, and you want mine. Think on it."

"I'll do so, Thomas."

My cousin smiled approvingly and stood up and moved away between the tents, swishing midges.

Kildrummie fell to us. A traitor within the walls set fire to the stables and the fire spread. After that it was soon over.

That same liege lord of whom we spoke then joined us at Kildrummie to supervise the hangings and to order cages made for two of the ladies we had captured, there to dangle from the castle walls in shame. God's blood, he came on horseback! That same angel that watched over him had brought him back from infirmity to inexplicable heartiness.

My face fell as I saw him approach, by all the saints magnificent as ever, and in the saddle tall and upright, exactly as a monk would draw if one said "Paint a picture of a king." I heard my cousin Tom beside me give a wicked little chuckle, and his welcome to my father was enthusiastic to the point of idiocy. I worked to emulate a similar display.

"The finger of God is on his Grace!" cried a lyrical monk.

Would it had been His foot, thought I ungraciously.

I swear there was a malevolent glint in his eyes as my father ordered the thanksgiving service for his recovery, and made sure we all sang "Alleluia".

With autumn's encroachment we went down as far as Carlisle, and my father took up abode at Lanercost, the Benedictine priory nearby.

I spent Christmas with my two young brothers at Northampton castle, rejoining my father in January for the Carlisle parliament, with my household and with Gaveston.

God, that priory was a dreary place! Bleak enough those northern reaches of the realm, but here the lands for far and wide had been laid waste by one side and the other in the ravages of war, and, besides, the bitter gales blew from the Firth, and up and down the crumbling stone of the old Roman wall. It was the vilest time of year, the bare forked trees bent into goblin shapes, the clouds heavy with rain.

Walter Langton told me that my father's health was giving cause for concern; infirmity of limb and the inclement weather had prevented him from attending the parliamentary assembly, and the Bishop and the Earl of Lincoln had gone in his stead. But I knew my father and his love of Parliaments. Bodily infirmity? Mental deviousness, more like.

His sweet Queen led me into her apartments and made me welcome. Such austerity as may once have been the feature of Lanercost was well spread over with the pomp and luxury we like to have about us. My father would sleep rough on his campaigns, but he made sure the Queen and he were comfortable; and there were Persian carpets on the flagstones, tapestries upon the walls, a great fire in the hearth, books, chalices, plates of sweetmeats; furs and velvets, cushions; and the great grey wolfhounds stretched before the flames.

And on the table, a map of Scotland; Robert Bruce had recently returned.

"Your father sleeps in the afternoons," she murmured. "He will receive you in good time."

"What is the state of his health?" I enquired, toying with the clasp of a little prayer book.

"Why, he is very well," said she, and looked up at me with those clear grey eyes in which I saw unswerving loyalty so plain that if my father had been three breaths from his last I would never have learnt the fact from her, did he not wish it.

"Better it had been if you had not brought the Gascon with you," Walter Langton said. "At least, not in such prominence."

"I like his company; therefore he rides with me."

"I speak as an adviser," said the Bishop darkly. "We have heard ill

135

tales in which Piers Gaveston plays part. You would do well to keep him from the King. It were rank folly to have brought him here at all, knowing what is said of him. But since he is here, keep him in the shadows of your company and let him tread as gently as he may."

"Foul-mouthed old man," I seethed. "What do you know of Gaveston save what you hear from rumour mongers? He is my friend, and that is all you need to know."

"He is a landless fortune hunter," Langton retorted, "and the world knows it."

"Landless he may be, but I intend to remedy that," I said stoutly. "I hope indeed to rectify that matter while I am here."

"What do you mean?" shrugged Langton. "If you hope to persuade the King to grant him property, you live in a dream. I know he will not do it; he has said as much to me."

"My father speaks to you of Gaveston? What business is it of yours?"

He smirked, comfortable, sure of his place in the scheme of things. "The King, your father, knows an old and trusted servant. I doubt you have that skill. I pray that it will come."

"How dare you speak to me in those terms?" I gasped. "If you pride yourself on your diplomacy, you show none in this instance. Have you forgotten who I am?"

The Queen then took my arm. "Dear Ned, be calm. All here wish you well. I have to add, alas, that it is true your father has no plans to grant land to your friend. It would be best if you refrained from asking such a favour."

"I have no intention of asking any favour," answered I, "merely his permission to give land of my own away. Ponthieu is mine. It's my desire to give it to Piers. I shall not miss it. I've promised it and he expects it. If to be a prince means anything, then surely I may give away what is my own to give."

They looked at one another doubtfully. Langton muttered something about wisdom, caution.

"No, you are wrong," I told him. "It was my cousin Thomas clarified the matter for me. He himself, he said, would respect Gaveston the more if he held land. He speaks for many. For Piers to own the fief of Ponthieu would make for harmony, and his acceptance amongst those he meets. I cannot see why there should be the least objection."

"A dream world," Walter Langton said, and raised his eyes to Heaven. "He lives in a dream."

136

It was true that in the afternoons my father dozed. Swaddled in furs he sat in a great chair, feet on a stool, hands loose on the neck of his hounds, eyes sunk beneath bushy brows, and a rhythmic snoring arising from his throat, giving intimation that he drifted in and out of sleep. How I mistrusted such a sleep! I swear he saw more when his eyes were shut than even did he waking. Every time he shifted, I twitched in apprehension; twenty-two years old, and I start guiltily to find his gaze upon me!

"Well?" growls he.

"Sire?"

"You wish to speak. You have sat there this hour intending speech. What is it?"

"Sire, the matter is — I wish to say that —"

"You were taught speech as an infant, were you not? Make use of it."

"Piers Gaveston —"

"Ah, no!" A monstrous growl rose up from his belly, and the dog made echo. I stood up.

"Sit down!"

I sat.

My father slowly moved now, leaning forward in his chair, his eyes a-glitter under those jagged fearsome brows, rays of malevolence burning out a passage in the air between us.

"We have spoken of Piers Gaveston before," said he, "and I was calm. Since then I have heard that name spoken more than I would wish it. I know the boy to be a worthy youth. Saint Peter's staff, I picked him out myself, didn't I? And you, Edward, you have not always been a trial to me. I shut my eyes to your spendthrift ways, your playing, and your lightness; you were brave enough when we first rode to Scotland. Fire and straw separate, each contained in their place, are not hazardous. Put them together and you have a burning byre. Gaveston and you, each in your place, are well enough. Together and — the burning byre. Don't tempt me further. Let me hear you never see him and you'll please me well. It is the only way."

"But sire, I — there is a matter — and if you care for Gaveston as you imply you do, you'll hear me out, for it is to his benefit."

"I will not hear you out!" he bellowed, and he was very loud when he did that. "You pain me. Get you gone, and come again when you are wiser."

"I grow tongue-tied in his presence," I confessed to Piers in my own chamber. "I am awash with self loathing. What a coward! I don't understand it. He's an old man. Why should I fear him? I feared him as a child. But Heaven and all the saints, I am a man, and still I fear him."

"Many do; you are not alone in that. And with cause enough — what about that page whose head he broke open? And anyway, I can do without Ponthieu."

I knew he lied; I knew he wanted it. Not Ponthieu itself, an unimportant little place. But to be styled Count of Ponthieu, a title. It would raise him in the eyes of all who sneered at him behind his back, calling him Lord Landless; and it was in my power to do this for him — if I dared.

I had the idea then of using an emissary. If Walter Langton were so firmly in my father's favour as he maintained, let him do it, let him speak on my behalf. Why not? That way he could prove to me his own importance and his self-confessed diplomacy. His vanity touched by my belief in him, the Bishop agreed to my request. Reluctantly, of course — whoever sounded out my father in this matter would be ill received and Langton knew it. But if the Bishop was as necessary to my father as he himself supposed, then surely he would be the man to put my reasonable proposition. Accordingly, while I waited in the chilly shadows outside the oaken door, a sullen guard nearby, the Bishop went about my errand.

The raised voices reached me even through the door; at least, my father's raised, the Bishop's indistinct and deferential. Then the crashing as some stool or bench went thudding. Like a kicked dog, Walter Langton scuttled out and grabbed me by the sleeve.

"If I had asked him for the crown itself his rage might not be greater. We have touched a raw wound here. There's no recourse but you must go yourself; he's asking for you, nay, demands your presence — go to him."

"But whatever did you say?" I marvelled. "Did your manner so offend him? It was a simple thing — how could you so mismanage it?"

"Lord Edward, I have pleaded for my reputation at the Court of Rome and won it; I am as silver-tongued as anyone. The fault was not mine, I assure you. All I can say is that maybe flesh of his flesh will succeed where mere politeness failed. He waits for you."

No martyr to a den of lions went in with more unwillingness to his fate than I into that room. The King was on his feet, half turned, dressed in the homespun clothes he liked, an artisan you'd say, were it not for his great height and his commanding presence. Beyond him, old Lacy, Earl of Lincoln, looking much as if he would be anywhere but here; and the elder Despenser, and Langton behind me, wringing his hands like a washerwoman. The justness of my cause filled me with righteous firmness.

"You had no cause so to berate this wretched messenger," I said at once. "I sent him on a simple errand with a most reasonable request. I cannot think why — "

"And did I give you leave to speak?" my father boomed.

I paused, and sucked my lips, eyeing him. I shrugged. The action certainly offended him. He came circling round me, like some prowling lion that waited for the moment when the claws went for the throat. I stood my ground, as nonchalant as I knew how.

"You wish to speak about Piers Gaveston," he said, dangerously quiet, "after I said we would have no more of that."

"I do. And what I ask is so patently reasonable that I don't understand your irritation. Ponthieu is mine. Therefore I may do with it as I choose. I wish to give it to my friend. I would have liked your approbation. But I do not see you can forbid it, even you."

To my annoyance, my voice sounded high and querulous, his low as a bear's.

"Your friend," he sneered. "Your whore, is it not? You take him to your bed and use him as your wench. Or is it the other way about?"

My face paled. My heart began to thud. I was aware of Langton, Lincoln, servants, ears pricked up and down the passageways, the very carved embossments on the pillars flapping in their eagerness to catch the accusations which he never should have voiced aloud thus.

"Lies — all that is lies," I stuttered.

"Lies, is it? I believed so once, against my better judgement. But I've heard too much, from those I trust, who have the wit to stick the prick where God intended it. I know about your kissing and your mauling, your unnatural embraces — you have not the subtlety to keep the matter secret — I don't blame the boy — you are the King's whelp, after all; your gold and glamour drew him and he went where wealth lies; it's a weakness prevalent among the landless. No, it's you, boy, that I hold at fault. We all have taken whores — but then we keep our counsel; herein lies your crass stupidity. Take the boy in some dark corner, rut there all you may — he's pretty, anyone can see it — and then let him understand his place. But never come again to me with talk of lands and titles. Christ in Heaven — are you imbecile as well as sodomite? What was my sin to have it so revisited a thousand-fold upon me?"

I had listened to this tirade with a slowly growing anger. My rage was ever slower to ignite than his; but once roused it was its equal.

"Well may you ask Our Lord, whose blessings you have only ever used to further your misguided follies!" I yelled back at him. "Did he rain his thanks down when you quartered Wallace or hacked off de Montfort's balls? And now you speak to me of Gaveston, as if he were a street whore. As you say, you know such well! My love for Gaveston is of a higher kind — we are David and Jonathan, friends for all time. Our love surpasses that of women. And Piers is noble, every whit so as the barons lurking about Westminster, whose nobility lies only in inheritance, assessing whether you are like to live or die. If I honour him by my high birth, he honours me as much by his devotion. And thus it is entirely proper I should get Ponthieu for him!"

My father sprang at me and seized me by the hair. The fist that wielded axe from Jerusalem to Stirling tightened on my head, and heaved me to my knees.

"You baseborn whoreson," said my father. "Do you want to give lands away now, you who never gained any? As the Lord lives, if it were not for fear of breaking up the kingdom, you should never enjoy your inheritance!"

"And what was I doing the while? Screaming. You will find, Robert, if ever you have the misfortune to be dragged by the hair, that this is what you do. The meaningful riposte, the cutting sarcasm or the bawling of abuse, these come later, on a separate occasion, and not while your scalp is parting from your ears. I was sprawled about the floor, hands flaying, screeching like a mandrake; I was in agony the like of which I'd never known. Believe me, he was striding up and down the while he held me; I was scrabbling on my knees, the Persian carpet tangled up with me, and when at last he dropped me I was on my belly like a many-patterned slug and somewhat more vociferous."

"Lecher...murderer..." I screamed the first things that came into my head. "My mother hated you — she prayed to die and so be quit of you — and God in Heaven, why do you yet live to pain us all?"

He lashed out with his foot; I rolled out of his path. He stood rigid. There on my elbow, glowering venom somewhat in the manner of the serpent leaving the Garden, I observed him. He was looking at his hand, which, claw-like, still retained the shape of his grip, and I saw there filaments of golden hair, and so did he, as if he had that moment just received the bird that carried a strand of Isolde's hair from Ireland and fallen instantly in love. This so far from being the case, he cast a glance at me. I swear that if we'd been alone, he would have come across to me and knelt down by me; I could see it in his face. But we were not alone. The Earl of Lincoln fidgeted, much ill at ease. Later he would rebuke my father; they were of an age. Despenser also looked uncomfortable. But Walter Langton, like the cat with the cream, had not time enough to mask his satisfaction. He never liked me. Now he relished my humiliation. I crawled to my knees, unravelling myself from the Persian carpet. I made to go.

"Don't you quit this place," my father growled. "I have not done with you."

"Well, I have done with you," I said; and went from them.

He had some kind of seizure in the night; they sent for me. The room seemed smaller in the dark. The fire was stacked high, crackling vigorously. The candles round about the bed illumined a little circle of intensity. My father lay on his bed like his own effigy, hands clasped in prayer, a great black fur strewn over him. Queen Margaret sat at his pillow, her long hair loose about her shoulders, a chalice in her hand. Physicians left the room as I came in; but Walter Langton hovered in the shadows, like a bat.

"Is he dying?" I said cautiously, unwilling to give free rein to my hopes.

"We think not," Margaret murmured. "Lord God has heard our prayers this time."

"Then why was I sent for?" I said coldly. "I am not needed in this place." My head still throbbed from his performance earlier.

"Come here, Edward," said my father, his voice rising up from his chest like the creak of a heavy door. I moved to the bedside. The Queen indicated a low stool; I sat. He moved his head and fixed me with his beady gaze.

"If I should die —"

"You will not die," I said.

"If I should die," repeated he, "I require this promise from you."

I waited. I thought it would concern Piers Gaveston; I thought that he intended to control us from the grave. It crossed my mind that I would have to break whatever oath he sought, and risk damnation; but I was wrong; his mind was on his own obsession.

"Scotland," he said.

"Scotland?"

"Never rest till Scotland be subdued. You will never rule England with Scotland wayward. Scotland must be crushed, and Robert Bruce paid in that kind we showed to Wallace. Ah! That I were there upon that day!" He twitched about beneath the fur. Raised upon one elbow he worked to make his voice stronger. I watched the wagging of his beard. "But I will be there! You will see to it. Edward, you will carry out my wishes!"

"Your wishes, sire?" Curiosity for a moment overlaid the revulsion I experienced to be so close to him. As from far off, the bell for Vigil chimed. Cold and sleepy, the monks would be shuffling down to pray. "Boil my bones down," quivered he in mystic tones. "Boil my bones down; carry them with you wherever you go. Always with the army. Ever present. Let the Scots know I am there. They will fear me dead even more than they do now. I shall be deathless, my legend enduring through the time to come. Promise me!"

The lively shadows on my face disguised my feelings as I worked to keep my expression properly sober.

"Father, I promise it," said I, the tremor in my voice suggesting I was moved by strong emotion.

He lay back on his pillow, with a long low sigh. Queen Margaret stroked his brow, and nodded; I had permission to withdraw.

I pulled my robe about me and swirled from the room, dancing down the icy passages, light hearted and half bursting with barely controlled hilarity. I flung myself upon my bed and rolled my furs about me, and I sniggered; then the merriment within me rose up to my throat, and with my face pressed in the furs I rocked and chuckled and I laughed until I ached.

Boil his bones down! God! what a revolting notion! What — was I to carry the resultant slime in a holy phial, guarded by the elite and accompanied by singing boys and a priest with a golden cross for fear the wolfhounds got to it and found it palatable? Ha! And why should he suppose that I would be in Scotland? Or that anyone from the court of England would go north at all?

I fell asleep still laughing.

Chapter Ten

THE OBSTINATE old King had defied the Heavens; he had not died. And at my father's orders we assembled in the abbey chapel, shivering in the February chill.

Before the altar Piers and I; upon the altar the bread and wine, the consecrated Host; to one side, Walter Langton, rampant, swelling with importance, the holy one chosen to show us the error of our ways, a proprietary eye upon the sacred vessels, much as if he had lifted up his hand and called "Let there be bread; let there be wine," and God said "Dearest Bishop, you have but to ask."

For whose benefit was the ceremony that followed, I wondered? For the nobles whom he dredged from Carlisle to witness it and understand that Piers and I were strongest contenders for the royal disapproval? Despenser was there, and young Hugh, and Hereford, Warwick, Thomas and his brother; all were invited. For himself, because he truly feared I'd give away my patrimony to all comers and he would forestall it? Or for Piers and I, to put the seal upon our subservience, in so public a display?

King Edward entered, with his folk about him. I smirked. It all had something of the preamble to a ceremony of wedlock. I sneaked a glance at Perot for an answering smile; but I should have known — he was immobile, pious-seeming as a cherub, and very dignified, slipping easily into that self-preserving dutifulness manifest whenever my father was nearby. Sly deceiver! I itched to tickle him and make him laugh.

Offering the consecrated Host to us as if he'd given birth to it, Langton took Piers' hand and mine, and laid them on it.

"Body of Christ," he murmured, "blood of Christ. Now make your oath."

"I, Edward, Prince of Wales, Duke of Aquitaine, Earl of Chester, Count of Ponthieu, do swear that I will give no lands to Sir Piers Gaveston."

"...by the body and blood of Christ," added the detestable Bishop who had seen me hanging by my hair and heard my screams. I properly responded.

"And I, Piers Gaveston, swear to receive no lands from the said

Edward. By the body and blood of Christ." Piers was quite white. The words are like to send a shiver down the spine even when one knows the ceremony's stupid.

What must we have looked like to the gawping group behind us in the shadows, we so singled out in misdemeanour? What did they think about it all? For there was no denying now, that we stood there, myself and Piers, condemned in love, marked to the world as men reputed to take one another in so-called unnatural acts. This knowledge must be in their thoughts now, though the oath we spoke pertained to land; and would they picture us about our so-called wickedness? I believed they would.

In their minds, our clothes would slither down our bodies, rippling like water; we would stand naked at the altar, and we were very beautiful. Ah, Piers especially! His arse, his lovely arse, all lightly furred with soft dark hairs — how they would desire him, and how they would deny it, but their hearts would know it true!

I led my horse into the stable, kicking the mud from my boots against the door jamb. The wintry light came in pale and sunless through the open shutters. It showed me the strewn straw on the earthen floor, the great cruck beams beneath the thatch; and the monks' horses tethered in their stalls. I called for the stable boy.

Piers detached himself from the shadows, unnaturally bright in the dim surroundings.

"I sent the boy away," he said. He looked distressed. "I have to speak to you, where we may be alone."

"What is it? What has happened?"

"The worst," Piers answered. "Your father sent for me. He says I must go back to Gascony. Ned — I am banished from the realm."

I stared. "But why?"

Piers made a noise of irritation. "Don't be naive. You know why well enough."

"But this is spiteful...petty...unnecessary," I cried. "We have sworn upon oath to cause no trouble. What more does he want?"

"Ned, he was curiously kind," said Piers wryly. "He assures me that he bears me no grudge. He says that it is for the good of the realm."

There was a movement on the ladder leading to the hay loft. A cat came down the rungs, a mouse clamped in its jaws. The cat fled, seeing us, and took its booty to the shadows. The straw rustled.

"Oh well," I snapped, "he would say that. No, I shall speak to him myself. He must be persuaded to change his mind. I'll talk to him..."

"It will do no good," shrugged Piers. "And truth to tell, I half begin to think I would be well quit of this place, this situation..."

"Don't talk so!" I cried. "I won't have you speak like that."

My horse fidgeted and shifted and tossed its mane, startled by my tone.

"I warn you, Ned," said Piers, his eyes a-glitter. "I do not choose to make a further show of myself by confrontation. I intend to go with dignity."

"Oh, dignity!" I spat, and turned from him and strode towards the door. I shouted for the stable boy to take my horse and I went in search of the King.

"But it would be folly to banish Perot!" I protested, and my voice grew querulous and strained. "Don't you see? It proves the rumours true."

"The rumours are true," said my father reasonably. "You have seen to it that all the world knows it."

"Not so!" I cried. "They may suppose it if they choose; but matters such as these are only to be guessed at. No one but myself and Piers can ever know the truth, and we deny everything. But if you banish him, you give credence to their worst fears."

"I know it to be for the best," King Edward said unmoved. "We are about to make our preparations for the Scottish war. I need your wholehearted support here. Diversion of any kind will make you a poorer campaigner. No one brings their sweetheart with them!" He said that with an almost careless good humour. The spring was on its way, the King's strength had returned and he was about what he loved best — preparing to invade beyond the northern borders, to lead his troops again, to crush the Bruce. Everything was simple.

Piers himself proved no ally to me. "The King, your father, has made a wise decision," he said in my father's hearing. "I for one am content to abide by it. And you should do the same, my Prince."

My father gave him an expansive hug. "You show a wisdom I could well wish I might see in Edward. And fear not, you shall not go empty handed. You've done me good service, young Gaveston. I've been pleased with you. You love a good tournament, just as I did in my youth — you'd go anywhere to take part in a joust. I like that in a man. Go you to Gascony with all I shall give you. Your absence will give Edward time to see some sense. By the month of April I shall look to learn that you have quit these shores."

"I shall obey your grace's pleasure," Piers said firmly, and I vowed to strangle him when we were next alone.

"I am not a hard man, Edward," said my father, shamelessly

145

content now that he had the chance of battle, siege and warfare. "Go with Gaveston to Dover. You see how generous your father can be to a dutiful son. Make your farewells. And then come directly back without delay. I shall look for you at Carlisle in May."

All the birds of April sang as we rode south. We were a small procession, guards and baggage, and the minstrels making music.

"You were there, Robert. You recall how fair a journey, and how foul our spirits."

"And God be thanked," said Piers, "that we have left that place behind."

He was preoccupied, subdued. That was his first communication, said with passionate intensity.

"I think it will be no bad thing," said he, "if I return to Gascony."

"How can you say it?" I cried, stung. "Away from me?"

"Away from you, yes, nowhere far enough! Away from courts and kings and bishops, and noblemen who pester me for reasons of their own."

"And who particularly?"

But Piers fell silent, sullen even, and some time elapsed before I could get the truth from him. A monument of woes, it seemed, of which I had known nothing.

"It started at Kildrummie," he said, "when Lancaster arrived."

"My cousin Tom? Whatever do you mean?"

"He told me he would watch me like a hawk. He said he understood my game. I told him there was no game. He said the game was thus: a landless knight attempts to make his fortune by leching on a prince. He said that he would make it his purpose to ensure it was a game I lost. I was angry but I said nothing. It's not in my nature to be silent, but I thought it for the best."

"You should have come to me about it."

"There was no point. He was only expressing an opinion, and it's an opinion shared by many. Everything depends on where you stand. It's perfectly reasonable that he should think thus. It will look so to a man who hates me, yet is loyal to the crown."

"You think he hates you?"

"I don't know. Despises, even. Despises in an unnatural way. Regard: The earls of Lincoln and Pembroke have as much cause to find me troublesome. And yet they speak to me when there is need, and without rancour, without jibe. With politeness and indifference, as I to them. But to Lancaster I seem to be some kind of sore, that he must scratch."

"And therefore he must speak with you and slight you. Well, he was ever sour, was Thomas."

"He...there was more," said Piers in a low tone.

"What more?"

"He made me clean his armour."

"He did what?"

"He sent for me once, to his tent. I should not have gone, but there were folk about and it would have looked odd if I had refused. It made me think of that other time, in Flanders, when he had sent for me, and wanted me as a boy of the camp. And that was in my mind when I went to his tent. He was alone. He must have sent away his servants. He was lying on his bed, on his elbow, like a Roman emperor, and eating grapes. It was a pose so carefully arranged I would have found it humorous, but I did not, because I was too wary, watching him."

I flushed. It seemed a parody of my own behaviour. I wondered if Perot had thought as much.

"On the ground between us," said Perot, "lay his armour — his chain mail and helmet, his leg guards and his gauntlets. He pointed to it. 'Polish it,' he said. I could not believe what I heard. I stared at him and hoped I had misunderstood. 'You heard me,' he said. 'Do as I say.' I said 'I am a knight in the Prince's household.' He said 'You are one of Prince Edward's valets, a yeoman of his chamber; I am sure you do as much for the Prince. Do it, or the King shall hear that you offended me.'

"Then I was uncomfortable because I understood that he intended to make trouble. He has more lands than anyone in England; he has power second only to the King. We laugh at him and call him Churl; we mock him and recall that we refused his lust. But Edward, as I stood there I was frightened in my heart. I hope I did not show it. I knew that if he spoke to the King I was finished. He could tell any lie about me. Who would be believed, he or I? And so I cleaned his armour."

I suffered for my darling, appalled at Thomas' spitefulness, astonished that I had not heard of this before.

"And what did he do?"

"Well, he watched me, obviously. He lay there on his couch and watched me, chewing grapes and spitting out the pips — with vigour, like the churl he is. And I was kneeling in the trodden grass, and clumsy in my anger, and not looking at him, but feeling his gaze on me, up and down my body, like a crawling thing. And he waited

147

till I'd almost finished and said nothing all the while, but ate, and spat, and watched. Then he stood up suddenly, and stood before me where I knelt encumbered with his coat of mail and before I knew what he was about, he took me by the ear and made me look at him. I winced; he was not gentle. He said — must I tell you what he said?"

"Yes you must!"

"He said 'Witch's bastard, know your place and you'll have no cause for fear.' 'Of you?' I seethed in contempt. I could have killed him with his own weapons; they were all about. Believe me, I was tempted! 'You understand me well enough,' he said, relinquishing his grip, 'Now get you gone, remembering.' I ran out of his tent and took my horse and left the camp and rode; and in a grove of trees I paused, dismounted, stood and wept against a tree. What business had I with a prince of England? Why must I put myself through these humiliations, why thus dishonour myself and no retaliation?"

"But you should have come to me!" I cried. "You should have come to me!"

Piers turned on me. "And what could you have done?"

I gaped at him. "I...I could have..."

"Nothing!" Piers snapped. "You have no power, Edward. You have no power over Thomas of Lancaster, none at all. You have no power at all. Langton controls your purse strings. The King, your father, controls you. So I said nothing. I made myself calm and I rode back to the siege. And I avoided Lancaster, and anyway he said no more to me. He had no need. He made his stance clear, crystal clear. And Ned, the worst of it all is something other, something curious and vile."

I waited, marvelling.

"When Thomas held me there in front of him, I kneeling and obliged to see his face, I saw there his desire for me. I saw it, like a demon sitting in his eyes."

"Oh, Perot!" I said in revulsion.

"So when he came to Lanercost, I feared. Of course, he dare do nothing near the King. Not so Langton! Every time I saw him, or so it seemed to me, he took occasion to speak severely to me about the way I was misleading you! Your father thinks it's you at fault; Bishop Langton thinks it's me! It is all too ridiculous. So when the King said I was to be banished the realm I was startled, yes, but my strongest feeling was relief. I am too vulnerable. My position is impossible."

"I'm sorry," I said meekly. "It's all my fault."

"Yes it is!" said he with a rueful laugh.

"But...you don't regret our love?" I cried in a panic.

"Well...was it ever love?" said Piers.

"You know it was...is!" I answered hotly.

"No I don't," he answered, "and there's the heart of it."

"I've told you so many times that I love you. What must I do more?"

He laughed. "Oh, turn your back on kingship and run away with me to Lyonesse."

"Is that what you require?" demanded I, desperate to prove my love.

"No," he said impatiently. "I wouldn't ask it of you, for the crazy thing is, I believe you'd do it. I know that you are not content — I know you hate King Edward. And he has other sons. Of course, the country would be in chaos as it waited for the brats to grow to manhood. Thomas would probably take command, and you in exile in some flowery hermitage would grow to hate me for causing you to break with your true purpose. No, no, I'll never ask for what I know is wrong. I merely question whether it was love or loneliness that drew you to me. Or the transience of lust!"

"What must I do? I swear it on my mother's tomb that you are my true love."

"I've had enough of oaths!" said Piers, and shuddered.

"Ah...", I said uncomfortably.

"When we stood there before the Host, and knights and barons witnessing our promises — our collusion — I felt so shamed!"

"So shamed?" I gasped. "Myself I felt such pride. I was so proud that we were bound in love for all the world to see."

"I felt like a freak at the fair."

"How could you? You were allied with me. Am I so disgusting to your fine nature? I hardly think so."

"No, it wasn't you, Ned. I see you as a victim, like myself. This wasn't why I ever came to England, full of hopes for glory, full of pride in my own worth. Not to stand up before the nobility of the realm like a naughty boy, known to them all as the one the Prince takes to his bed. For though that oath taking seemed to concern the gift of land, in truth it proclaimed us lovers. It would make them picture us naked. And then to banish me — what other interpretation could be put upon such a pronouncement but that I have become so dangerous a threat to your reputation that I must be removed?"

"Well, yes... he would be thinking of that statute: any man discovered in the act of sodomy to be burned alive. It would embarrass him beyond belief if that man were myself!"

"They certainly saw it so. The Earl of Warwick..."

"Warwick? He spoke to you?"

"Oh yes. He laughed at me. 'So you failed then, little catamite,' he said. 'You worked your best and all for nothing. It's back to Gascony! My commiserations!'"

"Warwick's a cur," I raged. "We always knew it."

"Yes. The Black Dog of Arden," Piers agreed. "Well, let him snarl. I'll be revenged on both of them."

"If I have anything to do with it," I agreed.

"No Ned, not you. I mean myself," Piers answered quietly. "I myself shall be revenged; the matter is between myself and them. I am not your thing and it is not for you to save my tattered pride. I shall do it, when the time is right. I have resolved it."

I ached with admiration. I believed he had no chance of ever doing so, and yet I believed he would.

"Well," answered I. "You take revenge on Thomas every time he sees you and lusts for you and all to no avail."

Piers grinned. "I suppose so. Piquant, but it's not enough. And the same is not so with the Earl of Warwick, alas. He has no troubled sentiments concerning me, as Lancaster has. He would merely like to tread me underfoot." He gave me a wicked little smile. "Pity it's not the other way about."

"What do you mean?"

"Guy Beauchamp is a monster; but he's handsome as Lucifer."

"Piers...you cannot mean that if it had been he that asked you to his tent...?"

My darling laughed and tossed his hair, and ducked the blow I aimed at him.

Ah, it was true that I was powerless. Of myself I could do nothing. It was gall to me to know that he was right. And even if I went to my father and complained — which I would never do — I doubted we would get redress. Instead I daresay he'd have found our protestations cause for humour.

"You know," I said morosely, "I think he'll never die. I think he'll live and live, and we'll grow old, unsatisfied and wrinkled; and crooked with age, I'll still be going cap in hand to him for pennies."

On a day of shower-bursts we sought shelter in a village somewhere in the midland shires, not wishing to go on and seek an abbey. A river curled beside the crop of cottages, its surface a mass of movement from the rain. There were dark clouds overhead, the trees a dull moss green, the river grey as lichen, and our track awash with puddled mud. The village took us in; we paid for what we had. Piers and I ate with their head man in his house, a low-beamed dwelling with a floor of earth and straw, and I conversed with him in English, and we talked of pigs and crops and market prices, and of his family, all of which was pleasing to me and refreshing as a contrast to the sound of abbey bells and monks' talk. The man thought we were odd, that much was clear; odd, but, it seemed, harmless; and he made space in his upper room for us to sleep, and went elsewhere. We spread our roll of swansdown over the straw and lay beneath the low thatch, and in the barn, hard by, owls hooted all the night.

"We are outcasts, fleeing from those who would do us harm," I said, "but for the moment safe. No one knows where we are."

"Outcasts? You are not! I am the one that's banished," Piers replied with some asperity.

"You think I am not so? He did as good as call me bastard. That smacks of some finality."

"He didn't know what he was saying; he was angry."

"He was angry, yes, but he knew very well."

"Edward," Piers said. "There could be no chance...? I mean of it being true?"

"If anyone but you said this," I answered mildly enough, "I might suppose it treason."

"But why should he say it?" Piers persisted.

"Because he hates me and can't bear to think he sired me. For his accusation to be true, my mother would have needed to deceive him and then confess, or for himself to pass some stranger's infant off as his own, some Welsh child born in April in Caernarvon, assuming the royal child had died at birth. Neither is a possibility. And I resemble my mother and my grandfather, and perish the thought, would even resemble him were I to grow a beard. No, he'd never accept as his one that was not — Plantagenets have too strong a sense of their own worth to abdicate their place to anyone but one of their own blood."

"And yet you say that if I asked, you'd come away with me and live in legend?"

"Yes, and so I would! But that's because there are my brothers, Thomas and Edmund. If there were not, I'd never renounce my inheritance, not even for my dearest love. And you would never truly wish it, would you, Perot?" I added sourly.

"Why do you say that? What do you mean?"

"When I said that I would quit the kingdom for you if you asked me, it was in answer to a question — did I truly love you? As I recall, you gave no similar protestation of your own love. You said you doubted it had ever been love. You tell me you'll be glad to leave England. I wish I thought you truly loved me. I wish I thought that even were I lowly born, you'd love me. If we were two boys born in this village, sleeping under this thatch, tomorrow working in the fields, would you be as you are — or would you leave this place and seek your fortune, just as you left Gascony?"

"That's monstrously unfair!" said Piers angrily. "For your sake I've endured the jibes of Lancaster and Warwick — accusations veiled and direct as to where I spend my nights — and now for your sake I'm kicked out and sent away and all the world knows why!"

"Yes, all that is true," I said. "But it was you, not I, who doubted this was done for love. If you suffered these things for love of me, then we are lovers such as minstrels sing of; if you put up with my love because one day there would be rewards, then that's a different thing."

"Why are we quarrelling? We are soon to part," said Piers evasively.

"I don't know. You are sent abroad and I am disowned by my father. I feel that I would like to know why. Is it for grand passion — or is it a great mistake, a muddle? I'd like to know, that's all."

"What can I say?" cried Piers. "I don't know the answer. It was you that pushed the idea of love, so long ago at Langley. It wasn't what I sought or wanted, I'll say that much. And then it didn't seem to matter what it was, since all that was required of me was to be your companion, to learn with you, and play, and ride, make journeys, and to hold you close when it was safe to do so. And then suddenly it was different — people eyeing us and hinting I had grown too dear to you for someone who had after all no lands to speak of, and who came from Gascony, that trouble spot of ill repute. And then that time at Lincoln, your father swooping on me like a falcon — *do you sodomize my son?*"

I swore beneath my breath.

"Your father uses direct speech," said Piers. "And he stood waiting for an answer. I was scared out of my wits. I blushed and stammered like a virgin. Fortunately he must have supposed me one, believing my denial. But the word goes round — no fire, no smoke — and Warwick calls me whore, and I must ask myself: do I want all this trouble?"

"And what do you reply?" I breathed.

"I say I don't. I say you pushed me into love and it was not my choice. And while it was mere pleasure, I was happy to oblige. But now it isn't worth it. I am abused and have no recompense. You have made me important in a way that embarrasses me, and neither of us has the power to go against those who cause us this annoyance. It is a situation too intolerable to be borne."

"Very well! Then rid yourself of it — and of me!" I cried. "And by God's breath I'll count myself well quit of you. By all the blood of Christ, Piers Gaveston, you are the most ungrateful creature on God's earth!"

"Oh, gratitude," he sneered. "Have I not shown enough, Prince Edward? Permit me to kiss your feet."

Distracted for a moment from my irritation with him I paused in the undeniably attractive image that his offer presented; but he lay rigid and sullen beside me, and I was reluctantly obliged to suppose his suggestion rhetorical.

"So, you don't love me," I said evenly. "And all these years — what, nine years, is it? — it's been for you — what? — pleasure only? At least I may congratulate myself that pleasure was a part of it!"

"Ned, we were boys, and friends, companions, knights. Why was there need to speak of love at all?"

"Don't call me Ned," I snapped.

He drew in his breath and then sat up. He scrabbled around in the darkness, heaving on his clothes.

"What are you doing?"

"Leaving your presence, my lord, and finding somewhere more suitable for one of my inferior position."

"Oh Perot, don't be stupid."

But he wriggled down the ladder and was gone, and where he slept that night I never heard.

It was sunny in the morning, very bright and sharp, the earth steaming in the heat of it; and when I'd eaten coarse-grained bread and drunk sweet ale I joined those villagers that watched the thatcher at his work. I stripped off my shirt and set about to help him. I stood knee deep in wheat straw, brought out dry from the barn. We used hazel sticks, iron hooks, and cords of brambles. We climbed by ladder to the eaves and fixed the yealms, with hooks and wove the hazel sways about them, piling other yealms upon the first, till they were thick and overlapping, all secured with spars and hooks. I did not stay to see it finished, but we parted from the villagers on very friendly terms.

"They'll speak of it for months to come," said Richard Rhymer as he unloosened his fiddle. "How the Prince of England came amongst them and helped thatch a cottage on an April morning!"

"That they will not," said Piers sourly. "They asked me who the tall young man was, he with the yellow hair and the muscles of a soldier. That's Lord Edward, Prince of Wales, Earl of Chester, Duke of Aquitaine, Count of Ponthieu, I said. And do you suppose that anyone believed me?"

We stayed no more in villages, fleeing our true identities. London drew us nearer, nearer, April drawing to a close, and Piers to get gone before the month was up.

Once we reached the city we could not pretend the situation other than it was. We had dawdled on our journey, but the moment could not be forever held at arm's length, and my father waited in the north, with Scotland to be conquered and myself to take part in one more year of our campaigning. If I delayed, the greater would be my father's anger and the resultant discord. Now the month of May was with us, when the heart should sing; but we must south to Dover, and my heart had no voice at all.

I gave my darling presents: tapestries, clothes; two buckram quilts, doeskin boots; gold drinking cups, a belt of silk covered with pearls; and a ruby in a gold ring from off my very finger. He would not be poor when he reached Ponthieu — ah, yes, Ponthieu, not Gascony, for we had planned he should not go so far.

"Who will know?" I said. "They'll all be in Scotland. Stay there and I'll come to you. Why, it's so close to England you shall hear me if I shout. You'll see, I'll work something out. I'll get leave to go across the sea; I'll find a way."

I gave him silk and sendal, I had him fitted with green velvet embroidered all with pearl, and gold aiguillettes, and a green tunic overlaid with green of a different shade, and all to match his eyes; and a green cloak with a clasp of gold. I did not talk of love. But everything I did, my care of him departing, and my gifts, my overseeing of his going, all these spoke of it.

On the quayside at Dover, with the castle overlooking us upon its craggy hill, we stood to make farewells. The great ship waited, and the wind true and the sea calm. There surely were the seagulls crying, there were seamen about their work, but no, there was nothing all about us and the only truth was our standing there about to part, and not to be together.

I had steeled myself to be calm and was determined not to compromise him with a display of strong emotion, such as would in his terms make him the minion of the Prince. I gripped his arms and smiled, and, hiding all the aching of my heart, I looked at him and tried to learn him like a book, to weld his imprint on my memory — his black hair blowing in the wind, his dark brows, his dimpled chin, his beautiful green eyes, his long dark lashes and his quivering mouth.

"Safe journey, Piers," I said.

"I don't want to go," he said hoarsely, and he stared at me, and fell on me and wept into my neck. His hair, flecked with sea salt, tangled in my lips; I sucked it hungrily. I was astonished. He seemed like a little boy. "I don't want to go," he said over and again, and tears poured down his cheeks, who had said he would be glad to go to Gascony and far from me. "It isn't true that I don't love you. I do love you. I can never be content away from you."

My heart was full. I had not been prepared for this. Now... now when we must part — a declaration of love — an unlooked for declaration of his love, and an embrace so fervent I could not doubt its honesty; and all this before the observers on the quayside, as if he cared not who should see.

"Oh, my love!" I answered, moved beyond belief. But this would not do. I must be strong, as I had planned. "Well," I said, "Be assured it will not be for long." Somehow I achieved a fine control and firmness, patting him and holding him, and marvelling. He tore himself away. And turned, a little distance from me. His face was streaked with weeping.

"Edward," he said. "Don't forget me. Promise me."

"I promise," I said stupidly. God's eyes, he truly seemed to think that I would do so once he quit these shores.

I watched the vessel leave. I spent some time in Dover, London, amassing gifts for him. I sent him horses, money. I heard that he lived very well in Ponthieu, and had done well in tournaments, and was a great success.

Where should I go but to Langley?

Hedgerows thick with hawthorn blossom, blackthorn, may; way-sides bright with daisies, cowparsley — things which last year were a joy to me — meant nothing to my saddened heart as I rode home. Choosing gifts for him, arranging for their embarkation, this had given purpose to my situation, had staved off my gloom, but now his banishment came home to me and with it the attendant sorrows. Langley was an empty place without him. Gilbert was there; but Gilbert was ill, and cause for further sadness. And then came the news of the death of my dear sister Joan. It seemed that one misfortune, one grief, now came heaped upon another.

"I was with you, sire. I worked to make you smile."

Robert the Fool was there; and worked to make me smile. I lay alone at night, and in the hollow darkness, came the idiot braying of the aged camel, mournfully across the quiet courtyard.

Agnes was there, the witch from Gascony, awaiting news of Perot.

"Should I make preparation for Ponthieu, my lord?" she asked. "My place is with him. Is he to return?"

"Sweet lady, if I knew the answer I would be a happy man," said I. "All I can advise you is to make your preparations, but to make them slowly, praying as you do so."

Then I looked at her and she at me. There was great meaning in that gaze. It was as if she asked for my permission for a deed she dared not name. A shiver passed between us, inexplicable and eerie. I nodded.

"And Agnes," I said in a low voice. "If you know any spells...use them now..."

I must go north; they waited for me. Messages came with speedy regularity and found me wherever I was — Lambeth — Northampton — St Albans — and the words were always the same: hurry — Scotland — the King — the army — Carlisle — Robert Bruce.

Robert Bruce had defeated the Earl of Pembroke at Loudon Hill in Ayrshire; he was rampant; he must be brought down before he achieved further successes; I must go north.

My heart was heavy and my spirit most unwilling. Lead weights dragged me back. Could ever man have gone more reluctantly upon business of the realm? I doubted it. My little troop edged slowly forward, with Robert gambolling beside till he was like to burst with effort; and the time slipped by, and June turned to July, and still I was slow footing it, inching my way north to face the spectres that would greet me there — my father newly triumphant, sword in hand, his gold and crimson banner gleaming; my cousin Tom, strong, high in favour, smirking not a little to see me returned without my Gaveston, and obliged to carry out my duties comfortless; Warwick, carelessly complacent, having seen the court rid of unwelcome interlopers; Langton, self righteously smug, he who had once been accused of adultery; and all the shifting sludge of faces watching me with curiosity to see if I could deal with the dashing of my hopes. No wonder I went at snail's pace.

A twist in the road, a turn in the track, and Fortune spins her thread and makes a little knot and so the weave goes on, a different pattern, other threads conjoining. One birch tree like another birch tree; the difference being that between the two trees, in that small space, the world became a different place, the time a different time, our journey something other than it was.

The horseman was a messenger. He drew his horse up short; a cloud of earth dust flared beneath the hooves. My men surrounded him. He stumbled from the saddle, seeking me. He fell upon his knee and seized my boot and kissed it, with the loud formality of one who knows that on this day he ranks with those that find a sudden fame and never afterwards attain the like.

"Most Royal Majesty!" he cried so all could hear. "I bring bad news." He handed me a letter. It had Warwick's seal upon it.

"You are sure of this?" I asked, re-reading it with close attention.

"The King, your father, died at Burgh Marshes. He lies at St Michael's church. The news is kept quiet till you come... Your Grace."

I dismounted then. I bent and grabbed the man by both arms, shaking him. "But are you sure he's dead?" I gasped.

"I swear it..." stuttered he. "The letter tells it. As God's my judge, it's true."

The men about me knelt and made obeisance. I raised the messenger and rewarded him. "Rest yourself," I told him. "And when you've rested, get you with all haste to Piers Gaveston at Crecy in Ponthieu. Tell him to come to England. Tell him God speed."

Then we continued on our way, slowly and with dignity, as befits those who mourn. Robert composed his fool's face to a monkish soberness, and I did likewise.

Yes, Robert was quiet for once; but it was my heart that was gambolling and leaping.

Chapter Eleven

CROSS THE purple of the pall that covered the bier of the dead monarch, the Earl of Warwick and I watched each other.

The church was dark, a stony refuge on the saltmarsh, place of flood and screeching birds.

"I was raised to believe him indestructible," said I.

"We are all mortal," said Guy Beauchamp. His voice was low and sonorous, with intonation like a priest's.

His face was long, the nose aquiline. His brow was broad, his eyes narrow, brown; the eyebrows well shaped. His mouth was wide and sensuous — the mouth that had kissed Piers in jest and scorn — a fine gloss of black stubble over the upper lip. His hair was dark and sleek. His expression was forbidding, arrogant; the eyes calculating, with a tendency to look from sideways rather than to meet the gaze full on. Piers thought him handsome as Lucifer. He was learned, was Warwick; he could converse with ease in Latin, welcomed scholars to his castle hard by Arden forest. He had the whitest hands, his long slim fingers always restless, toying with his rings. He was then thirty-four. They said of him that he was dangerous, and that whatever he caused to be done, his own hands were kept clean. *When he waylaid me, with his men, at Perth, said Piers, and held me to the wall and handled me, I was enraged. But when he took his hands from me, my nipples were as hard as beech nuts, and my cock was up. He hates me, that is clear. But when I recall his contemptuous kiss, I tremble.*

"I was with your father when he died," said Beauchamp.

"And I," said the ubiquitous Walter Langton, bustling forward.

"He spoke to us of his hopes and fears. He asked us to convey to you his dying wishes."

"I believe I know them," I replied with a dry smile. "Something to do with bones?"

"You are to bear his bones before the army," began Langton self-importantly.

"His bones will go where bones should go," said I. "Into the earth."

"But —" Langton bristled. Warwick said impatiently: "Have done with bones. The King's last words were about Gaveston."

158

"Piers Gaveston? The Gascon?" I said politely.

"The same," said Warwick firmly. "And he gave us a warning against Gaveston: That man is a schemer, said he, an upstart and a braggart. And I fear he loves the Prince inordinately. I foresee only discord if he ever should return. Be sure that he remains in Gascony. And since the Prince is malleable, kind-hearted, easily persuaded, I look to you, and Langton here, to be his good advisers in this matter."

"My father said so much?" I marvelled with raised eyebrows.

"With his dying breath," Langton promised me.

"And I took it upon myself to assure the King," continued Warwick pointedly, "that the Prince would never be so stupid as to bring the Gascon back to England."

I smiled, as if the sombre Earl had made some kind of quip. I turned to Langton. "You may accompany the remains of your old master to the abbey of Waltham, while we make arrangements for the burial and deal with matters more important. And as for Gaveston," I said to the Earl of Warwick, "he is on his way."

In Carlisle castle I received the homage of the earls, magnates of the realm. We were united, in good humour, optimism, mutual acclaim. There is that about a new beginning which inspires, and lifts the heart.

Loudest in his protestations was my cousin Tom. He believed his place in the new scheme of things was to be at my side, my lieutenant, my strong right arm. "We are of the same blood," he told me warmly. "We have been friends since childhood. Bound by indissoluble ties. Look to me for loyalty, Ned; ask of me what you will."

Bound also was he to the Earl of Lincoln, having wed his daughter Alice. Henry Lacy was of my father's generation, and from him I half expected fatherly advice of the kind I could well do without. But I misjudged him.

"I was with your father when he died," said he.

"You also! With Warwick and Langton?"

"We were all there with him. And my lord of Pembroke."

"And what were his last words?"

The Earl of Lincoln frowned. "There were no last words."

"No — warning?"

"Warning? No. Your father had enough to do to rise up in his bed and take his cup. He gave no warnings. No, he sat up, and he fell back, and he was gone, as a tree is felled. He died among his companions, and," he added with a wry smile, "he died with his face towards Scotland; he could see its hills across the Firth. He died well. But that is all past now, and it's what's to come that matters." He took a long breath, and his vast stomach heaved. Piers called him Burst Belly. He was monstrous fat. "At this time of change, the most important thing is to show unity of purpose, solidarity. I served your father all my life, and what remains to me of life is yours, my prince. That is, your Grace," he coughed. I could see it plain; it would be hard for him to learn to call this beardless boy by the same title as that giant. He coughed again. "There is a matter I would like to raise, and you will forgive the presumption of an old man..."

"Speak on, my lord."

"Your father believed that your affection for Piers Gaveston was of such a nature as no Christian man may countenance. He spoke to you in anger; he should not have spoken so. With my own ears I then heard you deny his charges, and declare your love was of that courtly quality of which there are so many fine examples in our songs and legends. If you can assure me that you spoke the truth, then you shall have no more ardent servant than old Lincoln, to the ending of his days."

"I spoke the truth," said I. "My love for Gaveston is pure." As you see, they are wrong who said I never understood diplomacy.

"I knew it," said the Earl of Lincoln, grateful as a suppliant who receives a gift. "There is no bar then to a great and glorious future, and I thank Your Grace for that."

The Earl of Pembroke, Aymer de Valence, was a man I liked and trusted. Though Piers in his habitual disrespect had christened him Joseph the Jew for his tall pale sombre mien, I knew him loyal and well-meaning. Dignified and courageous, he had been with me in Scotland at my side, and if, as he maintained, my father had entrusted my welfare to his keeping, I was happy to accept his care of me.

There were also gathered there at Carlisle castle Humphrey de Bohun, Earl of Hereford, my sister's husband, who had fastened on my spurs when I was knighted, a man who dressed well, but whose gloomy nature made him a poor companion, and sullen now because he had been promised lands in Scotland. There was my dead sister Joan's young son, sixteen years old, Gilbert de Clare, a kinsman of my childhood friend, who being yet untried, had been eager to go fight the Scots. There was old Despenser and his pretty son; Roger Mortimer of Wigmore, some twenty years old, a Marcher lord; there were the young earls of Arundel and Surrey, brothers in law; and the Earl of Oxford and my cousin Richmond, older men and tried in service. And there was Guy of Warwick. Here then were assembled all who had a part to play in what was yet to come. There lacked the one, the spark to set the stage alight. Where was he? Why was he not here?

But would he come at all? What of his anger and confusion, his disgust with courts and earls, his careless treatment at their hands, his fury at being suspected my lover. Why should he come to me at all? Was my poor love enough to bring him back?

"Did you truly think he would not come to you?"

"Yes! He had been badly treated. Everybody was against him."

"You're a fool, sire. Anyone could have told you he'd be back. There was more for him in England than in Ponthieu."

"Well, yes. There was myself!"

"And so much for your assessment of the barons of the realm. What of theirs of you? If only hearts were worn on sleeves, and honesty the juice greased Fortune's wheel!"

"You think I saw what I would see, and not what truly was?"

"I think self-interest bound you all. When one reign ends and another begins, the link is weak and there must be some rapid welding, everybody working to make fast the broken chain."

"I swear the general consensus was a good one, all auspices favourable, and the rejoicing loud. We were all so merry; it was one feast after another. You know it, Robert; you must admit it to be so!"

"Yes. You seemed all that a king should be: tall, handsome, strong; young as you were, a hardened campaigner, devout, courageous. As a figurehead you were what was required. So they clustered about you, the old nobility, most of them related to the crown by blood or marriage, others by past service and past battles. Lacy may even have believed your declaration. "

"Oh, I am sure of it."

"But Warwick with his lie made his position clear, and Lancaster was about as transparent as a wall, that is, we had no idea of what went on behind his eyes. If he vowed loyalty, you may be sure that he was after something."

"The Stewardship of England, yes, the which I granted him."

"And when he got it, was he then so kind...? No, they were a pack of hounds scrapping for meat. Each had his own place, each knew the other. That kind of pack has no use for an interloper, one moreover who comes in on top."

He sent me messengers. He was arrived in England — he was in London — he was with Walter Reynolds, while he waited for a sick servant to recover from the voyage — ah, some page boy! Piers was always good to page boys.

We quit Carlisle for Dumfries castle, there to meet those Scottish magnates true to us; and from the windows here I watched the southern road, beyond the Nith, beyond the Moss, beyond Caerlaverock, towards the shallow channels of the Firth. The August sunlight shone upon a land of emptiness, that would be grey and blank until he gave it colour.

It was no secret that I was a king in debt. My father, whom the known world owned as a pattern of kingship was in truth a bungler, wriggling worm-like from an economic shambles. We were sixty thousand pounds in debt to Florentine bankers. Nothing had been paid. We owed to the army, to our clerks, our household, to our bakers, merchants; it was wonderful he had got by for so long; well, such is reputation.

"It would seem to me," said I, "that Walter Langton, treasurer, is much at fault here. And should be replaced and even punished for his carelessness."

As I recall, no one disagreed.

"And there will be no more Scottish war," I said, and most of them that heard it raised a cheer, English and Scot alike.

"And now to the Exchequer accounts," suggested Lacy.

A messenger at my elbow: "Your Grace, Piers Gaveston is here!"

"At last!"

I ran to meet him; others followed me more slowly.

Across the great hall of the castle Piers ran to me like an arrow, and he knelt at my feet and took my hand and kissed it.

"Sire!" he breathed. I could feel the excitement coursing through his fingers and his lips, his breath hot on my hand. My own pulse raced. I bent my head to him and kissed him on the mouth, my tongue lightly circling the inside of his lips. I raised him to his feet and looked at him.

He was dressed all in white, white linen edged with scarlet braid, a scarlet belt low on his hips, its gold clasp winking in a sunshaft. The rubies I had given him glowed on his fingers. His dark red shoes were dusty from the road.

His face — ah, could a man who was already perfect in his beauty yet become more beautiful? I tell you, it was so. And that short absence from me served to underline what was now plain to me in sudden clarity — that boyhood was long over, that this was a man who came to me, my lover. He radiated strength and vigour and lightness of step, swordsman, dancer, knight at arms. My admiration soared when I considered that this was a man had ridden the length of England, but in that white tunic he might well have dropped from the gates of Heaven. How was he so clean, so bright, so impossibly untarnished! Laughing then I understood that no one who ate his pears with a silver fork was likely to burst in upon me travel-stained. I pictured him bathing in a sun-dappled brook, naked beneath the overhanging trees, and all the road-sweat gone from him, Roger his page lightly gilding him with perfumes, unravelling the fresh white garment from a chest, handing him jewels.

"You've done your hair differently!" I declared. Rolled curls over the forehead and at the nape of the neck.

"It's the French fashion," answered he.

"We must go talk," I murmured.

"The Exchequer accounts, your gracious majesty," said Lincoln at my elbow, sounding something like my father after all.

"But Piers and I haven't seen one another for three months!" I began, almost coquettishly. Then stopped short. It was the first time it came home to me that I was answerable to none. No one had the power to make me do what I would not. A lifetime of subservience to figures in authority is not so easily cast aside. I did so in that moment.

"Let the Exchequer wait," I said, and loudly to my friend: "Come, Gaveston; we have much to discuss."

"They watched you go and in little groups they moved about, and muttered."

Now in my chamber we were quite alone. The sun poured in through the arch of the window and made the dull stones rich as cider. We hugged each other hard. Elation, relief, excitement, these conjoined in our embrace. My mouth pressed against his; we kissed.

"So many days," I murmured. "So long without you..."

"Whoever might guess," he said, "that when we last met and said goodbye — whoever could have guessed that now..."

"I feared that you would not return."

"That I would not — " he stared. "Oh Ned! You must believe in me!"

"You were so angry," I began apologetically.

"I had cause. But — it is different now."

"Yes," I said blankly. "Yes. Is it? Why?"

"But naturally," he laughed. "Or had you forgotten?"

"Forgotten — ?"

"That you are the King!"

163

I grinned. "I am just the same as ever I was."

"No, my Ned, you're not; it isn't possible. You are the King. You can do anything you want." He looked at me, his eyes laden with implication.

"I can do anything I want," I repeated. Then I looked at him, intoxication bubbling in my throat. *"We can do anything we want."*

"We can do anything we want," he laughed agreeing, and with dancing eyes he backed towards the bed and dropped upon it, lying on his elbows, legs apart, blatantly inviting. I bounded to him, knelt between his thighs and pressed my cheek into his groin; beneath his clothes his cock grew hard; I hugged him around the waist, and my eyes filled with tears of happiness. We struggled with our clothes; and linens, satins, clasps of rubies, clasps of sapphires, slithered to the floor. Now naked, our warm bodies fell together on the bed and my hand clamped firmly on his prick. Commendable consideration made me pause.

"You are not too tired, after your journey?"

"I am never tired," he boasted cheerfully.

"Ah, yes — I forgot." I grinned and clipped his ear. We fought and laughed, our limbs entangled, blond and dark hair mingling. Did I say Piers appeared to me a man? — we were more like puppies then, scrapping and rolling in the sheer delight of our reunion, and in between our gasps we giggled: "Anything we like! We can do anything we like!" and then in foolishness carried away:

"Banish all women and give it out that men must marry men!"

"Send Lancaster and Warwick to a lonely monastery and oblige them to take the vows!"

"Naked banquets! Imagine old Lacy with his flesh a-wobble..."

"No more statecraft; only music!"

"Boys of exceptional beauty to be sold in Cheapside every Friday, decked in ribbons!"

"Perot, I can wait no longer; I shall burst."

"Here — all over me — cover me — ah, I'm ready too!"

We lay weak and spent, well content, murmuring fond things.

"Ned, I wish to say — "

"Your words are pearls, each one beyond price."

"You exaggerate, but only slightly. Now hear me out."

"There is nothing I would rather do than listen to your voice."

"Be serious, Ned. Listen now. There will be those that say — that say I came back for rewards and favours."

"To the dungeons with 'em!"

"But Ned, it isn't so," my love continued. "I can't make proof of it, d'you see? I can't pretend that you are not the king. But Ned, it was the man for whom I quit Ponthieu, and not the monarch. I can only say it and ask that you believe me."

"I don't care why you came back. It is enough you did so."

"Yes. But it is important to me to make it clear to you. That I came back because of love. Do you believe me? You must."

"I do believe you, dearest. I believe everything you say. Are the fires of Hell extinct? Tell me so and I'll believe it. Horses have two heads — say it's so and it shall be. England is attached to France — "

"Ned!" cried Perot in exasperation. "For once do not be slight. Remember how you once said to me was it true love between us, or a muddle? For me it's love. Don't laugh at my protestation. All simply, I am yours, now and for always."

"Well, thank you," I replied. I added thoughtfully: "I believe that is a gift surpasses any I may give to you."

"There's no life for me but by your side; I know no other. It's something beyond mere choice. There simply isn't anything else that I may do."

"Perhaps that potion was magic after all," said I.

"The potion?"

"That you brought from Agnes when we vowed to love each other for all time, and Gilbert said we looked like the famous lovers."

"Ah, yes, that." Piers looked at his hand and laughed. "I still wear the ring you gave me, the great ruby. But now I have to wear it on my smallest finger!"

"The earldom of Cornwall," I said then. "It's yours."

"Tristan's country?" Piers said, shining-eyed.

"The same."

"Ah, Ned, I could not," Piers said soberly. "What was I thinking of? And what were you?" he added reprovingly.

"I'm merely being practical," I shrugged. "As King I am surrounded only by the nobility. You wish to have access to me, I suppose? Then you must be an earl. And Cornwall is unclaimed. It's yours."

"Well, I for one will have no part in it," said Warwick. "The earldom of Cornwall has always been in royal hands. King Henry's brother Richard, then Edmund his son were earls of Cornwall last. If the title is for gift, then give it to your step-brother Thomas."

"Thomas is too young," I snapped, "and my decision made."

"I shall never put my hand to such an ill-considered act," said Warwick.

"Believe me, it was well considered," answered I, "and fortunately others are more generous in their sentiments."

We made my darling Earl of Cornwall. Lincoln witnessed it, and Tom, and Pembroke; also Richmond, Warenne of Surrey, Hereford and Arundel. The deed was done therefore in universal accord. I could not help but smile and raise my eyes to Heaven where I hoped my father's spirit raged above the clouds. Ponthieu? That cottage garden? With Cornwall went excess of land.

Next day I sent men to arrest Walter Langton, where he waited with the bier at Waltham. That man who thought himself so schooled in policy should learn in prison that it does not pay to displease princes.

We left Scotland in the capable hands of Pembroke and my cousin Richmond. All centred now on England. My plans were thus: to replace Langton in the treasury with Walter Reynolds, who would give me money when I asked; and to recall Archbishop Winchelsea, remembered warmly for his antipathy to Langton, living now in exile in Bordeaux, victim of my father's bitter hostility, and to have his firm support in all I did. I would then arrange a marriage for my darling that would further fix his place amongst the nobles of the land. The lady we chose was Margaret, daughter of my sister Joan, and sister to the young Earl of Gloucester, Gilbert, who had pleaded with me to set him a task to prove his worth and volunteered to die for me; but death was furthest from my mind, and I could only promise him peace and festivities.

"Ned," Piers whispered to me. "Show me my inheritance."

We can do anything we like!

And so we rode to Cornwall.

Tristan was the son of Blancheflor, sister of King Mark of Cornwall; his father was Rivalin of Brittany. Tristan grew to manhood, strong and handsome, witty, full of charms, and good at tournaments. His boat brought him to Cornwall and he landed on a rocky shore.

"Down there!"

Tintagel castle, the most beautiful place on earth — there Perot and I passed two nights and a day in legend. We stood at a window and the sea wind blew our hair across our faces. Below, far far below, the white waves pounded tawny rocks, and the sea stretched out towards the lost land of Lyonesse. High on the rocky cliffs the castle stood, turrets and towers, home to the Cornish chough, King Arthur's spirit, so they say.

Tristan came to Tintagel. Mark was king there. He lived alone; he had no wife. He welcomed the beautiful youth and brought him to his castle. He made a place for him. He knighted him. They lived in harmony there, far from courts and rumours, by the white waves and the pounding sea.

We had a fire lit in a hearth, and we sat on furs, and ate rough bread and rabbit stew; Richard Rhymer played for us the Welsh music that so pleased us and it passed over our senses like the shadows over grasses, while the candles flickered and we moved closer together, and one cloak warmed us both.

"September, was it, sire? That castle must have been a vile and draughty place. Where did you sleep?"

"On a straw pallet spread before the fire. We gave orders for the music to play on until we slept. We fell asleep to that music, in each other's arms."

"I cannot think you slept well!"

"We slept in Heaven."

We slept late. We were still aching from the long ride and there was the homeward journey yet to come.

I had heard there was a cave down on the shore, where Merlin nursed the infant Arthur, and Piers was eager as myself to visit it. But none of our party could make himself understood to the natives of the place; and none came forward to be guide. Therefore picture myself and Perot down in the cove amongst the shingle and the sand, climbing the rocks, searching for caves. We found one indeed, and entered it. The walls were wet and slippery to the touch; there were shifting pebbles underfoot. Dark rock pools were there, seeming to be filled with strange seaweeds, and little floating plants with curling leaves, such as oak trees cast in spring. The living rock made curiously carved partitions; the water dripped and slithered in their fissures. In the darkness we went forward carefully, feeling our way.

"Ghosts may be here," said Piers, and paused.

I stood against him, with my arms around his waist. "Merlin's ghost won't harm us."

"Merlin!" called Piers in summoning ringing tones. We listened, and we heard the distant crashing of the waves. When it became apparent that no ghost would come here at our beck and call Piers laughed and called out: "Merlin! Merlin!" in a series of foolish voices; and then kissed me; and we came away, cold, from the cave; and Piers grumbled about the sand and damp on his doeskin boots; and we climbed back up to the castle, and he swore he could see Ireland.

In the early evening a roseate mist lay on the surface of the sea and tinged the rocks with fine translucence. The seaweeds hugged their edge like maidenhair. We half supposed a phantom ship would rise up, coming from across the Irish sea.

That night we sent the minstrels to another room, and made love on our fur-strewn pallet by the fire, and lay and listened to the pounding of the sea and the whistling of the wind that stirred the straw flecks and teased the spluttering embers.

"It's special here," said Piers.

"It's Mark and Tristan," I agreed. "They're here still, living. And they recognise us and accept us."

"We'll drink then, shall we? As if it were the magic potion; for certainly this is a magic place."

We shared the chalice. "Now we are truly bound," said Piers.

"Were we not before?"

"No," he said, "because at Langley when you ordered a ceremony I gave it from good humour, and I didn't love you as I think you may have loved me. It was to please you, that was all. But now I drink, and take you as my lover for all time, knowing what I am about, eyes open; there's the difference."

"I knew you didn't love me then. I pretended otherwise. But it has been almost worth the self-deceiving to hear your words of love now in this place. The spirits of Mark and Tristan stand beside us, listening and being glad."

"I love to play before an audience," smiled Perot, and he put his arms around me and we sank back down into the furs.

"Will we return? We should; they will expect it," he said, after loving me.

"We shall return; I promise it."

And as we rode up country towards Exeter, across bleak wilderness and wooded valley, time and time again I gestured to the lands we traversed, laughing, saying: "All this is yours. How do you like it? Ponthieu? Who wants Ponthieu? All this is yours. And more!"

The generous Parliament at Northampton granted money for the funeral, marriage, coronation. We saw my father finally to rest in the abbey at Westminster, beside his father and his brother, and, duty done, I heaved a great sigh of relief, and set off to Berkhamstead for frivolity.

This castle I intended Piers should have, both as his right and for convenience sake, for it was a stone's throw from Langley; here he should hold court. At present Queen Margaret had abode here, looking after young Meg, and here Piers was to be wed and all was set for celebration.

It is a very fair castle, built of flintstones, with the wooded slope of the great common just hard by, and the massy beechwoods that surround it every shade of gold, red, tawny in the sunshine of October.

"You remember, Robert, how very happy we all were, as we rode down to Berkhamstead, determined that the day should be entirely memorable...more than a mere ceremony, but a festival of joy!"

"You were happy, sire. Young Margaret, what of her?"

"Oh, she was content enough. She was getting the most handsome man in the realm as bridegroom, and his star in the ascendant, therefore hers. And this marriage came at a good time for her: her mother newly dead, her stepfather like to fall back to obscurity now that the Gloucester estates had reverted to young Gilbert. At fourteen, a good marriage was exactly what she needed to begin her future. She proved a good wife, did she not, and bore my love a daughter?"

"One child in five years; hardly fecundity."

"Piers was otherwise engaged."

"Queen Margaret then; I do not recall that she was well content. But maybe I was mistaken? Her dark looks were mere sadness at the recollection of the ceremony in the Abbey two days previously?"

"Ah, yes, I believe that lay at the root of it."

Queen Margaret was yet a young woman, widowed, barely two years older than myself. I did believe she truly loved my father, hence her sober garb, her dull expression. She embraced me, yes, but she looked sour at me.

"It is too soon," she told me, shaking her head. "Your father buried; you should mourn, as I do."

"Madam, it will come as no surprise to you to learn I have no cause to mourn," I said, annoyed that she had chosen to haunt the celebration like some spectre. "If the merriment disturbs you, you have leave to spend the time alone with your thoughts. But don't choose sorrow, dearest lady," I said winsomely, of a sudden remembering the affection we had held for one another these past eight years since she first came to Canterbury. "Life should always be more dear to us than death."

"And where in your philosophy lies wisdom?" answered she, a

little tartly; but I smiled, since I would have no discord at the wedding of my sweet.

It's true that for the moment I was jealous. There had been no need to woo the girl, but Piers was courtly, charming, debonair, and everything he undertook he did with relish. I had heard him whispering to Margaret, cooing like some dove: "Dear lady, we are no strangers to one another. In your mother's household I have seen you grow from childhood to young maidenhood. The King, your uncle, is my dearest friend. You know me as a knight devoted to your family. Could you begin to think of me as a husband — one who would cherish you and treat you kindly?"

Sickening, would not you say? And all my glowering he received with smiles, and what offended me as much as anything was that I knew his protestations genuine. He would be kind to her; he spoke in all sincerity. And it would not be difficult for him. Meg was a lovely child — all Joan's children were — tall and pale, with auburn hair, good natured, yet with that sudden wildness of spirit that all Plantagenets possessed; she was my favourite of Joan's children. I was glad to see my dear ones so conjoined.

"I shall be wearing peacock blue," said Piers.

"You cannot; I am wearing blue," I snapped.

"You always wear blue; you should try something different."

"Why must you wear blue? It won't match your eyes."

"I can't always live in green. For my marriage I fancy peacock blue."

"Why can't you wear one of the tunics I've already given you?"

"What, old clothes for my wedding? No, I have had this one specially created. I designed it myself," he added with a smirk. "It will be trimmed with rabbit fur, and all my jewels will be silver. Edward! It's not every day that a person weds the King's own niece, a lady of the Plantagenets, daughter of Gilbert the Red, a hero of our time. It must be peacock blue!"

I gave way; I always did. "Oh, very well. I'll wear yellow." The thought began to appeal a little. "And all my jewels shall be gold. I'll dazzle like the sun. I'll be the sun; you the moon."

"To the blessing of the Lord and of the Lady," Piers added delightedly.

I pondered this. "Best speak of God alone, my sweet. You know how easily the rumours start."

"What rumours?"

"You know what I mean. Be careful speaking of the Lady, and if

170

you must do so, cross yourself and quiet the tongues by making believe you mean Our Lady, Mother of Christ."

"I won't tell that kind of lie," said Piers stubbornly. "My mother's religion is as holy as the other. Holier, and older."

"When I was at Langley, Perot, and you were across the sea, I spoke with Agnes," I said, now reminded of that disturbing little encounter. "I said if she knew any spell, then cast it now. Within two months, Perot, my father died."

"So what?" Piers answered gaily.

"So? What? You tell me."

"Something else happened after those two months, dear Edward: I returned! If Agnes cast a spell, she would have cast for true love's triumph. Ah, Ned," he cried, and hugged me. "You make goblins, then you live in fear of them!"

He could always laugh away my doubts.

The wedding was a sumptuous affair; I spared no expense to make it so. It was myself that threw fistfuls of silver pennies over Piers and Meg as they emerged from the chapel, and kissed them both and wished them well. Then to the feast! The triumph of the table was a stag with a jewelled dagger protruding from its roasted flanks, and when Piers drew it forth, out gushed red wine, to cheers from the assembled throng, and to a screech from Piers who leapt back, fearful of his peacock blue becoming splashed and stained; I laughed to bursting at the sight.

My father's dear friend Despenser, and now my own dear friend, sat by my side, and Hugh his son, for from this day we were all related to one another by ties of marriage — Hugh was already wed to Eleanor, Meg's elder sister; and Gilbert of Gloucester was with us, and their stepfather, dear Ralph de Monthermer, campaigner by my side in Scotland; and Lincoln was present, still believing at that date that we must all show solidarity; and all Piers' household; and the Queen's; and I noticed Agnes, dark and silent as the Queen herself, and wondered if spells would be cast this night.

"Later," I said in Piers' ear, "later, come to me."

He crept into my chamber in the night, barefoot and shivering from the flagstones. It was the first day of November, and the autumn chills were on us, for all that the sun had shone upon the ceremony. He reached for me and tried to warm himself upon me.

"Beast," I muttered, unresponsive.

"Why? You told me to come and here I am."

"Don't play the innocent. You've been with her!"

"God's arrows, Edward, where else should I have been?"

"You were in bed with her!"

"I was! You saw me put there."

"Did you consummate the marriage?" I seethed.

He began to giggle. "Ah, so that's what this is all about!"

"How astute you are!"

"This is true; I'm famous for the rapidity of my perception."

"You will be famous for two black eyes tomorrow if you annoy me further."

"Annoy you, dearest? I but did your bidding. Wed the lady, said my sovereign, and obediently I made my vows."

"And then — ?"

"And then there was a banquet, and may I say, Ned, that it was superb!"

"Did you — and she — ?" I stuttered, gripping him by the throat. "I want to know."

He disentangled my wrists. "Do you expect me to lie passively while you strangle me?" he enquired mildly. But he was laughing; I could hear it.

I threw myself upon him and rolled him on his belly. I made him spread his legs.

"You did! You did your duty, all of it. I know it."

"Duty, dearest? It was pure pleasure," said he, all provocation. I responded as he very well intended. Weak with laughter, and no doubt with passion spent, the wretch lay at my mercy, and I was in no way gentle.

"Ouch! Edward, you will tear my skin —"

"At least you'll cease your laughing," I panted.

"I am silent!"

"You? You are never silent! Well, let's listen to your groans now, and your cries, the which offend me less."

"Ah! That hurts."

"There's more —"

"Ned! You're really hurting me —"

I gasped in exertion, every thrust a joy to me, my rampant jealousy receding with each gratifying howl beneath me, and somewhere in my mastery of him I spent seed and rage and lay upon him in exhaustion where he snivelled on his fist.

"Brute," he said.

"I'll bathe you," I offered, penitent.

"Tyrant," he said.

"And rub your shoulders," I added.

"If the good folk of England only knew what manner of monster was about to undertake protection of their welfare," he continued. "My shoulders *and* my back."

"Anything at all. Just ask."

He snuggled into my arms. We kissed, a long slow kiss, and had become again the dearest in each other's hearts, before we fell asleep.

Queen Margaret spoke to me before I left. Waylaid me, almost, waiting in the passageway.

"Attend me in my chamber, Edward," she said, while her servant opened the door for us and we went through into her room, its shutters drawn against the wind, the candles giving light and shadow. The fire in its iron basket blazed and spluttered. I noticed that we were alone.

"Tell me that it is not true," said she in icy tones. "Piers Gaveston came to your room last night...his wedding night. Deny it if you may."

"Madam, I need no longer make account to you for what I do, or what my friends do," I said calmly.

"So it was true. I had prayed otherwise."

"Presumably you made sure of your suspicions before this little court enquiry?"

"I sent a man to watch," admitted she, as if shamed by the admission. "He saw."

"Then would you have me lie?" I shrugged. "You know all that is to know."

"May God forgive you, Edward," she replied.

I bowed and turned to go. "I daresay He will do so."

Then Piers and I returned to London. The dignity of our leaving was somewhat marred by the screech Piers gave as his bum hit the saddle.

There was no doubt of it: Piers was flirting with my cousin Tom. I watched, amused, and marvelled.

There we sat, Thomas visiting us at Langley, halfway through November. The crowning and my wedding fixed for early in the coming year, there now remained the year's end with its Yule festivities to enjoy, and more — Piers planned a tournament.

And now he was all deferential, winsome, asking Tom's advice and fluttering his lashes, and lo and behold, Tom was falling for it. To think I had been wary of the two of them in close confinement! I had assumed that Tom would behave haughtily, Piers truculent, but no,

173

both were polite, nay, more, affectionate. Of course, Tom had decided to support me, for whatever reasons, and that meant supporting Perot also; but this warmth was a delight to witness. I must suppose that Tom believed Piers worthy of his patronage now he had become a landed earl, or did he think that Piers by his attention to him signalled that he would welcome a return of Tom's advances?

"You will come to the tournament at my castle," Piers cajoled, "and bring as many as you can? It means so much to me that the great men of the realm so honour me."

"At Berkhamstead?"

"No, at one of my other castles," Piers said modestly. "Wallingford."

A little flicker crossed Tom's face, I thought, perhaps at this reminder that from landless Piers had risen to a choice of castles. There was no need for irritation on his part; cousin Tom had more castles than he knew what to do with. It seemed, however, that he remained firm in his intention to promote harmony.

"I shall be there; they all shall."

As a boy I used to wonder which of all the castles might be Camelot. I must admit I had never considered Wallingford a contender. But now I saw that it was so. This great castle, a simple enough place beside the river Thames, glowed in a haze of rose, and glimmered like a star, although as I recall, the day was dull, the month December.

Our company foregathered there, and gave itself up to gaiety. The lists were set up in the fields, and we sat beneath a canopy of red and yellow, while the common folk came from round about, and our trumpets blared commencement. Knights and horses in bright colours — the knights in their embroidered surcoats, the horses in their long emblazoned mantles — massed in serried ranks, their squires attending further off. Two parties of knights — the young men of Piers' household, and the ranks of older barons — rode at one another to begin the tourney.

Tom had brought them all, even the Earl of Warwick. Sword and mace were the weapons, swords blunted and rounded, and all chain mail well padded. There would be no danger, and through skill alone each knight would work to unhorse the man he rode against. Piers' knights were palpably superior, younger, lithe and supple, insolently sure of themselves. Down went their opponents, one by one. All those unhorsed retired to fight again or nurse their dignity; and then came jousting, this with lance. At the far end of the field the knights hung up their shields, and any would-be challenger came to touch the shield with his lance if he wished to take on its owner.

Piers rode from shield to shield and touched them all. I would have thought him weary from the fray, but he must have been possessed. He rode with Meg's fur sleeve upon his arm; she had been named the Queen of Beauty in his honour. The winner of the joust would win the prize from her hands. It was a silver circlet. The champion would then hand it to the lady of his choice. And it began to seem that the champion would be Piers.

Down went the Earl of Hereford to his lance. Elizabeth my sister rose up in her seat; but Hereford got up and limped away. Down went the Earl of Arundel, thrown like a sack of grain — a flurry of panic here as he lay inert, but no, he stood. Down went Warenne of Surrey, that great unmannerly lout; he shook his mailed fist as he left the lists.

I knew well enough what Lancaster and Warwick would be thinking: Down go the old nobility at the lance of an upstart. Came Lancaster, pounding towards Piers; their lances touched, and Lancaster and lance went flying. Tom's page came running forward, but Tom hurled him away, his rage apparent even behind his helmet, his weapon embedded in the ground. Piers rode back, circled, changed his lance, then took on Warwick. As they rode towards each other the clods of earth flew, and the ground shook beneath the thudding hooves. Lance struck shield with horrid resonance — and Warwick fell, unhorsed, the mighty Beauchamp spreadeagled in the mud. Piers turned, and looked, the slits of the helmet showing nothing, nor needing to do so. His triumph was complete. He had downed them all, and he was still in the saddle and not even grazed. The crowds began to cheer, admiration of his prowess their strongest emotion, overriding any other. His page now helped him to take off his helmet.

Piers rode lance in hand to where his young wife sat, beside me, and lowering his weapon he received from her the silver circlet.

The lady and myself looked down at him with eyes that shone with adoration. His face was drenched in sweat and streaked with grime. He looked superb.

And now he turned his noble steed, and from his lance tip offered up the silver prize to me. I received it and formed the words of thanks and praise.

And I had thought him mere Gawain. By God's blood, this was Lancelot in all his glory.

Chapter Twelve

SIRE, WILL you grant and keep and by your oath confirm to the people of England the laws and customs given to them by the previous just and God-fearing kings your ancestors, and especially the laws, customs, and liberties granted to the clergy and people by the glorious King, the sainted Edward, your predecessor?"

"I grant and promise them."

"Sire, will you in all your judgements, so far as in you lies, preserve to God and Holy Church and to the people and clergy, entire peace and concord before God?"

"I will preserve them."

"Sire, will you, so far as in you lies, cause justice to be rendered rightly, impartially and wisely, in compassion and truth?"

"I will do so."

"Sire, do you grant to be held and observed the just laws and customs that the community of your realm shall determine, and will you, so far as in you lies, defend and strengthen them to the honour of God?"

"I grant and promise them."

The deed was done; and I became God's Anointed. I looked at Piers and smiled. Ah, if only he could have been crowned king beside me, in place of the mewling mawkish French chit I had been obliged to wed! If the nobles might be subject to his will, ceasing their wrangling and the petty complaints that had so plagued us of late!

This very morning, this twenty-fifth of February, the day of my coronation, they had come to me whingeing — Warwick threatening to refuse to carry the sword of state and to bear a ribboned garter in its place. I had to palm them off with promises.

Why were they taking against Piers so much, I wondered petulantly? It was true that he had beaten a good number of them in fair combat in the lists and some had taken their unhorsing in poor spirit. This was not Piers' fault; they should learn to take defeat with grace. Indeed, his triumph had been so absolute that some had put it down to sorcery. The fools — they simply could not believe one man so skilled in all he did. And though the silver circlet should have gone by rights to some woman, it was a very kind gesture for Piers to offer it to his liege lord; none but the most carping could think the deed anything other than delightful; I don't know why Lancaster and Lincoln had been so peevish. And did Warwick need to ride away so suddenly and not remain for the banquet at which Piers was to preside? It showed a monstrous churlishness; I cannot have been the only one to think so.

How I chortled at the way Piers had teased Thomas into conciliation! Why, he must have planned it all along, to bring the barons to his tournament and to joust with them all and bring them low. I'll make them sorry for the slights they showed me, he had promised; I'll do it by myself, without your help; I'll be revenged. And I had not believed it possible, and yet he had done so, all carefully and cunningly, confident in his skill and prowess, marvellous to behold. He was exceptional in everything he undertook.

A few months earlier at Westminster, during Christmastide, all had begun so merrily — at least, it would have been merry if Lincoln had not scowled so; and then there was the brawling between Piers' retainers and Lancaster's, and the knowledge that soon I would have to depart for France and bring my bride home. Yes, that did dampen the spirits a little. And Lincoln then began to be my father come again in portly form.

"This unseemly romping," he began — I had been chasing Piers about the palace — "must cease of course when Isabelle comes to England. This is understood, I trust?"

"Running keeps the heart in trim," I grinned.

"Let us consider dignity," said he, ponderous in speech as in bulk. "The Earl of Cornwall should comport himself as befits his title. And less like a young puppy."

Lurking behind a pillar, Piers began to bark and whine and slobber with his tongue. I giggled.

"His foolishness seems to be what Your Grace admires," said Lincoln sourly. "Your fawning upon him ill befits the future king."

"I do not fawn exactly," I said carefully.

"You hold his hand, you nuzzle in his ear, you fondle him."

"You take delight in watching us, I see," I smirked.

"I wish I could not help it. If I am in your presence I must see him, since you behave so all the time you are together."

"But he's so beautiful!" I sighed ecstatically. "Don't you think he's beautiful, my lord of Lincoln? Isn't he the loveliest thing you've ever seen?"

"Pah!" said the Earl of Lincoln in a heartfelt manner.

"I simply cannot keep my hands from him," I said. These were all the kinds of things I had longed to say to my father and never dared; out they now tumbled, frivolous and foolish. "It is a rare malady, of which these are the outward manifestations."

"Yes, I have heard as much," said Lincoln darkly. "It is commonly spoken of that he has bewitched you. I begin to think it true."

"No, my lord!" I cried in sudden alarm. I had been playing; I had no intention of sailing into deep waters. "No, my lord, the malady's name is Love."

"Prince Edward!" cried the Earl of Lincoln in kinder tones and with some exasperation. "Your Grace! What would your father say to hear you talk so?"

"Finally and at last," said I, "my father is irrelevant!" And I struck the table with my fist, as I had seen him do so many times. I found it a very satisfying gesture; but it hurt the fist.

"You told me, Edward," said old Lacy, "you gave me your word that the Gascon and yourself were pure true friends. My own eyes, day by day, have witnessed that I would to God I had not seen, the which persuades me that the love between you is of a questionable nature. If I am wrong, may God forgive me for the foulness of my thought. I say this as your father's friend. Now as an earl of the realm I say: Root out the dalliance which offends us all, and do so before you bring home your bride, or by God's blood, before we know it we shall be at war with France."

But we were not. We were in that peculiar harmony which the marriage of two royal families promotes between neighbours strong in mutual distrust. In January, in the church of Notre Dame at Boulogne, I wed the Princess Isabelle, with pomp and splendour and all rites due to such a union. Kings and queens attended, archdukes and princes; gifts flowed to and fro, many wedding presents for the new bride and her spouse — and France was very rich just then, with money plundered from Knights Templars with great vigour and excess of zeal.

To me the Princess seemed barely more than a child. It comes to me that I had no idea of her exact age — I was betrothed to her when she was eight years old, and somehow it had always stayed with me that she was eight. Of course, this was not so, but nothing about the youthful Princess contrived to give impression of maturity. She must have been in fact about fourteen. She had plainly been pampered horrendously from birth, the idol of her doting father, Philip the Fair.

His nickname remained long after any cause for the claim. Piers called him Philip the Foul.

Isabelle I received with a nonchalance bordering on ennui. Pretty? She was fair enough, and considered like to bloom and bear good fruit. I remember from our wedding night the uncompromising whiteness of her thighs, so startlingly without hair, smooth and inflexible as pillars.

"Edward!" she breathed in my ear. "I am so happy you are mine!" She had a high pert voice that grated on my ears. I winced to find it in such close proximity to me. I winced also at her assumption. Hers! She seemed to think that I was her possession now, the latest in a string of such bestowed upon her by the puissance of her father. All I could think about was my darling, sleeping alone — or, said my jealousy, with John his page — but nonetheless awaiting me, longing for my return.

I simply cannot understand why so many people took offence when I left him regent in my absence.

"The regency should have gone to me," said Tom of Lancaster.

"We were surprised," said Warwick, "that the regency did not go to Thomas of Lancaster, blood of your blood, greatest in rank and claim."

But I was gone barely a fortnight. It was not as if I were thrusting a new king upon the realm. If there were disagreements, they should not have been allowed to fester in so short a time. And Perot had no real power as such; indeed the work that was required of him was mere administration, book work with clerks, the issuing of licences, grants, ecclesiastical benefices. I think it shows my understanding of my own responsibilities that I left England in the hands of one whom I completely trusted. I said as much to Tom. He laughed. He was, in those days, affability personified when in my presence.

"It occurs to me, Ned, that your friend — and mine, I hope - - might have borne himself with more humility in his high office. It's common knowledge that when the Earl of Warwick came to him on business, the Earl was made to kneel. Do you not see, my coz, that Warwick treated so is Warwick in ill humour?"

My lips twitched. "It were no bad thing for Guy Beauchamp to practise some proper meekness. Indeed I had heard he knelt to Piers' command. I wish I had been there."

"Had you been there, the situation would not have arisen!" said Tom impatiently. "It was your absence, and your friend's assumption of your royal authority that proved the cause of the resultant discord.

Yes, Warwick knelt — and all the others who came to Gaveston as suppliants, for he insisted on it. So, he has had his little triumph, and believed for two weeks that he was a king — a fanciful dream lived out to feed his arrogance; and what has he achieved? A hearty resentment of his person, and my lord of Warwick bristling like a mastiff. You should have spoken to him, Ned, before you went — warned him not to offend the old nobility. God's teeth, he should have known it for himself!"

"Bristling like a mastiff!" I said amused. "A muzzle would well suit the Earl of Warwick for his wild vindictive tongue."

"Enough of that, Ned," Tom warned. "He knows that Gaveston calls him the Black Dog of Arden."

"Oh, has he heard that?" I laughed. "It serves him right. The name becomes him."

"Get Piers to curb his wit," Thomas advised darkly.

"You don't understand," I said indulgently. "His life has not been easy. He suffered for my sake at Warwick's hands when I was powerless to help him, and you yourself were not kind to my darling in the past. Let him enjoy to strut a little; he deserves it; and besides, he looks so handsome in a place of power; authority looks well upon him."

"I don't see it myself," said Tom, polite enough. "Beauty he has, yes, but arrogance of nature sits a little askew on one who rose through favour."

"And ability," I protested.

"Ability?" said Tom wryly. "The only thing we know him skilled at, to our cost, is jousting."

Recalling Wallingford put me in great good humour; Tom also at that time was mellow enough, and in my company he let the matter pass.

"It is no business of Lancaster's how I comport myself," said Piers huffily. "I believe I may be permitted a regent's privileges. Why not? Anyone would have behaved the same. It's not given to many in this world suddenly to rule England! If I am to play at king I must enjoy a king's prerogatives. And it was so good to see the Earl of Warwick on his knees, and after all, I granted his request. Why should he grumble?"

Happily I returned from France, the ship half sinking under the weight of French gold! From the side I leaned to watch the slow approach of Dover, the new Queen by my side, her ladies gibbering and pointing, and I in my good humour pleased to point out land-marks to the child and appease her curiosity as to her future home. I could see Piers waiting; there were other nobles present, to be sure, but beams of radiance spiralled forth from him alone, utterly obscuring the rest.

He wore a crimson cloak and mantle full and wide, fastened with a golden clasp, and oh! a dear little cap, the same crimson, close about his ears; and on it a wonderful jewel — emerald and garnet with a white cameo in the middle; I remember it because it pricked my cheek when I embraced him. Oh! How I caught him to me there on the quayside, forgetful of all else save that we were together! I held him in my arms and kissed his lips and hugged him to me, and the warm scent of his skin reminded me of times of pleasure and the promise of pleasures still to come. His eyes were dancing, full of love and laughter.

"My sweet lord," he whispered saucily. "Should you not look to your Queen?"

How jovially we set about to prepare for the coronation! That is, Piers and I were jovial. Oh, such a whirl of discord now about us, buzzing like a myriad summer flies, a constant background to our joy, the inconsidered mutterings of the discontent. And where was Arch-bishop Winchelsea? I wanted him to crown me, and he knew it; but he sent messengers to me of his illness and his inability to travel, so we had to make do with the Bishop of Winchester instead. However, there were so many good things to consider — clothes, banquet, celebrations — and, loving all festivities, Piers and I threw ourselves wholeheartedly into the process.

The table was all spread with papers — several of them Piers' designs for his coronation robes — and over them Piers sprawled, his elbows on the table, facing me.

Tom came bursting in, unseemly in his haste. Ignoring Piers, he said to me: "And is it true? Is he to bear the crown?" He jerked a thumb at Piers.

"My lord of Lancaster," said I, raised eyebrows, very calm. "Are you referring to the Earl of Cornwall?"

"If you choose to call him so," Thomas scowled. "Yes, even he. He is to carry the crown of Saint Edward and walk in next to yourself?"

Tom looked flushed and clumsy. The plum-coloured tunic that he wore did not well favour him. His jaw had gone to jowl, I noticed, and his neck was red. He was heavy in his movements. "Yes, that is so," I answered. "Wherein lies your grievance?"

"I would have expected to bear the crown myself," said Tom, as if explaining to a simpleton. "I am the next to you in blood."

"You are to bear the sword Curtana," I said. "Had you heard that also?"

"I would have liked the crown," said Thomas, sullen but appeased.

Piers sniggered pointedly, and Tom, reflecting on what he had just said, looked momentarily discomfited.

"You understand me, Edward," he continued carefully. "It is important that at the coronation no one is seen to be slighted. The eyes of the known world will be on us. We must tread daintily. You do understand this, and does the Earl of Cornwall" — he said this with ironic emphasis — "understand it also?"

"Walking daintily?" laughed Piers. "Yes, I have always done so. I am famous for the elegance of my bearing." He flicked a dazzling glance at Thomas. "Can the same be said of you, my lord?"

Tom drew in his breath with a sharp suck, and said as he left the room: "Edward, I have sworn to be your man and true to you. But as God is my witness, those whose company you keep would try the patience of a man more steeped in sanctity than I!"

"Regard him," said I fondly to Elizabeth. "He is as perfect as a man might be; yet I have heard only grumblings and hostility towards him."

I sat in a chair by the glowing hearth, Perot on a low stool beside me, leaning against my thigh. I parted the thick black curls at the nape of his neck, and fondled the smooth skin beneath, and bent my head and kissed it. Piers sat comfortably, accepting all my adoration placidly. Beyond us in the shadows, Richard Rhymer played his crwth, and Bruno and Swift, my wolfhounds, dozed, all legs, and snoring slightly in a warm contentment.

"No one has, I believe, questioned the Earl of Cornwall's visible attributes," said my sister, walking up and down, her skirts twitching on the flagstones. "What they have taken against is that he is here at all!"

"But he has always been here!" I laughed. "Always by my side, since we were boys together, and in Scotland in the wars...he is no new star sudden risen."

"And yet that is exactly how he does appear," said she, pausing now, and contemplating us. "My husband says that you were ever thus, touching hands and lips, looking into each other's eyes and such, but that it was more tolerable on the march — he says these things are habitual when men are far from home and may be shrugged off as camaraderie. And of course at Langley it was hidden. Now suddenly you are much on show, as players on a little stage — we all are, of necessity, enclosed here at Westminster, all together, awaiting the crowning. What kind of king have we, ask the folk? They study you — and they see Piers. Always Piers. They see you touching him. And let me tell you, Ned, were he a woman, they would still feel irritation. It is a truth that no one likes to sit and see two lovers fondle continually in a place where all can see. I don't know why it is, but after a while it sets the teeth on edge in an observer. And you, you are inseparable. Why, I have even heard it said: there are two kings!"

"And so there are!" I cried and ruffled his hair. "He is myself, and I am him." Piers carefully tidied his tousled locks.

"No, Edward," said my sister patiently. "Fool's talk is not appropriate. You are Plantagenet and will become the Lord's Anointed. The Earl of Cornwall is another being, and he is very much in the way. I shall say it to his face, since if I wish to speak with you, Ned, I must speak with him also, you never being apart."

"Edward! I shall quit the country; I shall go beyond the seas," said Piers, jumping up, and looking mortified. "I am a burden to you."

"You are not," I said comfortably. "Sit down; your place is here with me. " Piers sat, and once again I put my hand on his shoulder soothingly, and wove my fingers back into his hair.

"It's bad policy, that's all," Elizabeth said, taking no notice. "If you had — God forbid — so singled out the Earl of Arundel or Surrey, the hostility would be directed towards them. Give your favours out, one here, one there, and keep all well content."

"Rule instead of me," I laughed. "You are the better fitted. The Earl of Cornwall and myself shall find a little hermitage and there live out a life of peace and love, with minstrels our companions. A hermitage about as big as Langley, with a good stable and good hounds!"

My sister disentangled my fingers from Piers' hair and held both my hands in hers. She looked me in the eyes. "When will you be serious, Ned? Your pleasure in Piers' company is that of a new wed husband to his lady. But Ned, you have a lady — a sweet young wife, and she should be the object of your but too palpable affections. What *of her in all this?*"

I looked at Perot, he at me, and we both shrugged and laughed.

What of her? She was a child. A little sharp-faced pretty child, surrounded by her ladies as the centre of a flower is by its petals. I had already ascertained she could not bear the sound of the crwth and thought the Welsh savages; she was frightened of my dogs; she did not want to see my horses; she found England cold and would not step out of doors, but sat and conversed with her kinsfolk, here for the coronation. All we so far had in common was a love of finery. The marriage had been consummated; I had done my duty. Therefore what of her? She was irrelevant.

Piers kept his coronation clothes a secret; but the nobles were to wear cloth of gold. Would they behave themselves with dignity? Their voices resounded in my head: Send the man away; send him from our shores; if you do not, we shall disrupt the ceremony and you never shall get as far as the anointing. Peace, I told them, we shall talk of it more; this is a happy day...

"Speak the words swiftly," I said privily to Bishop Woodlock, "especially if you suspect impediment. Do the deed and let's have done and waste no time; do I but end the day crowned in the sight of God I care not how it's done."

Yet we were stately, Marshal leading the procession, carrying the gilt spurs, close behind him Hereford with the royal sceptre, and Tom's brother Harry with the royal Yard. Tom in solitary splendour bore the blunted sword Curtana, then came Lincoln and Warwick with the two great swords of state. Roger Mortimer of Wigmore, old Despenser, Arundel and Oxford carried in the royal robes upon a chequer. My dear friend Walter Reynolds, soon to be bishop of Worcester, followed, bearing the paten for the chalice, and John Langton of Chichester the blessed chalice.

All this while, Piers and I were waiting to enter and take our place, and Piers was carrying upon a cushion the great crown of Saint Edward. We were hid from view. He took the crown between his fingers.

"Edward? May I? You permit?" he breathed. I understood.

"Yes! But quickly! I can hear the queen approach." I put the crown upon his head.

"How do I look?" he whispered, his eyes glittering with excitement.

"I adore you!" I whispered.

Piers flashed his dazzling smile and carefully removed the crown. Within a moment it was back in place, demure upon its cushion.

My young wife and her escorts joined us, with a flurry of silks and velvets, a glitter of gold. Had she seen? Had that French encumbrance to me seen my handsome lover with the crown upon his head? I did not think so. I cast a terse forced smile in her direction and gave her my arm.

184

My darling glided forth to follow Chichester, and I followed, and Isabelle, with my eyes upon the graceful shape before us, Perot in purple velvet which, smooth and clinging upon his hips, swung in a wicked rhythm from the shifting contours of his arse.

And so, my fingers gripped about the carved gilt-painted chair my father built, the Stone of Destiny beneath my bum, the words of promise uttered, and the crown upon my brow, now I could breathe in some relief... Finally I was King!... I looked at Piers and smiled, and mouthed a kiss.

When I recall the banquet that followed, I see Perot in that purple velvet trimmed with pearls, his hair so sleek and smooth that every movement of his head showed undulating waves of light, his smile a radiance. He was magnificent. You would have thought he was the king.

> *"You go too far, sire. What of yourself? It was you that were magnificent, and let us not forget it in your panegyric of the beloved! Your father come again, they said, your father young. Tall, golden, noble in your bearing, you were all that could be wished for in a new-crowned monarch. Though you recall the gripings of the discontented barons, let me well remind you that the realm gave thanks that day and counted itself blessed."*
>
> *"Yes, thank you, Robert; it was so. But, near to Perot I could never think of anything but he. I fear I may have been... a little besotted."*
>
> *"Your Grace, I do believe you were."*

Satisfaction that the ceremony had gone without mishap, excess of wine, good humour, and the heady pleasure of each other's closeness, may have caused us to be careless. I know we paid small regard to the assembled throng. I know I had my arm about him, and my cheek against his, and our fingers intertwined. We drank our wine with arms linked, gaze to gaze. It seemed to us that all our troubles would be over now, for I was king, and as my darling said to me: You can do anything you want! A lifetime of pure pleasure lay ahead. Small wonder we were merry.

I was aware of no dissent whatsoever. To be sure, there was much coming and going, and some quit the banquet early; but all by me were well content — dear Despenser and pretty Hugh and Eleanor and Meg; and Edmund and Thomas my young brothers, now aged six and seven, a little tipsy further off; and Robert was in good form, fooling and tumbling, turning somersaults between the lark and partridge pies — in those days, Robert, ah! your hands and feet had wings!

The Earl of Lincoln stood before me, crimson-faced above his cloth of gold. He hardly could frame words, so great his rage and his embarrassment.

"Do you not see, sire? For God's sake, have a care — do you see nothing? Her Grace's kin have left the banquet!"

"Weary so soon?" I said in scorn.

"Weary, sire, of witnessing your pawing and mauling of the Earl of Cornwall," answered Lincoln, spitting out his words like undigested gristle. "As are we all."

"My lord, if my friend and I have given you offence," said I," you have our leave yourself to retire."

"You have monstrously insulted the entire French party," Lincoln spluttered, "all men to whom respect and honour is appropriate. What your sweet young queen must be suffering is beyond supposition. I can stand by no longer. I am here to say Your Grace may no longer count upon my goodwill. It cuts me to the quick to see our crown degraded so. It never would have been so in your father's day."

"This ancient song?" I said with a great yawn.

The Earl of Lincoln turned to Piers. "And you, who have seen fit to dress yourself in royal purple, so that you stand out from the general throng in arrogance as you do in effrontery, I tell you: Get you gone, my lord, in good time, or by Heaven you shall encounter those shall make you go!"

"What does he mean by that?" said Piers uneasily, as Lincoln waddled away.

"Bluster," I replied.

"No. Lincoln is a moderate man and has moreover the all-pervasive influence of one who was close to your father. What if I went to Wallingford and waited there for a while?"

"There is no need, my sweet. I won't be separated from you. Nor should we allow the threats of observers to put an end to anything we like to do. So if I wish to kiss you, I shall do so. Remember — *we can do anything we want!*"

And Piers received my kiss, in earnest of our shared belief.

In such sweet work as that, we saw, heard nothing; all was taste and touch. As we drew apart, Piers reached for his goblet and took it in his hand and stood. I watched him, and made ready to respond, my own wine at the ready. The Earl of Warwick, gleaming in his cloth-of-gold, loomed on us suddenly, and lunged across the table, seizing Piers' wrist, twisting it, and causing him to drop the goblet so the wine spewed vividly upon the whiteness of the cloth. Piers gaped; he was completely taken by surprise. He stood, leaning forward, his wrist still gripped by the angry Earl.

"I have watched long enough while you unman the King," growled Warwick, "and I bring this warning, Gaveston: if I am a Black Dog, look you to my bite."

They faced each other in a glowering silence. Then Piers, breathing quickly, curled his lip and smouldered with a passionate insolence, into Warwick's face: "My lord of Warwick, it would appear you wish to clasp my hand. Are you too coy to ask for an embrace?"

Guy Beauchamp flung Piers' hand from him as if it scalded his palm. He lurched at him and reached for Perot's throat. The table's width prevented him achieving it; and it became an undignified scuffle as they went down head first amongst the dishes. I screeched my orders — "Guards!" — but in the instant Despenser and Richmond were beside us, and, beyond the table, Hereford and Arundel dragged Warwick off. As he went, half hustled, half willingly, he called over his shoulder, almost frothing at the mouth: "Look to it, Gaveston! Look to your life!"

Piers, hunched over the table, his long hair in disarray, stared after him. White faced and panting, he put his hand to his throat.

"Ned?" he said uncertainly, and looked at me.

"Very well," I said. "We fortify the Tower."

Despenser said that we were close to civil war; I didn't believe him.

"Is it possible that so many would knowingly commit high treason within a week of our coronation? What would they gain if they were all in prison, tried and executed?"

"By whose forces, sire?" said Despenser drily. "What makes up a king's power? The loyalty of his barons and their armies. The armies of Lancaster, Warwick, Hereford, Arundel, Lincoln, these are what make up the strength of your power. You cannot afford to have them on the opposing side, or what remains?"

"Tom is for me!" I cried. "And cousin Gloucester. And Richmond — Oxford — and I believe I can yet count on Pembroke."

"Be wise, dear lord," said Despenser my friend. "Don't cause any of them to be obliged to choose."

And so we circled about one another in a dance of mutual distrust. We fixed for an April parliament at which all grievances were to be aired, and listened to rumours, went into huddles, suspicious, probing, making use of spies.

Secure within the Tower, but uneasy in its proximity to the city, and possessing yet my family's long wariness of Londoners, Piers and I made plans. I issued orders which changed the custodians of some dozen of my castles for men I could be sure of — Scarborough, Nottingham, Northampton, Chepstow, and the Tower itself; while the Cinque Ports and Dover I gave over to one Kendal, Piers' man. I learned that the barons were doing likewise in their own lands. I arranged for men and weapons to be brought both to the Tower and Windsor. All this while, the barons and myself made no reference to our business, but each knowing what the other was about.

Once, when I dined with Elizabeth and Hereford, the lugubrious lord said that the matter was a simple one: the barons merely wished to redress the things that were done before this time and the oppressive acts which had been done and were again being done from day to day to the people of this land. And I said: "My lord, if you think that is a simple matter, you are far wiser than I, for by God's truth, I know not what you mean."

"He means the Earl of Cornwall," said Elizabeth.

Certain of the barons sought audience with me at Westminster.

I was sitting playing chess with Piers in a window seat in an alcove warmed by the bright spring sun. That sunlight picked out every golden thread of Piers' sleeves, collar, tunic, and the glowing gold and amber of his rings. The sun god of the rising year, I thought adoringly.

"Sire, is it ever possible to speak with you alone?" the Earl of Lincoln demanded in aggrieved tones.

"What matter is so secret that it must be kept from the Earl of Cornwall?" I replied a little wearily.

"Then if the Earl of Cornwall wishes to hear that which is to his detriment, let him remain," said Hereford.

"I see you have not brought the Earl of Warwick with you," Piers observed. "I trust that he is left on a leash, well muzzled!"

"It was our intention," Lincoln interrupted, "to forestall the more public display of hostility which surely is inevitable when we gather for the parliament in April — by a few quiet words in your ear, sire?"

Warenne of Surrey, who was something of a lout, swelled like a frog as he worked to make his jest. "But Your Grace's ear is forever stopped by the Earl of Cornwall's tongue, and so you understand our difficulty."

Lincoln frowned at him for his coarseness. "In all expediency, sire, it is good if sometimes you should meet with us without your constant accessory."

"I am the Earl of Cornwall," Piers said with great dignity. "In my own right I merit nearness to the King. And I am one whose loyalty is not in dispute."

"Our intention was to ignore the Earl of Cornwall," said Hereford firmly, "and to speak to Your Grace. If you were to send the man away before the April parliament, we might simply get down to the business of the realm — king and magnates, with one purpose: the government of England."

"I urge it, sire," said Lincoln. "We shall never enjoy friendship with France while he remains so visible an eyesore."

"I have been called many things," laughed Piers, "but that one I strongly deny."

"They know you gave away the young Queen's wedding presents to this Earl," continued Lincoln. "They are beside themselves with rage."

"The wedding presents were gifts to the royal treasury, and mine to do with as I chose," said I. "The Queen is perfectly well provided for."

"It is the principle behind the act," said Lincoln. "Gifts for the Queen were given to your — "

"Bedfellow," said Surrey. "And they understood that also." There was a vibrant pause. Surrey continued sullenly: "So what? Why should I not say it? Your Grace is always looking at him in a lovesick fashion. And while you do so, you can see no other thing. We understand it — we have behaved the same with wenches. We may stand here and spout till we burst; we are invisible to you who see only him. I know enough of lust as does any other. And all I say is: none of us bring wives or whores to any council meeting."

"I believe I am as good a soldier as yourself, my lord of Surrey," Piers responded glittering-eyed. "I do recall at Wallingford I gave you proof of that, and will again if the lesson is forgotten."

"Surrey spoke in haste," said Hereford, a little nonplussed at the plunge into obscenities. "We merely fear — we fear — "

"So, Hereford," said Piers, still glittering, sleek as a snake. "What do you fear?"

"Your Grace," said Hereford, averting his eyes from Piers with difficulty, as if he thought that Piers would suddenly uncoil and dart some venom from his tongue, "it's said that you are bewitched."

"Bewitched!" I guffawed, leaning back.

Lincoln hastened to dispel the baldness of the accusation. "It does not seem entirely credible, sire, that one man may so captivate another to the exclusion of all else, without the cause be supernatural."

"But look at him!" I said laughing. "And tell me if one needs a supernatural aid to find him beautiful."

"My lord," Piers murmured in amusement, "it was their professed intention to ignore me. Do not encourage them to break their vow."

"But do you see, sire," Hereford said urgently, "if so be you were bewitched, you would not know it. This, I understand, is the success of sorcery."

"Well let me tell you plain, my lord of Hereford," said Piers at once, "I never have required the aid of sorcery to get me anything I sought. All I have ever done has been achieved with what you see."

"But then you do know sorcery?" persisted Hereford.

"My lord, you overstep the bounds of what is proper," I reproved.

"His mother was a witch!" cried Hereford to all, as if in some court of law he had proved some conclusive point.

"Do you deny it, Gaveston?" said Surrey curiously.

"No; I glory in it," Piers replied.

"You see!" said Hereford triumphantly — and patently confused. It was customary to shrink and squirm at such an accusation, and here was the Earl of Cornwall seeming to take pride in it, nay, revel in so damnable a charge.

Lincoln looked unhappy. I believed he would have preferred a plain acceptable denial. He was uneasy in these darker regions.

"And so, my lords," said Piers, and eyed them one by one, the sunlight dancing on his cloth-of-gold, "be careful what you do. I may call down Beelzebub."

"Your Grace, send him away," said Lincoln, plainly discomposed. "He works to make us mad. Let him be gone by April, and let us prevent our festering unrest from bursting forth in words and deeds we shall regret."

"I know you mean well, Lincoln," I replied. "But no one tells us whom we may or may not have about our royal person, and I wish that to be understood."

"We understand it, sire," said Lincoln with pursed lips; and they withdrew.

"Archbishop Winchelsea!" I cried warmly, with a welcoming embrace. "My dear old friend! How good to see you safely returned! My friend! I look to count on your support in troubled times."

He did not look as hale as I remembered him, the much maligned old man. My father's persecution of him had long ago brought on a seizure, and his face hung slack at one side, and his hand twitched in repose. Yet he preserved his pleasant corpulence and apple-cheeked good countenance despite infirmity, and greeted me with equal warmth.

"Your Grace, I bless the day — and look to give you that support, so long as it be consistent with my conscience and my duty towards God."

I smiled, and in uneasiness recalled my father's voice: By the blood of God, he sets himself to be a second Thomas Becket...

I later heard that he was dining with the Earl of Lincoln.

Easter saw my love and I at Windsor.

At that point we believed the barons were to come against us. My sources told me they were arming, and were planning to seize Perot by force. We lived in half belief, half disbelief. I knew they would not do it, since we all must live by law; and yet I feared they would. This precious time alone together must be savoured, every moment tasted to its fullness. The April parliament loomed close upon us, and would bring confrontation. Here in this fortress, let all time be still.

Time is a gift, spun out for us by the loving hand of the eternal — the mother goddess, Piers would say; the Lady who gives only good things to Her children. Time is the means whereby we understand the unravelling of love's intricate threads, and bind ourselves into that dear captivity.

I see the room at Windsor where we slept. The bed is covered with a crimson velvet cloth, edged with gold orphrey, and the hangings, drawn back, are of azure, flecked with threads of gold; the jutting tester, azure also, fringed with gold. Piers lies there naked, like a prince from Faery, discovered sleeping in the world of mortals, only to vanish when the huntsmen break the briars. His long black hair so fine and sleek spreads on the pillow, his arms slung wide across the coverlet, his hands trailing at the bed's edge, as if the fingers were in water. His eyes are closed in sleep, his dark eyelashes quiver, and his throat's arched till each pulse beat shows its throb of life's vigour. Smudges of black curls upon his chest; below the navel a line of dark hair to the lovely bush about the crotch; his prick lies dozing. Now he moves, and one knee raises, and his warm inviting thigh now calls my hand to stroke the silky hairs and rouse him. That fine pretence of sleep no longer deceives; his lips are smiling; and the rogue's awake. I fall on him, and silence protestations with my kisses, and tickle him from dignity till we're both laughing, rolling, limbs entwined, and his nearness so inflaming me that I cannot wait to place my prick in a more apt conjunction with his body, but must come where I lie, melting into sperm upon his belly; and he hugs me close.

Standing at the window, Perot turned and looked at me. "Why do you suppose that Warwick hates me so?" he said reflectively. "He above the others."

"I can find no reasonable cause," said I from the bed.

"I understand the strong dislike between men who are different from each other in their nature," Piers continued. "I can understand he finds me an annoyance, and I do provoke him, I admit. But to threaten me with death...even by implication — this is a very power-ful hatred. Why? What have I done to cause so fierce a response in him? Why not shrug me off as beneath contempt? *Why do I matter to him at all?*"

"It's more than I can comprehend," said I.

"Lancaster now — he dislikes me, but he has more reason, because I do usurp his place in your affections, or so he sees it. But if I were kind to him, I believe I could make him eat out of my hand. With Lincoln it's a straightforward irritation because we smudge the reputation of high office with outward shows of our love at inappro-priate moments; we don't behave as your father would have thought proper. But Warwick — I don't understand it. With him it is pure hatred, to an unnatural degree. But why? I wish I knew."

> "Sire, I think that Warwick hated something in himself, a dark root whose growth he feared, and Piers its outward sign; and he must tear it out."
>
> "Roots be damned. There's no defending that black dog."

"If I went back to Gascony," Piers murmured dubiously, as we lay in bed, "it would be for the best."

"That's not like you, to talk of flight," I answered.

"I find this place oppressive. We are in hiding, aren't we, waiting for our foes to show themselves. I don't like it. I'd rather go to meet them."

"Be gloomy if you must, but let's have no talk of Gascony," I shuddered. "For the best? How best? How could I rule without you? Rule?" I laughed bitterly. "How could I live?"

"I would prefer to stay," he smiled, agreeing.

"We are lovers, Perot," I said ruefully, "and you have heard the songs, the stories. Lovers always have to suffer. Lovers always seem to bring out jealousy in those who have not that richness in their own lives. I don't know why it is, but it has always been so."

We were despondent that day. News had come to us that Gilbert had died, Gilbert our childhood friend, companion in our escapades at Langley. He was our own age. We knew he had been wasting; even so, one hopes, and we were sad, remembering.

"After death..." I began.

"I never think about it," Piers said swiftly.

"After death, when we go to God's judgement..."

"I don't believe we do," said Piers.

"What do you mean by that? Of course we do."

"I know the priests would have it so," said he. "And naturally I let my confessor think that I believe it. But my mother's way is different. It's somewhat more agreeable," he grinned.

"What is it? Tell me."

He leaned up on his elbow. "Death is a boat," he said. "Like King Arthur's boat, the one that took him to Avalon, with Queen Morgane. It is transparent. It floats along the surface of the sea and then a lovely land appears, where magic apples grow. We eat of them and we become immortal."

"And good and bad alike are brought there, without judgement?"

"Yes. In death they become changed. There is no good or bad. The Lady cares for every child of Hers."

"And so, I suppose, the Afterlife so pleasant, you have no fear of death?" I said admiringly.

Perot hugged me. "No amount of magic apples takes away the fear of death. It terrifies me."

All around the castle, now made strong by our defences, beyond the great park, empty fields and woodlands stretched away, the river winding, gleaming grey, towards London. Daily we expected that our foes would be upon us, blackening the empty fields with armies, bringing the woods alive with shouts of hate, staining the river with soldiery. Each day when we looked from our high walls, the same still fields, the same quiet woods stared back at us, a silence heavy with menace.

With that same dread silence clamped about us, closing us in on all sides like a vice, and our own sorrow working on us from within, making us silent each in his own turn, we lay in that great bed in one another's arms.

Then Piers said: "Look at us. What fools we are! We are alive, aren't we? And tell me, which is stronger, death or love?" and he turned to me, and kissed me till I knew the answer.

Chapter Thirteen

RIDICULOUS THINGS — they accused him of ridiculous things. And they came armed to Westminster, as men did to my grandfather.

Even as I fended off the hatred, I could find it in my heart to marvel at the work we were about — grown men, like yapping dogs, all barking like a pack out in the field; and we the country's government. What did it matter to the nation that a handsome Gascon lived close to the King? Whom did it harm? What law did it contravene? What business of the realm did it prevent? And yet this inoffensive fact had become so distorted, had so swelled and festered in the minds of the accusers that they could see nothing else at all, nor would be swayed from picking at it, scratching at it, till it must be cauterized or burst.

Disinheriting the crown? What did that mean? Removing the King from the council of the realm? Any councillor might come to me; I was accessible enough. Sowing discord between King and people? The discord was all sown by others. Making himself a peer of the realm? Was this not done with the full consent of those who now accused him? And, foulest of all, committing treason through the usurpation of the property of the crown. Treason, no less, and he my most loyal subject. Property? True, he now had lands, as does befit an earl of the realm — as did they all; and how were their own lands acquired but by the kindness of some predecessor of mine who knew how to reward services rendered? If kings may not give gifts to those that serve them well, I wonder they be kings at all.

Such charges would be laughed out of a court. Let him be tried then, I said scornfully, let these base accusations be proven! He is already judged, said they. How so? And here as fine a piece of casuistry as I had yet seen: The coronation oath is invoked, saying that the community of the realm determine law and custom, the which I have sworn to uphold. And who are the community of the realm? My people, as represented by these hounds that howl about me.

No armies came to us at Windsor, and when I returned to Westminster I sent Piers to Wallingford, well out of harm's way. My Queen, who might have been expected to support her husband, joined her voice to the clamour, saying that her father watched all that we did, and looked to find my friend removed.

"If not," said Isabelle, lifting her chin, and her little pointed nose thereby, "he will become your implacable enemy. And I do not need to say to you, my lord, what it will mean to have the enmity of so great a power as France."

I laughed in disbelief. "Do you threaten me, madam?" In comparison with myself she was so short of stature; somehow I could not take her bluster seriously.

"It is the might of France that threatens you, my lord," she answered. "A wise man will understand what that precisely signifies."

I did not fear Philip; therefore her hints were meaningless.

"I would have thought," said I, "that if you have some influence with your father — and I suppose you have — it would not be beyond the bounds of possibility for you to avert the disaster you foresee, by gentle persuasion."

I looked at her curiously. I had always assumed such to be the strength of the female. But looking at the girl, I half began to doubt it. Even in those early days, there was not the gentle about Isabelle. I think she loved me; I was assured that she did. To me it felt more like possessiveness. Close to her — and I rarely was so — I understood the feelings of the small craft sucked towards the weir. And now she spoke with a brittle intensity.

"Maybe I do not choose to influence my father. Maybe the fear of war with France is what is needful for you to act in the way you should."

"I think, madam, it is not for you to tell me what that should be."

"Who else should tell Your Grace, if not your wife?" she counterbalanced.

"We share a difference of opinion as to the duties of a wife," said I, carefully reproving. "I do not believe that they include the shaping of the policy of the realm."

"But this realm is mine now, since we wed, and I want everything that's best for it."

Mine now — that was Isabelle's refrain.

She all but stamped her foot. There was nothing endearing about Isabelle. I could picture her as an infant: but I want that gown, that pony, that castle!

"I came here to be Queen of England, Edward," she continued. "Since I was eight years old that was my destiny. A country of my own to rule. A country almost as great as France. I was determined England should be mighty, under my command."

I began to laugh. She was so puny. Under her command!

"Edward!" She saw my amusement. She screeched at me. "I will not be made ridiculous!"

I thought her so.

"Indeed, my dear? And whom do you suspect of finding you ridiculous? Who," I almost sniggered, "would dare do that?"

She turned away. She said between her teeth: "I won't have them laugh at us in France."

"Who laughs?" I frowned.

"They must do; they all must do. The situation is so ludicrous."

"Is it? I don't see it myself."

"No?" she snapped. "It isn't droll then, that you love a man and not your wife?"

I laughed dismissively. "Don't be silly. Your position is unthreatened. You are the Queen, my wife, with all honours due to you. You have nothing to complain about."

"You think not? I have heard of kings and queens that do not share the same bed, but it is rare for you and I to share the same castle, the same air!"

"Affairs of state keep me from you," I murmured.

"Affairs of the bedchamber, I think," said Isabelle, muttering, picking at her clothes, talking almost to herself. "I knew about that kind of man, of course — pitiable — beneath contempt — a figure to despise — but I never did suppose that I myself would be obliged to consider the matter closely. What must they be saying of me, at my father's court? Laughing behind their hands — pitying me, I who was so proud and splendid! But they shall see — I will not be pitied! No one shall laugh at me!"

And then indeed she stamped her little foot. Her face was pink and flushed. She turned and looked at me.

"Send him away, Edward," she said sharply. "Send that man away! There are too many people against you."

And even then I considered her irrelevant. I thought she was merely passing on the message from her father, and I guessed also that certain barons may have sent her on this errand, using her youth and ingenuousness to work upon me. I never credited her with opinion of her own, and as to her emotions, they were a pit I had no wish to delve in. For all I knew, she had none, save the fear of being found ridiculous.

"What would content you all?" I asked them in gathering perplexity. "Must he live quietly at Wallingford? Or at Tintagel?"

Exile. They all agreed.

I refused.

And so off we go again in circles of words around walls of obduracy. I recalled how my father had strode from this place — "The air of Westminster does not suit me!" — and just as he did, so do I. But though we quit the thing that so displeases us, it yet remains and waits for us, inevitable, to be confronted. And April turns to May.

Now Pembroke comes to me and tells me in a sombre voice that nothing stands between myself and civil war but Lincoln's tenuous grip upon the seething barons.

Joseph the Jew! He must have heard that Piers so called him. He would not have been best pleased. He was tall, much of my height, but his thinness made him seem too long of limb. He had a lovely wife, Beatrice de Clermont Nesle, daughter of the Constable of France; they said he was besotted. Perdition take the lady; she was to bear more blame than she would ever know.

I liked the man. It grieved me that he threw in his lot with those who took against Perot. Our distress indeed was entirely mutual.

"You know, sire, my unhappiness to find myself so placed. I beg you, end this horrible impasse; it lies within your power. Be generous. Listen to the barons. Although they seem to show only hostility, their anger is prompted only by their love of you."

"Reason with them, Pembroke. You have always been a mediator."

"Your Grace, they are beyond mere reason. They are incensed, perhaps unnaturally so. They can see nothing beyond the Earl of Cornwall's presence. I put it to you, sire — the time has come to consider the peace of the realm. It must be placed before all personal consideration. You see their implacability; they came into your presence armed..."

My grandfather, King Henry. *"What, am I taken captive?"* he had said. *"No, sire"* they replied, *"but you must banish your Poitevin friends and swear observance to our councils. Swear, touching Holy Gospel, swear..."* De Montfort was their leader... He was not afraid to fight the Lord's Anointed. My grandfather was weak. He ruled in name only. My father said that I resembled him.

It isn't so. They'll come to see it isn't so...

My fingers clenched. I gestured Pembroke from my presence. I said that I would give the matter thought.

It seemed to me that at this moment the best thing would be to call the barons' bluff, to take them by surprise by seeming to agree to their demand. They would find us dignified, amenable. They would, as a result, appear foolish, to have so frothed about for nothing, for taking fright at so trivial a situation. I wrote to Piers. He agreed. He said that he would come to Westminster and accept the judgement of the barons. He said the health of England must come first, and for that cause, and my wellbeing, he would go willingly wherever I would send him.

He said as much at Westminster.

Could there be any sight more noble, I thought, warm with pride, as I watched my darling make that sacrifice: himself, for the good of the land.

"I understand it to be impossible for His Grace to rule with the support of the great men of the realm if I remain," said he before them all, in quiet tones; subdued, as one who had much struggled with his conscience, duty triumphing over inclination. "And therefore I submit my will to the will of the people, and my body to His Grace that he dispose of me as he think fit."

The emeralds on his fingers matched his smouldering eyes. He wore dark green brocade, and a belt of silver with an emerald clasp. His black hair was as smooth as silk. I thought: how soft and vulnerable he looks, how slight of build! Hard to believe the strength of arm and shoulder that brought down his adversaries at Wallingford! I felt the earls must think as I did. This willow-slender knight, this Gawain with the lovely eyes, the dignified demeanour — this was no monster, threat to England's peace. Could it have been that they experienced some shame, some sheepishness? It seemed the wind was gone from their sails, the air from the pig's bladder of their pontificating. Their wishes, however, were unchanged.

"Within the month," they ordered.

"That is too soon," I countered.

"Mid June," they said, "and all his titles forfeit."

"Impossible," I said enraged.

"Accept," said Piers. "Do as they say."

And now Archbishop Winchelsea rose up like the whale of Jonah, and he whom I had reinstated and returned to glory, vomited his thanks: "And if he goes not from these shores and if he should return in secret, be he excommunicated, in the name of Holy Church."

We rode to Langley, Piers and I, amongst the hawthorn blossom and the melodies of many-throated birdsong.

Piers sang some love lilt as he rode — that irritating one with the monotonous tune it was — "in May I pluck a flageolet". There are so many verses too; I might well have lost my reason by the end of them.

"How can you sing, buffoon?" I cried. "It's plain enough we are ruined, ruined!"

But he would sing. He could have made a living as a troubadour. The way our luck was running, he may yet have to.

"Imbecile," I groaned. "You must see how it is. Exile. Excommunication. Threat of war. Complete capitulation. How will we fare? Whatever will we do?"

Piers looked at me and laughed.

"You'll think of something."

Our spirits rose when we reached Langley. The month was June; the woods were full of honeysuckle, and every hedge a welter of wild roses. Here it was possible to believe that life could be lived in some simplicity; and after weeks of wrestling with the many-tentacled opposition, mere peace and quiet was to be cherished.

One day we entered by the wicket gate into the clover fields where the new priory stood, a lovely gabled building two storeys high, made with the grey-gold flint from hereabouts and dressed with Totternhoe stone. In its church, perpetual Masses sounded for the souls of long-dead Plantagenets.

"I envy that same man that digs a ditch," I said.

We stood and watched him, Wilfrid, a worker farming Langley's fields, and one it was a joy and pleasure to observe for the pull and stretch of his great muscles. He would have been a little older than ourselves; it's difficult to tell with peasants; their faces, wind and weather-tanned, are dark and leathery, crinkled from good humour or from hardship — at Langley from good humour only.

Our Wilfrid had a head of tousled hair, chestnut-grey, the colour of tree bark; and crooked eyebrows sloping towards the ears, and a direct gaze that held much of the quizzical. He had hitched up his tunic in his belt, his big arse bending in his well-worn hose, thongs about his calves. His arms were bare and brown, and furry as a bear's.

When he caught my eye, he touched his brow, and gave us both a narrow gaze, as if to say there's some as don't know what it is to work; then he returned to digging.

Piers sat down on the grassy bank and extended his embroidered shoe. He leaned back in the buttercups; he wore rose-coloured silk. Wilfrid shook his head, marvelling as clearly as if he spoke, that one could be so indolent so close beside one that plainly toiled.

"Does he talk, your Wilfrid?" Piers said lazily, playing with a grass stem.

"Of course he talks, fool. But of essential matters only. I have never yet discussed philosophy of life with him. He digs a most exquisite ditch. I envy him his skill."

"In digging? It looks easy enough."

"Would you like to try it, beautiful?"

"Not me! But you, I think...?"

I took off the outertunic; I climbed down into the ditch. I took the spade. In palpable amusement Wilfrid stood and wondered.

"Sit with my friend," I told him, "and tell me if I dig as good a ditch as you."

The spade cracked earth. The crumbled soil came up sweet-smelling, rich with worms and grasses. The sun struck warm upon my back. I dug. At first I worked to impress my doubting friend, but finally I worked to make a ditch. How long I dug I hardly knew; but what I learnt was this: that, digging, all my thoughts were in that spade.

When, panting and sweat-drenched, I drove the blade back in the soil, and turned to them, I marvelled that in all that time I had not thought of earls or Piers or exile, or indeed of who I was. I was a man that dug.

Piers clapped and gave me praise. Wilfrid climbed down in the trench beside me and took back his spade. He eyed me thoughtfully, and with that crooked gaze, conveyed his comprehension.

But we got philosophy enough when Thomas visited. The purpose of his visit was twofold, I guessed: to convince me of his good intent as he waited for the confirmation of his Stewardship of England, and to gaze on Piers in his disgrace.

Ample opportunity had he for gazing. At my request Piers sat immobile while the portrait painter worked to make a likeness. Therefore we all found our sights directed towards Piers. A sunshaft lay upon him, as if God's finger pointed down from Heaven to show us where to look.

"Where will you go?" Tom wondered.

"It is not yet decided," answered Piers.

"France or Ponthieu must be out of the question, with Philip out for your blood," Tom mused. "Would even Gascony be safe?"

"I have no plans to go to Gascony or Ponthieu," said Piers imperturbably. "I think I shall become a sea pirate."

Thomas squinted at him, not entirely sure whether he were jesting. "I wonder at how well you've taken it," said Thomas grudgingly. "I did not think you could be so serene in time of trial."

"It's my philosophy sustains me," Piers replied piously.

"You read Boethius?"

"But naturally," said Piers. I did not think that he had done so.

Thomas spoke. "'Is the insatiable discontent of man to bind me to a constancy which belongs not to my way? Herein lies my very strength; this is my unchanging sport. I turn my wheel that spins its circle fairly; I delight to make the lowest turn to the top, the highest to the bottom. Come you to the top if you will, but on this condition, that you think it no unfairness to sink when the rule of the game demands it.'"

"Precisely," answered Piers.

"I hope that I may know your fortitude if ever I should feel Fortune's impartial cast," said Tom a little sanctimoniously. The richest man in the kingdom, the greatest landowner next to the crown, High Steward of England, it seemed most unlikely that such would ever be his lot.

Now Tom was gone.

Piers and myself lay in the long grass of a clover meadow near the river. The breeze brought scent of cut hay, and the grasses nodded and shifted above our heads. Pale blue dragonflies hung and darted on the heady air; bees bumbled by. We were completely out of sight; we heard no sound of humankind. Midsummer! Our favourite season...

"Undress me," Piers cajoled, and stretched his arms behind his head. I hurried to comply. I had a sudden picture of ourselves disguised, he as a lord, I as his servant, escaping unobserved, living in some deserted place, a little hut in a forest, unknown, unseen, vanishing like elves into the dusk. However many times I must have seen him naked, every time was new and precious. Now he lay amongst his clothes, nude in the grasses, with the clover heads twitching in the little breeze and the questing bees observing this new source of sweetness.

I kissed his throat, his chest, the little curls upon it, and I tasted his fine sweat laced with the perfume of the fragrant oils he used. I kissed his belly, nuzzling his crotch. My mouth closed on his cock. He spread his legs wide, giving himself up to my ministration, moaning comfortably, arching his back. I lay there filling all my senses with his pulsating closeness. He nudged me with his knee.

"To it, Ned."

Before he dressed he stood and stretched, and I lay on my back and looked at him. Knee deep in quivering grasses he stood there for a moment, naked against a sky of azure, shimmering. I ached with adoration.

Then he swooped and knelt beside me on his hands and knees and looked into my eyes.

"Oh, Ned. Whatever will become of me?"

The idea came to me in the middle of the night.

"Ireland!"

"Ireland?" Piers moved beside me sleepily.

"It answers all our needs. It's as close as France, without the nearness of Isabelle's relatives."

"Do you mean that I should hide there?"

"No, my love! I mean that you should rule there!"

The King's Lieutenant of Ireland left the port of Bristol with all ceremony.

"Grant me this," Piers had said, "that I may quit the country with some dignity and not be made to sneak out like a thief."

"You shall depart in splendour."

His vast household went with him: steward, treasurer, chaplain, chamberlain, armourer, confessor; clerks, pages, messengers, yeomen of the chamber, falconers, armed retainers, archers, yeomen, horses, goods and personal possessions. His brother Guillaume Arnaud went with him; and Agnes; and Matilda the washerwoman, and the women servants. And with the King of England there to see them go, no man could say this was a poor hurried departure. It ranked with many a royal progress. Why, it took three days to load the ships.

That is to tell it bravely. The night we quit Langley, we lay and wept floods of tears and showers of anguish, and Ireland, which had seemed so near, then seemed as far as Trebizond.

"As we sailed towards Ireland," Piers told me afterwards, "a mist obscured the horizon. The sun cast pools of silver, then pools of gold, which ran alongside the ship. In the distance there occurred a curious illusion, a long curve of gleaming foam as if the sea broke on a hidden strand. Shadows, that could have been mountain or cloud, showed to our left; we followed their course; with always a little ahead of us that pool of molten silver. I thought myself approaching Lyonesse."

Let it not be thought that I sent Piers to Ireland on an ill-considered whim — the man who governed that wild country must be soldier, statesman, captain, lord. Only the most able could have done what Perot did, and I knew it when I sent him for the task.

The year that followed was a paean to his rapturous successes. It was Wallingford again, acted out amongst the mountains of the barbarian.

News of the hero thundered to our shores. Gaveston's troops have won a mighty battle — Gaveston's army has subdued the wicked O'Byrnes — Gaveston has put down revolt in Thomond and in Munster — Gaveston has captured the outlaw who burned Castle Kevin — on Gaveston's orders Castle Kevin is rebuilt. Now they are building roads for trade and communication; now protecting Leinster; now restoring peace where there was anarchy. The Irish nobles give him their allegiance, and admire the fashion of his clothes, his courtly manners. Now the turbulent clans of the Wicklow mountains accept his overlordship; and now he is in Dublin, passing laws.

"My dear," he writes to me. "I am at Isolde's Tower. The walls are nine feet thick and forty feet high. A silver moon shines and the town is quiet. Your Tristan looks towards England. The dragons all are conquered, but the wound does not heal while I am from Tintagel."

"And so, from the very day of his banishment, you have consistently worked for his return," said Tom. He stood facing out of the window, there in the small chamber at the palace of Westminster. "But he must not come back! You must see that, Ned." Tom turned slowly round, his face a frown. "Ned! It was not well done!"

Thus did my cousin dismiss the months of labour and diplomacy, in which largely alone and through my own efforts, I had sought to convince all those concerned in this affair that they were wrong. And not without success.

My policy had been to pick them off in turn, one by one, away from each other, and with reward, bribe and concession, achieve my purpose: Perot's return and reinstatement.

Winchelsea proved a disappointment to me, and would persist in constant references to excommunication. Even for one who cherishes a belief in a Pagan afterlife, there is no joy in being excommunicate upon this earth; and it was necessary that this edict be revoked. Winchelsea was implacable. To think I had longed for his return from exile! He might as well have perished in Bordeaux. Fortunately, he was of necessity subordinate to higher authority.

The Pope, "for the love we bear towards the Most Holy Father in Christ" received of us jewels, land and castles. Encouraging us to take what wealth we might from the Knights Templars in England for holy purposes, he imposed a further vexatious condition upon us, that we free Walter Langton from prison. This we did, restoring him to his old bishopric and later to high office, in an uneasy truce.

"Bishop Langton," I said, a little uncomfortably, I must admit. "I hope that we can learn to bury our past differences, and learn to work together."

"Differences, Your Grace?" said Langton smoothly. "I was ever your friend."

It was his nature to be loyal to the crown. He might have served me well enough had the times proved peaceable. But I was to find him in the months to come a weak man, hesitant when I most needed his support, a spent force, fearful of the barons.

Meanwhile, so caring of us was the pontiff that he sent a mission to us, in the promotion of concord, and some of these men went to Ireland. If all went well, Pope Clement would grant absolution from the threat of excommunication; and he was softening daily.

Dear Pembroke went at my instigation to Avignon, with Richmond, further to convince the Holy Father of our mutual harmony. All was progressing very well.

As to my dear wife's father, here again the wretched Templars served as pawns. It was not good what we did, but we were not vicious, as they were in France; and if persecution may be termed gentle, ours was so.

In order further to convince King Philip of my kindliness, I made love to my wife.

You may well imagine the enthusiasm with which I entertained the lady at Langley, the place above all whose essence was Perot, whose fields and gardens, stables, woods, all spoke Perot, whose great hall was the scene of our first meeting, whose inner chambers, passage-ways and window alcoves breathed his presence.

I believe that Isabelle and I would never have been close compan-ions, even had Perot not existed. I did not like her; we were not well matched. She came to me young, and she was child-like, petulant and strident. It's not that I refused to love her because she was woman; I have given love freely to the women in my family, and I've known women that I could have loved in body, had they been mine to love — my father's young Queen when she first came to England, for example, before she took against me. It was unfortunate for Isabelle that she believed Piers' absence meant that she would replace him in my affections, that with him gone I would see her anew and could not fail to be enamoured. And yes, she was in a way beautiful, if you take her face feature by feature; but the soul that shone from behind her eyes was brittle, fierce and petty, and this I saw when she would have me see what she supposed her beauty. As for her taking Perot's place, the opposite was true — in his absence I thought more on him than ever. He missing was more real to me than she, reclining on her couch.

"We are lovers at last," she murmured, well content, it seemed, and truly it was said she loved me. She said so herself. She said that I was strong and handsome; she admired my yellow hair. She did not handle my body; all this admiration was conveyed behind the safety of the bedclothes. Then she giggled and said male parts were amusing. In her lovemaking she showed not finesse but appetite. She was in a quiet way quite terrifying.

When we went riding in the woods she turned to me and smiled and said: "I'm glad you sent that man away. You were under his thumb, Edward. Everyone could see that he manipulated you, and you were pliant in his hands. And do you know, I believe that he would have liked to be the king. I saw him, when he put the crown upon his head, your crown, before the coronation. He has dark ambitions. He could be a dangerous man, an enemy. Everyone says so. We are well rid of him. Now we can be King and Queen, as it should be."

My polite silence was received by her as my assent.

And in the evening, looking up from a letter which a messenger had brought from France, she said: "My father thinks I should have my own lands, across the seas, lands I may call my own."

"Very well, my dear," I answered. "You shall have Montreuil."

"Montreuil is not enough."

"How right you are! You do deserve another, one more worthy of you. I have somewhere else in mind...Ponthieu. It's yours."

I thought that this would raise a smile from Perot when he heard.

And there was no more talk from Paris of potential enmity between us. But the curses of the Templars echoed through the palaces of France.

"I have no animosity towards Gaveston, none at all," shrugged my young nephew Gloucester, Joan's son. "He's good to Meg. She's desolate with him gone. No, all I want is action. This is the first summer I am come to court and this is the first summer we have not gone north to fight the Scots. Grant me a chance of glory, sire; that's my dearest wish."

And Richmond: "My voice was never raised against him."

Lands for this pleasant pair.

It was not so easy with the others; it necessitated many meetings formal and informal; but time, that gnawed at my bowels like the legendary snake, proved also my ally. The days and weeks that passed seemed to erase the memory of what had caused them irritation. I speak of Hereford, of Lincoln, of Pembroke. What did they recall? — Piers as they saw him last, slim and slight, subdued and courteous, standing there in sober green, no threat to England's peace at all, but simply a misguided youth who had a little overstepped the mark of what was done at Westminster, and now regretted it. And here was I, to all intents and purposes, an affable and wiser man, pleasantly acquiescent and agreeable to all. Why, at their request I sent Despenser away for fear his constant presence should offend, for fear no baron might come to me and find me close with other than himself. What this perpetual affability cost me in secret tears and anger shall go unrecorded; enough that it be said I found myself full often pounding down to Langley, seeking Wilfrid and his spade, and digging half a field till I was calm again. For months my hands were raw with blisters.

But at last I even won the Earl of Warwick.

"No, I shall never consent to his return," said he, when I first sounded him out in the summer when Piers left England.

"But, Warwick, why?" I cried. "Be fair with me and speak your mind. What is it that so causes you this rancour?"

"Sire, you would not thank me if I spoke my mind," said Warwick, with a crooked smile.

"I ask it and demand it," I replied.

"Very well," said he, and toyed with the great garnet on his forefinger. "The crux of it is this: for all his prowess and ability, Piers Gaveston's a whore; and that he is a royal whore in no way mitigates his offence. And if it were a woman so displayed, so fêted and so lifted from her proper sphere, it would be no different. A favourite's place is in the bedchamber, and not before the public gaze."

"Even if your vile suspicions were true," I said without a blush, "which they are not..."

He interrupted me. "A different man from Gaveston — fouler featured, a man less free with waspish jest — might somehow dissipate the general tenor of distrust which he induces. But there is that about Gaveston which..." he paused and laughed, "...which, elegant and perfumed as he always is — calls to mind the odour of musty sheets after a night of lust. Certain women I have been with have the same effect. And since you ask, sire, it should be between us plain enough that such is not appropriate beside the throne, nor at the sanctity of coronation, nor in the council chamber. And therefore I do not consent to his return. I say let him remain beyond the seas, and let him stew there."

Intransigent, would you not say? But you shall hear how even he...

The matter of Perot was perhaps dwindling in importance to them. As Tom pointed out, there was a sea of heaving troubled waters rising, beside which Perot was of small account — legal issues, grievances, purveyance, imposts, matters of the realm. Now they could be discussed.

"Certain obstacles had previously prevented their discussion. No such obstacles now remained."

Visiting me at Langley, Tom stood pensively before Piers' picture.

"It is best he's gone from both our lives," he said. I wondered at the time what relevance Tom thought Piers had to his life; Piers never gave Tom a second thought. But none of us knew what was in my cousin's mind, did we? I gave a fatuous smile. Gone from my life? I did not think so.

Tom was becoming dreary. He would turn to me and say that we should talk of grants and prises and church franchises. We sat once at a table, a great pile of papers before us, clerks at our elbow. I sucked my quill and wondered what Piers was doing now.

Tom put his hand on mine and pressed it warmly. "Edward! Cousin! This is how it should be! We two working in close harmony, striving for the good of England; no distractions and no irritations!" He sounded incongruously like Isabelle. "Now we should consider the Exchequer, and, if I may say so, your household expenses. Ned!" he said reprovingly, but with a twinkle in his eye. "You're spending too much money!"

I fended off this patronizing patter.

"And then there's Scotland," Thomas continued briskly. "Bruce is stronger now. King Robert, as he calls himself. Young Gloucester's pressing for a summer campaign; it might be no bad thing — bind us in one purpose. We might discuss it all together before we meet in any kind of Parliament. We have to work together, king and magnates, for the good of the realm."

Did we so? What did I need of recalcitrant barons, if the Pope himself supported me? And on my birthday, Clement issued his papal bull of absolution; now there was no spiritual bar to Gaveston's return. Winchelsea was powerless and Philip of France was docile. I believed the barons were largely indifferent, and if there were dissension in the form of undercurrents, I felt strong enough to dam them.

"My Lord of Warwick, even you?" I said carefully. "You cherish no resentment and you will put no bar to the return of Piers Gaveston and his reinstatement?"

The Earl of Warwick laughed and shrugged. "The news of his return, though not the most joyful to my ears, will be received by me with equanimity. Your Grace is King; you may do as you please."

Capitulation! This, and the papal bull — all my efforts had born fruit. The way was clear for Gaveston's return.

So wherefore Tom's long face, his rough dismissal of my hard fought struggle, and my victory.

"Ned! It was not well done..."

"I think it very well done," I replied huffily. "Why are you so sour, Tom? Or is it merely in your nature?" I was mortified to find him so malcontent.

Then Thomas looked at me, as if he would impart some fact of great moment; then he hesitated, his face, of a sudden, haggard.

"Ned...there are things that you don't know," was all he said. Then he shook his head and made a sound of exasperation. He would say nothing further; and it was shortly after that he took off to his castles in the north; but Tom was ever unpredictable.

> "Sire, did you not think Warwick's change of heart a little odd?"
>
> "No! Everybody had backed down. I assumed he had thought better of his previous antagonism and joined with the others in the general amnesty."
>
> "It could not have been so..."
>
> "No."
>
> "Tom's ambiguous words to Your Grace then could possibly be interpreted as in the nature of a warning. He knew something, but feared to say — or chose to remain silent, for his loyalties both to Warwick and yourself."
>
> "It's possible. How well, with hindsight, we may make our guesses at what then seemed of no consequence."
>
> "I take it that your cousin Thomas promised to put up no resistance to Piers' homecoming?"
>
> "...I believe I never asked him."
>
> "You did not ask the Earl of Lancaster?"
>
> "Robert, he had been so long so agreeable. He was good humour

itself. All those months that Piers was from me, Tom was a good friend to me — companion, adviser — but we rarely spoke of Perot."

"And the rumour was about that Piers would be recalled."

"Yes; once I had the Pope's approval, it was a foregone conclusion."

"And then Tom suddenly went north..."

I did not give it thought. My own journey lay westward, to meet my love returned from Ireland.

Chapter Fourteen

AND SO, which of them did you sleep with?" I demanded, seizing a leather glove with which to beat him. "Don't think you can fool me — which of your pages did you fuck? Or did you fuck them all?"

"Enough, Ned, let me be," groaned Perot, laughing, running, half undressed. "I am not well — I was seasick on the boat that brought me. Oh, that Irish Sea!"

"The vanquisher of the mountain rebels brought low by a mere *mal de mer*? I don't believe it — excuses to deceive me!"

I did not care a fig for his small amours. Let him have them all, those pages, those sweet lads, let him have anything he wanted. He was right; it simply gave me pleasant cause to chase him and to handle him, to reach for him, to marvel that he was now with me once again, after so long. Our romping excited Bruno, who leapt up in happy recognition of our long lost friend, pinioning him in a mighty embrace, his great jaws panting, his tongue seeking Perot's face.

"Deceive you, Ned? Never! I would not dare. Oh, call him off!" Piers laughed, nuzzling him. "I will be devoured. What, Bruno, will you eat me?"

"Heel, Bruno!"

"Heel? In his case that means thigh."

"All your household boys are pretty. You choose them for their good looks. I know that you were tempted, far away from me, from civilisation. How many was it? One — six — all of them?"

The stones of Chester castle could never have witnessed such a scene in all its days, the noisy playfulness, the shouts, the tears of joy, of lovers reunited. Reunited moreover in a welter of dogs, for Piers had brought me back two superb Irish wolfhound puppies to join our merry companions of the hearth and field, and all must join the merriment.

I held Piers with his back against the wall. Eye to eye and breathless, we paused now, every sense alert and vibrant. Willingly submissive, laughing-eyed the while, he teased, provoking me.

"Ned, I forget. It cannot have been more than a dozen."

"A dozen! Could you not be faithful to me, as I was to you?"

"I was faithful in my heart!"

"In your heart? It's made of stone."

"No, truly. Feel it — put your hand here — there upon the nipple — ooh, delicious!"

I pounced. My lips closed on his throat; I sucked a rose-red stain upon his skin. He put his arms around me, and between his thighs his passion flared. I seized him roughly, pulled him to the bed. Bruno pounded contentedly along with us. I had to put him from the room.

Piers settled in the sheets, his face all creased with hilarity as I returned, muttering between my teeth; it is no easy thing to shift a reluctant wolfhound.

"Ah, Ned, you've strewn the sheets with petals," he admired.

"All the flowers of midsummer," I said appeased. "The waysides between here and Wales are now completely bare."

"Ned, is it true you took no lover while I was away?"

"As God's my witness, villain," I scowled, climbing into bed. "You forget, I think, that while you are not averse to fat-arsed page boys, I am your devoted slave. I gazed upon your picture, hand on cock, and that was all the loving I did these long dreary months. While you were adding to your reputation with a soldier's talents and the skills of an administrator, I was solely dedicated to the matter of your coming home. Working, sweating...digging..."

"Digging?"

"Digging. If you but knew the blisters and the back ache you have caused me! And all the little lies to Isabelle, and all the promises I don't intend to keep, and kind words to those I would sooner see dangling from a tree. If you but knew... All this, I think," I said, reclining back, my arm behind my head, "deserves reward."

"My pleasure to comply," said Piers, and put his face against my belly. As his tongue moved over the hardness of my cock I knew such happiness as never words described. He was here; he was with me; we had won.

Next day, my gifts to him were brought in, and were placed in agreeable disarray about the room — a velvet cloak trimmed with fur, a belt with bands of silver and gold, gold drinking cups and spoons, a dozen silver pots; a silver ship with four gold oars, an ivory box decorated with silver, an enamelled silver mirror and an enamelled silver box with inside, two diamonds and two emeralds, and a cameo in a gold ring; and a belt of pearls.

"This is all I could bring in a hurry," I said. "There will be much more."

Piers sat amongst it all, clad in his breeches trimmed with orphrey, his bare knees jutting up from gold and silver, looking at himself in the silver mirror.

"And they consented to my return?" he marvelled.

"Oh yes. We'll have no trouble now," I answered airily.

"Even so... I shall tread cautiously."

I laughed. "You could not do so if you tried; and I love you for it."

I could not take my eyes from him. I thought he had grown more virile in the year of his campaigning in the mountains. His face was suntanned more than he preferred, and yet it well became him. His neck and shoulders that so skilfully bore lance and sword, were sinewy and puissant, and his thighs were taut with muscle. He was then twenty-six, and I had been his close companion twelve years or so, and seen him grow and change, and always beautiful.

He caught me looking at him, in the mirror, turned, and smiled his dazzling smile.

"I will be good and docile, never fear. Polite to Lancaster, respectful to Lincoln, charming to my lord of Pembroke; and I shall control my wilder urges and not take the Earl of Warwick in a passionate embrace. Ah, what a pity that man wastes himself with women!"

"That's foolish talk," I frowned. "He has accepted your return. Ignore him merely; don't provoke him with your all too visible sensuality. You called him a black dog — and you can't even handle Bruno!"

"Ah, the lovely wicked Warwick," Piers wriggled shamelessly. "I know he longs to stand on his hind legs and press me to the wall and lick my face...and wouldn't anyone?" he added, blowing me a kiss. "When do I meet with them?"

"At Stamford, I suppose, when we are due to parley," I replied. "And they will make demands and I shall promise everything they ask."

"And then?"

"You know the way my father treated promises..."

We encountered the Earl of Warwick in Stamford town and our horses jostled in the street. It was plain enough there would be confrontation. With Warwick in his customary black, and Piers in gold, it was like the meeting of the night and day without the intermedium of dawn.

"Piers Gaveston," said Warwick cheerily. "If I am not mistaken, you shall go from hence the Earl of Cornwall once again, and some other titles more. I swear you rise more swiftly than the arrow from the bow."

Piers inclined his head in a graceful acknowledgement of a compliment perceived.

Guy Beauchamp curled his lip. "One step taken against the peace of the realm, Gaveston, just one step — I warn you, all your witchcraft will not save you from the dogs that prowl."

Piers put his hands together in a pose of prayer, and bowed his head as one who promised piety.

"My lord of Warwick," I said angrily. "This comes not well from one who promised peaceful intent. Your language to the Earl of Cornwall is insulting, uncouth and unnecessary. Did you not swear to me that you accepted his return?"

The Earl of Warwick spat out his response before he turned his horse's head and rode away.

"Sire, I lied."

The business done at Stamford, Piers and I rode south to Langley, and there passed the summer's heat in pleasures.

There was, down by the river, an old cottage with the thatch in disrepair. I undertook to mend the place. It was no mean boast, but I could thatch as well as anyone I knew. Now thatching, unlike digging, takes a skilful hand, a perfect eye. We had a good leggat at Langley for the shaping of the thatch; and I was a neat hand with the shearing hook; and while I worked, Piers sat about or dozed in the wheatstraw by the heaps of golden broom, and his page Roger atte Halle carried food and drink to us. The heat of August was such that I stripped off my shirt and worked in peasant hose with thongs about the legs, and leather knee pads, and the sun blanched my fair hair to flax, and browned my arms and shoulders. Any hint of cloud or storm had me working the harder; I wanted no rain on my creation. Piers said that he would cut a design out of the thatch to go upon the gable end, and, balancing on the roof's edge, I grinned to see him squatting in the yealms, exclaiming as the straw thatch pricked his fingers, whittling away, absorbed in making his design. He showed it to me, finished, and I climbed down the ladder to give it my full consideration.

"Do you like it?" he said dubiously.

"What is it?"

"Can't you tell?" he queried, frowning.

"No, truly."

"It's plain enough, I would have thought," he answered huffily. "A royal leopard. It's a compliment to you."

"I see." My mouth twitched. "Thank you."

"Ah!" he stamped. "You don't think it looks like a leopard."

I had to admit it. "More like a mushroom."

He threw it on the ground, and would have trodden on it, but I bent and rescued it. "No, spare it, darling. I like it anyway. Leopard or mushroom, it shall go on the roof."

Piers grinned. "I have not your skill with straw, my love. And up till now I had believed I could do anything. I am not perfect after all."

"You are, you are!" I laughed and kissed him. "To the littlest curl of the hair on your crotch you are perfect."

"Oh, very well," he said, as if conceding a reluctant defeat. "If you say so."

We slept in that cottage under my thatch, close to the calling of the owls that quartered the meadows, close to the river and the golden floating water lilies, and the kingfisher perching on his alder bough. A shack it was, no more, with room enough for our bed — a feather mattress spread over with black satin sheets and a coverlet of purple.

We swam in the sun-warmed water.

"I know, Robert, that you consider every river icy whether the sun shines or no, and Piers was not unlike yourself in this. He could not stay long in the water. I see him now, his dark hair like some strange and beautiful sea weed, clinging to his shoulders, and his glistening body moving amongst the finely etched bulrushes as he splashed his way to the bank, defeated, while I swam on."

"So you didn't get as far as Berkamstead?" he asked me saucily when I returned, with the horrid smugness of one already dry and clothed. He rubbed my shivering carcase with a towel. "Did any say to you, Ned, that you are the handsomest King was ever crowned, with the finest limbs, and," he pummelled it, "the most beautiful bum ever to sit on throne?"

"Oh, Perot!" I cried. "If only we could wish all that away!"

"Don't be ridiculous," said Piers brusquely.

"Oh? You like Westminster so much?"

"Possibly more than you do, Ned," he grinned. "But you would not enjoy to play at peasants in the snow, admit it, and you have grown accustomed to the trappings of regality."

"I can't answer you there," I replied, "for nothing can be proved except by trial. But in all honesty I believe I could be happy poor and humble, if I had you by my side."

"You would be unhappy then," said Piers and bit my ear and ran

214

off, calling over his shoulder: "for I'd not stay with you."

I shook my fist at him and squelched after him barefoot, and vowed to make him sorry for his callousness.

That night, he stroked my brow for me, my head lying in his lap, his fingers gentle on my temples. From time to time he bent and kissed me, and nuzzled my ear lobe with his stubble.

"Yes, I would stay with you," he said, "and trudge the roads with you, and hold one shaft of your trundling old cart, and heave sacks for you, and rub your cold hands warm, and curl up in the straw with you at night, and never grumble. I would do all that; I swear it."

> "But as you say, sire, nothing's proved, except by trial."
> "Peace now; I believed him."

Of course, we were not continually together. After all, I did have duties elsewhere, though you might be forgiven for supposing otherwise, since all the talk is of Perot. Sometimes Isabelle was at Langley; and Piers' wife, Meg, being at Berkhamstead, he would often stay there.

I do recall one time I took my boat upon the Gad and rowed by night, all night. The shadowed meadows lay upon my right and left, and wind-sound in the summer trees, and all the while the calling of the owls, the splash of oar, the scuttling of the creatures in the reeds. The stars of the Heavens lit my way, and I was halfway to Berkhamstead before I was aware of it, and still I rowed, and saw no one, and rowed; and near the dawn I gained the water meadows near the castle, and I walked up to its walls, like Gawain to Sir Bertilak; they let me in.

"God's blood, it is the King!"

"Oh, Ned!" cried Piers, appalled, admiring, possibly embarrassed. "You rowed? You must have been possessed."

"I had to see you..."

It was that simple; I had to see him.

He took me to the little chamber that I used, and led me to the bed, and here I slept.

By the light of day we all behaved as if the event were eminently reasonable. I commend sweet Meg, who made me welcome.

Would you believe these men were magnates of the realm, to hear them whine and howl and scrap? My hunting braches were kinder beasts than these. I did not think it lay within the duties of a king to pacify unreasonable clamour such as this. How may one govern in conjunction with baronial support, when such support is vigorously withheld? I speak of the York council, that is, what should have been the council, did the councillors attend, and not make protestations in the ante chamber.

When I appeared, with Piers beside me, clad in dark red velvet, we met such verbal affray as gave us pause.

"What, is he here?" Thomas cried, "the so-called Earl of Cornwall, this man that follows you around forever fawning for the favours from your hand? However large the council chamber, there's not room for myself and Gaveston in one same place."

"But you were pleased enough to work with me at Westminster, Tom," I protested reasonably. "This was as it should be, you said. All I require is more of that."

"You shall not get it. Men of equal rank may work together, but not with minions and bitches."

"You are all of equal rank here, Tom," I said gently.

"Not so; for some cling to their titles with a tenuous grip, while others are secure by their inheritance. I shall not come where he is."

"My views are known, sire," agreed Warwick. "I would go further. I would say that though my loyalty to Your Grace is not in question, when I see that rosebud that you wear about your royal person, I greatly itch to hack it off."

"No man may reach you, sire," said Hereford. "It is well known — if one would get a grant of land, a manor, pardon, knighthood, one must make plea to Gaveston. I will not stand for it, and therefore I will not attend our council."

Oxford and Arundel joined their voices to the general dissent. I hesitated.

"These people have made their position clear enough," said Piers. "Plainly they have work that's more important. Let us not keep the others waiting. You and I, sire, have the work of England's governing to set about. Shall we go in?"

I smiled. "We shall." I turned to the fuming throng. "We shall convey to you, my lords, news of the council's business when the work is done. You have our leave to retire, to hunt or play, or whatever it is that keeps you from your duties to the realm. Come, my lord of Cornwall..."

It was at York that Piers and I began to be pursued by calumny of a personal nature. Some songs had been composed concerning him, and some contrived to fall into our hands, and the more daring sung the words beneath his window — vile poison; I will not repeat them, even if I could remember them.

"I recall them well enough, sire. The first verse was:

I came to court and thought to see the King,
But in his place I merely saw his thing.
Should you wish lands and wealth and knighthood too
Give Piers a kiss and he'll get them for you.
From nothing he has risen to be great,
Let him remember other upstarts' fate;
Though handsome, rich and clever he may be,
Through insolence we may his ruin see...

There was much more."

"There may have been; I forget. Close your mouth, Robert. I don't doubt your skill in memorising street filth, but I wonder at your patent pleasure in preparing to give voice to it."

"The tune's so jolly!"

"Well, we may laugh off scurrilous ballads; the other was more dangerous."

"The rumours, sire..."

"...concerning our royal person."

"The rumours that Your Grace was a carter's son. Our King keeps company with common folk. While other kings lead armies into battle, ours digs ditches, ours consorts with thatchers and works with his hands. He swims at dawn; he rows a little boat. Did Longshanks ever thus?"

"Could I but have found the source I'd have had his head on London Bridge. I ordered the arrest of any found spreading rumours."

"But rumours, sire, are whispers in the dark."

"It seems the only way to prove yourself a true Plantagenet is to go north and ravage Scotland," I observed with cynicism. So that was what we did.

Piers and I believed a Scottish war the most appropriate course of action at this point. He was always one for deeds. Fighting in a just cause pleased him and well suited him, bringing all his soldierly qualities to the fore; he was a leader of men.

"I have in mind that Scotland shall be all for you that Ireland was," I said to him at Christmas, which we spent at Langley, while the snow fell. "It's well known how bravely you acquit yourself in Ireland."

It was one of those pleasant occasions when Isabelle had been prevailed upon to visit Meg at Berkhamstead. We sat before the hearth in my bedchamber, dogs sprawled about us.

"If we could only do the same with Scotland, your reputation would be made. Your position would be unassailable. We might arrange for you to be Lieutenant there, but with more powers than Pembroke had. Success in Scotland, eh? If we two could together achieve what my sweet father strove all his life to do and failed, we would be invincible."

"You're right," said Piers. "And why not? I believe it possible."

I hugged him. "In your company I believe all things possible."

And it was true. Perot had even softened Isabelle's bad humour.

As if through a richly-coloured window, gilded over with the intricacy of its perfection I see that Christmas, with its shifting scenes of great contentment.

We had a visit from Italian musicians to augment and diversify our music making; we learnt new songs at their direction. We lit a bonfire in a glade in Langley Woods and dressed in deer hides and antlers to celebrate old Yule, and a Green Man from the village led us, covered in boughs and berries, prickled by holly, and we knelt to him in the snow by the rising of the moon. We rode amongst the woodlands, with our furs about us, and our falcons on our wrists, and the trees and pathways white and glistening. We heard the wolves that howled in the dark places. We threw stones in the frozen river to see the ice crack. We sat up all night in the stables with the horse which had the strangles, a candle glowing in the straw; the horse recovered.

In the great hall there was dancing; and such was Perot's glamour that he bewitched even Isabelle, and danced with her and paid her compliments, and I half believed she credited him with desire for her — she was very vain — and certainly she mellowed to hi.n in the torchlight.

There were games — the silly one with the bees' antennae, where you sit in a circle and the bee bobs his head, and you mustn't let the antennae touch you; and where each is an animal and one is blindfold, and the captured one makes his animal's noise. I believe it due entirely to Piers' presence that the festivities caused us such delight; laughing and singing was the way of it. And he and I together, on the furs beside the hearth in the bedchamber when we could be alone, the firelight turning his dark skin to amber, and from kissing it, the taste of sandalwood upon my lips.

We were full of plans. That ancient map of Scotland now unrolled before us, we leaned across it on our knees and elbows, squinting at

Forfar, Banff, Dundee and Perth, choosing where to set up our headquarters. We had no doubt that we could vanquish Robert Bruce; the question was merely how soon. There was that about Perot which promoted optimism. Scotland was to bring us glory, that much was sure; and furthermore, it would take us away from Westminster, where, as my father and my grandfather found before me, the barons of the realm were prone to bring their grievances and seek to turn them into laws.

A gutful of this now awaited me.

It seemed that while Perot and I had been at Langley, revelling in the bounty of the season, celebrating Yule with mummers, jugglers, minstrels, opening the hall to all comers poor and humble, sharing all we had, and dancing, drinking, dressing up and making songs — it seemed that while we had been doing this, the rest of all mankind had been whispering in corners, plotting, making lists, and waiting like the demons at the Day of Judgement to pounce upon us with the forks of their hostility at the Parliament in February.

Méchant they were — that is, without song. Unable to enjoy, unperceiving of the sweeter things, inimical to love expressed. They broke the result of their deliberations to us in the persona of the Earl of Lincoln.

He was short of breath now when he spoke, and so unwieldy in his movements that I sat him down, concerned that his legs might buckle from the weight.

"My intention is to forestall a scene of violence and danger," he said.

"You are to be commended then," I said drily. "A noble aim, would you not say, my Lord of Cornwall?"

"We cannot but admire the Earl wholeheartedly in this instance," Piers agreed, elaborately impressed.

"Sire, hear me out." No easy matter, with the pauses and the puffings and the dabbings of his brow. I did so, not much relishing the substance of his speech.

"For his own safety, sire, the Earl of Cornwall must not come to Parliament. Your Grace recalls the difficulties we encountered at York? The matter now is worse."

"Thank you for your warning," I replied. "The Earl of Cornwall stays with me."

"I have no fear of anything that Lancaster and Warwick may devise," said Piers, "and am well able to defend myself."

"Lancaster and Warwick," said the Earl of Lincoln, "together with every other, all promise to bear arms if you, my lord, come to the chamber. What, would you provoke a brawl or worse, when we should govern?"

"I provoke?" cried Piers enraged. "As God sees us, let Him judge who provokes!"

The Earl of Lincoln turned to me, ignoring Piers. "Edward!" said he, in a different manner, warm, beseeching. "If you love him..."

"You presume..." I gasped.

"If you love him, as you say you do," the unrepentant Earl persisted, "send him from this place. My fragile hold is all that lies between him and their anger."

"We refuse," said Piers at once.

"No," I said, putting my hand on his arm. "No, I must think on this. This good Earl's argument persuades me more than threat or clamour. My Lord of Lincoln, I may have news for you to carry to the earls; but go now..."

"Ah, no, Edward, I won't be packed off out of the way," Piers spluttered, much offended. "They will think I am afraid of them."

"They've never accused you of fear, come now," I remarked with a laugh. "It is your lack of fear to which they take exception."

"May I perhaps make some speech before them, saying that I go unwillingly, if I do go?"

"I see it now — as an infant you were forbidden to play with fire, and now you can't resist it!"

"I have my reputation to consider, and my pride."

"And I your safety!"

Piers gave an expressive snort. "What can they do to me?"

"I understand they have in mind perpetual banishment. Piers, I can't go through all that again, the grovelling and whingeing and concessions in order to achieve your reinstatement. If you are by my side — where God knows you should be if there were any justice in the world — there will be confrontation. All the old issues will be raked up — Winchelsea will sing his song of excommunication and that's a timeless chant I'd sooner do without. Rather than bring matters to a head, I would prefer to sidestep; it's so much easier. For my sake, quietly disappear."

"We play into their hands," Piers protested.

"My love, we're different in our natures, you and I. You're such a fighter — this indignant streak that makes you want to win at all you do — small wonder it was you victorious at Wallingford. If anyone goads, you answer back in kind and worse. And if your words offend, you laugh and shrug, uncaring."

"If I were different, I would be less myself."

"I know it. But in this instance, please be ruled by me."

"What, like a good little subject?" he said irritably.

"Yes, for once!" I laughed. "I'll deal with this in my own way, and you'll find that once it's done, there'll be clear roads ahead, and Scotland waiting, and the chance of glory."

Piers dropped upon one knee, his hand upon his heart. "Sire, I am yours. Do with me as you will."

However insincere my love's surrender, it was entirely charming, and it melted me. I raised him to me in a strong embrace, and felt his lean hard body all the length of mine.

"Where shall I go?" he murmured in my neck.

"I create you Keeper of Nottingham castle. Take with you whom you will, and wait there till I send for you. Believe me, it will not be long."

It was February when I met with my nobles and they had their say.

I dismissed their demands as gibberish. Seemingly, I was led by evil counsel — I had squandered the vast fortune left to me by my father — I had lost Scotland — I had extorted and squandered. And the remedy for such monstrous ills as these? Ah the surprise of it! — reform. And under whose direction? Who but themselves!

Their plan was that a select council should be created to ordain reforms and right the general wrongs; they had it well prepared in fine detail. I would have added that all was done with the greatest respect, had it not been that they pursued their points home by appearing armed at Westminster, fearing, as they said, for their own safety.

And who were these ordainers? Well, my cousin Thomas for a start, and the Earls of Warwick, Gloucester, Hereford, Lincoln, Richmond, Arundel and Pembroke; and loud-voiced Winchelsea and a crew of bishops, and a smattering of other folk, these they were who set about to keep an eye upon the King about his lawful business.

I had nothing but contempt for their manoeuvres, and since it was plain that we were to play at games, I would join in with equanimity — I love amusements. We are not hostile, sire (though we come armed, like men-of-war) and we, the ordainers of reform, shall make no ordinances which shall not be to your honour and advantage and to the good of holy church and the people of the realm, as was sworn by yourself at your coronation. You, for your part, must maintain the Great Charter and protect the church's franchises, and give no gift except that we permit it; and we shall sift through the Exchequer and the Chancery, and see where the money goes. We shall work on this throughout the coming year.

Beyond the windows, beyond the cloudy skies without, I saw in my mind's eye the windy hills of Scotland, and I felt the freedom of the wildernesses far from Parliaments that would constrict and bind; and I saw the northern castles, grim beloved sanctuaries, and my lover's laughing windblown face, and we together riding, and the wide expanse of tawny sand that hugged the sea's edge. I thought: All this is mine once the business here is done.

"Agreed," says I and lying through my teeth. "It shall be as you say."

As I told Piers, my way was best.

When I decreed that all should meet at Berwick to join forces against the Scot, I knew very well that any man believing himself working for the good of the realm as a Lord Ordainer would refuse. It has been thought I showed naivety, requesting the attendance of the lords; that I was shocked and disappointed when they did not join me. Not so. I knew what I was about.

Leaving the good old Earl of Lincoln Keeper of the Realm in London in my absence, I went north, and the Queen with me. And I took with me the Great Seal and Exchequer, and when my Chancellor old Langton wavered, I dismissed him and replaced him with my good friend Reynolds. In effect, I took the government north with me.

I was joined by my young nephew Gloucester, eager for glory, and by Warenne of Surrey, whom I suspect was eager to be far away from Winchelsea, who pestered him with accusations of immoral living; I grant him lands and castles. The only other earl with us would be the Earl of Cornwall. In the summer months we separated to raise troops and make our preparations; and by the following September we met at Berwick with our armies. Our communal determination made our spirits high.

It was at Berwick that Piers confessed to me that he and those about him had been obliged to lay low an assassin. It was a Yorkshireman, a villain of vile degree, whose plain intent had been to murder Piers.

"It was his life or mine," said Piers. "These men will swear to it. He came at me with his dagger but the fool was clumsy and I had drawn mine and pierced him before he could close in. My men were on him in an instant; we dispatched him. It was his own fault. He deserved it. But I have not been easy till I could explain to you: we have done murder, whether we would or no, and we pray you pardon us."

"Which I will do most willingly. You did not learn then who sent him, or if he made his foul attempt from private grievance?"

"It was over in an instant; there was not time."

"Keep men you trust about you, Perot. God be thanked that you were saved."

Then we commit ourselves to warfare.

Warfare — well, in part it was; but mostly it became that deadly game of seek and find which plagued my father in his day, and though we flit from east to west and places in between, we had no confrontation that autumn. Certainly there was time enough to ride through the October mists with Perot by my side, and our beloved Welsh about us; and to laugh to think of the Lords Ordainers puzzling over the niceties of reform in some dull room, to the scratching of their clerks' quills; but we would have liked a military success, even had it been a small one.

As winter came on, each commander took up his position in a line that stretched from Roxburgh to Berwick. We almost tricked Bruce into capture, but failed; and after wintering each in his own castle with his own wife, we had achieved little, and so Piers took his army north to head off Bruce in Galloway. And then, while he was gone, news came to me of an event that filled me with despondency and sadness: Lincoln was dead.

I should not have been surprised; the old man had been in indifferent health, and far too ponderous for his own comfort for long enough. And though we had not been the best of friends I know he always wished me well and worked for the stability of government. I much regretted he was gone. I understood immediately the symbolic importance of his passing, over and beyond the actual. I knew well enough the Lords Ordainers fret and fumed because I took the Exchequer north; I knew that Lincoln's firm and kindly hand held them in check; and worse, I knew that Lincoln's great expanse of land would pass now to his daughter's husband, Thomas of Lancaster. My blood ran cold to contemplate the vastness of wealth and territory that would now be Tom's; it were not good that any subject of the realm so rivalled monarchy.

And as he must, Tom would be obliged to swear his fealty to me for those lands, and I must verify his overlordship. We would have to meet.

And what had I to show for my absence? Gloucester and Surrey were harrying Selkirk and Ettrick; Perot and Robert Bruce were prowling round about each other by Perth and Dundee, each looking for that great deciding battle. But while we sought open ground, the

Scot hid in the hills and woods; and there was no encounter. I was short of money to pay troops. I had a hornet's nest awaiting me in London. I was caught up in the same toils as my father. And I was not even with Perot.

It was my Queen who stated what was only too apparent.

"Edward, what are we doing here? My father sent me into your keeping to be Queen of England, not to moulder in an obscure northern castle. You and Gloucester live in a little land of fantasy, fending off the troubles that accumulate about you; and that Gascon goes prancing up and down the Highlands like some knight errant seeking dragons that never manifest themselves; and nothing is achieved. This foolish interlude must cease. We simply cannot stay in Berwick all our lives!"

I sent a message to Perot to join me and consider what to do.

Thomas Earl of Lancaster (and Lincoln, Leicester, Salisbury and Derby) came north to do homage for his lands. I waited in Berwick castle, with Piers and the Queen; and servants came to tell me Thomas was at hand. We looked across the Tweed for sign of his arrival; there was none.

Messengers ran between us. Thomas was a little further south and had set up camp at Haggerstone Castle. His messenger brought the news that Tom refused to cross the Tweed; the business was an English business and must be done in England.

"Make him cross the river," Piers said. "Does he dictate terms to us?"

For once Isabelle agreed with Piers. "The king must overrule dissent with his authority."

So there followed an exchange of messages, and more refusals and, on Tom's part, threats of civil war, neither of us giving ground; the river Tweed then taking upon itself an importance greater than it merited, the boundary between authority and anarchy, hostility and amity. It was myself that broke the impasse; only I, it seemed, could see that we were making ourselves ridiculous.

Accompanied by Piers and Isabelle, both aggrieved, considering themselves the injured party upon my behalf, I crossed the Tweed and met with Thomas, and received his homage.

"And, Tom," I said, "no more threats to the peace of our realm over matters which are not in themselves important."

"The principle is important," Thomas said. "And I am glad to have the opportunity to speak with you face to face, sire. You have been too long absent from where duty should keep you."

"Thomas, greet the Earl of Cornwall."

"As I was saying, sire, matters in London..."

"The Earl of Cornwall, Thomas..."

"I have paid my respects to Her Grace and to my lords of Gloucester and Surrey. I see no one here whom I should greet else. And meanwhile, sire, I tell you as your trusted adviser that you are required at Westminster — or wherever you decide to hold a Parliament. The council of Ordainers finishes its work this spring, and its results are to be brought before you, and you must be there."

"Must, Tom? Inheritance of land has gone to your head, and made you careless in your choice of language."

"My passion for reform, Your Grace, has so possessed me that I speak with honesty, and forget to sweeten plain truth with honeyed words."

"Common politeness has also been forgotten, Tom," said I, reminding him. "We still await your acknowledgement of the Earl of Cornwall."

"And I refuse to give it, sire. There have been changes in the south while you have been away, and it will become apparent to you, sire, that evil counsellors have no place there."

"Tom, what are you about?" I cried appalled.

"The good of the realm, sire; surely the same aim as yourself."

"My aim, at present, is to defeat the Scots," I answered carefully. I marvelled he had grown so bold. Was this what Lincoln meant when he warned me that his hand alone restrained the barons who came armed to Westminster? Tom must have read my mind.

"Without the Earl of Lincoln," he began, "your government in England flounders somewhat. The unrest in England should be your first consideration."

"The Earl of Lincoln," I said thoughtfully. "I deeply regret his loss."

"On his death bed," said Thomas clearly and with every nuance expressed, "the Earl of Lincoln directed me to free the people of England from their vexations, and to shift evil counsellors from the court, and also," he continued, "foreigners". He spoke the word as if contained therein lay every vice imaginable.

Piers stood in haughty silence. His hand strayed to the jewelled hilt of his dagger. I stepped forward, between him and Thomas.

"I never believe," said I in icy tones, "deathbed exhortations that accord with the intentions of the man who tells me of them. Thomas, you have leave to go, and learn meanwhile of foreigners good manners."

"Get me a victory against the Bruce!" I said in desperation to Perot.

"I'd give all I possess to grant your wish," my darling wailed. "What can I do? He won't be drawn out of his bolt holes. I have never seen a place that's so devoid of Scottish troops as Scotland!"

I summoned Parliament to meet in August. I ordered Piers to quit his pointless campaigning. With everything for his well being save my presence, I left him at Bamburgh castle, well secure.

Bamburgh castle — they said that it was Joyous Gard, Lancelot's home. How fit a dwelling for my darling! More to the point, it was a castle on a crag beside the northern sea, impregnable. The image of that fortress on the rock beside its glowing sands, its wild seabird-ridden surf, would never leave my thoughts, I knew, as with a sinking heart, I rode away from Scotland, south.

Chapter Fifteen

FLIES BUZZED in the rancid heat. Two of them settled intermittently on the rim of the silver goblet; I flicked them absently away, distracted from my thoughts.

What a vile place was London! The foulest and most stinking town one was obliged to set foot in! Close-packed houses, twisting streets, meat markets, offal-stricken gutters, smoke and stench,and worst of all in summer!

At Bamburgh now, the sea winds would be clean and tangy with the scent of seawrack and the flowers of the cliffs, the dune sand fine and soft amongst the marram grass. Up in that rose-walled castle, Piers would lean upon the window's edge and look towards the sea, towards the islands with the flocking birds, his dark hair whipped across his face, his green eyes pensive. I liked that image of him standing there alone; but of course, Meg was with him. Meg was newly pregnant. Did I feel resentment? I don't think so. Maybe a little. But the idea pleased me. A son perhaps for Perot, to be born in January, as they thought. I would stand godfather, give gifts.

Irritably I turned back to the scrolls before me on the table. The Ordinances. The legal means whereby to curtail the God-given rights of an anointed monarch. All that awaited was my royal Seal.

Forty one clauses for my perusal, and at the heart of them the hatred for Perot, the magniloquent language barely a disguise for spite and malice.

What a monster they created here! He had misled and ill advised me and enticed me to do evil in various deceitful ways — he had provided me with evil counsel — he had drained the treasury (of what? there was nothing in it) and sent money abroad (as everybody did); he had estranged me from my people — he had received lands and gifts, and led me into hostile lands, (our flight to Scotland) thereby putting me in danger (if we could have found a foe); he had returned from exile without consent (of whom?) — oh, there was more, and all too stupid to be credited. The recommendation for his villainy was that he should be banished to perpetual exile; and herein lay the full thrust of their venom — not merely from the shores of England, but from Scotland, Ireland, Wales, and all the dominion of our lord the King on both this side and the other side of the sea, thereby excluding Gascony and Aquitaine and any of our lands that bordered France.

Small wonder that I felt despondent, angry, persecuted. Small wonder that I felt monstrously alone.

"Before you paint a picture, sire, of solitude, we should recall that you were ever with the household and your cherished household knights. The Queen was by your side, your cousin Henry Beaumont, and the elder Despenser; the Earl of Gloucester spoke for you, and Richmond; Reynolds was your friend, and the unlikeable Ingelard Warley, keeper of the wardrobe, who was known to be his friend. Your brother Edmund though a mere lad at the time, was always loyal to Your Grace. Nor were, of the barons, every one hostile to you."

"Even so, these good advisers all advised me to give in."

"While it is true that Lancaster and Warwick, and Winchelsea of course, made great clamour, I believe the mass of those concerned, the justices, the aldermen, the knights of the shires, had no particular axe to grind, but merely thought they acted for the best."

"They would reform my household! What...control whom I appoint, and me never to quit the realm nor go to war without I ask them! They would organize my life as one would provide for an idiot!"

"There was a throng about me... But without Perot I was alone."

My cousin Thomas sat down opposite me.

"I wonder you dare show your face, Tom," I said grimly, looking up from the papers at my elbow.

"Bellowing at each other across a council chamber is not perhaps the best way to promote harmony between us," Tom agreed with a little grudging smile.

"Or across the river Tweed," I said. "A bull would envy you, Tom, the strength of your bellowing."

"Then quietly, Ned, as cousins, as we have done in the past... I come to you in friendship."

I pursed my lips, and gestured to the Ordinances. "Do I not see your hand in this?"

"You do. And if you could but read it with detachment, you would see that everything contained therein is for the best. For instance, the Florentine bankers, Ned, to whom you are in debt...these have to go."

"The crown has always used them, as you well know, to prevent us going cap in hand to Parliament. Why they should of a sudden be a cause for dissidence...but to the Devil with the Frescobaldi — it's

Piers you're hunting down, as usual. Leave him, Thomas, let him be; and you can have the rest."

"The Ordinances are a carefully composed piece of work," said Thomas severely. " No one section is more pertinent than another."

"Don't stoop to barefaced lies," I snapped. "I say again: cease hounding him and I'll discuss with you all that does not impinge upon my personal sovereignty. As a gesture of good intent," I added with a crooked smile, "I'll give up every Florentine you care to name."

Tom leaned forward, reaching for my hands. Stupidly I permitted it.

"Instead...if you were to give up Gaveston..." he breathed.

Lord knows how he misinterpreted my silence. He began to speak, quickly and fumblingly, his thumbs digging into my wrists. "This could be the time to make a choice, Ned. Think...think back...remember when we were boys together and how close we were...what might have been...how much we loved each other. I never wanted enmity between us. I want us to be intimate, as once we were. This could be the time, Ned, to choose wisely; to choose what's best for England, for the community of the realm. A new beginning. I can help you. Make a choice, Ned. Cast him away. I am stability; I am the voice of the people, and the barons of the old blood. Make a choice — choose what I stand for — any other choice means anarchy and chaos!"

His face was tense, lardy with sweat. His eyes were bright, expectant. I swear he thought to get a good response. I looked at him as if he were a halfwit, barely meriting reply.

"Between you and he," I said, "there is no choice."

His grip on my wrists hardened, then as suddenly he let me go. His face twitched.

"Remember this," he said, as he stood up. "I came to you in peace. I warned you. If there is trouble now, you are the cause."

He went from me, and I was left with my heap of documents, flicking the flies.

Two months later, from the constant haranguing, rumour spreading, gathering of armed retainers in the city, I was persuaded in my mind that there would be some form of civil war if no way out of this impasse could be achieved. I took the only course; I set my seal upon the Ordinances, which were then proclaimed about the land. My capitulation was political; I assumed that in the tradition of the monarchs of my family, I would find means to wriggle clear, that time would aid us, and some way out of the difficulty would be found, once the flames of ill feeling had died down. A tried and trusted remedy.

"Gaveston must come south," they insisted.

"He cannot; it is not convenient."

"He must. He must hear what is ordained."

"It is not convenient. The Countess is with child."

"Oh!" chortled Arundel, working his pea brain to make a jest. "By immaculate conception?"

"If he does not make the journey of his own accord," said Warwick, "he will be fetched."

Archbishop Winchelsea said: "Your Grace agrees to his permanent exile. He must be gone from England by November. Failure to observe the Ordinances will result in excommunication. Your Grace agrees."

Promises made under duress are no promises at all. I set about to issue letters of safe conduct for Piers to travel south. At least I would have sight of him.

"I've no intention of standing before them like a man on trial," Piers said haughtily. "Nor of hearing accusations read, none proven. I have never found these people worthy of respect and now do they set themselves up as judges. God's soul, I have done nothing wrong! They know it well enough. These things they say about me are beneath contempt. I've never been ambitious for lands and titles. It was enough to be with you and share your life. All you've given me has been given through your generosity, not through my greed. And on such paltry charges which are plainly made from jealousy and spite, must I go travelling?"

"I'm sorry," I said stupidly. "I couldn't think what else to do."

"It isn't fair!" he said, and stamped his foot.

He sounded like a little boy. I put my arms around him. This small room was for a moment haven to us. It was almost November, very dark and dim without, the candles flaring in the wind draughts, the fire burning low. Brightest in the room was Perot, in white and gold, tricked out with orphrey and gold thread. He gleamed as he moved, and now he shook free of my embrace and strode about. "It isn't right," he reiterated. "I spend more time away from you than with you. It shouldn't be like this. What can we do? There must be something."

"I don't know... I must think..."

"Well, soon, please, Edward," he said pettishly. "I'm tired of scudding to and fro, now here, now there, on the whim of men who should be subservient to you. Why were you not more forceful? Why do you permit them so much power?"

"You do no good to either of us to censure me," I said stung. "I did what was best for the general good."

"And what about the good of Gaveston?" he blazed.

"God's teeth, but you are selfish," I flared back.

"I must look after myself, it seems," he scowled, "since you cannot. Or will not."

"That's a foul accusation — and from you who say you are my friend."

"I am your friend, though much good may it do me."

"You've had good aplenty from my hand."

"And lost it again. Am I not plain Gaveston again by reason of the Lords Ordainers? Why is it other earls are earls as if the earldom came like skin and hair growing upon them, and mine is like a little hat that comes on and off at whim? Oh! You think that's droll, do you? I assure you it's not so, and if I had my way..."

He stopped, hearing a commotion at the door; we turned to look. The door swung open with a crash, and brought into our presence Hereford and Warwick and my cousin Tom, with Pembroke, Arundel and Winchelsea lurking behind.

"And did I summon you, my lords?" I seethed.

"Peace, Your Grace," said Hereford. "Our quarrel is not with you. But there is no way we may speak with him save in Your Grace's presence."

"The Earl of Cornwall has no business with you," I replied.

"We see no earl; our business is with Gaveston," said Warwick, prowling forward. "We heard he would not come to us, so we have come to him."

"I'll hear them," Piers shrugged coolly, with a glance in my direction. "It's plain enough we'll get no peace till they have spouted."

"Yes, you will hear us," Warwick growled, "and not because you choose to, but because we order it. Now stand your ground and hear the Ordinance against you which I shall read."

It seemed to me that it had gone to Warwick's head a little to be suddenly so close to the one he had worked so long to topple. For more than a year those very men had been together closeted, entirely to pass judgement upon Piers, and had wound themselves into a mode of hatred from which it would be difficult to break away. They could no longer see Piers Gaveston; they saw a fiend created by their own overheated fancies, as if in some dark place they had been brewing something in a cauldron, adding the odd dead rat, the bat dropping, the lice-infested liver, all to summon up the vilest thing they could imagine, and now it stood before them in all its superhuman foulness. Whereas in fact the opposite was true: Piers stood immobile, golden, like an archangel enduring the jealous ravings of Lucifer.

"Read it and have done," I said. "Then go your ways."

Warwick began the list of accusations, holding out the scroll to arm's length, like a player to an audience. The allegations unrolled — the evil counselling, the wrecking of the treasury, the accroaching of royal power, the acquisition of property to the diminution of the crown — the rest of it. Warwick paused and took a breath.

"Is that all?" Piers enquired with studied insolence. "Well, it was beautifully read, my lord. I love to hear a fable. You have a charming voice; do you also sing?"

I winced. I knew it the reaction most likely to cause Warwick to behave as he did now. He let fall the scroll, and in a swift and sudden movement drove one fist into Piers' belly and the other to the chin. I have never seen a man thrown back as fast; Piers lay sprawled upon his back. I ran to him, bent over him. He sat up blearily, his hand to his mouth, blood trickling between his fingers. I eased him to a chair, and he sat draped along its edge, his arm against his stomach, and his hand on mine where I knelt beside him, protective and appalled.

The Earl of Warwick hung over us like a raven, and with no break, as it seemed, in his harangue, continued. He was not even breathless.

"As a result of this decree, Piers Gaveston," said he, "your lands and titles are forfeit and you are declared an open enemy of the King and his people, to be exiled for ever from England, Scotland, Ireland and Wales, and all dominion of our lord the King on both this side and the other side of the sea."

Warwick hammered home the positive finality of the sentence, place by place, blow by blow.

Piers raised his head, the back of one hand gingerly against his mouth, and eyed the earl askance. "So many places where I may not go," he mused ironically. "And where may I go, my lords?"

"To Hell," said Warwick plainly. "Now our business here is done."

"And plenty soon enough," said I. "What manner of lout did you bring in with you, my lords of Hereford and Lancaster? Return him to his kennels."

"Wait!" said Piers, straightening up painfully, wiping his mouth. "My lords, I demand the right to answer all the charges you have brought against me."

"It is refused," said Warwick curtly.

"Surely I may speak in my defence?" Piers cried. His hand, that still gripped mine, was tight with anger.

Now Lancaster came forward, his pleasure in the unfolding of the scene clearly apparent. "Your guilt is proven, Gaveston; you have no defence."

"But what of justice?" Piers demanded. "The common man, it seems, has rights I am to be denied."

"You have been pleased to live your life so far above the common," Tom said scathingly, "that you receive now more than common dealing. And as for justice, for your crimes it has been meted out to you, by the consent of those who make the laws."

"Against the wishes of the King?" Piers said contemptuously. "What kind of law is that?"

Winchelsea inserted himself between the two, plainly disconcerted. "Come away, my lord of Lancaster...my lords..." he looked about beseechingly. "This is not why we came." He turned to Piers. "Now Gaveston, get you gone. Return, and by the terms of the Ordinances, you risk your immortal soul. There is no more to say."

The lords muttered agreement, and withdrew.

I jumped up and closed the door behind them. I was quivering with fury. I returned to Piers, who sat still in the chair, hugging his stomach, sucking his lip.

"I am not hurt," he spat, when I would minister to him, his denial unconvincing.

"They are brute beasts," I murmured, kissing him.

"Well, it shall test my ingenuity to find a bolt hole acceptable to the Lords Ordainers, will it not?" he laughed a little ruefully. "I'll tell you what I'll do — I'll take ship and I'll sail to and fro between the Thames and Tintagel. And you shall row out to me, and aboard ship there'll be a special cabin all decked out for pleasure. We'll make love all night, and in the morning you'll return to Westminster and perform your kingly duties; and then when you have need of me again..."

"...next evening..."

"...you'll return and I'll be waiting. Yes, that has much to recommend it. I'm surprised we didn't think of that before."

I put my arm about his shoulder.

"There must be those shall speak for me," said Piers. "I'll work at it...send to the Pope...I must be heard...so much to do." And then he ran his fingers through his hair and gave a wry smile. "And just at present, thanks to Warwick's sweet caress, I doubt if I can stand upright."

"Warwick shall pay for it," I promised. "And legally or otherwise, I shall not let them part us. Trust me...trust me..."

Piers sat up in bed, dishevelled and dozy. Roger his page in attendance sorted through the clothes that he would wear when he arose. I sat down on the bed and handed Piers his wine.

"Wake up."

"I am awake."

"My sister Margaret writes that she will be happy to receive you in Flanders."

"Well, that's good news, I suppose, if I can get past Philip the Foul who has promised to imprison me in his darkest dungeon," he said laughing. "It's no easy thing, eh, Ned, to be the lover of the King of England. One flits from one crazed foe to another!" He sipped his wine, looking for the moment supremely at his ease. "Ned, must I go to Flanders?" he said winsomely. "Your sister doesn't want me — how can she? I will be such an embarrassment at her court. God's soul, I will be an embarrassment wherever I go — the King of England's bedfellow kicked out of England by his barons in a legalised rebellion! And Flanders is uncomfortably near to France. Would I feel safe there? A would-be murderer from France could make the journey in a day."

"I think that my wife's father's intentions stop at incarceration," I said tersely. "Be easy. Margaret and John will ensure your safety in Brabant. And it will not be for long."

"I am too ill to travel," Piers said stretching, looking fit and hale. "My guts still ache. Send the ship away without me."

"You'll make your preparations for departure and go sweetly," I said firmly. "Or I shall set the Earl of Warwick on you and he'll hustle you across the seas thrust in a barrel."

Fools that we were, but we were dogged by humour and frivolity, and forever found amusement in the vituperation of the earls, finding them ridiculous.

On the night of Samhain we made a working to the Lady. We lit candles and made ourselves an altar and burned incense, and knelt and offered up our prayers. We asked for safety for all travellers, especially those who must go beyond the seas. We asked for Her protection.

"May the waves which rise and fall at Your breath be calm and steady, may the Gods of Going watch over the ship, and may Perot with Your blessing go in peace and soon return to whom he loves...oh, may he soon return!"

Our parting, on the Thames-side quays, was noisy, colourful and brave. A mizzling rain fell on us, everyone was swearing at the damp, their coiffures spoiled, their furs teased into horrid jagged points, and puddles ruining their shoes. We were determined to be merry. Piers, retainers, mine, in scarlets, golds and blues, swapped quips and rudery; our minstrels played for all they were worth, to the detriment of fiddle string and drumskin; and the small craft round about the ship came up to gawp and marvel.

Piers and I embraced and kissed and wept and pretended we did not, and joked that we seemed always to be making farewells at quaysides, and talked of when he would return. He had been busy; he had obtained letters testifying to his loyalty and good character, with signatures and the royal Seal; he lived in hope of stating his position to a jury, in despite of earls. I feared for him across the seas. Philip the Foul had taken prisoner the man we sent to put our case to the Pope. Out there in that wet greyness, nameless threats surged with the shifting waves. And more, it was November, and the seas were wild, and Perot would be seasick. Desperate as it seemed, the safest place for him was surely England, under my protection. What was I about, to send him from me?

We saw him aboard, and all those with him, and we waved, blew kisses, and watched them go; and laughed like fools to show how careless we were, how unrepentant, how insouciant.

When I turned my face towards London, I could not see its towers and roofs for the rain that blurred my eyes.

"Your Grace need never feel alone," Hugh Audley said, beside me.

Hugh Audley, one of my household knights, a man from the Marcher lands, black haired, dark skinned; he had a look of Piers. I put my arm around him.

"Thanks, good Hugh," I smiled, but I could say no more; there never would be anyone for me but Piers.

At night I paced the bedchamber. Whether fury or despondency was uppermost with me I would be hard put to say.

Isabelle, in her night gown, her long hair loose, attempted to pacify me. I flung myself into a chair. I put my head in my hands and covered my eyes. I felt her, ineffectual, about me, patting, touching, speaking.

"Edward...come to bed. Could you not put him from your mind now he is gone? It's finished; you must see that...it's for the best...it's for the best. We should be glad...at least we can begin to know each other, which we never could while he was there. Edward, I've changed since I first came to you, all unknowing of love's ways. Let me be your friend and your support. I can be strong for you...we can be strong..."

I half believed her. Her voice was urgent, low, like one that cast a spell. I let her raise me from the chair and lead me to the bed. I was so tired. If, against such odds, there had been conception from that night, it would have been a child conceived in desolation and unhope.

It was in the arms of Hugh Audley that revelation came to me.

It has often seemed to me that at passion's culmination there comes illumination. Piers had been gone but two weeks; and sweet Audley offered comfort, and the need for pleasure's sure escape had been too strong for my resistance. But he brought more — enlightenment. I lay, my arms about him, staring into darkness, seeing what I'd been too blind to see before.

This. I had worked to avert civil war. Civil war is evil. I had made my decisions based upon that premise. Piers was gone. And what were the barons doing? Were they safe at home, each in his own castle, tending his own patch? They were not. They were meeting, holding tournaments; they were armed. Now it is understood that tournaments without the King's approval are the means whereby soldiers gather, weapons are massed, and war games practised. I had been stupid and naive. It was civil war they sought! Even now they were preparing for it. They had worked to send my most able captain from me, and, like a fool, I had permitted it. They remove those closest to me, those most loyal — I had given them Despenser, my most faithful servant. I had been too tractable. My heart beat faster. What was their intent? Where would they stop? What must be done?

"The answer's plain," I said.

"The answer, sire?" said Hugh and nuzzled closer.

"We must confront."

"We must?"

"We have been too gentle, too considerate," I said. "That time is past."

In the early light of dawn by candle's light, I wrote a brief and secret letter and I sent it to Flanders; and then I made some preparations for a journey.

With a small entourage I rode through the November mirk towards the west country. We did not spare ourselves. I saw the sun rise on the downy mists that curled wraith-like across the sleeping fields; and watched it set in crimson-turquoise radiance ahead of me the way that I would go. We came to Cornwall.

I reached Tintagel before Piers, and therefore I had time to oversee its readiness. It was more comfortable than when we came to it before, through Piers' custody of the place — God's eyes, there now were

236

beds, carpets, tables, silver drinking cups. I ran about the rooms, arranging things, giving orders, making sure it all was well, and all the while with half an eye cocked to the sea, and every sense attuned to the first tidings of his approach.

"Let me know the moment you observe the ship..."

I was down there on the beach, my feet in shingle, my cloak blowing about me, and my hair half in my eyes and mouth, elation wilder than the waves upon the rocks possessing me. Late afternoon it was, the ship in the bay now, and the rowing boat approaching, flung like driftwood on the brine. I ran into the sea, drenched to the waist, and hauled Piers from the boat, and he half drowned and retching, staggered with me to dry land, and there we sprawled, like mariners cast ashore after a storm, laughing, hugging, incoherent. And when we stood up, then we flung our arms about each other, and we danced and danced, ungracefully, sinking in the shingle with each step we took. We must have looked much like those pictures of the ones who dance with the plague outside the city walls, doomed, ecstatic, oblivious.

I kissed him, weak with happiness. "Everything is ready for you at the castle..."

I took my Tristan home. How eagerly I helped him from his wet clothes — was ever Mark in such haste to see his nephew stripped? I daresay that he was. I sat and watched with hungry eyes, as Piers sat naked in his tub, obscured by steam. I dried him, put a robe about him, cuddled him; our servants brought a meal and wine. I had to touch him, to be sure that he was well, was here, unharmed and safe, here in this precious place, this secret place where no one knew about our presence except the ghosts of legend, who understood the workings of true magic.

Come the night, we lay in bed, in a room full of warmth and shadows. Replete, content, we talked a little, and made love, and fell asleep, peculiarly tired and drained, sleeping fitfully, waking to make sure the other was still there, and that we did not dream it.

Yet it was dream-like. Mist hung on the grey rocks, making land seem insubstantial. Surf pounded all day long. The moon turned sea and rocks to silver-rose and washed the shadowed sands with mystery, the sea a mere soft whisper. Were we in Lyonesse? — this place was not affixed to earth.

Every time we drank, the magic potion worked its curious enchantment. Though we knew the wine to be from Bordeaux and the cup from Wallingford, the sanctity of fable blessed it, and it was as if with every sip we further bound ourselves each to the other.

Down in the cove, we built an altar to the Lady who had brought him home. We gathered driftwood, enough to make a little fire. We left it drying, then returned, and found we had to send for brushwood; it was too wet to burn. The normality of this was reassuring; we were becoming more ethereal than was comfortable. A fire was lit; we drank and ate beside it, and gave thanks. I said I'd heard the souls of drowned sailors took up abode in the flying gulls. Piers shuddered and said grimly that no wonder there were so many of them. He was no mariner.

The fire spat and burned low. Piers stood up, dark against dark rocks, and ran his finger slowly along the granite. Against the noise of sea sound, he said: "Ned, we must have done with all of this."

"I know it," I said, looking at the fire. "You understand...I sent for you because...I have this crazy notion we should be together, at whatever cost. Even if...I mean, unleashing certain forces, dangers..."

He crouched beside me. "I know why you sent for me. You don't have to persuade me; it's what I wanted all along."

"But don't you know we risk...it will be dangerous...?"

"We're fighting for our love, Ned," he replied. "The right to be together in the open, not secretive, not living to the dictates of others — not running away and giving in. It's odd, isn't it, that something so reasonable should also be dangerous! But what else is so worth fighting for?" He looked around. "This land is Mark's and Tristan's; but we are not them. Our way lies the other side of Tamar."

Wallingford and Windsor have their foundations in more solid ground — if not in actuality then in terms of the world's opinion.

But in Piers' company as we rode towards them, I thought what magic clung about us would suffice.

Chapter Sixteen

WHEN LANCELOT saved Guinevere from burning at the stake and took her to his castle Joyous Gard, and Arthur was obliged to go to war against his friend, was the ensuing conflict a war of love or hate? Mordred led the barons — why? Through an honest disgust at Arthur's failing leadership and a desire to rule a different way — or through jealousy and spite, and pleasure in destroying? Or for desire of Guinevere? What followed? Muddle and confusion. I begin to think that by the end of it, none knew why they were fighting; and as for love and hate, it's well known they are horns on the same goat.

So, as we made our plans in York that January, though we were full of conviction, sure of the rightness of our cause, I knew quite well that Tom of Lancaster believed his cause as just, and I could not but suppose it likely that in time we all would grow as much bewildered as those heroes whom we saw as patterns for ourselves.

But it seemed to me we were engaged upon a war for love as surely as any that were writ in legend. Piers and I were lovers and we wished to live that love on our own terms; our foes wished to prevent it, and rather than that love should triumph, they would go to war for it. All else was irrelevant, trimmings and excuses. In this matter, you were for love or against it, and on that basis, chose.

Gathering together all those necessary for our welfare, we had passed as merry a Yule at Windsor as I ever recall. There is a certain relief, a certain feeling of well being that occurs in reaching a decision, taking a stand after vacillation. A gaiety followed, almost to the point of foolishness and lightheadedness. Isabelle, perhaps, was the least susceptible to it; but her own preoccupations did not mar the general festivities, and she had Meg to talk with. Meg, true to her bold lineage, vowed that her condition should be no bar to our journey north, and that she would give birth anywhere, beneath a hedge if need be; to which Piers responded that no son of his should begin life so, and all attention should be Meg's when her time came. The two Despensers joined us, and Eleanor, Meg's sister, and it was comfortable to be surrounded by so many that wished us well. Robert the Fool was —

"To be honest, Robert, you were not so nimble, were you? The stiffness in the limbs was setting in; but you were jovial, and joined in the playing."

God's soul, how well content we were! We acted out the barons hearing of the news of Piers' return. I played old Winchelsea, pot-bellied, twitch and all, calling down doom and clanging the bell; and when Audley played Tom, he could not get it right, so I played Tom as well, crying: Reform, reform! What, me want to be king? oh no, not modest me — jealous of Edward? never!

Piers' Warwick was a gem, played on all fours, with barking and snarling, a fur rug on his back; and Piers' clerk Philip Eyndon playing Pembroke was a fine creation: I am for the King — and yet I am for the earls — I want only what's best — well, I think I'll go to war; that's best!

And Robert nearly split himself in three, portraying Hereford and Surrey and Arundel explaining what they thought of Piers. It was when Piers began a vivid rendering of our dear neighbour Philip of France, brandishing a great iron key and looking for a suitable oubliette, that I had to intervene and hustle Piers away, for fear of Isabelle's taking offence; and tears of mirth streaming down my face.

I say that all necessary for our welfare was contained within that castle; there remained yet one thing, and when the Chancery clerks brought me the Great Seal, which had been in the possession of the Lords Ordainers, we were complete.

So, northward.

Two great households weaving their way in cumbersome procession the length of England in the January weathers, no easy matter, and a sight most marvellous to behold. Piers had with him Meg, redoubtable and hugely swollen, and Agnes to attend her, and every gift I'd given him in chests and coffers — his jewels, his armour, goblets, silver pots and ornaments, his wealth of clothes — borne by nine pack horses, and followed by his own horses, forty-one destriers and one palfrey. He took with him even more than I.

I took with me one very peevish queen. It was small joy to travel in close company with Isabelle. She had supposed when she left Berwick and came back to Westminster that she had seen the last of England's northern reaches. The natural truculence of her affections became exacerbated by ill fortune — which was what she understood the northern exodus to be.

"My father did not send me into England to become a traveller...my father did not send me into England to shiver upon icy roads far from sight of comfort...my father did not send me here to lurk about the shadows of your goodwill while Gaveston basks in your best regard..."

"I often wonder myself, madam, why your father sent you," I replied at last.

"Choosing to ignore your rudeness," she replied with dignity, "I believe the friendship of our two realms was to be further augmented by an heir to the throne. We have been wed these four years, Edward, and my father writes to me of his anxiety."

"Let him take a posset," I said sourly.

When we reached York, the Queen and I and our household took up abode at the abbey of Saint Mary, the rich and beautiful Benedictine house beside the river, just outside the city wall.

Isabelle, thankful to be in one place at last, modified her discontent; and Meg, whose relief to be no longer in motion possibly exceeded that of Isabelle, gave birth to Perot's daughter. Joan, she called her, after her mother, my beloved sister. It was an easy birth, said Agnes complacently; but I did not enquire further, believing any woman fortunate to be attended by a witch's skills.

"Not too sad to be cheated of a firstborn son?" I teased Piers.

"I always wanted a daughter," he replied indignantly.

"So many skills my darling has," I laughed. "And now the power to give life. Now this deserves, I think, some amethyst and jasper, and a little gold, and emerald, and a big beautiful ruby for the child."

Immense good humour hung about me as I joined the Queen that evening. Even she for once was placid. She was fond of Meg, and glad to find her well, the infant healthy. To be the parent of a newborn heir then seemed a very pleasing prospect, and it may perhaps have been in our thoughts that night when she and I lay close, the minstrels strumming in a room nearby, the hearth fire glowing warm. The son that we conceived from the encounters of those winter nights was begotten out of love — but love of whom for whom I would not care to say.

It was now a matter of some urgency for us to raise an army; and Piers was here and there — at Nottingham, at Scarborough, at Newcastle — to see what could be gathered in the way of troops.

Moves of policy were mine. First, Piers must be created Earl of Cornwall once again and all his lands and titles restored, and more added. Orders were given to fortify the castles up and down the land, to eject any custodian who might be disloyal to my person, to replace him with one trustworthy; to hold London for the crown; and our men in Gascony to come with troops, as many as could be brought. From London we heard news that the barons were foregathering, with Tom as leader; and that Winchelsea had once again read sentence of excommunication against Piers. It was a hustle-bustle time, with messenger and rumour flying back and forth.

"My dear," said I, "we seem to have a letter come from cousin Tom. Ill-mannered churl that he is, he does not pay respects to the lovely infant, or commend your prowess in the skills of procreation..."

"He ever lacked politeness," Piers agreed. "What does he say?"

"I am to surrender you at once, or — if that happy prospect does not please us — he has given us another choice."

"I long to hear it."

"It is this: you must go to perpetual banishment immediately. Which shall you choose?"

"Neither choice calls up unmitigated delight," Piers answered soberly, with merry eyes. "This is not a man who understands the secret of making others happy, is it, Ned?"

"I fear not. Yet it seems unkind to refuse both his kind offers; he has obviously given the matter much thought. We may offend him by refusal."

"Dear sweet, I may seem hard and cruel," said Piers, "but — it's reprehensible, I know — I believe that it would not grieve me if I offended Thomas. Of course, you may in your great wisdom, disagree?"

"No, no," I said airily. "I too could bear to offend cousin Thomas. We'll send a negative reply."

It was at York I learned that Isabelle was with child.

I dearly wish to say that from that moment all was well with us. But she must spoil the gladness of the moment.

"My dear — " says I, quite overcome and sentimental, reaching for her hand, putting it to my lips.

She smiled; but not with warm affection and pure love, as Piers did; no, a little smile of triumph, as if to say: well, he cannot do that for you.

"Perhaps now you will see at last where your true inclinations lie," said she. "We know now I am fertile. I can give you many children. Man and wife, as it should be. As everybody knows it should be. And you might spend more nights with me. And we to be together always..."

"I am so very pleased to hear your happy news," I said, now merely polite. "You must convey the tidings to your anxious father."

It was plain enough that York was not the best of places to dig in and make defence. Berwick or Scarborough seemed both better propositions for our purposes, and Scarborough the likelier of the two; therefore we sent men-at-arms and foot soldiers to the castle, in anticipation of our needing it as refuge. But we had yet another die to throw — a truce with Scotland. If Bruce was ally, all the northern reaches would be ours. To this end, we took off, with our baggage, north to Newcastle, leaving Meg and the child with Eleanor and Agnes at the abbey; but Isabelle I judged it best to bring with me, and by April we were in the castle there, with everything for our well being, and all Piers' goods and treasure, awaiting news of our negotiation with the Scot. Which proved a failure.

And now misfortune struck.

I found Piers sitting head in hands, and when I went to him, he looked at me strangely and said: "Touch me; I am on fire." And then he fainted on my shoulder. I screamed for servants; and we carried him to bed. For two weeks then he was possessed by fever.

I stayed with him day and night, a physician from the town attending, and a monk from Tynemouth, brother Robert, assisting him. It was a dreadful time. The fear for Piers was very much increased by the knowledge that we should be elsewhere. We had not planned to stay so long at Newcastle; we were here without an army, or any garrison worth the name; we must get Piers to Scarborough castle, a place of safety, and he was in no way fit enough to travel.

Of lesser trial, but trial enough, was Isabelle, who, since the confirmation of her pregnancy, had somehow persuaded herself that I would never leave her side, and that this fact of nature gave her claim upon my heart. As I bathed Piers' streaming brow, the Queen sent constant messages that she wished to see me; and always for nothing or to grumble. She who might have proved to be my support, proved yet another burden...

"Sire! Now have done — cease upbraiding that wretched woman! First, she was newly with child and looked to you for strong affection; and furthermore, you had no time for anyone but Perot whom she hated, and, sire, not without reason..."

"But he was raving — disordered in the head — drenched in sweat — I had to wring the sheets — my mother died of fever. I was distraught. And Piers was never ill — I was beside myself with mortal

terror — I could not give myself up to matters of no consequence — she should have understood!"

"Plainly she did not. I heard her say if Lancaster or Warwick took the castle, it would be no bad thing."

"Then she was more lunatic than he, and with less cause. I'm glad I did not hear that she said that. And I fearing for his life..."

"But he recovered."

"God be praised! Or was it the workings of the Lady? I prayed to both, you may be sure. Fifty candles to the goddess of healing, with no very clear idea to whom I made my supplication. The day when he sat up and was himself again, a hundred more in thanks. And for a week, I would not quit that place though we were most uneasy there; but I must have him well recovered."

It was about the Feast of Beltane when I knew him to be thoroughly restored. We sent our servants out into the fields to gather mayboughs, and we twined the garlands round about the bed. Where Isabelle was I cared not, but on that warm sweet-scented night of May I lay with Piers as a lover once again, though my emotion at the joy of his wellbeing threatened to prevent love's consummation. Ah, the fervent kisses of that night, the remembered taste of his perfumed skin freed from the stench of fever... Little starry blackthorn petals drifted on to us and settled in our hair, and wayside daisies. A celebration to the Lady truly, for the Lord does not smile overmuch on pleasures of the flesh.

In the morning I leaned on my elbow, looking at him. My eyes drank in this most precious of sights. I watched his lips, his clear dark skin, the lovely eyelashes. I moved the sheet from him and kissed my way from neck to toe in simple adoration. He lay and sighed and moved a little, just enough to show he did not sleep, that all my ministrations pleased him. There are sultans out in Trebizond and Persia much the same, with slaves to do the kissing. My servitude was chosen, and complete.

I traced his outline with my palm, moving up again towards his face, and placed my finger tip upon his lips; he licked my finger sleepily.

"Out of bed now, lazybones," I said.

"Am I in bed? I thought I was in Avalon."

"You are not. And look — here come Roger and John, peeping round the door, afraid to disturb us. Come in, Roger. Roger?"

Surely the youth's face was a curious chalky white, his manner clumsy, his speech somewhat inarticulate —

"Sire — oh my lord — "

Philip followed, equally distressed, and more vocal.

"Sire! The Earl of Lancaster is at the city gates!"

We leapt apart and out of bed, white faced, appalled as they.

"They say," and clearly Philip had a better sense of number, "he has one thousand horse and fifteen hundred foot soldiers!"

The pages moved about like those in a trance, handing us our clothes all anyhow, stupid, trembling, shaking. And we — if you have ever seen two full grown men awash with cold panic, you may well then picture us. We scarcely had the wit to dress, and none to think, and planning was beyond us. We gibbered like idiots. We were possessed by one thought only — to get away.

Down the dark stairways we ran, accumulating as we went a motley crew of those who would escape with us — a huddle of frightened servants, and yourself Robert the Fool, who were no fool at all. We toppled out by the postern gate, and took fast horses towards Tynemouth.

We tumbled from the saddle to huddle in the priory above the bay, while we sought ship to get us clear of this place of hazard. Its peacefulness the further emphasised our fear. Through fine stone tracery warm mocking sunshine poured upon us.

"The Queen?" said Piers of a sudden.

"God's blood! I had forgotten her!"

Servants were dispatched to Newcastle to bring the Queen and all our baggage, goods and horses, and all Piers' treasures; but we had not time to stay and see it stowed. We passed a dreadful night, sleeping not at all, but watching, watching, servants at every window, monks to ring the bells if troops were sighted; and, a ship being got for us, we embarked at once, at dawn.

"Oh, must we go by ship?" Piers groaned, alarmed afresh at the sight of it, and the sea ahead of us.

"A thousand horsemen — fifteen hundred foot — " I reminded him unhappily.

He could not dispute the fine logic of my argument. We went by ship.

Swiftly down the sea coast sailed our vessel, the wind good and the sea calm.

Scrying the shoreline for signs of pursuit, we saw only a wilderness of rocks where seabirds massed, and craggy cliffs of crumbling limestone overhanging white sandy bays. We saw the towers of churches built on hilltops; and wooded creeks and inlets and the fishing villages that hugged their slopes; the singing of monks wafted to us on the breeze.

For the first time since our flight, we had occasion and tranquillity enough to marvel at our situation and to dwell on our predicament. We began by giving thanks to God for our deliverance, and to the Lady, for we were very much convinced that powerful forces had been with us to deliver us. But this elation rapidly evaporated. Doubt set in. Should we have fled? Should we have remained, and treated with our foes? Surely we could have come to terms acceptable to all? Look at us now — the king of England, sitting in a boat in the well of the deck, surrounded by the welter of provisions we had cobbled together in our hurried flight — barrels of ale, casks of wine, cheeses, honey from the priory garden, bunches of herbs and a sack of flour, some tallow candles, and a heap of fleeces, strewn together in confusion. Where the pomp and ceremony, where the trappings of high office, where the jewels and gold?

The latter was the cause of Piers' greatest misgivings. Queasy of gut, but grateful not to be as seasick as he had been on his previous voyages, he could not rest for thinking of all he had left behind.

"Everything I own..." he wailed. "Jewels beyond price...my gold and silver...armour...horses...and my clothes — my velvets, furs and silks — "

"We'll get them back," I promised.

"From Thomas?" he screeched. "For it will all have fallen into his hands," he added gloomily. "Oh! How can I bear it!"

"I repeat, we'll get them back," said I. "Your state is not as wretched as my own. This is the Lord's Anointed this, in the only clothes he possesses, and this gallant crew" — I gestured to our patchwork of retainers — "my court."

Our eyes met and we both began to smile. We were in such a cast the folly and the humour of it now began to make us merry. We were never those by nature morose, as Thomas was; and laughing came as easily as breathing.

We were safe! We were together! We had escaped a monstrous army and outwitted pursuit. Scarborough castle waited, fortified, impregnable. Moreover, it was the month of May, the month of love and song and brave adventure. Seeing us so merry, all the rest grew so, and gaiety spread; and Richard Rhymer struck up a song of woods and nightingales, and then it was all song, all hilarity; and we nearly lost Robert tumbling from the mast, and we convulsed ourselves when Roger discovered to his chagrin that pissing to the wind brings back its own rewards.

The great keep of Scarborough castle showed now on its massy cliff, and we veered towards it.

We leaned and watched the slow approach of land.

"To arrive by sea..." Piers mused. "One feels oneself a stranger, bearer of tidings, bringer of war..."

"Wanderers and outcasts, seeking refuge. Saints and heroes come by ship."

"And ferocious savages. Norsemen ploughed these seas before us, and claimed this very place."

"As we shall claim it," I said firmly.

As Piers and I prowled around the castle's fortifications and assessed its defensive capability, we both agreed it was impregnable.

The sea whose arm encircled it on three sides, the great height of its cliff, its ditches, banks and baileys, and its sturdy curtain wall, would prove the first encumbrances. The great keep, itself on firm foundations, soared up, strong and mighty, one hundred feet high, grey turreted and strongly buttressed; herein lay cellar, hall and chambers; and in the bailey a well. Already such provisions as we had contrived to send were here assembled, and our garrison of sixty men.

It pleased Piers very much to discover that there was a second well which was named after the Lady, a well which had miraculous powers.

"So I shall drink at the waters of the Lady's well and I shall be sustained," he said.

"Thus your soul," said I, "but you are in accord with me — the place is unassailable."

"I believe so. What troubles me is the smallness of our provisions. I had not understood we had so little."

"Easily remedied. I shall send more."

We were much heartened at this juncture by the arrival of Piers' brother Arnaud Guillaume and his small company. Piers and he embraced, and Piers took him to view the walls and their defences.

I stood at a window in the higher reaches of the keep. My fingers traced the smoothness of its stone. The sky was very blue. Dear God, thought I, direct us now. Have I done right? It seems the best — give guidance if You will — I see no better way.

Piers is to remain at Scarborough, custodian of the castle, Arnaud with him. They will be secure, completely safe. I will return to York, the seat of government, and raise troops, and send provisions to the castle so they may hold it for as long as may be necessary. I shall return as often as may be, and bring all I may bring...it seems the best... I see no better way...

I moved about the bedchamber, assessing what was needed. Hangings for the bed — some lengths of velvet and some trimmings, several curtains to be hung on rails to partition off the room, some Turkish carpets for the walls and floors — some damask tablecloths. Piers should have every comfort; I would be happy furnishing the same.

Therefore the night we passed together was a time of greatest happiness. Naturally I saw no need to engrave upon my senses every nuance of his many attributes, to sink deep into the well of every minute... Yet one does remember and absorb when the most dearest one is close — the crinkling skin when his eyes laughed, the thickness of his hair — the shadows on the muscles of his thigh, the intricacy of veins about the foot, the ruby on his finger, that same ruby which I gave to him at Langley when I first in arrogance insisted that my love deserved response, and we made vows.

Those vows had led us by so many tortuous paths to this place, to this castle on this crag, this towering tawny-coloured keep where now the moon shone through the windows and cast its silver on the stone.

We lay close in each other's arms, the feather touch of breath upon each other's skin. I had once asked him if what bound us had been love or muddle; and I smiled affectionately at the memory of the callow youths that we once were. For my sake he had suffered taunts and jibes and banishment; for his I had taken ignominious flight in the clothes that I stood up in, turned my back on a dishonest peace, and risked a civil war.

It seemed to me our story had much in common with those knights who so inspired my boyhood; and now I did not need to ask if it were all done for love.

Chapter Seventeen

O PEN THE castle to no one but myself," I charged him, "and if it should so be I am in enemy hands, then not at all. In that case it were best you get to Gascony with Arnaud Guillaume, and await events."

We stood at the top of the flight of steps that led into the keep. Below, those who were leaving with me gathered, with the horses we'd procured not without difficulty, anxious to be leaving.

"I'll send news as soon as I reach York," I promised.

"I'll be so much in touch you'll think me with you," he replied.

"And since your jewels were mislaid..." I said; and took from my neck a gold chain with a great ruby and clasped it about his, and all my rings, all rubies, fitting them on his fingers, kissing those fingers. He took my face in his hands and held me with a long slow kiss.

"I'll soon be back," I said, much moved.

"And bring provisions!" he said, laughing. "Oh...and Edward, don't forget to include all my clothes and all my perfumes. Ned!" he added poignantly. "This is a matter of some desperation!"

I swore it.

As I descended the steps he added after me: "And my green silk with the fur."

Thus I quit Scarborough and rode to York.

I found Isabelle waiting there in a fury so uncontrolled that she could barely speak. Unfortunately for me this happy state of affairs was all too brief; her voice was soon recovered and I the victim of her all too justifiable venom.

"You abandoned me!"

I could not deny it.

"You abandoned me for him!"

"He had to get away," I said, mildly enough. "You, on the other hand, were in no danger. You are the queen, and well respected."

"Not by you, my lord!" she spat.

"No word of welcome, then, for my return? I was also in some peril."

"Why should I welcome you? What do you care for me, or for

our child?"

"I cannot think it good for him for you to rage so. Won't you be calm, and sit, and tell me all that happened since I left you?"

She would, if sullenly. Her news was dire. Thomas of Lancaster and his army had arrived at Newcastle, had pursued the rumours of our flight, had found the Queen at Tynemouth, and, as Piers had feared, his entire wealth and treasure.

"The bird has escaped us," Tom said, "but he leaves behind the wherewithal to line his nest." And gleefully it seems, he strutted to and fro, inspecting Piers' household goods, his jewels, the gold and silver drinking vessels, velvets, clothes, the armour, chests, all that we had had to leave behind. Where was it now? Queen Isabelle did not know, and plainly did not care.

"I believe you fret more for Gaveston's jewels than for our royal person," she declared, about to shout again.

I pacified her. "No, no, of course I was anxious for you. I hurried back here, didn't I? I'm here with you now. You spoke to Tom. What did he say?"

Her brown eyes blazed. "He was kindliness itself. If only you possessed a tenth of such consideration for me! He said he was my friend. He agreed that you had treated me abominably. He gave me comfort in my distress."

Did she hope to make me jealous? "What possible comfort could Tom of Lancaster give?" I said, with a fine curl of the lip.

"This comfort," answered she, and there was unashamed malevolence in her reply. "That he would never rest until he had separated you from Gaveston."

"I pray God he may never rest," I said, and crossed myself, and shuddered.

I ordered the assembling of provisions; I acquired fine clothes such as might fit any slim and well built Gascon that liked to dress with elegance — tunics in shades of green, silver belts, velvet cloaks, and many choices of clasp and buckle, and breeches trimmed with orphrey, and several pairs of shoes, and much besides. It took a few days to gather this together; meanwhile I wrote to him and he to me. At last the goods were ready to send off, and under guard they wended their way toward the coast.

"I will come when I may, dear," I wrote, "but I must begin to gather troops."

He wrote to me. "Your provisions have not arrived. I much regret this, as you may suppose. I have bad news. They say Lancaster's forces lie between this place and York, the intention being to keep us well apart. This morning we perceived a great army assembled round about us, which, as far as we may ascertain, is digging in for siege."

God be praised — it was not Lancaster who led the besiegers, but Pembroke. But faint comfort that, since he was dedicated to the surrender of the castle, the capture of my love. Warenne of Surrey was with him, and Henry Percy; my procession of provisions must have walked straight into them.

My spies recounted to me that the army of besiegers was large and well equipped, in short, too great for such small forces as I then had to go against. This must be resolved through diplomacy.

I did not think that Pembroke could be so stubborn. He refused outright my order to abandon the siege. For two weeks messages passed between us. He assured me on his honour that no harm would come to Piers, but that Piers must surrender, and when he did so, he should come under escort to my presence, there to discuss terms.

Piers smuggled out a note to me down through the postern and out by sea. "The plain truth is we have no food. Is there nothing you can do? Would you advise me to surrender? If you could arrange it so that I fall to Pembroke whom I trust, and if he promises that Lancaster and Warwick shall have no part in it, I am persuaded such a course would be the best we could take. For truly we shall die here otherwise."

I saw in my mind's eye that so small heap of provisions in the cellar of the keep — a little heap surrounded by expanse of floor, pathetic and inadequate as a berry on a dish. And more than sixty men to feed from it.

"Sire," Pembroke wrote, "as regards the earls of Lancaster and Warwick, neither is present here at Scarborough. Whereas it is true that Lancaster was here, he is now gone. But Your Grace, I stake my life upon the honour of the Earl of Lancaster. We are all agreed that no harm shall come to the person of Sir Piers Gaveston. Your fears are groundless. You have my word on it."

"There is nothing to eat here," Piers wrote, "and we see no point in holding out further, since Pembroke promises to bring me to you upon very generous terms. Therefore I propose to surrender myself to him; I trust you think I have done right. Also, my love, he promises me access to the clothes you sent me in the baggage, and you will recall I had none with me when we fled but what I wore."

Scarborough castle, the first that fell because the commander lacked a change of linen... I smiled wanly.

"I would not have you starve," I wrote, "and therefore, since the

Earl of Pembroke gives his oath in respect of your safety, I agree it best you should surrender."

They came to us at York, to the abbey of Saint Mary. We were all assembled — Isabelle, and Meg and Eleanor, and Agnes with the infant in her arms, and our household knights and pages, fools and minstrels. It was the twenty sixth of May.

A curious business, half informal, half severe, none knowing quite how to behave, the situation curiously untoward. I greeted Pembroke, but my eyes were only for my darling, standing dignified and handsome in his dark green sendal, two guards beside him, clad in Pembroke's colours. A couple of quick strides brought me to him. As I reached him the guards drew their swords and would bar me from him.

"Your Grace, Sir Piers is under guard," coughed Pembroke.

With every ounce of majesty I stood to my full height and looked the guards in the face. There was no need to speak. Both men replaced their weapons instantly. I put my arms around Perot and hugged him to me in a strong embrace. Perfumed! Kind Pembroke had done all that we demanded. Piers responded with a fervent rush of warmth and our lips met in a greedy kiss.

"How I have missed you!" I gasped. "These three weeks — and are you well? You seem so." I held his arms and gazed at him from head to toe with hungry eyes. "I feared you would be gaunt and thin — but you are beautiful as ever — even more so! Ah, how good it is to see you!"

"And you, dear sire," he said. "Well, we have seen some times together, Ned," he smiled, and gestured to the scene about us. "And so, what now?"

I took his hand, and led him to the ladies. "Your wife...your child...all well."

I stood by fondly, while Piers embraced Meg, and received his child, and took the sleeping infant in his arms. I sensed that those about us quietened their vigilance; it must be plain to them that here in this sanctified place, here was nothing dangerous, no cause for conflict. I turned to Pembroke.

"My thanks, my lord, for your chivalry. I believe our business next is to discuss the Earl of Cornwall's situation now and in the days to come."

"That is my intention," said the Earl of Pembroke.

Aymer de Valence, Earl of Pembroke...at this juncture from a background figure, a part of a group, a voice now dissident, now supportive, he steps forward to take a chief part in the work that followed.

A little under forty years of age he was tall and rangy with a long pale clever face. His nose was large and long, his mouth thin and good humoured. He wore his hair cut close, a small fringe across his broad brow, like the old Normans in the tapestries. His eyes were bright and honest; you would take him for a monk.

The three days that we passed in negotiation were not unpleasant, for all that the entire abbey clanked with soldiery and that Piers and I were not permitted that complete and careless freedom to which we were accustomed. Pembroke took his duty seriously, the representative of the Lords Ordainers. His comfortable assumption of their good intent was all pervasive, and the terms he offered on their behalf were better than we hoped.

A Parliament was to be called for July, at Lincoln, at which Piers was to speak in his defence; this pleased him mightily. If nothing could be decided, he was to return to Scarborough, the place to be fully provisioned. Until that time, he should live at Wallingford under guard; and I to visit him as often as I chose. My lord of Pembroke undertook to bring him there, to travel by slow stages south.

I hesitated. I looked at Pembroke, willing with all my heart to trust him. I must hand my dearest treasure to him. To be sure I hesitated. He understood.

"Your Grace," he said, "we have sworn upon the Host to protect him with our lives. And I myself have pledged my lands and property. By all that I hold dear, and by my honour, dearest of all, I swear to Your Grace the safety of Piers Gaveston. And sire," he added, eminently reasonably, "whom do you fear? The Lords Ordainers are of one mind. We act only within the law. We are all committed one to another. There is no danger."

"Well, certainly I do not begin to understand the workings of the minds of you and your fellow Ordainers," I replied reluctantly, "and concerning the Earl of Cornwall," I added pointedly, referring to Piers by his proper title, "I see I must take the word of one who speaks for all."

"That word is given," Pembroke said. "I swear it before God." Then he gave a little smile. "The guard about Sir Piers is not because I fear for his safety. It is to prevent him escaping."

"But I too have given my word," Piers interrupted haughtily.

"The only other reason for the guard about Sir Piers," said

Pembroke looking at me steadily, "is my own fear that — persons unknown may attempt a rescue."

I clasped my hand on his and burst out laughing. "Dear Pembroke...I too have given my word."

Three more *preux chevaliers* would be hard to find.

"I assume that the Earl of Cornwall and myself may be permitted the privacy of the abbey gardens to make our farewells, my lord," I said in a tone which brooked no refusal.

As merry a May morning it was as ever I have known, if sun or carolling of birds or brightness of flowers has to do with merriment. Nor do I recall ourselves that we were sad — after all, we would be meeting soon at Wallingford.

"By midsummer," said Piers.

We wandered under the trees. "By midsummer." I agreed. "We'll hold a tournament, shall we? And come the evening, light such bonfires as they'll see from London. Did you know," I added, "that a tournament is now reckoned to personify each of the Deadly Sins? What was it — pride in one's own strength, envy of others', wrath in combat, sloth in placing pleasure before devotion, covetousness of others' weapons, gluttony at the feast — and lechery after!"

"Then we'll indulge in all of them! Particularly those that happen after dark."

"Do you like Hugh Audley?" I enquired abstractedly.

"I do. Are you suggesting he should be included?"

"And Roger also; I believe you're close with him?"

"I believe I am. How long have you known?"

"Oh, I don't know; it's not important. But here is something of great importance — urgency, even. And I'd like your serious and considered opinion."

"Yes?"

"I've been thinking of growing a beard. What do you say?"

"I think you'd look delightful. What, one with little points? It would make you look more like your father."

"Do you think so? Well, that may be no bad thing!"

We laughed. We had reached the abbey garden wall. A little door hung open, and, beyond, the river, gleaming in the sun.

We saw a little boat there, lying tied against the bank, oars resting. We looked at one another, and had darted through that doorway and into that boat as quickly as the deed could be done. I rowed us rapidly downstream. We chuckled to see the wretched men at arms in great confusion, some running down the bank, some reaching for their

254

arrows, but not daring to let fly.

"They've heard about our great escape from Tynemouth!" Piers grinned.

"How far could we get, do you suppose? Remember, I am something of an oarsman," I added modestly.

"I don't know. If the Norsemen came this way, we must at length reach the sea."

"Yes, by the Humber. There, a ship."

"To where, outcasts such as we?"

"Norway no less. And then by land to — anywhere we chose! Disguised as monks."

"Or nuns."

"I am too tall."

"It was the reason you fled the nunnery. The Abbess swore you were a man."

Behind us, far behind us, I could see the start of our pursuit. "We could elude them, Perot," I said, "if we so chose..."

"I know it. But..."

"We gave our word," I said, and groaned.

I rested on the oars. "Well, and so the honourable course is ours. I'll take occasion of this interlude instead to kiss you."

The long leaves of a willow overhung the water, and beneath its canopy of green we leaned and kissed, knee to knee, with all the strength of passion's warm intensity. We gently drew apart.

"I love you more than I can say."

"And I love you, Ned."

"Till midsummer then," said I.

"Midsummer..."

I pushed the boat clear of the bank, and slowly rowed back to the abbey. A horde of irate men at arms lined the grassy rim beside the wall, and Pembroke waiting by the landing stage, his face a conflict of emotions.

"My Lord of Pembroke," I greeted him good humouredly. "You look a little discomposed. Whatever were you thinking?"

"Your Grace knows very well," he answered dourly. "Permit me to assist you to dry land."

With Roger, his page, and Philip, his clerk, Piers quit the abbey in the company of the Earl of Pembroke and his men-at-arms. Beautiful as the god of the forest Piers rode, upright and splendid, all in green, with a green feather in his cap, and the sun upon him. I ran alongside for a while, ever thinking of more things to say, both of us laughing at the foolishness of it, till Piers said finally: "Go back, Ned! You have miles to walk!"

At the bend of the road he turned, knowing I would still be waiting, standing there. He blew a kiss.

"I love you," I said, to the air, and all the birds sang, stupid jocund fowls, and all the wayside bloomed with an excess of daisies. It was the twenty-ninth of May.

It is well known that action is best antidote to anxiety, and I went busily about on matters of troop raising, and diplomatic flurries concerning France and Avignon. It seemed to me that foul Philip and I might come to some agreement concerning the exchange of an army of French troops for a certain patch of land called Gascony, the which he lusted after. The plain distressing truth was that the combined forces of the barons who opposed me made a greater army than I could personally muster, hence desperate measures.

Piers wrote to me whenever the cavalcade paused upon its way to Wallingford. "The Earl of Pembroke is a cultured and pleasant companion. He reads Ovid from the Latin, and translates with ease. I enclose one of the verses. You see that Ovid advises the seeking of pleasure as of prime importance. Leave everything for love, work to be together though the sun burns or the snow falls. You and I, my dear, have proved his good disciples..."

Hugh Despenser was there then, my father's trusted friend and mine; his son Hugh was not with him, or no doubt the good man would have but oh so gently moved him to my notice — Your Grace recalls my son Hugh? — which he ever did when Piers was from me. I grew to expect it, and I always smiled at it. And it was Despenser who came frowningly to me then, a letter in his hand. So gently, so unobtrusively, did chaos begin.

It was the thirteenth of June.

"Your Grace, do you know aught of this? My son's man Robert of Harrowden — rector of Deddington — has written to my son. My son says that the custody of the Earl of Cornwall has fallen to my lord of Warwick."

"No, Pembroke has him. You are quite mistaken. It must be some false rumour."

"But my son says otherwise."

"Give me the letter."

The letter was as vague as Despenser's account.

"Deddington? Where is that?" I demanded.

"Oxfordshire, Your Grace."

"Deddington? Is it close by Warwick?"

"I assume it."

"But why should Pembroke — ? No, Pembroke's honour is unimpeachable." I spoke so to persuade myself. "Your man must mean that the Earl of Warwick has joined forces with him. The situation is as before. Nothing has changed. It is unfortunate that Wallingford lies so close by Warwick's lands. I hope he does not mean to lay siege to Wallingford. But Piers will write and let us know."

No messenger came. After a day or so I sent a man to take the road to Deddington, if he could find so undistinguished a place, and to enquire the whereabouts of Pembroke's troop and send me word at once.

"I don't understand it," I said to Despenser, bewildered. "If a problem has arisen, Pembroke should have told me. If all is well, I should have had communication from Piers. Where are they? Surely not — Christ save us — at Warwick? Aymer de Valence has sworn to me that Beauchamp is not to have a hand in this — he swore it — he has pledged his lands and honour..."

I think it entirely to my credit I did not go mad, but acted with composure and as if I had my wits about me. I sent a letter to the Earl of Pembroke, to be received at Deddington by Robert Harrowden the rector and forwarded thence; I sent a letter to the Earl of Warwick querying what I had heard, demanding explanation and assurance; a further to young Hugh for clarification about what he seemed to have heard upon this issue.

I wonder if there be a torment so refined as waiting for news, none coming. With every start of the new day the certainty, the expectation of a messenger's arrival; with every day's close the disbelief that night has once more come, and yet no tidings; again the renewal of hope at the start of the new day, and all begins as before. Six days passed like this.

And yet, unknown to me, I was a happy man. I basked in happiness. The happiness of a man who does not know what is to come, who does not know that he will never know true happiness again, and therefore, by default, is happy. And all the while the abbey doves cooed, purred and crooned upon the ledges; and I grew to hate the sound of doves.

I was sitting, in abstraction, with my fingers in the fur of Bruno's neck, gazing at nothing; it was early afternoon, and warm. Robert sat at the window, silent as myself.

"I watched a butterfly, sire, lost among the scents of flowers."

Despenser came in, very quiet, the door left open behind him, and some movement there. I looked up instantly, all senses suddenly alert.

"Your Grace," he said, his soft voice loud in the silence, "these men have news for you."

He beckoned in Roger atte Halle and Philip Eyndon, who had been lurking by and now came in and flung themselves upon their knees. Their hair, their clothes were white with dust, they plainly were exhausted to extremity. They blurted out their news in incoherent unison.

"He's dead, sire, our master's dead! They killed him, sire! We rode...we came as fast as ever...we wanted you to hear it from his friends. This is no thing to hear from strangers..."

"Dead?" I said stupidly.

As an interpreter from a foreign court, Despenser, upright, said: "These servants of the Earl of Cornwall have ridden up from Warwickshire. The Earl of Cornwall has been murdered."

"By Warwick," I said. I swear, I had guessed it.

"By Warwick and by Lancaster," Despenser said.

"God's soul, the fool, the idiot!" I said through my teeth. "I told him to keep clear of Lancaster and Warwick."

"The Earl of Pembroke..." Despenser began.

"Not Pembroke, damn you, Gaveston!" I shouted. "What was he thinking of? To be such a fool..."

Roger and Philip retreated a little at my outburst. Had they expected me to weep?

"Lancaster?" I said, the fact now penetrating to my brain. "Lancaster was there?"

I stood. I screamed: "But where was Pembroke?"

"He was not there," gasped Roger terrified.

"Now...wait..." I said, my hand out, every finger spread, as if to ward the truth away. "Pembroke was not there? How could it happen then? How was it possible?"

"Without law and suddenly, a mob in tow. It was the act of savages," Despenser spat.

I looked at the two quivering at my feet. "Could there be some mistake?"

"No, sire, none."

"But then how did he die? I don't understand this. There must be some mistake. You think that he is dead?"

"We know it, sire," they said.

"But how?" I screeched.

"Beheaded, sire," groaned Philip from the floor.

"Oh God," said I.

The silence tore at me. "Speak," I gasped. "Must I demand it word for word, all that you know?"

"We were imprisoned," Philip stuttered. "We weren't there. We heard about it afterwards, when they cast us out; we heard it in the town."

"Imprisoned? Where?"

"In Warwick's castle...all of us were taken there..."

"He was killed in Warwick's castle?"

"No sire, no sire, on a hill."

"Christ give me patience...on a hill? What hill?"

"I don't know. Somewhere outside Warwick town. We were not there, you see...the people told us..."

"Where — is — he — now?" I said and hung over them so fierce they shrank down on the floor.

"The friars took him to Oxford."

"Oxford? Ha! Dead he travels to and fro?" I said, a certain craziness uprising in me.

"They said the Earl of Warwick would not take him...and Lancaster has gone away...and so the friars took him to Oxford. To the priory there. We had it from a man who saw them go. A man who knew the shoemenders."

"There were shoemenders? They paused to make him shoes?" Yes, this was indeed madness, I decided calmly. Madness is thus. One talks of shoemenders. It is all so very reasonable. Why should there not be shoemenders about a death? They had as much right to be there as butcher, baker, candlemaker.

Philip burst into tears, and too convulsed with weeping, could not speak. I turned to Roger.

"What is this about shoemenders?" I asked politely.

"I dare not say, sire," he replied.

"He dare not say," said I in quiet tones. Then I spun round and slammed my fist upon the table. An inkwell leapt into the air and spilled an ooze of black across a parchment. "Get them from my sight, Hugh. Get these jesters from my sight!"

259

They fled.

"Sire — "

Without looking at him I said evenly: "And you, Despenser. Go, or I won't answer for your life."

The door closed. Then there was a howl of pain and rage the like of which I have never heard — a trapped wolf came close to it, in Langley woods — a scream of fury and such sounds of wreckage as would cause all within hearing to tremble where they stood. Blind wrath possessed me, giving me a madman's strength — I overturned the great oak table, and the monstrous chair; a coffer I upended, and from a wall cupboard I hurled goblets, dishes — pewter, gold and silver, all went indiscriminately — some stringed instrument I smashed — holy pictures — a recess curtain I tore down — and to the crashings now was added barking, yelping, as the frightened dogs upon their hind legs clamoured to be let out at the door; and in amongst it all crawled Robert, who had stayed with me, and judged my throws, and against all odds, avoided maiming. I stood stock still staring at him, gawping at his obstinate loyalty. I knelt down with him in the ruins, clawed him to me, sobbed into his neck.

"Did time pass, Robert? I recall we had the letter from the friars...?"

"And it was just as well, sire, since it gave us proper confirmation. The first coherent words you said to me were: 'What if it isn't true?' and you began to hope it; therefore I was glad when they wrote to us from Oxford, asking for instructions. Were they to proceed with the embalming of the body, and did Your Grace wish the heart to be left in place or to be removed?"

"God's soul, this moves too fast," said I upon reading the letter. "Bring back the wretched Roger and poor Philip. Let us know more..."

"They are with the Countess, sire, and Agnes."

"Ah..." That there were others than myself who mourned jerked me to some semblance of action, and I joined the stricken group about the cradle, Meg, ashen-faced, and Agnes, like an avenging angel, dark-browed, radiating an intensity of anger. Where Isabelle was, no one knew nor cared.

A curious lack of knowledge of the facts drove us to half stupidity; and then I said to Robert: "Go to Deddington on this most precious errand. Ask everyone, the passer-by, the villager, the guard — discover every detail — spare me nothing — I must know — and bring the truth to me where I shall be — where we all shall be — at Oxford..."

Chapter Eighteen

THIS, THEN, is the account that Robert brought to me.

"You tell it, Robert; write it as you heard it then, from witnesses that saw it; write down the circumstances of his death, his murder. Ten years have passed since then. It ought to be possible to speak of it, dispassionate, as clerks do, simply stating what occurred. Therefore proceed now, if you will."

Sometime in the afternoon of June the ninth, they came to Deddington, a sprawl of houses round about a church and market place. Everybody saw them come, it seems. I had no difficulty here. A troop of men at arms, two earls and their retainers — it was quite a sight, and everybody came to gawp.

My Lord of Pembroke thought to lodge his prisoner at the castle, and rode confidently forward in its direction. But when they arrived at it, they found it to be in a sad state of disrepair —

"And this is so, sire; it's a small dilapidated place, holes in the wall, and birds' nests where should be defences."

A tumbledown place this castle, Pembroke found, with one chamber only barely fit for use; and a dovecote, empty, in the overgrown bailey. The stones had been plundered to build houses; it's a sorry sight, more grass than stone. My Lord of Pembroke was exceeding vexed, and looked a fool before his soldiers; and naturally Piers was monstrously amused and laughed heartily, for after all, it was not his problem. He dismounted and sat on the grass amongst the daisies, with Roger and Philip. They passed the time in making daisy chains, while Pembroke rode about in irritation. His intention had been to leave Piers guarded in the castle, and taking the opportunity of its nearness to Bampton, to visit his wife, the Lady Beatrice, who was lodging there, and to return the following day to take Piers on to Wallingford. His lady stayed for him, and lo, there was no castle!

At this juncture up came Robert Harrowden the rector, offering his humble house for their convenience. And it was not so humble either.

It's a two-storeyed building just beside the church, in the church's very shadow, with many rooms and a chapel, fronting on the market place. The Earl of Pembroke, very pleased to have his face saved, rode to view the place. It pleased him, and he set up Piers in that abode, a little troop of guards with him. This done, the Earl of Pembroke rode to Bampton, thinking that Piers would be dining with the rector and secure there, since the guards were left.

"Whereas in truth we never saw the rector," said Roger atte Halle. "Oh, we ate well, and were treated much as guests, and were it not for the perpetual presence of the guards, who sat about and sprawled and played at dice in the manner of guards, and joked with us the while, we would not have felt ourselves creatures in captivity.

"You must understand, there was never any sense of threat or menace. It seems so unbelievable now. But the sun was shining, and the journey south was quite agreeable, easy, without hurry, and the Earl of Pembroke and our master so at ease together, each polite and affable toward the other, discussing poesy and such. And at Dedding-ton, that business with the castle — it was all so droll — the villagers all gathered about in groups, giving advice as to where we might stay, and of course, they were so very rustic in their speech and habits it made us laugh; and there we sat and made our daisy chains, which irritated my Lord of Pembroke the more — it was a situation of amusement, of the ridiculous. And the rectory was very agreeable; we were happy to lodge there; and when my lord of Pembroke rode away, we settled to the night without a qualm.

"Outside, the sounds came to us of the setting up of trestles for the market on the morrow. We leaned from the upper window and watched. Some of our guards looked up at us, and warned us that they saw us, therefore not to make attempt to escape; but we shrugged. Why should we escape, we thought? We were on our way to Walling-ford, and Pembroke had sworn our safety on his life.

"We slept in a big room at the front of the house. It had one bed and a trundle, and since it was my turn — am I to tell all that passed? everything? — well, as we travelled, you see, we three being together, when we were private we could sleep in the same bed and give some comfort to each other, and that night was my turn to sleep with our master (Philip on the trundle bed) and he had the use of me, which suited us both well. We often wondered if the guards outside the door could guess how pleasantly we passed our nights.

"Well, after we had had our pleasure, and had washed ourselves, I combed his hair and perfumed him and saw that all was well with him, and then we slept. And we had eaten well and drank and were content from what we did, and we slept very well, and thought no harm, and heard no sound, the market tables being then in place, till morning.

"But the morning was a different matter. I awoke all sleepy-eyed and found my master was not in the bed. I looked and saw him at the window, all naked from sleep, his hands gripped on the window ledge, his body stiff like an animal's that hears a prowler; and I heard then a great noise beyond him, out of doors.

"'What is it?' I said, now alert.

"'Christ save me, I am done for,' he said in a low voice.

"I leapt out of bed, Philip also. We joined him at the window, and below us in the market place we saw a mess of men and horses, riding to and fro, with weapons drawn, and some dismounted, making for the door below us. And the Earl of Warwick in their midst, on horseback, with a brandished sword the which he jerked at Piers and cried in a loud voice: 'Get up, traitor, you are taken!'

"And Piers backed off into the room and he had barely time to take a piss and pull on his breeches before they burst into the room, soldiers with the Earl of Warwick's badge. I handed him his shirt, he heaved it over his head, and they took hold of him and dragged him out and down the stairs and out into the market place. I saw it from above; I saw him hustled out, barefoot and undressed, and held before the Earl of Warwick who then sheathed his sword and cried to all about him: 'Well! we have him now. The witch's son shall feel the Black Dog's teeth!'

"'I am the Earl of Pembroke's prisoner,' Piers shouted. 'You have no right to take me. On his honour he has sworn my safety.'

"'But he is not here!' roared Warwick.

"'My lord, he swore on your behalf as men of honour...'

"'But I should remind you, Gaveston, that I am no man of honour, but a black dog,' Warwick sneered. 'And you shall expect from me such as you would look for from the same. And this dog has stood by for long enough and watched you batten on the King, and now this dog breaks from his chain. And you shall ask yourself what you deserve from my hands, Gaveston. Bind him!'

"'My lord, I am a knight of the realm,' cried Piers, struggling in the grip of soldiers. He was very angry. Surrounded and held by the soldiers of the Earl and in his shirt, he looked so proud and haughty and sure of his own worth it would have made you weep.

"'You are a traitor to the realm,' said Warwick in reply, and leaned down from the saddle and drove his fist into Piers' face. It was because our master looked so arrogant, you see, and should have been in terror but was brave. And when he raised his head again his face was bloody and his hair hung forward and the earl looked satisfied.

"'No traitor wore a jewel like that one,' Warwick said, and reached down for the ruby on the chain Piers wore about his neck and grabbed at it. But Piers twisted from him, and he grasped at nothing, and Piers laughed at him through the blood that trickled from his nose, and Warwick all enraged cried: 'Take that jewel!' And soldiers tore the ruby from him, breaking the clasp, and handed the great jewel to Warwick who held it to the light and said in awe: 'This must be worth one thousand pounds!'

"'So now you would add thieving to your crimes,' jeered Piers in scorn, but you could see he was distressed, it being the King's gift to him. And there were other jewels they took from off his hands; but one ring with a ruby would not come; they left it on his finger.

"'You'll have no need of rubies now,' said Warwick. And then he oversaw the binding of Piers' wrists with rope, and the end of the rope handed to a soldier on horseback who rode forward, and Piers on the ropes' end.

"Then some remembered us, and Philip and I who were now dressed, were brought down and our hands bound, and we were sat upon one horse and brought along; but Piers was walking. And they took us all to Warwick, and Philip and I were put in a prison cell and kept there till it was all over; and then they set us free, and we learned from the servants in the castle what had happened; and then we rode to York on stolen horses."

That was a market such as never had been seen at Deddington. Through the stalls they rode, my Lord of Warwick's men, apples scattered, pots crashing smashed in the wake of the horses' careless path, the villagers enraged, bewildered, asking themselves what was this all about — who was this prisoner? The rumours passed about. A traitor to the realm — an enemy of the King — an enemy? no, that's Piers Gaveston, the man who loves the King, but loves the King too much, if you know what I mean — and lies with him as a woman... Whatever the truth of it, it were plain enough he should be gone from Deddington and they were glad to see him go, and mess enough to clear up from the soldiers.

But how came Warwick's troops to Deddington? Where had they come from, I enquired? From Warwick, obviously. But who had told them come? Who had told the Earl of Warwick Piers was here? Who had gone the twenty five miles between the two places and brought the Earl, so horribly in time? They did not know; but let us say the rector of Deddington was not at home that night and his horse gone from the stables, and the rector is young Hugh Despenser's man..."

"I'll not hear Hugh slandered, Robert. I have it from his own lips that the rector was in Banbury; there is no more to say. Enough that Warwick came. And in such strength that Pembroke's guards put up no fight. An unbelievable piece of wretched ill fortune."

"Exactly, sire, ill fortune, no more, no less, just as you say. Coincidence perhaps. It shall be just as you declare it, sire, whatever I may think. To return, therefore, to that vile journey towards Warwick..."

"Yes, tell it, Robert, smoothly and concisely, and without emotion. How Piers was dragged at a ropes' end, barefoot and bleeding, along the rutted track towards Banbury, over the bridge across the Swer brook, walking, running, stumbling, at the whim of some villain of Warwick's, till his feet and knees and wrists were bloody, and his arms and shoulders aching, and how the Earl's men made the usual foul jests to one another, and answering with boorish guffaws, and when he fell said 'How do you like the taste of mud who once ate off silver?' And raised him with their hands about his arse and handled him there, saying that he liked it and he did that with the King. And where's the King to save you now, they said? And how the Earl of Warwick rode alongside him, in such good humour that there seemed a kind of madness in it. 'Come, Gaveston, you are too slow,' he said, 'it is not like you to be backward; you were not thus at Wallingford.'"

"You are a brave man, Warwick," Piers said. "When the King hears of this, he'll kill you for it —"

"Ha! Would you threaten me with Edward?" Warwick answered with a cynical laugh. "Call on him now, why don't you, Gaveston? See if he hears you!"

"Oh, judge and jury I have sat against myself for that day's work! I did not even know... I slept in scented sheets...and he was treated as a felon...ten miles barefoot and tormented...that's right, Robert, tell it calmly, pleasantly, dispassionately..."

Towards the outskirts of Banbury on the downward slope of the hill, there was an alehouse on the roadside, where they paused, some of the men dismounting, others in the saddle passing round the ale; but all their sights upon their prisoner, now on his knees, his head between his outstretched arms, exhausted, leaning on a log. And even now they would not leave him alone, but in an insolent camaraderie would have him speak. One stood, his boot upon the log, leaning over Piers, and said: "Are you the King's whore, as they say?"

"Ask him to tell us what they do!" And all the others laughed, because they knew full well and some had certainly done as much themselves. But the prisoner preserved his silence, and in a cheerily vindictive gesture then, the guard reached down and half upended him across the log, and clawed the breeches from his hips and bared his arse, and for the entertainment of his friends he pulled out his own prick and stood astride his prisoner and made as if to bugger him, but stupidly and working for a laugh, and saying: "This is what they do!"

The Earl of Warwick, coming from the alehouse, cuffed the man about the ear so hard he fell down flat; and looked at Piers' backside and bellowed: "Cover him!" and glared so fiercely that they ran in clumsy haste to stick Piers' arse back in his breeches. Then Piers sat sprawled in the grass, entangled in the great snake of the rope, the end of which was handed very deferentially to Guy Beauchamp, who took it between his dainty fingers with distaste.

"On your feet, Gaveston," said he.

Piers raised his head and gave him a slow look, as arrogant as ever though his face was smeared with blood and grime and though he should have then been awash with humiliation and shame...

> *"Oh, Piers was always glad enough to show his arse to guards! That which the church is pleased to call the parts of shame to Piers have ever been the parts of pride, and rightly so, with him. Oh yes, there would be many who would die the death if they were taken captive in their shirt and in a pair of close-fitting breeches trimmed with orphrey. Not my love, not Piers... And why do you suppose the Earl of Warwick so enraged, eh? Why did he strike down the guard? Because the man made clear what was understood at heart: they lusted after him, they all did. All this talk of treachery and traitor to the realm, the poor disguise for jealousy, the official language of those who are too poor in spirit to be honest about their desires. They longed to see him naked. Christ! I sometimes think we are all sodomites at heart..."*

"Stand up," then says the Earl of Warwick, and the Earl looks down at Piers, and Piers up at him, and the long slack rope between them. With a flicker of the eyes, Piers indicated his bare and bleeding feet.

"I refuse," he said. "Get me a horse."

And Warwick grunted and slung the rope down in the grass and called the innkeeper.

An ugly mare it was they found for him to ride, all skin and bone, upon which it was supposed no man could sit with dignity, and thus the troop continued towards Warwick town. My lord, we know that, bruised and bloody and begrimed and on that nag, the Earl of Cornwall would have been exactly like Sir Lancelot when he rode to Sir Meligant's castle in a cart — a noble knight is noble always. And now they could go quickly — twenty miles or so, to Warwick town.

"And he'd not have been despairing even then. He always did believe the best...expected good things... Ned will save me, he'd have thought. When they tell the King, all will be well... And therefore, even when he saw the towers of Warwick's castle, even when they led his nag across the drawbridge, he would not despair... I wish I could have seen him one more time. I wish I could have told him..."

Of the nine days that followed, I could not ascertain all the details, only the events. But I have spoken to those both within the castle and those out in the streets. This is what I pieced together. Certainly he was put in a dungeon, at the bottom of a tower. And then others came to Warwick.

The Earl of Hereford, Humphrey de Bohun, was first; then the Earl of Arundel, Edmund Fitzalan. At last the Earl of Lancaster (Derby, Leicester, Salisbury, Lincoln...) Thomas Plantagenet, cousin to the King. Then there was much discussion.

They knew this up and down the castle, everybody knew it — Gaveston was taken prisoner and lay within their very walls; his lordship had invited all the earls and it was like to prove the end of Gaveston — this was freely spoken. And a few days later, lawyers came. And it was supposed they did not dare to have him killed and yet they wished it, and Thomas in a loud voice was heard to say: "While he lives, there will be no safe peace in the realm of England, as many proofs have hitherto shown us." But it was said my Lord of Arundel refused and would have no part in it. Hereford, on the other hand, supported Lancaster, and said they should make oaths to bind themselves one to another.

Then the Earl of Pembroke came, and as soon went.

"I have pledged my lands, my honour," Pembroke told them, "and by implication, yours. We speak with one voice, I told the King. I am dishonoured by this deed — and what of yourselves? I gave my word — our word — to the King. He accepted it. He trusts us to behave as knights. You have behaved as curs, and now as shifty deceivers."

But they would not be reasoned with.

The Earl of Pembroke was beside himself with rage and would not stay. And the justices they brought in made a case which said if the Earl of Cornwall was a traitor he should die a traitor's death; and if it could be proved the Ordinances had not yet been revoked in Warwickshire, then legally he was a traitor; and they agreed that this was so. And they brought Piers up from the dungeon; and he was in chains.

In the hall of the castle were assembled at a table the earls of Lancaster, Warwick, Hereford and Arundel, and the two justices, with clerks and servants. I had this from the very guard that brought Piers to the table. He received him from the gaoler and he led him in to stand before those that would judge him.

Was that the Earl of Cornwall, he thought when he first saw him, so dirty, stinking and so dark? Was that the man the King loved? It was hard to credit it. An eight days' beard blackened his face, his hair was foul and tangled, and his limbs were stained with filth, and the manacles about his wrists weighed down his arms.

"And I wondered why they sent for him at all," said the guard, "because they would not let him speak. They read a list of crimes; they called him traitor; and they said that by the rights they had as Lords Ordainers, they were empowered to sentence him to death.

"'The King himself said I may speak in my defence' said my Lord of Cornwall; but they would not have that, and said he was not brought to speak but listen — that was my lord of Lancaster.

"'Does the King know what you do?' then said the Earl of Cornwall. 'Dare you confess as much to him?'

"Poor soul, he swayed upon his feet; I had to hold his arm for steadiness; and I thought I saw great unease upon the faces at the table then; but no one answered, and the lawyers read a rigmarole I did not understand; and Lancaster ordered Gaveston removed.

"'Let me see the King...' he then beseeched. 'For God's love, let me see the king.'

"But they did not reply. They gestured us away and stood and made to go and I was told to take him to his gaoler, and as we shuffled from the hall, he wept; his face was streaked with tears.

"We stood beside the doorway for a moment, and as we paused, the Earl of Warwick was beside us, all in black, with gold threads and gold buckles and a gleam of jewels about him, and I waited, thinking he would give me orders. But instead he looked at my Lord of Cornwall, who returned the look, as if there was much to be said that never would be said.

"'My lord,' said the prisoner, his voice all hoarse, 'I beg you, let me see the King. I know he wishes it.'

"'I know it also,' Warwick said. 'It is not possible. It is too late. God's teeth!' he suddenly cried in anger. 'You fool, Gaveston, you fool! Why did you make it so easy for me to capture you?' And all in a movement he took a kerchief from his wrist and doused it in the water of a hand basin set in the wall, and washed the Earl of Cornwall's face, grime, tears and blood and all; at least, all that can be done with water..."

"*He had the power to halt what they were about. Don't ask me to believe the Earl of Warwick blessed with a sudden sensibility. He was a brute, no more, no less.*"

"*I merely say what passed. He gave no orders, certainly. He turned away; and Piers was led back to the dungeon whence he came.*"

Anyone at all could retell what happened next, for all the town turned out to see it.

Out from the castle came a great procession, over the drawbridge and down into the town. Thomas Earl of Lancaster, Bohun of Hereford, Fitzalan of Arundel, and a troop of men-at-arms in colours of the same.

"Not Beauchamp."

"No, not the Earl of Warwick. It was remarked upon."

Now what was heard was that at first the people could not tell which was the traitor, for every one who rode seemed noble. Then Piers was seen, between his guards, and dressed in green. He was bareheaded and very beautiful — sleek and perfumed, and his face all washed and shaved, and his hair smooth and combed. And though the crowd came as to see an entertainment, laughing, blowing trumpets, catcalling and dancing up and down the road, the Earl of Cornwall was as regal as a king and looked straight ahead and calm as if he rode at Langley. You would have sworn he had no fear of dying.

"*Oh Christ! At heart I know him terrified.*"

Down through the streets of Warwick town and out beyond its boundary they went — across the Avon and across the water meadows, taking the road to Kenilworth. And everybody wondered why they went so far, so far from Warwick, and so far...

"Into the lands of Lancaster. My lord of Warwick washed his hands of the bloody business — Beauchamp's hands were ever white and clean. But Tom was made of sterner stuff and would not flinch now, no, not Tom."

At the juncture of the lands of Lancaster and Warwick lies a little scrubby hill, where brambles grow, and a dark grove of trees. They say that it contains the bones of Saxon dead; a place of death. Here the procession paused. The mob still followed, yammering and cavorting as for a carnival, banging drums and blaring horns, with yapping dogs about their heels.

Enquiring closely, I had converse with two men who stood at the front of the crowd and saw it all. They heard one ask why there was no priest. The man's an outlaw, they were told, a traitor to the realm, a witch's son.

"Let him do magic now then!" they laughed, and nudged their friends. "A witch's son — let him do magic, eh!"

"Back!" Thomas roared, and drew his sword to force the throng to clear a path where men at arms could make a place of execution.

The ground was dry and sandy, tufted with rough grass; with boulders jutting from the earth and stones; the soldiers kicked it into smoothness.

"Bring him forward; bind him," Thomas ordered, and they took Piers from his horse and tied his hands behind his back.

"There is no priest for the excommunicate," said Thomas loudly, and looked at Piers for his response.

"I want no priest of yours," said Piers contemptuously.

"Then look to your soul yourself," said Lancaster, and turned his horse and rode a little further off.

"I will," said Piers and he began to pray.

"But not to Our Lord. His prayers were to a woman," said my close observer. He added dubiously: "It might have been Our Lady."

"It was not," the other said, and crossed himself.

" I hope the Lady answered him," said my informant. "Whoever she was."

"Well, it was soon over for him. They stuck a sword in his belly; they pulled it clear; they shoved him face down over a stone, and they struck off his head. A quick death. I've seen worse. Remember the man they hanged at Hampton, that would not die...?"

Already it had paled for them into a certain insignificance; they had seen many deaths; this one over, they went home...

"Sire?"

"It's all right, Robert. I have cried for it before."

Thomas of Lancaster rode forward now, amongst the general jollity and clamour, the cake sellers and the fiddlers, the pedlars and the drummers, and the crowd that gathered round for pickings. Tom could clearly see the guards that hung about the corpse, rooting for gold and clothes. One of the men was kneeling, struggling to pull the ruby ring from off the finger, failing, as the others had, reaching for a knife to hack the finger off.

"No!" shrieked Thomas with his sword drawn, and he would have killed the guard if the man had not fled from him. The crowd shrank back, alarmed, and Thomas rode his horse about and stared down at the mangled corpse.

"Are there no shoemenders here?" he cried. There were.

"Have you the tools of your trade about you?" They had not.

"Then get them — instantly — you will be well rewarded."

And trusting no one now to guard the body, Thomas dismounted, and his men made a circle about him, and he stood there, like a knight, with drawn sword, and waited.

The shoemenders have a shop in a narrow crooked sidestreet in Warwick town. They work in a low room open to the pavement, where the floor's of beaten earth, and the air smells of leather and cord. A trestle table was piled with leather scraps, and a wooden last, and bags of nails and needles, and knives, and many thicknesses of twine. But this same table, on that day, was the place where, on Thomas' instructions, these men washed the tarnished corpse and sewed the head back to the trunk. Of course, this is not uncommon practice; but the sensibilities recoil...

"It was well done," says one. "It was our finest work."

"We were well paid," another says, and will not look me in the eyes.

"He was a fine looking man," the first says, laying down his hammer.

"We made him good as new," the other says, and gives a rough laugh, as men do that must protect themselves against a show of human weakness.

At night the Earl of Lancaster came. Then the room was shuttered, full of candles; so the table seemed a bier; the body, covered with a homely cloth, a thing more sanctified, an effigy.

The Earl of Lancaster drew the cloth aside and looked upon the corpse. They stared at him respectfully, curiously, rich men from the coins he gave them.

"Leave me," then he ordered, and they scuttled from the room.

"Why do you think he wished to be alone?" I asked the shoemenders.

But they shrugged. They'd waited in the street. The workings of the nobility were not theirs to question. They were paid; the work was good; they wanted to forget it.

> "He would have kissed his lips, Robert. Alone, in the shuttered room, with the candles burning."
> "Yes, sire, that was my thought also."

Then he called them back. Brusque now, authoritative, a man who had recovered self command. He gestured to the covered corpse. He said, with something of a sneer: "Take that to the Earl of Warwick."

They carried the body on a hurdle to the walls of the castle, at first light of dawn.

A servant informed them that the Earl of Warwick would not receive it. The Earl of Warwick wanted no part in it. The Earl of Warwick was not at the castle. The Earl of Warwick said to take it to Oxford, to the Dominican friary, and to let him hear no more of it.

"May God have mercy on them all," he said.

This, then, was the tale that Robert brought to us at Oxford.

When we came to Oxford — Agnes, Meg and I, with household knights and Piers' own servants — we were met by the Abbot and escorted to the friary of the Dominicans, and thence into the church. It was afternoon, but the church was dim and lit by candles. Before the altar, upon a bier, the coffin open, Piers lay. I could see his face as we approached; it showed pale and translucent in the candlelight.

"It has been most beautifully done," said the Abbot. "All traces of the blood and gore are gone; I would not have credited possible a work of such excellence."

I shuddered.

"The embalmers are still here, of course, and very pleased with their success. Naturally they yet have more to do before they finish, but Your Grace will be pleased with what you see. The Earl of Cornwall looks as if he sleeps. And shall you see them, sire? They would be happy to explain..."

"No," I answered curtly. "My mother was embalmed. It was

272

explained to me then. Reward them handsomely; but keep them from my sight." I felt oppressed and hemmed in by this man. I gestured. "Clear this place."

At last I was alone with Piers. He smelt of balsam and every kind of spice. I leaned close and I kissed his face — his closed eyelids and his eyebrows, his resting lashes, and his forehead. I kissed his hair; it smelt of rose water. I kissed his lips. I was surprised, and a little hurt, to find them cold.

The monks had bound him in white linen, to the jaw. His arms lay by his side, hands visible, and on one finger the ruby I had given him at Langley, which no one had been able to remove. I saw that they had cleaned his nails; they were pale and immaculate. I put my hands on his.

I was aware that Agnes was beside me now. Her arms were full of roses. She picked one out and handed it to me, a vivid crimson against the whiteness of the linen.

"It is midsummer," she said.

"I had forgotten."

"It is a good time to be with the Lady."

"Is it so?" I said bleakly. "Well. We said that we would meet again at midsummer. It was a special time for us."

"How beautiful he is..." she lamented.

"They said he looks as if he sleeps. I never saw him sleep so. Even in sleep he was graceful, sinuous. Never so concise. And he would not have chosen to be dressed in this unadorned white linen. They meant well, of course." I gave a brittle laugh. "The embalmers have laden him with a powerful array of scents. A veritable herb garden. You know what they do to preserve a corpse? Oil of sandalwood in the anus of course he was no stranger to."

She sensed my gathering hysteria. She channelled it.

"Now tell him, sire, that you will be revenged. He waits to hear."

"Of course," I breathed. "One more final gift...a vow..."

"Yes, sire. We will both promise it."

Agnes the witch and I clasped hands across his body. We vowed to mete out justice to Thomas of Lancaster and Guy of Warwick. We promised expiation, amongst the scattering of rose petals.

"He shall not be buried until they are buried also. I swear it. We shall be revenged."

"My prayers conjoin with yours, my lord," Agnes murmured. "And if I can do more, I will."

I leaned down over him. "They all shall die, my darling. I shall do

273

this for you; pain for pain. I swear it by our love."

Then Agnes and I came from that place, and left Piers free for Meg's gentler ministrations, and the weeping of his pages.

The Earl of Pembroke came to me at Oxford, possibly the bravest man in the kingdom, I reflected, as I raised him from his knees.

What could I say? He was more wretched than myself, and as much betrayed as I. Since the moment of Perot's abduction, he had worked ceaselessly and in vain for his return. He had sought help from the Earl of Gloucester, and the brat had told him: "We all agreed that Gaveston should be taken. If you have sworn away your honour and your lands, my lord, all I can say is that you be more careful how you swear in future."

He had prowled about Oxford — he had appealed to the clerks and burgesses of the university to back his voice with their legality. His remorse threatened to engulf him. It was for me to pacify him, reassure him, comfort him. He swore to be my most devoted man henceforth; and he has been so.

Having sent orders to the mayor and citizens of London to fortify the city on my behalf against the entry of the earls, I set Philip and John, two most faithful of his servants, to watch over the body of my friend. I had the linen cloths removed and exchanged for cloth-of-gold. I made arrangements with the friars that Piers should lie there in that place until his burial at some future time; that is, when the sentence of excommunication had once more been lifted, and Piers had been avenged.

And then I rode to Langley, and I walked down from the palace, and I strode about the meadows seeking Wilfrid where he dug; and he saw me coming, and he handed me his spade.

Chapter Nineteen

GOD BE praised," they said. "His Grace the King and the Earl of Lancaster are reconciled. And now, the kiss of peace."

It had taken more than a year of tortuous negotiation to bring us to this moment, to Westminster, to this banquet, where the magnates of the realm were gathered with their ladies and their servants, where the wine flowed and the excellence of the fare was praised by all. A palpable air of relief hung over everything, of gratitude, of satisfaction, of a task well done. And Tom and I sat side by side, with Isabelle and Alice, and we laughed at every antic of the Fools, and cried appreciation when the minstrels played well, and drank noisy toasts to harmony. And now the kiss of peace.

We stood; the conversation died a little, and the feasters turned towards us, Tom and I.

I took his face between my fingers and I kissed his lips.

"I'll kill you for it, Tom, I swear it," murmured I, an ambiguous smile upon my face.

Tom returned my kiss. "Remember, I am Simon de Montfort come again," he said in low tones, "and I shall break you."

Then we sat down, and the banquet continued, and the music played, and the observers clapped their hands, to see the thing so happily resolved.

It was my consuming passion for revenge which alone sustained me during that first year without him.

Pembroke and I, with a good sized force, had ridden into London, summoning the mayor and aldermen. I spoke to them myself. That cold fury which was habitual with me then may possibly have lent my person some forbidding aspect —

"Or more likely the new beard upon your chin, sire! Your father as he lived, we all agreed."

Whatever the cause, when I demanded pledges of their good intent they gave them.

"If you fail," I said, "my men will undertake the task themselves."

The gates were shut against my foes, who lurked in Hertfordshire, while we sent to France and Avignon for aid. The Pope, a good Gascon, loaned me one hundred and sixty thousand florins for my cause, and King Philip sent a batch of lawyers with the dismal task of scuttling to and fro between a king and that king's sullen barons. We ordered Lancaster, Warwick and Hereford to appear unarmed at Westminster, to discuss the Ordinances. Discussion was not our intention, and they guessed it, and they would not come. Gloucester and Richmond ran between. Legal terminology was the stumbling block.

My demands were that they come unarmed to Westminster to receive my royal pardon for their crime, and that Piers' goods, captured by Thomas at Tynemouth, be restored. A pardon — did that seem like capitulation? It was not; you cannot have the barons at large, hostile, loose in the kingdom. Returning them to the fold is the first step to enclosing them.

They replied that since they had heard that the King had become annoyed with them — a hollow laugh on my part here — they would indeed come to Westminster as he required, but first the King must agree to maintain the terms of the Ordinances — and these, of course, proclaimed Piers traitor. And if he were traitor, they had committed no crime, and therefore had no need of pardon. The goods they were asked to return were a felon's goods to be forfeit to the crown. I would not receive the goods on those terms, and I insisted upon pardoning the earls, thereby branding them murderers, and not the executioners of an enemy of the realm, as they would have themselves described.

We stuck on this...

In the November after Piers' death, Isabelle bore our son, conceived in York in greatest happiness.

A son! I could forgive her all her little spitefulnesses and her hatred of my true love...the gift of a son...marvellous indeed!

I knelt beside the bed where Isabelle lay, and kissed her hand. She lay there flushed and — yes, I must admit it — beautiful, her long hair loose, her look one of immense satisfaction.

"My lord is pleased?"

She knew it, smiling.

"It is the only good thing that has happened this year," I said, "and I thank you for it with all my heart."

The nurse then handed me the child. I held him in my arms and cradled him, much moved. So helpless and so precious, this small child must one day be king, and take on that so heavy mantle; he must keep the peace, and fight when need be. He must know more than his father ever did. A lump came to my throat.

"He shall be called Piers."

From the bed Isabelle gasped. She sat up on her elbow, open-mouthed.

"Peter then?" said I, prepared to concede an anglicised form of the name.

Isabelle began to scream. She sat there screaming. Her face went scarlet with her screaming. The nurses looked at me in horror. You would have thought I'd done my wife an injury, the look they gave me. It was down to me to save the Queen from apoplexy.

"Oh, very well," I said reluctantly. "Edward."

Apart from this hiccough, Isabelle and I were on good terms. For her part, she was so relieved to have her rival gone — although she had the wit not to admit as much to me — that her character much improved and she was pleasant in her nature, which she never was before. For my part, I was grateful that she showed only sympathy to me, and that she said "They never should have done it." It was enough; I warmed to her; and for a while, the bond of parenting drew us together. It was plain enough young Edward was a healthy beast, and neither could detect in him any symptom of decline, and England had at last an heir.

Further good news followed: Archbishop Winchelsea grew sick and died; and I filled the see of Canterbury with some satisfaction with my old friend Walter Reynolds, Bishop of Worcester, and I hoped that Winchelsea would spiral in his grave.

"Your Majesty," said Walter Langton. "I beg you to accept my heartfelt condolences upon the death of the good Earl of Cornwall." So long ago, those merry days when Piers and I had trespassed in his woodlands... He would recall them with far different sentiments than I. And yet I swear his kind words were sincere, and I accepted them with all my heart.

Isabelle and I spent early summer with her father — this the man who swore to imprison Piers if he should catch him — but I am a liar and a diplomat now; everything I do is for my purpose, and I need French aid and I am gushingly polite to Philip and much in his favour for fathering a son; he had doubted my capacity. Isabelle and I were further bonded by escaping from the burning palace in our nightclothes; such shared intimacies promote a certain unity. And if on the nineteenth day of June I chose to be alone and ride off by myself, well, that was my affair, and no one questioned it.

If I say that the court was a different place without Piers, you understand, I mean not to state the obvious, but to describe the change of situation. It was Lancaster and Warwick now who were the embarrassment. The general consensus was that they had been wrong to act as they did; that what they did was murder, and had no semblance of legality. About me I had loyal support, while Lancaster and Warwick lurked in their own castles, sullen and guilty, procrastinating over peace terms, haggling over the choice of words in the messages sent to them. My papal envoys said unless they changed their tune, were I to take up arms against them I would not be to blame. Pembroke wanted it. He longed to see them downed. Despenser urged it. London rattled with unrest — Pembroke and Despenser had to flee an angry mob. Perhaps the papal threat had impact — Hereford and Arundel came snivelling back to court to make their peace. Then Lancaster and Warwick capitulated. They would agree to all my terms — the jewels and goods restored to me, and gone the reference to felons, traitors, Ordinances. They said they did it for the common good.

Then my nerve failed me. No, I could not meet with them. Fifteen months ago they had killed Piers. They yet lived, and I had vowed to kill them. What was I about, agreeing to permit them to return, and pardon them, to a clamorous chorus of approval? Forgive them? It was a lie. I might say the words, but my intention was to see them dead. This was no better than the dumb show of the player, an entertainment to buy time.

"It's impossible," I told Despenser. "I shall not be able to prevent myself from ordering their execution — why should we wait?"

"Remember what we planned, sire," murmured he. "We will be stronger when we come back from Scotland. You will then be supreme in power. Hold back now; your time will come."

"Be it so then," I said grimly. "And meanwhile let them know they are to beg for their forgiveness on their knees."

When Lancaster and Warwick and Hereford made their public apologies to me there in Westminster Hall, beneath the great beams of Irish oak, admitting their regret and their remorse for all to hear, it was, I suppose, a kind of victory for justice, a kind of triumph for myself and Piers. But it was not enough, oh, nowhere near enough — a grain of sand where I would have a desert.

Let them humbly apologise — it will not bring him back — let them admit their fault — their slaughtered corpses are the only reparation I will take of them.

From the dais where I sat, I looked at them upon their knees in poses of humiliation. I heard their noises of regret. Christ save us — they were sincere as I! Remorse? They did not know the word.

Serenely I gave them full pardon, planning retribution.

As was my wont, I rode over to Oxford to explain it all to Piers. I always brought with me gifts for the Dominicans, and cloth-of-gold to drape the coffin, scented candles, nothing but the best. There I would remain in the half light, the church empty save for he and I.

"It's all going very well, my love," I said. "We're going north. At last I have an army. As I understand it, by the time we arrive at Berwick we'll have some two thousand horse and fifteen thousand foot soldiers. And our beloved archers from Wales. The cavalry will be our main thrust. And you know, my love, that cavalry are invincible. Do you remember how we sang at Langley when we heard of the victory at Falkirk? Invincible — invincible! We shall be knights upon a mission. I expect us to be well into Scotland by midsummer. Midsummer, eh, my love? Will the Lady watch over us, do you suppose? Never fear, I'll make appropriate offering! The deaths of three earls...

"They all desire it, you know, war with Scotland. There's nothing better calculated to unite those barons that support the crown than to take them north and promise them a battle. My father knew it well enough — I can almost see approval written on his face. It has befallen well for us — we have a challenge tossed to us: to come within three leagues of Stirling castle by midsummer, where Mowbray holds it yet against the Scot. Summons sent to all the earls. If I have gambled correctly, certain of them will refuse. And we don't want Lancaster and Warwick with us, do we? We want them waiting quietly at home, gnawing their nails and wondering what we're going to do. And this is what we're going to do: we're going to turn our army round, our great army, our by then successful army, and we're going to annihilate the Earl of Lancaster and the Earl of Warwick...and then we can begin to be at ease. One day I'll come to you with news, good news... I must be strong till then. How am I? Well enough. I suffer from a stomach cramp, yes, constantly. The physicians don't know what...yes I went to Agnes. Do you know what she said? *It is the sword with which they slew him.* She gave me no potion; she said there was no cure. She said grief hidden and denied comes forth as pain... Meg and Joan are well; no need to fret about them. I'll have more to say when next we meet. I feel that all goes well for us at last, my darling. This Scottish campaign is the turning point. A pilgrimage..."

"Dear sire," Despenser urged beseechingly. "Give the Earl of Cornwall Christian burial. The sentence of excommunication is quashed; there is no bar now to a more fitting resting place."

I gave a crooked smile. Despenser thought my conversations with a coffin morbid. He made no secret of it. I guessed that once Piers was below ground, there would be more space above for Despenser to invite me once again to view his son — "Sire, you remember Hugh..."

"Peace, friend," I told him fondly. "I have made a vow concerning Piers. I have every intention of overseeing his funeral with all magnificence when I have attended to some other business. It will be done when I return from Scotland..."

Granted we were exhausted, and because of this, the army took all night to cross the stream to make for higher ground, for level ground, where a cavalry charge would have greatest effect. And it is true we were dispirited because of Henry Bohun's death — it never should have happened — skull cloven by the axe of Robert Bruce in a combat Bohun should by rights have won. And the damned terrain, the streams and marshes, and the pits dug by the Scots so covered over we scarce could put foot down with certainty; and the woods that hid the foe... Although all this were true, it is ever with bewilderment that I recall that shambles, that disaster which we termed a battle.

Yet all the signs were right. We had the greater army — the pride of English knighthood — the will to win — the cavalry, the invincible cavalry — and it was Midsummer morning, and I made my prayers to all the gods and the Lord Himself to fight for us and grant me this first step towards my vengeance. I knew that we would win — I knew it in my heart — the mounted knight is invincible, invincible. And when at last the Scots came forth from hiding, and I saw that they relied on infantry, upon those hedgehog schiltroms that my father scattered at Falkirk, my spirits rose.

"The first part of my revenge," I breathed. I turned to Gloucester. "Success is sure. And those who went against me shall rue this day. I have not yet forgotten the wrong that was done to my friend Piers."

"Your Grace, it is too soon to talk of victory," said Gloucester frowning. "I wonder if low cunning might not be more appropriate for us at this stage. Their infantry are tightly packed. If we could make them break their ranks before we began, it would be the better for us."

"Our cavalry charges will do that," I replied with confidence.

"It has been put to me," said Gloucester, "that if we retreated to the baggage train and let them glimpse the gold and silver, we might tempt them with rich pickings; and then attack from vantage."

"Hide behind plates and tents, my Lord of Gloucester?" I said in scorn. "Is that the language of a knight? You who pleaded so hard for a chance of glory!"

The youth responded with an oath of fury. "Do you doubt my courage?" he demanded. "Must I prove myself by deeds?"

And impetuously forward rode he, with a charge of cavalry, and was instantly slain. We followed him into the mêlée, angry and appalled. Our mounted knights charged time and time again; hemmed in between the streams, the damnable streams, we had no space to make an impact, and the schiltroms held, and more than held, advanced.

Our archers who, as at Falkirk, made to shoot into the Scottish ranks, were scattered by the Scottish horsemen; we fell back. And all the while I fought I knew that we must win — the omens all were right — it was midsummer — it was my revenge — courage alone must do it — we were King Arthur and his knights, the Scots mere hill men, cattle raiders. My shieldbearer was captured, my shield gone; my horse killed under me. They brought me a fresh horse and I began again, fighting in the thick of it, for Piers, for our revenge, for legend, and, God save us, for my very life! My horse veered from the struggle, the bridle sharply pulled back by one who fought beside me.

"Sire! Come away! The day is lost!" Pembroke, with Sir Giles d'Argentin, both heaving at my rearing horse in vain.

"We must fight on!" I screamed. "Too much depends on it. I'll die here rather then retreat! Leave me be, God damn you, leave me be!"

"Forgive me sire, but I must disobey you."

They dragged me from the fray. About us all was chaos. But the truth was plain enough — we were mown down in thousands. We made for Stirling; but they would not let us in, for fear we would be captured when the garrison surrendered. We fled to Dunbar castle, pursued. Brave Pembroke trailed back to the scene of slaughter, to bring his Welshmen home by land across the moors. Myself took ship at Dunbar to Berwick, and one more ignominious flight by sea.

Shaken, disbelieving, we crouched about the deck, counting ourselves fortunate to be alive. The belief of a lifetime is a hard thing to dispel. Cavalry are not invincible. The mounted knight — Sir Lancelot — can be brought down by the spikes of a hedgehog.

Extremity removing every barrier of rank and station, Roger Damory put his hand on my knee.

"Don't give up hope, sire. We shall rise."

The lovely Roger, household knight, an Oxfordshire man, a hero. His hair was fair and soft, and his eyes hazel. He had a wide smile, and Lord knows I needed signs of other than despair. He was broad shouldered, strong, slim hipped. I would discover soon enough his arse was neat and pert, his prick rapidly responsive, and his body hair a tawny gold. At that precise moment all I saw before me was an understanding friend.

"Thank you, Roger," I said gratefully. "I saw you in the fighting. You bore yourself so bravely. I am so sorry it was all to no avail."

"And you, sire, were a lion," he responded warmly. "This is a setback, no more. We shall retire, regroup..."

"I fear that this encounter with the Scot is something more than a setback," I said gravely. "I staked all on a throw, and I believe I lost."

The full extent of what the battle had cost us was revealed when we arrived at Berwick and began to learn the dismal truth. Young Gloucester dead, and all the mighty Clare inheritance in disarray as a result; the Earl of Hereford a prisoner, Sir Robert Clifford killed, and many other knights; men slain and drowned in the treacherous streams, and countless others cut down as they fled; our costly baggage taken, Stirling surrendered; and the Scots exultant.

For myself, the personal cost was incalculable. The glory I had anticipated so fervently was turned now to humiliation. The swift arrow of my revenge, so sure in the arc of its impetus, was checked in its flight. They brought news to me then that in my absence, Lancaster had used the time to raise an even greater army than before. Now he would be invincible.

What was there left? The warm thighs of Roger Damory, as I took him to my bed.

Roger Damory? I think we all know well enough I went with him for comfort, and he went with me for lands.

"I am Simon de Montfort come again," said Thomas. "His terrain fell to me long ago. Now I take on his mantle. I am the steward of his inheritance. I am the power now."

It must have been plain to everyone except Thomas that he was in no way the de Montfort come again. Simon de Montfort was handsome, witty, courteous. He was also arrogant and single minded, greedy for land and power. But he took an oath to uphold the Ordinances he had contrived against the King, and for that cause he split the kingdom and rose up against the Lord's Anointed. He curtailed the King's authority, nay, he ruled England. They wrote songs about him when he died:

> *Ore est ocys*
> *La Fleur de Pris*
> *Que taunt savoir de guerre*
> — Now is slain
> the flower of chivalry
> so skilled in warfare

His charm, his courtliness, his elegance: no, Thomas was not he. But that Thomas believed himself so, there lay cause for great disquiet.

York — I hated the place. I had bad memories. They crowded in upon me, diminishing me.

Now in York castle, Thomas came to me before the Parliament began, to tell me of his plans. At Pontefract his monstrous army waited, straining at its leash, and I — the heart had gone from me; and all I could think was: here at York it was that I heard Piers was dead.

"It was never my wish that we should be enemies, cousin," Thomas said. His tone was sanctimonious, as if he were a tutor, older and wiser than myself, about to reprove a wayward pupil for some lapse of taste. "I offered you the hand of friendship time and time again. But you refused."

The fault was mine, you see; ungrateful wretch that I had proved to be. I sat hunched in my chair and saying nothing.

"I knew full well why you had gone to Scotland," he continued, walking up and down, his long sleeves rustling against the skirts of his velvets. His shoes with the long pointed toes did not suit him; they made his feet ungainly, like duck's feet. On Piers the same style had looked wonderful. "You thought to use your victorious returning army against me. But you are not your father, Edward. I imagine you will not forget the Field of Bannock. The judgement of Heaven against a perjured king who had forsworn his oaths, who had denied the Ordinances." He grunted complacently. "You will always fail. You're weak, and stupid, and anyone may lead you. You were always so."

I recalled our boyhoods. *Do you think we could be changelings, Ned?* — the rumour that he put about that his own father was the first born, and cast aside because he was deformed, and therefore Thomas rightful heir to the throne. I remembered his great dejections, when he retired to dwell on such wild and raving fancies, nurturing his discontent in one or other of his gloomy castles. I pitied him.

Moreover, he was growing ugly, I observed, and his skin was pitted. I do believe I saw a redness round the eyes; a sty was forming. They do say that envy festering must manifest itself in outward signs.

"I shall not forgive you for that you thought to march against me," Tom said. "No king should use a subject so. I should not have to protect myself against your evil machinations. I should not have to be obliged to defend myself, to hold an army in readiness for fear the King will suddenly attack. And there are other wrongs against me, Edward."

He stood still and faced me. With an effort I succeeded in raising an ironic eyebrow. "Other wrongs, my Lord of Lancaster? What may they be?"

"You should not have made me kneel to you at Westminster," he growled. "You should not have agreed to that hollow ceremony. That was a mistake, and you shall pay for it. Nobody so humiliates me and goes unscathed. And I tell you now, dear cousin — and I think that it will come as no surprise — I made apology for what I did to Gaveston but it was for the peace of the realm I spoke the words. I lied. By all the saints, I tell you now I'd do it all again. If I could kill him twice I'd do it, and this time I would hang him as a traitor, from the nearest tree, and leave his body for the crows. He should have hanged at Warwick. It was only his kinship to Gloucester's sister that saved him and gave him the nobleman's death. If I had had my way he would have hanged... we were too good to him..."

I could not speak. I trembled; I hugged my arms about myself, and rocked, like silent idiots are seen to do.

"They say you've taken up with Damory," said Thomas with a sneer. "You've soon forgot him then?" He laughed. He stood with feet apart and looking down at me, thinking himself supreme. Perhaps he was. I offered no resistance. He frowned. "I warn you, Ned, if I thought you intended to replace Piers Gaveston with someone else I would be most displeased. I would not tolerate it." He eyed me narrowly. "I would not have thought you'd wish it..." Then he shrugged. The possible emotions of a character so broken and pathetic as I must have seemed to him at that time were not his concern. Just now he was riding high and he was here to relish it.

"You have been informed of my intentions at the Parliament," he said in a brisk and purposeful manner. "A complete reform of the royal household — officers to be replaced by men of my own choosing — not only in the court, but in the kingdom. And I want Despenser removed, and Langton; and the Great Seal in the hands of whom I choose. You have agreed to this. For the good of the realm. Edward?

You have agreed? I don't want vacillation and hostility in public."

I made a noise of disbelief, a laugh almost.

"Edward? Is there a problem?"

"No, nothing," I replied. "I am unwell. I am not myself."

"What ails you?" he asked curiously, plainly seeing in an instant himself regent of the realm for the infant Edward, and the formality dispensed with, that of lip service to a puppet king.

"Stomach cramp. A sharp and constant pain." I looked at him between the eyes. "As if a knife were twisted in my gut."

He understood me well enough. He gave a snort of some contempt. "Would you spit words at me to make me feel remorse? I feel none; save your breath. You are much like your grandfather, King Henry," he continued. "A man of straw, devious and weak. I wonder if the dead return and inhabit the bodies of the living. King Henry lived in dread of the de Montfort. They say he was afraid of everything — thunder, lightning, war — but that he feared de Montfort most of all. And Simon told him "I have never seen such deception as I have seen in the English King, a man who breaks his word time and again — just as you have done to me, Ned. Ha!" he laughed. "The comparison goes further — they sent Simon to Gascony to put down the upstart lordlings there. And he ruled with a rod of iron, and put the Gascon lords in chains."

I listened to him. Every word he spoke was tightening the noose that I envisaged about his bulbous neck. I would be fair, though instinct cried for savagery. He would be paid in kind; his kinship to the King would save him from the traitor's death. A sword, an honourable execution... But I said nothing.

I forbore to point out that Simon died a hideous death. I made no reference to all the little flaws he overlooked in his interpretation of the way things had befallen. Enough that it be said I was not Henry; and I did not fear nor Lancaster nor thunderstorms.

Just as well. It rained continuously that autumn while Tom strode here and there pontificating, making changes. Pembroke came to me and asked permission to remove himself from court; his hatred of my cousin made it so that he could not bear to be present with Tom in such flagrant prominence. I thought Pembroke's course a wise one, and I left Tom to his triumphs; my mind was on other matters. I went to Langley.

And now at last my fine control broke down. That simple and debilitating gut ache grew and spread, till I was pain made flesh, and every breath an effort. I prowled the fields and woods of Langley in the rain — it never ceased, that rain — sometimes on horseback, sometimes on foot trudging like a peasant. I dug useless trenches which the downpours filled; I crawled through mud and sludge, in some vague wish to lose myself in the earth, my hands and knees in the slime of sedge-filled cart ruts; and with the relentless rain rustling the undergrowth I knelt there hugging my tormented body, marvelling that mental grief should take a toll so physical. And all the while I let him come to me at last, that beloved friend whose image I had since his death forbid my presence, as if by holding him at bay, I could preserve the superficial self command which was my poor defence against the agony I could not bear. Now I had no defence; my arms and heart were open, and he entered, overwhelming me.

Not as he was in death, so still and neat and grey, and perfumed like a censer, but vibrant, living, moving, graceful. Turning his head to grin at me over his shoulder, flicking his hair back from his face and laughing, with that dazzling smile. He always laughed. He was hardly ever sad. Sad when we parted, yes, he cried that night when he must go in banishment to Ireland — and on the quayside by the ship in that November rain... I could have said so much more to him — you never have the chance to say it all — did he understand how much I loved him? — did I make it clear enough? — could I have done more? — Oh, those wasted nights when all we did was sleep! — when I knew him there beside me and I simply said goodnight and did not drown his skin with kisses — the smell of his skin, the sweat and the sandalwood — his mouth opening to mine, his tongue, the play of tongues in the mouth — the light touch of his eyelashes on my cheek — and still it rains — I see him in the rain, wet hair sculpted to his forehead — licking the rain from my face, shaking a wet bough, pressing me against a tree, his tongue on my eyelids. *I want him here*, I screamed, *I want him now...*

The silence of the rain-drenched woods without him...the silence of the swampy fields...the silence of the swollen river...and I mudstained and sodden, screaming.

Down by the reeds that cottage I thatched, still standing, and the thatch good; drooping there at the end of the roof the mushroom shape that Piers swore was a royal leopard. It's not our place any more; a cottager has it and has made a garden for his herbs and beans.

I took the boat upstream and sat there drenched and stupid at the oars, recalling how I rowed to Berkhamstead and took them by surprise because I had to see him, and they said God's blood, it is the King! And now Berkhamstead was another empty place — the place where I raped him for the pleasure he had taken with his bride — he lay under me so beautifully, warm and writhing, noisy, not quiet and silent as he now lies... Those times I see him at Oxford — it was always he that talked the most, not I. It's hard to talk when the other one is always silent in reply.

I want him here at Langley. This is where he belongs. I said I'd wait until we'd taken our revenge. I can't wait that long. It will be easier for us to be together here. Will you understand, my darling, if I bring you home?

And still it rained, as we brought him to Langley.

Crows perched on the gaunt trees, and the wagon ground its way slowly through the puddles of frozen mud, breaking the brown ice. The monks' robes were bespattered to the waist. I rode beside the coffin, which was draped with cloth-of-gold, my hand upon it in protection, all the way from Oxford. It was the dark time of the year; it was December.

Our procession came up to the priory, just north of the palace wall, tawny-grey flint, with narrow windows, a half circle of bare trees about it, and some holly, soughing, bending in the wind gusts.

In the church he lay that night, I with him, keeping watch, none else about, just he and I, with the flickering candles and the wailing of the wind, the sound of owls. The sky behind the moon was almost emerald in its shimmering coldness. I recalled the clamorous vigil before we were knighted, when they brought the war horses in to shift the would-be knights and let the monks pass through. There was more holiness here. But it was comfortable and easy too. This was our place; here we could be together.

"Forgive me, Perot; I'd have wished to pay them blood for blood before this day; I was not able. Be patient; we will have our vengeance...but you'll rest more content at Langley. Our cottage yet stands. Do you remember — and how we — and all the things we did? You know, I took the boat out in a rainstorm and I thought to row to Berkhamstead? Old habits, you know. Well, we have a powerful gathering for you tomorrow — archbishop, chancellor, treasurer, justices, four bishops, thirteen abbots — fifty knights — you will be well attended! Pembroke is here; he's like to weep, I think; he takes it much upon himself. Despenser, he was ever loyal, and Hugh his son is here with him; and Henry Beaumont, and Elizabeth, with Hereford — a changed man, Hereford, but we'll not trust him overmuch, eh? And Meg, of course. Would you object if she were to remarry? I think it would be best for her. Your daughter will be raised at Amesbury, with my sister Mary... Isabelle is here, and not so sour as once she was. It will be a fine spectacle. Perpetual Masses to be sung, for my sake if not for yours, to ease my mind as to your soul's safe journey... just in case there is no Isle of Apples...only Heaven." In spite of myself, tears came to my eyes, and my voice faltered. "And I believed myself so calm. Tomorrow — ah — I hope I shan't disgrace myself with snivelling..."

"You will, Ned," I heard him laugh.

One day, when I came through the wicket gate between the palace and the priory, I found Agnes waiting for me, muffled in a cloak against the wind. A white mist hung over the low meadows. An east wind blew, bitter chill.

"I must speak with you, sire."

"Not here; let's go inside — either back to the church, or to the palace."

"No!" she said, and she startled me with the vehemence in her tone. "Where have you been, sire — hanging over his beautiful tomb once again? — pressing your lips upon it, thinking you are close to Piers? — whispering to his coffin? It brings you comfort, yes I know, but I will tell you of a greater comfort."

"I wish you would," I said soberly.

"One small tomb does not close love in," she replied, loud against the wild wind. "Piers is here — and here — and everywhere. He is above ground, not below. He is certainly at Langley. He will be here still when these stones, these walls, are long forgotten. As you will be, sire, yourself, in the air, in the light, in every blade of grass. Understand it, sire; and cease your grieving!"

"It is too soon..." I murmured. "You don't know, Agnes...it's like a living pain that gnaws my heart."

"I didn't promise you release from pain," she said. "No, you will never lose that. But leave these priests, this tomb; Piers is not there. He is with you, with me. Love is stronger than death."

I stared at her. We both were shivering, our cloaks whipped by the wind.

"He said that to me once," I mused. So long ago, at Windsor, when we feared attack, and fought our fears down with the passion of our kisses.

"And have you not some business in the world?" she challenged. "Will Thomas of Lancaster rule England, who slew Piers? Does Warwick live to boast of what he did?"

In the evening, she brought scented oils, and did as she would for

Perot, massaging sandalwood and lavender into my skin with practised hands, and the fire burned bright in the hearth and the candles glowed about us.

"Do you cast a spell?" I smiled, my face in the pillow, my naked body warming at her touch. "I seem to melt; and yet my muscles all grow stronger."

Her hands worked on me, satisfied.

"I did this for his mother also," she said, kneading. "She was my love, as Piers was yours. She was a most beautiful woman, the Lady's own child. Oh yes, and she knew secrets..." Her hands paused. "Sire..." She bent her head until her face was close beside my ear. "You wish to take the Earl of Lancaster by force of law. But leave me Warwick..."

Chapter Twenty

WHO COULD possibly suppose a time when Thomas Earl of Lancaster did not reign supreme? He strode the stage of policy as if he were indeed the King he thought he should have been, and I some figurehead, placed here, placed there, nodded at, brought in from time to time to sign a document.

Christ! not a thing was done at that time without Tom's consent. We needed his approval for each act of administration. All council meetings had him at their head. If he came late to Parliament, we waited for him. An hour, a week, two weeks, we waited for him. And I had sworn not only that I'd have his death, but that I'd bring him down by force of law. No wonder that I lay awake of nights...

But there was one thing Thomas had forgotten in his assessment of the situation when he took control at York, when he dismissed me as a reincarnation of my grandfather, weak, vacillating and confused. Simply this: King Henry was his grandfather too.

It was not the noose of my own designing, envisaged round about his neck, that worked to topple Thomas from his pinnacle of power; it was his own vile character.

Let us suppose for an instant, that Tom of Lancaster was right, that he was champion of the people's liberties, against a careless king. I knew what was said about me after the battle at the Field of Bannock — *the King has ruled for six years and has done nothing praiseworthy or memorable.* But what did Thomas offer in exchange?

He was a swine, was Thomas; everybody knew it. On his own lands he took away the rights of those entrusted to his care; his gangs of marauders drove the people's flocks from the grazing lands and he took the commons for his own. He terrorised the monks of Tutbury, ransacked their priory and drove them out; he took the rights of grazing and fishing from the monks of Rievaulx abbey. He threatened his tenants — he was a harsh and brutal landlord, a robber baron foul as any that lay in wait about the mountain passes in wild lands and slaughtered travellers for their gold.

Everyone deserted him in time, sickened by his persistent nastiness. His wife, the wretched Alice, left him, and ran away to a squire of low degree with whom she said she could be happy. Tom was unlovely; there was no doubt of it. Who liked him, answer me that? Who was his friend? The Earl of Warwick only, and he was bound to him by spilt blood.

"My lord of Warwick, welcome...welcome to Westminster." My voice was smooth as silk. I put my arm about his shoulder, reassuring him with camaraderie.

He had the grace to look uneasy, shifty round the eyes. Perhaps he was convinced by my demeanour; perhaps he thought me simple. And reasonably so — I had no influence at all and Tom was blatantly in the ascendant.

"Your Grace," said Warwick; but there were no words appropriate. The shoemenders had taken Piers upon a hurdle to the walls of Warwick's castle; he would not receive them. Go back whence you came, he sent word, I want no part in it...

I suspected him of some remorse. It did not matter. It was too late. My heart was hardened. As far as Warwick was concerned, my heart was stone.

That spring at Westminster, the Earl of Warwick was taken with a stomach cramp.

"Poor wretch," said I to all and sundry. "Why, I had one such affliction myself; it lasted more than two years. I am only lately recovered from it. I pray his lordship will be more fortunate. Of course, we live in troubled times. Sickness and disease...they blame it on the rains..."

We were a kingdom racked by pestilence. The rains, unceasing, spoiled the harvests and caused misery and blight. The wheat had to be roasted in the ovens before it could be ground to flour, and food was scarce. Plain simple crops — beans, oats, peas, barley — cost more than was ever previously remembered; and men were killed in the open country for the food they had about them. Sickness followed famine. It was eminently reasonable that the Earl of Warwick should be taken ill. Others were so.

When I last saw Guy Beauchamp he was sitting in a chair beside a window in Westminster Palace, and his sallow face was very pale and strained. He leaned his elbow on the chair arm and, his chin between finger and thumb, he looked at me with his hard assessing eyes.

"It may well be the air of Westminster," he said. "None of us who live amongst our own hills and woods love Westminster. Your father, as I recall, detested the place. The air breeds sickness, and the water tastes of piss."

"I never have liked Westminster myself," I said. I laughed. "If it's not the dead dogs in the river, it's the fear the citizens are planning a rebellion. There's always something vile here."

"And therefore I propose to leave for Warwickshire," said Guy. "The air is sweet and clean there."

He will pass the hill where they killed Piers. He will return to the great hall where they would not let him speak, above the dungeon where they kept him for nine days. I grew as pale as Guy.

"I shall regret your absence, my Lord of Warwick," I replied. "But you will soon return, no doubt."

The Earl of Warwick looked me in the face. "Your Grace knows better than I do whether that be so," he answered.

A madness in me longed to gloat over him as he had over Piers, to taunt him with the unlikelihood of his ever seeing Westminster again, to say: and this we did for Gaveston. But I must be serene; the rumours would start unbidden soon enough, without my fomenting them.

"My lord, I pray for your recovery."

He died that summer at his castle. He asked to be buried without pomp. Because his son was yet an infant and a minor, all the Warwick lands passed to the crown in trust.

They were all beautiful in their way weren't they? Roger Damory — Hugh Audley — Will Montague — and every one a scheming little beast. Their shamelessness perhaps delighted me. Here there would be no pain, no talk of love, no loss. Accessible, amenable, they made no demands upon my heart, and left me free to remember.

In the council meetings where Tom presided, it gave me a piquant pleasure to recreate Piers in my mind, to call him up as spirits have been called, and to arrange him above their heads, draped upon a bed, suspended there, in all his beauty. Naked on a velvet cloth he lay, upon his belly, each arse cheek touched with light, the slender hollow of his spine a long curved shadow; his thick black hair curled against the dark skin of his shoulders; and then he turns his head and looks at me; the dimple of his chin shows now, the whiteness of his smile.

That was a waking dream. The others, those out of my control, were another matter altogether.

I would be riding, solitary, through a forest, in the dark. Suffocating brambles surrounded me on all sides, but they melted away like water as I passed. I came to a green glade. An ancient chapel stood amongst the moss and bracken. A light glimmered at its window. The door swung inward and I passed through. Upon a bier with a cloth of white samite lay a dead knight, the knight of legend, whose wound bled, and would always bleed until — until what? the wrongs of the world were righted? — the Holy Grail were found? — the unknown question answered? Always I would wake then, in a cold sweat, knowing that the knight was Piers, terrified of what I'd see.

And then the dreams of startling sensuality, when he would come to me naked and lie beside me and begin to make love to me, this so real that I could feel his lips upon me, and the thickness of his hair; perfume, like a beanfield in flower, or the apple orchards at Langley in full blossom, drenched my confused senses; and in my dream I knew that it was reality that was the dream. Then I could hardly wait to wake and tell him we were wrong — he was not really dead. And I would shake myself awake to bring him this good news, so we could laugh at how we had been fooled; and I would find myself in a tangle of moist sheets, and one or other of my wretched valets holding me till my shivering ceased. Then anger against Piers engulfed me.

Fool, I told him, stupid careless fool, that sat and made a daisy chain at Deddington, and could not guess what was to follow. Possessor of the King's life-source, to take so little care of it. Why didn't you escape that night? How could you not know...? You fool, you careless laughing fool...

I all but drowned that wintertide. I had a boat out in the Fens; a current took my boat away too quickly; the boat spun round and round, and when I reached out to the bank to grab an overhanging bough, it pulled me from the boat and I went down into the icy waters. I began to swim, and struck out for the bank. And then I paused, the waters closing over me.

Instead of fighting then I rested. Death is a boat... I thought of Avalon, the Isle of Apples, where Piers would be, and if I let the river take me, we would meet there; we would be together.

But terrified, my companions hauled me to the bank and pulled me clear, and I lay gasping like a fish while they pummelled me and covered me, and took me to a reed hut; gave me drink.

I thought with some amusement that it would have been an inappropriate demise, for every one who stood there on the river bank was a working man, a craftsman, villager — men who had never seen the court... The king is crazed — his ways are not those of a monarch — you would swear he liked the company of common men above that of the men of rank he should prefer...

Apropos of that, we had an odd thing happen then. A claimant to the throne appeared at Oxford!

They called him John of Powderham. They captured him and brought him to me at Northampton castle, where I sat with Isabelle in the great hall, a certain curiosity possessing me.

The man had made such a great noise about himself he could not be overlooked, but must be given audience, and in he came, between his guards, a tall man, fair haired, but with a countenance so disfigured that one shrank from him. They said when he was taken he had had a cat and dog with him, and understanding that he was possessed by evil spirits, it was assumed these his familiars.

"Welcome, brother," I said, leaning forward with a smile. "Tell me your story."

The villain broke free from his guards and rushed at me. They seized him once again; it was an ugly scuffle. Struggling in their grip of him, he screamed at me: "You are no brother of mine, therefore greet me not so! I am the King of England! I am King Edward's son! My story is well known. Dare you hear it?"

"By all means," I said pleasantly.

"As I lay in my royal cradle," said the poor crazed man, "a great sow ran loose and bit my face, and so they wrapped me in a blanket and removed me from the palace, and a carter's son was put in my place. You know it — for you are that carter's son! You sit upon the throne in silks and velvets, but you cannot disguise what you are. The world knows you to be a common man — you dig and thatch and row a little boat. You have no drop of King Edward's blood within you. By single combat I will prove it — give me a sword, and we shall see which one of us is king!"

His foul face worked in rage as he writhed between his guards. Beside me, Isabelle began to scream. Her ladies rushed to her.

"Take him away," I said, and as the man was hustled screeching from our presence, I turned to comfort my poor wife. "Come, Isabelle, there is no need for this!" I was surprised to find her so distressed. I thought she would have been amused. "The man is crazed, possessed. He has been tried, found guilty and will hang. Forget it. I had thought to make you smile." But she was trembling, shivering. "Isabelle!" I laughed reprovingly. "Hungry sows did not run loose in the royal apartments of Windsor castle!"

But she looked at me strangely, and I thought: She hears that story from a madman's lips, and by God's truth, she half believes it!

"Your Grace," said Edmund my brother, seventeen now, tall and handsome, "There must be no more of this!"

"Of what?"

He frowned. "Rumours and fools. Mutterings about royal change-lings. Fuel for the fire of your enemies."

I shrugged. "There will always be idiots..."

"This one came to too great a prominence. You did well to have him hanged. Edward, you should show more anger."

"Ah...you think I am not angry?"

"I think that you preserve a kind of indolence which the observer takes for weakness. I know this not to be so, but I yearn for proof. In our father's day — forgive me, Ned, but no one ever called him weak. As I understand it, those were glorious days. They are not so now."

I curled my lip. "True. No one can call these present days glorious."

"Ned!" he pleaded, boyish, ardent. "Take arms — make a stand — go against Lancaster. I'll go with you. I long to see the crown restored to glory."

"Glory proves elusive," I said cynically. "I would settle for satisfaction."

And for revenge, my heart added.

I sighed; and drifted into one more reverie.

When I was not dreaming of my love, I was rehearsing Lancaster's downfall. My intention was that he should die as Piers had — a hollow trial, a hurried execution; but first he must commit that kind of crime for which I legally might mete out such a punishment. He must take arms against me; yet he must not win. So delicate the matter — I could not go against him till he trespassed...but my army must be greater; it was not. So I must bide my time — ah, blood of Christ, if I had known how long I'd have to wait...but I did not; I lived in hope, and I began to hope when Tom himself played into my hands by virtue of his weaknesses.

His flirtation with complete authority teetered to a halt; he wanted power, but he could no more handle it with ease than I, and neither could he work with others. He always said we were alike! Sullen and morose, he did not seem to know his own mind, and when he encountered opposition from his kind, he retreated to his solitude, and sulked, frustrated as myself. The means whereby he sought to clip my wings checked his own powers of flight; and all became a stalemate in a foolish game of summonses, refusals, legal wrangling, moves and countermoves. The King must work within the frame-work of the Ordinances; but the King would not accept them; and agreement never could be reached, because each saw his own truth only, and denied the other's.

Around this seething unrest at the core of government, there lurked perpetual threat from Scotland. Our northern lands were plundered by the Bruce. All but cousin Tom's lands. Why not these?

Tom, who should have been the barons' leader, now proved no leader through his own inadequacy, and, soon as his back was turned, I reinstated those he rid me of; and thus about me I had Reynolds and Despenser, Pembroke, Hereford and Surrey, Arundel and the bishops, and, in those days, the Marcher lords, the Mortimers; and my two brothers now grown to young manhood, Edmund Earl of Kent, and Thomas Earl of Norfolk. If Tom would make a wrong move, I would have an army...

He would not.

To reassure him of my good intentions, I invited him to Langley, and he came.

We were wary and polite. I had a second son by then, John, born at Eltham in July. Tom had no children. I took a pride in showing him my sons. I sensed his gathering unease.

"Frightened of me, Tom?" I laughed. "You have all but deprived me of my kingly rights. What can I do to you?"

"I have heard rumours...the Earl of Warwick's death..."

"Is much to be regretted, Tom. Some trouble of the guts, I hear?"

"Swear to me, Edward, you had no part in Warwick's death."

"I swear it. Tom, I was not there..."

"But I have heard that there are poisons which lie inert in the bowels and breed and fester, and do their work a month hence, two months hence..."

"I know nothing of poisons. You wrong me, Tom. You are quite safe at Langley. You shall eat from my dish, drink from my cup. Trust me."

Late in the evening, he and I sat in a little chamber by the fire, my dogs dozing, and our goblets brim full. As I spoke to him, I understood why it was I had wanted him here with me in this unaccustomed intimacy: I must talk of Piers.

"Four years since his murder, Tom," I said, quite lightly, as one would speak of the flavour of the wine. "Four years all but three months. I always hold the date apart, with gifts to the Dominicans who guard his tomb."

"If we continue to talk thus," said Tom, "we shall be in deep waters."

"I prefer it. Or are you afraid?"

"No. If I had been afraid, I never would have had him killed."

"Do you regret it?"

"No."

"Do you dare say that to me? You are a brave man, Tom, I grant it."

It seemed that Thomas also wished to talk. I had no difficulty prising from him his recollections of that fearsome deed. He seemed almost glad, I thought, to speak about it freely.

"I stood beside his corpse," said Tom. "The men at arms would have gone at him like crows that peck the sockets of the head. One had a knife to hack the ruby from his finger; and another would have had his balls." He curled his lip. "Such are the privileges of the victors. De Montfort's corpse was shared out by the fistful. I hated Gaveston, I own it. But I would not have him defiled. And when the man, thinking to please me, offered me the head held in his hands, I looked at it and I was glad. The eyes were open, but frozen; not as they were in life, so bright, so dancing. Since that time, I often thought: yes, I was glad; but why? It was for this, Ned: I was glad because at last you could not have him. Neither of us ever could again."

"Neither of us?" I blanched. "What had he to do with you?"

"You always did have everything I wanted, Ned." He tapped his fingertips on the table, one by one, in a meticulous irritating pattern. "I envied you your father — not simply because he was King; he was a hero also...whereas mine was gentle, ineffective. I despise the weak. And then you would one day be King — younger than me, and often stupid. I should have been King... I envied you your silly disposition, always simple, always laughing, light of heart. You had it all, Ned. And then Gaveston."

"Well. Most of what you envied you have taken from me," I said bitterly. "Are we now better matched? You have even had a taste of kingship; was it to your taste?"

"Not much," he said, with a grudging smile. "But my nature is such that I believe I never could be well content. It is a curse upon me. I have learnt to live with it."

"So all in all, you killed my friend so I should not be happy. An achievement to be proud of, Tom. And all those noble words you flung about were thin disguise for your wretched envy. We knew you wanted him. We knew you tried to get him to your bed. We laughed about it, Piers and I. We knew you wanted him."

I had made him angry; but then, I was much provoked.

"You laughed then, did you?" he hissed.

"Yes! And when we kissed and hugged before your face, we did it

297

to enrage you, knowing you desired him!"

Tom turned his face to me. In the candle shadows his eyes glittered.

"I did not ever mean to tell you this," said Tom.

"Then do not..." I said swiftly.

"When he was a prisoner..."

"I don't want to hear it."

"You do. I even think it's why you brought me here. You guess it and you want to know for sure. You want to hear everything about him, even this, and even from the lips of one you hate."

"Then tell me — yes, it's true — I want to know."

Our tones were low and passionate, like lovers.

Tom said: "I went down into the dungeon where they had imprisoned him. I stayed with him and talked with him. A conversation much as this. And...I made love to him."

"I don't believe you," I said instantly.

"Believe me or not, as you wish. It doesn't matter. He was vile and dirty, but I cried with the beauty of it. Ah — you think I used my power against him because he was at our mercy; it was not so. I asked his permission; he said he would put up no resistance."

"I doubt whether he would have been able, chained," I said savagely.

"It wasn't so. If he had told me to get out, I would have gone. Believe me, I was the suppliant, he the bestower."

"You are going to tell me that he wanted it?" I sneered in disbelief.

"He seemed to find it amusing," Tom shrugged. "He laughed. But afterwards he wept. I was surprised; I knew I had been gentle. I said why — ? And he replied Because now you dare not let me live. I said If I can make amends... He said Let me see Edward. I said that was not possible. Then I'll settle for a bath, he said. You must have heard the details of that day," Tom turned to me. "They must have told you Gaveston was brought out of the castle clean and shaven, perfumed. Whom do you suppose that you can thank for that? I gave the order. I arranged for him to ride with dignity. I found the clothes for him to wear. I stood there like a servant, taking his requests — "and green's the colour that best suits me" — I did all that was required..."

"Except bring him to me," I seethed.

"Well, that was not possible," snapped Tom. "We had agreed that he must die." Gone the reflective almost holy tone of his previous recital. He pounded both his fists upon the table, then he dropped his head between his arms. "He was too beautiful to live," he wept, "too beautiful to live."

A tangle of emotions possessed me then; I fought them down.

"Look to receive no mercy from me, Tom," I said tersely, "when the time comes. I have given my word that you are safe beneath my roof. But after this I make no promises."

And after that, Tom came not south again, but lurked about his northern castles.

When Tom's wife, Alice, fled from him and sought comfort with her loving squire, it was with the connivance of the Earl of Surrey, and from that time onward there was warfare between them in the north. Tom's presence in the kingdom was akin to that of a wolf at large that now and then came from his lair and ravaged the land about him. We suspected him of being in league with the Scots; we knew him to be attacking castles in the north, and he would not come south to any Parliament or council to answer our charges. He distrusted everybody. He sent messengers to say he would not come to Parliament till those who worked against him should be punished for their crimes against the Ordinances. He said Damory and Audley planned to murder him. When I sent messengers accusing him of lawlessness, of brutality, of assembling armies contrary to our country's peace, he replied that these armies were to uphold that peace and — a final insult — to serve the King. He said because he was Steward of all England by the King's consent, he should be treated with respect, and his approval sought in all we did. Everybody was ashamed of him. He was a canker in the flesh of the realm.

When I took my army north to keep the peace, I prayed that he would come out and fight me. If he would do so, I would have him legally, for taking arms against the King. I led the army up and down outside the walls of Pontefract castle. He was within; he did not answer.

"God damn you, Thomas, fight!" I seethed. What must I do? I could have taken him then; I had an army; we had come to keep the peace; we were strong.

His men leaned from the walls and bawled abuse; but they would not come out. We could do nothing. We came south, the thing yet unresolved.

Betwixt Tom and myself the barons scurried to and fro and worked to make us friends, and Tom and I swore countless oaths we would not keep, Tom that he never wished to deprive the King of any of his powers, nor would he ever; I that I would observe the Ordinances; Tom that he would gather no armies about him, I that I would banish from the realm all those whose presence vexed him.

To speak of which, Hugh Audley and Roger Damory were doing very well. Audley was now wed to Meg; and Roger to Elizabeth, Meg's younger sister. Piers liked Hugh Audley, and would have approved, and, yes, Meg liked him too; you may rest assured I would not have married her against her will. And when it was appropriate, one or the other, Damory or Audley, would come to me at night, and sometimes both, and we would play.

I might have gone forever so, drifting, waiting, contenting myself with half measures, dabbling in frivolity, enduring bad dreams when I slept alone, and every nineteenth of June winding my sorrows about me like a shroud... I might have gone on so for ever, had not Hugh appeared and taken me in hand.

Hugh Despenser.

It was hardly necessary these days for his faithful father to edge him towards me — "Your Grace remembers my son, Hugh?" — for he had been much thrust upon me by the Lords Ordainers as my chamberlain. They said he had a lawyer's mind and would assist me with his clear-headed detachment. Naturally, I hated him.

When I was flirting with the angelic-faced Damory or tickling Audley's ears, I was aware of Hugh Despenser well enough. I thought him grave and sober. I guessed he never made a move that was not well thought out and calculated.

> "Oh, sire, you never spoke a truer word! Do you not find it challenging to note that when the Lords Ordiners are at their most strong, young Hugh is working with them, and when through disarray they fall apart, young Hugh is to be found about the person of the King?"
>
> "No, Robert, I was wrong; I thought he could not be spontaneous in word and deed; but I was wrong."

I was with him at Westminster. It happened that we were alone, and Hugh was shuffling papers at a table.

"You have our permission to retire," I said. I found his presence irritating, and the rattling of those parchments grated.

Then without preamble he came over to me, and he stood before me, and without more ado, he held my face between his hands and drew me to him and kissed me full on the mouth and said: "I love you."

Against this simple and straightforward attack upon my heart I had no defence. I was completely taken by surprise. Naturally I returned his kiss. The sudden passion of that first embrace over-whelmed me. I had never thought to feel that shock again. I wonder whether it had been because he spoke of love? That was a word I never thought to hear again in this world. Eight years had passed since Perot's death.

"You love me?" I stuttered stupidly. "Are you sure?"

"With all my heart," said Hugh.

"I insist that young Hugh Despenser never made a spontaneous gesture in his life."

"I don't know why you must call him young Hugh, Robert; neither of us were young, Robert; we were both thirty-six. But it was true that he was handsome... He is, isn't he, Robert? No one has such lovely limpid brown eyes, such a mischievous mouth when he smiles; and what of his hair, his chestnut hair, and the firm line of his jaw, his slender neck, his long slim fingers tracing subtle patterns on my own? And to think he loved me all this time, and dared not say! And if you were to see him naked..."

"Christ save me, sire, from such an impropriety."

Once more at Langley I made my way into the church, that holy place, that place where Piers was lying. As was my wont, I came to talk with him.

"I never asked you, darling," I said, sitting with my arm about Piers' tomb, "I never asked you whether you liked Hugh Despenser? Do you like him? Never fear, he won't replace you in my heart, but Piers — he loves me, he really loves me; and I believe that I am beginning to love him in return. The world now sees it.

You would laugh to see it all begin again, the mutterings of some of the barons, and that most damning epithet they've already used against Damory — "worse than Gaveston!" Poor Damory's nose is very much put out of joint by Hugh, and he and Audley screech at me like fishwives: you like him better than us! Is he better in bed?

And there's the surprise, Perot! He is a good lover! When I first lay with him, I thought we'd share a dignified encounter — rather pure. But he knows whore's ways and he left me gasping. And you see, he loves me..."

"If ever you should try to replace Gaveston with someone else, I would be most displeased," my cousin Thomas had once told me. It seemed that he was not the only one to find displeasure in the notion.

What a hornet's nest I stirred up when I accepted Hugh

Despenser's love. Both Damory and Audley went off in pique.

Then there was Isabelle... She had changed towards me. Even I, who noticed little about my wife, could not be unaware of this. When she first came to England, everybody said how much she loved me. She even said as much herself. She seemed to think if only I could rid myself of Piers then she and I would ipso facto become happy. She used to snap and rage and force me to acknowledge her existence. Tantrums, threats, insistence upon her rights and status as my wife. We achieved two daughters, Eleanor and Joan, as well as our two sons, as a result. The estrangement had begun with the appearance of that madman John of Powderham — he with the disfigured face, whom I permitted to approach us. I think that she became somewhat unhinged. She is an arrogant woman, and she has a superhuman sense of her own worth and dignity; and now it seems she's married to a carter's son — it's all too much for her! It's laughable, of course; I pity her. She tolerated Damory and Audley; but with Hugh she senses something different, something more akin to Piers. But she says nothing. She has become more silent, more withdrawn on those occasions when we find ourselves alone. She eyes me with an odd look sometimes; Lord knows what goes on in her mind. I never think of her as eight years old these days! It's plain that I annoy her. Her answer in the past has always been to howl for banishment for whomsoever caused annoyance to her.

"How will she deal with this one, Robert? She can hardly banish me!"

The trouble blew up over the Welsh lands which I gave to Hugh. Damory and Audley wanted them. They took up with the lords of the Welsh Marches, one of whom, Roger Mortimer, became their leader. These Marcher lords have always been a trial to the crown, and Mortimer now became something of a troublemaker — rough, loud, warlike, eager to take offence. Worse, he put himself in touch with Lancaster, who by virtue of owning lands in the Marches, was a Marcher lord himself. Tom was the force behind the growing discontent. Not only was he stirring up the Marcher lords, but he was summoning his own Parliaments in the north and making a great noise of righteous wrath. Yes, he could not believe it was all happening again — that the King had dared to fall in love, and did not care who knew it.

Cursed London backed my enemies. The Marcher troops rode towards the city. Roger Mortimer had of a sudden grown vociferous

and full of self-importance. Damory and Audley joined him —
anything to be rid of Hugh. And Hereford changed sides again — I
had always said we should not trust him. Roger Mortimer took over
Clerkenwell, and Hereford set up at Holborn. Audley was at St
Bartholomew and Damory at the Temple. All were threatening to
burn London from Charing Cross to Westminster. We could not reach
the safety of the Tower; and Hugh and I must lurk at Westminster in
hiding.

"Well, this is like old times," I observed drily. "You have to see the
humour of it. How Perot would laugh to see us thus!"

But Hugh, alas, did not possess Piers' sense of the ridiculous, and
urged me to take matters with due seriousness.

"Your very throne is now in danger!"

"Nonsense! I am the King."

My lord of Pembroke took me to one side and he grew very grave.
"The barons have said that they will withdraw their homage. Let us
not put their vainglorious boast to the test, sire. They have threatened
to set up another ruler in your place..."

"My cousin Tom? Do they mean Tom?"

"It is irrelevant. That they should say what they have said is cause
enough for our unease. Consider, lord king," he continued, soberly,
"take heed of the danger that threatens. Neither brother nor sister
should be dearer to you than yourself. Do not, therefore, for any living
soul" — and here he looked at Hugh and paused — "do not for him
give up your kingdom. He perishes on the rocks that loves another
more than himself."

> "More than himself? But that's the only way to love, Robert, isn't
> it? Piers knew that. We knew that love is everything and that all else
> counts for little. Love is stronger than death, Piers said. Love is
> strongest of all. I've lived my life by that and I believe it to be no bad
> thing."

I had to laugh at this one: Hereford suggested that Hugh should be
placed in the custody of the Earl of Lancaster! They must have
thought me an idiot. It was Tom who was behind it all. He sat up there
in his cold castle, Pontefract, like a great spider, weaving, plotting.

Well...I had to banish Hugh. Hugh was surprised, and not a little
hurt.

"My love," I said to him, "that is the way of it when you become the
lover of the King! But never fear — I'll get you back — I always did.
I'm skilled at that now, bringing my lover home. Banishment? That's

just a little game I and the barons play. You'll soon grow used to it."

"Where shall I go?" he asked.

I laughed: "Piers recommended piracy."

Chapter Twenty-One

ALL HALLOWS Eve, outside Leeds castle...

A clear bright night with a brilliant moon. The dark trees rustled, and beyond, the skies took on a greenish glow in the eerie light. Owls hooted. And circumstances were much altered with me.

Beside me my brother Edmund said: "We have an army now. Never has there been such loyalty. Nothing stands in our way. If you but give the word we can go after Lancaster. But dare you do it, Ned? Dare you take this gamble?"

How insignificantly it all began: Bartholomew Badlesmere changed sides. Lord Badlesmere was a Kentish knight, constable of our castle of Leeds in Kent. He had been steward of my household; but he betrayed me by defecting to the service of my Lord of Lancaster. I despised him; but Tom had no time for him either. The isolation of Bartholomew Badlesmere was the reason for the situation in which we now found ourselves.

For reasons best known to herself Lady Badlesmere, secure within Leeds castle, had refused admittance to Queen Isabelle, on pilgrimage to Canterbury. Isabelle in a state of great fury had been obliged to pass the night at the priory of the Black Canons nearby. The throne had been insulted. In order to punish the treacherous Badlesmeres our army laid siege to the castle. We had with us Pembroke and my two brothers Edmund of Kent and Thomas of Norfolk, with levies from the shires. We guessed the castle neither would nor could hold out at length. But we played a dangerous game here — Richmond, Surrey and Arundel had not yet declared for us, and Lord Badlesmere, at loose, was like to seek for help against us from his Marcher cronies, from Hereford, and from Thomas. Would Thomas come south with his armies, and would the Marcher lords take arms against us, in support of Badlesmere? Would we at last confront?

We sat at Leeds awaiting the outcome of events, and the October winds blew and the dark came early. It was quite plain to me that this siege, this small thing concerning an insult to the Queen was like to prove of wider import. A foolish thought occurred to me — a memory of long ago when the fortune teller came to Langley and warned Tom and myself to beware of bees. I had long since, after Bannock, understood that she meant other than the honeymakers. For which of us would the custodian of Leeds castle prove the ill omen? And if Bannock was my bugbear, which was to be Tom's? I chid myself for childish fancies. The Marcher lords and Hereford were even now at Kingston by Thames, assembling. This was no time to think of gipsy prophecy.

"Edward! Richmond is here — and Arundel — and Surrey... this is something like an army!"

At the end of a week the castle surrendered. We sent Pembroke as mediator to ascertain the Marcher lords' intentions.

"They're breaking camp — dispersing," he told me. "They do so upon orders from my Lord of Lancaster. My Lord of Lancaster says Badlesmere may stew in his own juice."

Almost by chance, it seemed, I found myself in this so novel situation: I was in command of a large and victorious army. I had the support of almost all of the magnates at my court. The Marcher lords had taken up arms against their King. I had therefore a mandate to attack the Marcher lords.

"Only one course is possible," said Edmund. "We should go westward and follow up our victory."

They all agreed it. Pembroke, Richmond, Arundel and Surrey, my brothers Kent and Norfolk, they were all of one accord. But that which made my pulse race and my heart pound and my spirits soar was knowing that the Earl of Lancaster had mustered troops to aid the Marcher lords. If we were now victorious against Mortimer and Hereford, against Damory and Audley who were with them, then Tom himself must be our next target. Tom was a rebellious subject; we could go against him — and all within the law.

And he knew it. He sent blustering messages south; we ignored them.

All Hallows Eve I recollected was the Feast of Samhain, one of the Lady's days. I knew it for an omen.

"Piers," I thought, "*it's now...it's to be now...*"

I looked up at that shimmering sky, that glowing silver orb.

Lady, I said, grant me at last the fulfilment of my vow.

Westward, in pursuit...

And now my own dear Welshmen flocked to my banners. Sir Gruffydd Llwyd led them. Joyfully they wreaked havoc in the Marcher lands. They were superb.

We reached Worcester on the last day of December. Crossing the

Severn we arrived at Shrewsbury, and our foes retreated before us up the river, with skirmishing and the burning of bridges. My Welshmen put themselves between our enemies, cutting communications, harrying in the rear. We expected confrontation now.

"I don't understand it," Pembroke murmured. "They are surrendering in their droves — hundreds of them — Mortimer's men, surrendering to us."

I laughed in amazement. So! Roger Mortimer, so loud at Westminster, so arrogant in bearing — was this the great commander of the forces against the King, a man who could not keep his men, an ineffective leader? Under safe conduct he came forward to make terms, and Audley with him. Roger Mortimer! He with his great military reputation and his threats against the peace of the realm! Faced with our armies he had buckled like a badly made weapon. Pembroke had been entirely wrong to fear him. To think that he had warned me against him on that ridiculous occasion in Westminster Hall, when I had been obliged to banish Hugh! And we had chased after him, the breadth of the land, supposing him strong, supposing him an opponent of might — well, he was nothing.

"Take him to London. Let him cool his heels in the Tower. Let him meditate in solitude upon what transpires when a subject goes against his King!"

Audley we sent to Wallingford a prisoner. A pang of sadness I had, seeing him led away. How sweet he once had been, young and endearing, thinking to comfort me when Piers was sent from me...so long ago, as it now seemed; but it must only have been some eleven years past. Swiftly I put such thoughts from me. We had long since tired of one another. He was a fortune seeker, greedy for land, and now a traitor. I was well rid of him.

"The others have fled north," said Pembroke. "The Earl of Hereford — Roger Damory — Mowbray —"

"To join with Tom —"

"Such is their purpose, surely. He is at Pontefract."

"What — must it be a siege? I would sooner a battle, quick and sharp."

But first, consolidation of our gains. We received the surrender of the Marcher castles. The last to fall to us was Berkeley. As I rode into the courtyard on that winter day, in triumph, I permitted myself a smile of satisfaction — it was plain the letter B was never like to prove my downfall.

I sent a messenger to Hugh in exile that he should come now with all speed and join me. Victorious on all sides meanwhile we rode towards the Midlands to gather reinforcements. When we reached Gloucester we received good news.

"Lancaster is out of Pontefract."

Why ever had he quit the safety of his bolt hole? What was his plan? Did he, like me, long to confront, to bring our anger out into the open? Did he hope, as I did, to bring our childhood sparring to its grim conclusion, a combat in the field, where face to face and sword to sword we would at last discover which of us two had the right to play King Arthur?

They said that he was now besieging Tickhill castle, up near Doncaster, which was held by my constable. I could not credit his stupidity. This move would gain him nothing; it would waste him time.

"It is believed that he intends to seek the aid of the Scots," said Pembroke.

"Then would he indeed be traitor to the realm," said Edmund grimly.

"He must be prevented from joining up with them. Whom have we in the north that is dependable and trustworthy?"

We sent urgent messages to Andrew Harclay, commander of Carlisle. He was to take an army and move towards Tom's forces, putting a wedge between Tom and the Scots. Ourselves rode towards Coventry for the mustering of our army prior to moving north.

Warwick castle was now ours; then Kenilworth surrendered to us. Like plums these strongholds of our foes dropped into our hands.

Warwick castle! I should have flattened it to rubble. I should have brought the siege engines we had at Caerlaverock, the one we called The Werewolf — that would have seen off Warwick's insolent stones. Later, maybe, when the other was accomplished...

I shuddered as I crossed the great hall. Here they had led Piers in chains up from the dungeons. Here they had sat in judgement, Lancaster, Warwick and Hereford, gilding their savagery with a thin disguise of legality. Here my darling had stood and pleaded for a hearing; here they had refused him. If I could have killed the Earl of Warwick twice over I would have done it. There yet remained the Earl of Hereford, and Tom, my cousin Tom, the source of all my woes...

"To Kenilworth, Ned?" Edmund asked.

"Later...there is something I must do."

For Pembroke and myself there was a grim pilgrimage to make, that bitter February day.

We rode down slowly through the twisting streets, away from the castle, through the snow. The sky was white. A glowing ball of sun hung there, immaculate. We rode towards the river, pewter grey between its snowy banks. We crossed the bridge, the silent water meadows, and we found the ugly hump of the hill that swelled up from the furrowed snow. There we dismounted.

No, I had not meant to weep. For what lay ahead my heart must be as steel, my resolution firm. And Pembroke also had made the same resolve. But when we turned to one another, silent, our eyes were wet with tears. And then I knelt down in the snow and I began to pray, but no words came, and when at last I found a voice, I prayed for vengeance.

We came away. I shivered, more than cold and snow might justify.

"My lord..." said Pembroke awkwardly, intending comfort; but there was none to give.

"This is a vile place," I said. "It reeks of death. I'll have them build a cross. It might allay the ghosts..."

"I think not," Pembroke said.

We rode to Kenilworth.

Now I remembered how I had come to Kenilworth, a boy, when Tom was sick in bed, and brought him dogs and comfort. I gave a brittle smile. We'd talked of Mark and Tristan. It is my favourite story, I had said. Mine also, he replied; do you believe that they were lovers?

"Sire! sire!" Those ransacking the cupboards and chests of Tom of Lancaster's castle, which had been Simon de Montfort's castle also, brought papers to us worthy of our interest. Letters were discovered, letters between Tom and Robert Bruce, proof of his rebellious intent.

I read the letters sourly. Small wonder Thomas' northern lands were spared from Bruce's pillaging! Well! so much the better for our cause. Now our army was the force of right and law against plain treason.

"Yes," I said with satisfaction. "We have him now." My voice was cold and hard. I spoke of the cousin whom I once had loved. No love remained. Soft and sweet he thought me then. And now? What did he think me now — weak and ineffectual, broken down by grief and submission? I looked across at Pembroke. "You would not credit it," I murmured. "My cousin in his treason signs himself 'King Arthur'... You know, as boys we used to play at knights. But both of us would be the King. It was a matter that we stuck on, neither giving way." I

309

looked about me, at the lovely painted walls, the wainscotting, the window tracery. "I used to love this place. I used to think it could be Camelot. The walls, you see, in summer, glow," I laughed apologetically, "much like the colour of a rose. Kenilworth," I spat in sudden hatred. "By rights I ought to burn it to the ground."

"You haven't time, sire," Pembroke said, "for such a pointless gesture. We have unfinished business in the north."

At Lichfield, Hugh was waiting for me with a good sized army and the comfort of his presence. We embraced. I held him close.

"Hugh," I smiled ruefully. "We are an army on the march. Since you and I last met I feel that I have been perpetually in motion. My mind is possessed by one thing only. Forgive our lack of ceremony. I would have liked to receive you with all honours..."

"It is enough to see your face, dear sire," said Hugh. "I ask for no more than to be in your sweet company again. The days away from you were long and lonely; the nights worse."

"For me also, my dearest," I said tenderly. "With you beside me I have everything I could desire. Oh Hugh! Dare I believe it? It seems possible at last that we may force the Earl of Lancaster to confront us — to take arms against his king — to show himself before the world for the traitor that he is! A world without the presence of Thomas," I laughed, "seems a concept too good to be true. Paradise on earth. And you and I free to pursue our love. For if I were so fortunate as to defeat the Earl of Lancaster in battle, I would know true power at last!"

"Ned, I have never heard you speak so," Hugh said, curious, intrigued. "Power? You speak of power..."

"As long as I have ruled," I said, "the Earl of Lancaster has been a hindrance to my peace of mind, a bridle to my desires. A life without Tom would be a cloudless sky, a calm untroubled sea, an unimaginable bliss."

"And — power, you said," Hugh murmured.

"Yes, I would gain at last that actuality of power which is my due. And darling," I said warmly, "what is mine is yours."

"Then let us drink to Lancaster's downfall," Hugh smiled. "I have a mind to sail that calm untroubled sea with you...and love and comfort you."

"Dearest Hugh...it is so good to have you with me."

We learned that Tom was now near Doncaster, now near Burton, burning and plundering as he went. We were at Derby. We circled round about each other in the northern reaches of the realm. Crossing the Trent, my army worked to cut off Tom's escape should he attempt to return to Pontefract or to retreat further north, to the safety of his ally, that enemy of our kingdom, Bruce; but he eluded us.

Now came Sir Andrew Harclay to us with his army mustered from Cumberland and Westmorland.

"What do you here?" I cried impatiently. "You should be close to Lancaster, and hot upon his trail!"

"I come expressly to warn Your Grace about the Scottish situation. I wonder if your Majesty is fully cognizant of just how dangerous matters have become — the raids — the pillaging —?"

"God's teeth, of course I know, man! This is nothing new. By Heaven, the Scots must wait! We are about matters of more urgency! Take your levies north. Get me the Earl of Lancaster!"

Surrey and Kent dug in around Pontefract itself. My forces took Tutbury, where Damory was. It surrendered. Roger Damory was killed; he took a long time dying. I had to come away. God's soul, the man had shared my bed. My hardness of heart was like to crack; I could not afford this weakness. I gave him honourable burial.

Then news was brought to us that Lancaster was fleeing to the Scot and far advanced towards his goal.

"God's teeth," I swore, "we've lost him. Once he joins Bruce we'll be perpetually at war..."

It was the month of March. We set about to make attempt to follow him.

And then the end came, sudden, unexpected, and incredible.

"My lord! My lord! Oh, sire!" The man was breathless, mud-bespattered. He was Andrew Harclay's man from the north. He was brought into my tent. Upon his knees he stuttered out the news.

"Lancaster is taken, sire! At Boroughbridge!"

"What?" I was ice cold, trembling, pale. "Again — what did you say?"

"It's true, sire. I was there."

"Oh God!" I turned, gesturing wildly. "Fetch wine — fetch wine for this good messenger and me. Now sit down with me, good young man, and tell me all you know. And many times, if you please," I laughed, lightly, stupidly, "till I believe you."

I called for Hugh, for Pembroke. Around us servants, soldiers gathered.

"Boroughbridge," I echoed. "It begins with B." They must have thought me crazed. I turned back to the messenger.

"Our troops were assembled about the bridge across the river Ure," this angel said, this weary mud-bespattered Gabriel.

"Boroughbridge," I repeated. "Near Ripon, is it not? A little to the north of York? Yes, I recall it now. And you were placed about the river..."

"We were in schiltrom form."

"Ha!" I marvelled at fate's ironies. "So — Andrew Harclay placed his trust in the hedgehog pikes?"

"It was a trick he learned at Bannockburn, sire."

"Quite, " I said drily.

"The schiltroms were flanked by archers," he continued. "We saw that Lancaster had split his forces. It was my Lord of Hereford who led the foot soldiers. They came at us to rush the bridge. But we were stronger. Men from York came day by day to swell our ranks, while it was plain to see that Hereford's men were deserting in their dozens. And when Hereford was killed — "

"My Lord of Hereford is dead?"

"On the bridge, sire. A spear thrust upward through the wood and pierced his belly."

My sister's husband... I was then half relieved that Elizabeth had died before this day, for she had loved him.

"And my Lord of Lancaster?"

"He led the cavalry. He tried to cross the river further down to attack us from behind. But our archers foiled him."

Tom's cavalry — that invincible cavalry, in whom all knights had ever placed their trust — Tom's cavalry had floundered in the river. Had Tom, like me, staked all upon that dream of King Arthur? Did he, like me, look scornfully upon the hedgehog spikes, as Harclay's archers unleashed their rain of rattling arrows from the sky?

Tom's men deserted, spilling away from him like water. There were parleys, negotiations. Tom surrendered.

But I, I remembered to give thanks to the Lady. I believe it was Her festival of spring's beginning. There are some tall stones at Borough-bridge, where sacrifices were made, and ceremonies. Their tips are pointed, like arrows. I believe these were Her weapons.

We arrived at Pontefract in a snowstorm.

Edmund and Surrey were waiting for us at this, Tom's northern stronghold, now fallen to us.

God, but this castle was a cold place! I paced about it, half unsure as to how to behave in the possession of so much success. This was the very place where Tom had lurked, a viper in the bosom of the realm, plotting against me, plotting with the Scots... What dark revengeful thoughts these walls must have absorbed! What silent witnesses were they of Tom's recurrent glooms!

They said the tower he had built here was the one in which he planned to hold me prisoner. I stood within that tower, grim-faced and appalled. Had he some private fantasy that one day I should stand before him here, defeated, my forces overwhelmed by his armies and the Scottish hordes? Did he suppose that I would abdicate my crown?

And what then? Was I to be held prisoner, chained, as Piers? Fed only at my cousin's pleasure...starved? What was there to be done with a deposed monarch? What else but murder, in some vile dungeon, secret, horrible, the matter well hushed up, the news given out that the King had died of grief or apoplexy? And my sons, I thought then in fresh horror, what of them? Edward, nine years old, and John his younger brother? What had been Thomas' plans for them?

"God's blood," I seethed. "Let he who thought to take me prisoner be brought here, prisoner himself."

When Thomas of Lancaster was brought captive to his own castle I was watching from an upper window, Hugh beside me.

I saw Tom led within, encircled by guards. Now he was beneath me, safe ensconced in his own dungeon. I turned away from the window. I sat down, leaning my chin in my hand.

"Edward?" Hugh said tenderly, concerned.

I looked up at Hugh with a rueful smile.

"What am I become, Hugh, prying like a spy on those below? What did I hope to see? Verification of that which even now I find hard to believe — complete success?" I laughed cynically. "I know pain and defeat and self doubt and anger well enough — they have been my constant companions these ten years. Where is the corresponding joy I should be feeling now? It seems I have no talent for success."

Hugh sat beside me and took my hand, caressing it with gentle soothing strokes.

"Triumph is wasted on me, Hugh," I said. "I saw Thomas captive, bound, led to the dungeons. I felt — nothing. I long to gloat — I cannot bring myself to make the effort. I should be even now down in the cell with him, jeering, taunting, reminding him of all that he has done to me and all I mean to do to him in my revenge. I ought to make him grovel, and beg forgiveness of my slain friend. What a failure I present! Vengeance is within my grasp; and all I want is simple justice."

Pembroke came to me.

"Sire...the Earl of Lancaster asks whether he may be permitted a private audience with Your Grace."

"No," I said, brushing my fingers through my hair. "No, I will not see him."

"He begs it, of your goodness," Pembroke added.

"Ever the mediator, Pembroke?" I said smiling. "No, I will not see him until I see him at his trial."

We sat in judgement on him.

We tried him in the hall of his own castle. We sat at the high table, myself and Despenser, amongst the magnates and barons, with Pembroke, Surrey, Arundel, Kent and Richmond. Robert Baldock read out the list of crimes of which Tom stood accused; and Tom stood, bound and chained and guarded.

Odd, I reflected, as the list unrolled, odd to be the accuser. I had had so much of Tom's own accusations. Our court was of as dubious a legality as his own, I daresay; but if the King is the fount of all authority, then this assembly of his judges had the edge, I think.

He had plundered the Earl of Cornwall's jewels and horses at Tynemouth — he had come armed to Parliament — he had obliged the King to pardon him for an offence against the crown — he had worked for power in the north — he had negotiated with the Scot. In short, he had committed treason. There was no defence.

"May I not speak?" cried Tom, plainly appalled. The fool! Had he not understood his treatment was to be the same as Gaveston's?

"You are permitted no reply," I answered coldly.

Tom's eyes blazed. "This is a powerful court and great in authority where no answer is heard, nor any excuse admitted!"

"It is much like the court at Warwick," I replied. "Read out the sentence."

He was adjudged a traitor. There was no other conclusion possible. He should be hanged, drawn, beheaded. We could have given him this traitor's death — we had the right. But we were fair, so very fair; and therefore he would be spared the first two punishments; he would be beheaded, as befits a knight.

I watched him where he stood, outraged, bound, defeated. He had not believed I'd ever truly have him killed — he was my cousin, a Plantagenet; I was soft hearted, I was Ned — weak, ineffective, fond of dogs and horses, pretty clothes and music. I could not do it, could I?

"Ned!" his eyes said, "Ned!"

But I am not as I was when Piers was alive, and he has made me so. I turned to Pembroke.

Even to the end, I was scrupulously fair. "Is there, perhaps, outside the castle walls, a little scrubby hill?"

The Earl of Lancaster was led upon a sorry nag out to the hill a short way from the castle. A jeering mob pursued — somehow one such always materializes at times like these, to play its part. They pelted him with snow.

I, like the Earl of Warwick, waited within the castle, warming my hands at the fire. They came to tell me he was dead. More chivalrous than Warwick, I gave orders for his burial before the high altar in the priory at Pontefract.

Two months later, at York, I repealed the Ordinances.

"And it is decreed that henceforth and for ever at all times, every kind of Ordinance or Provision made under any authority or commission whatsoever, by subjects of our lord the King or of his heirs or contrary to the estate of the crown, shall be null and have no validity or force whatever; but that matters which are to be determined for the estate of the King and of his heirs and for the estate of the kingdom and of the people shall be treated, granted and established in Parliament by our lord the King, and with the consent of the prelates, earls and barons, and of the commonality of the kingdom, as has been accustomed in times past."

Perhaps now I would hate York the less.

I doubted it.

It was at York that first was brought me news of the miracles that were daily as it seemed occurring at Tom's tomb. A deputation from the priory stood before me, bearing a great document with every miracle enshrined in fine illuminated lettering.

"We beg Your Grace," they finished, " — indeed, we see no other course — we do beseech Your Grace for your permission to make Thomas Earl of Lancaster a saint!"

I turned to Hugh, who stood beside me, as he would always do henceforth.

"You hear it, Hugh? They wish to canonize my cousin. A saint, no doubt, would be a great asset to a priory, would it not? Pilgrims — gifts — fame far and wide. They are no fools, these monks. But I must disappoint the reverend fathers; they have made their journey here in vain. Get you back to Pontefract, my holy ones, and pray. Permission is refused. Would you have Canterbury jealous? We cannot have a flood of martyred Thomases; it would be greedy." I felt the risings of hysteria. "They want to make the Earl of Lancaster a saint. Tom, Earl of Lancaster, a saint..."

Then I began to laugh.

"There, Robert, all's complete. Have done and finish it. The time of trial is over. My enemies are vanquished, and my lover waits for me. I have appeased Piers' shade.

"But more than that. I am grown entirely strong. I take what I have learned from him into the days to come, with Hugh. Piers showed me it is not the mounted knights which are invincible, but the true lovers; that after all the pains, love triumphs, though the world's against it. I bless him for this knowledge. Who would have guessed, so long ago, when he rode into Langley upon my birthday, with his careless smile, his dancing eyes, and his beloved witchery, that this would be his gift?

"And I hear the answer clear as if he spoke: 'I would! In truth it was my intention all along.'"

"Well, let my darling boast; he has good cause. But you, Robert, I daresay that you the clerk, with a clerk's precision, want the last word. Take it; I have done."

I watch him go, the King — tall, handsome, flaxen-haired, majestic, well content, a golden aureole about him as he goes. Hugh Despenser is waiting.

I could call the King back — it's not too late — and I could tell him...what? What could I not say? Take care, my love, Hugh Despenser is not Perot. I could point out what is clear to me but not to him: love may be stronger than death, but in these calculations, take account of hate also, of spite and jealousy and expediency; and the long-borne humiliations of she whose passions you have never worked to understand. I could say: Perot simply loved his king; it is not so with Hugh Despenser.

But I have not a Fool's freedom since I took the part of clerk; and what's a clerk but a hand that writes, and what's a clerk's place but to listen, watch, and after, set it down?

POST SCRIPT

Roger Mortimer, of small account in 1322, escaped from the Tower of London and fled to France. He became the lover of Queen Isabelle and together they worked to overthrow Edward, who was obliged to abdicate in favour of his son, Edward III.

History tells us that Edward was murdered in Berkeley castle. However, as with so many royal murders, rumour and mystery surround the event.

In the nineteenth century, a long letter was found in the binding of a volume, dated 1368, belonging to the bishopric of Maguelonne, and preserved in the departmental archives of Herault. The archivist who discovered it was convinced of its authenticity. It was a letter from the Pope's notary, Manuel de Fieschi, a senior clerk of Pope John XXII, a canon of York and archdeacon of Nottingham. The letter, addressed to Edward III, purports to be Edward's confession — an account of his escape from Berkeley, and how a hapless porter, killed in the escape, was substituted for the body of the King. Edward fled to Corfe castle, and thence to Ireland, Normandy, and so to Avignon, where he was seen by the Pope. He went then to Paris, to Cologne, and finally settled in a hermitage in Lombardy.

Nobody was ever convicted of the King's murder, and Edward III refused to allow any trial. He may well have believed the letter to be true.

Also by Chris Hunt:

STREET LAVENDER

If you enjoyed *N For Narcissus* you will want to read the story of Willie Smith's first meeting with Algy. In the busy West End streets of 1880s London, young Willie quickly learns to use his youth and beauty as a means of escaping the grinding poverty of his East End background.

"I read all 343 pages in two compulsive sittings... Both a funny study of a young gay's mounting consciousness and a voyeur's guide to the seamy side of Victoriana" — Patrick Gale, *Gay Times*.

"The rhythm of salvation and perdition — from reformatory to male brothel to good works among the teeming poor, via a superb episode in Bohemian Kensington — is fearlessly sustained. The effect of this harlot's progress with a silver lining is irresistible" — Jonathan Keates, *Observer*.

"A gem of a book. Chris Hunt's done a marvellous job intertwining a solid narrative full of good humour and wit with a message of real social conscience and insight... Really, you haven't had so much fun reading a gay-themed novel in years." — John Preston, *Gay Chicago*.

ISBN 0 85449 035 3 UK £7.95/US $12.95/AUS $19.95

N FOR NARCISSUS

If you enjoyed *Street Lavender*, you will want to read this sequel, following the subsequent adventures of Algy and featuring several other of its characters (including of course the irrepressible Willie Smith).

It is 1895 and Lord Algernon Winterton has long settled down to respectable married life, taking on the role of the perfect Victorian gentleman. Anything in his youth which might have suggested otherwise has been forgotten. Until an old associate makes an unexpected appearance, stirring up disquieting memories that cause Algy to try and recapture former passions — which proves a highly dangerous step to take at the time of the trial of Oscar Wilde.

A fin de siècle love story taking the reader from elegant English homes and Paris salons to the slums of East London and Montmartre. Once again Chris Hunt has painted a revealing portrait of late 19th-century life, charting the persecution of gay men in Britain in the wake of the Criminal Law Amendment Act.

"Chris Hunt has carved a comfortable niche as the author of highly readable historical epics set against a well-researched historical background... Writes in a fluid vein that admirably encapsulates the time, well positioned with myriad details which bring the period vividly to life for today's reader" — *Gay Times*

ISBN 0 85449 139 2   UK £7.95/US $12.95/AUS $22.95

GMP books can be ordered from any bookshop in the UK, and from specialised bookshops overseas. If you prefer to order by mail, please send full retail price plus £2.00 for postage and packing to:

GMP Publishers Ltd (GB),
P O Box 247, London N17 9QR.

For payment by Access/Eurocard/Mastercard/American Express/Visa, please give number and signature.
A comprehensive mail-order catalogue is also available.

In North America order from Alyson Publications Inc.,
40 Plympton St, Boston, MA 02118, USA.
(American Express not accepted)

In Australia order from Bulldog Books,
PO Box 155, Broadway, NSW 2007, Australia.

Name and Address in block letters please:

Name
_____

Address
_____

_____

_____